JAMES McGEE

Crow's War

GRAFTON BOOKS

A Division of the Collins Publishing Group

LONDON GLASGOW
TORONTO SYDNEY AUCKLAND

Grafton Books
A Division of the Collins Publishing Group
8 Grafton Street, London W1X 3LA

A Grafton Paperback Original 1989

ISBN 0-586-20328-1

Printed and bound in Great Britain by
Collins, Glasgow

Set in Bembo

For my parents . . .
Whoever heard of a writer called Magoo,
f'r crying out loud . . . ?

'We of the Game are beyond protection.
If we die, we die. Our names are blotted
from the book. That is all.'

KIM – Rudyard Kipling.

Chapter One

Came awake. Fast.

Old habits die hard, I suppose. Or maybe it was just nerves. God knows, they'd been shredded enough over the years. Nevertheless, it was still a curious sensation; coming to like that. Quickly and not entirely sure where the hell I was. Knowing only that I had been jolted into this semblance of awareness by a combination of sounds invading my subconscious.

My initial diagnosis was that it might have been a too-close-for-comfort fragment of the dream that had caused me to surface so abruptly. Because the visions that had occupied my fitful sleep had not been at all pleasant. In fact they had been vivid and frightening and very, very real.

It was a dream I'd had before. Frequently.

A battle zone. Mind and body cocooned in gut wrenching apprehension as the choppers hit the LZ, ears bombarded by the belching BRAAAAAAH of the X21s laying down covering fire as the grunts ran helter skelter from the trees. Then the clatter and whine of the turbines as the Hueys lifted and wheeled away, accompanied by the shriek of rocket, the shockwave of violent explosion and the rattle of small arms fire as the VC broke from the edge of the rain slicked forest like marauding ants.

I focussed then.

The heavy WOP WOP WOP of chopper rotors that had seemed so loud and insistent at once dissolved into nothing more pervasive than the arthritic creak of the ancient ceiling fan revolving above my head with rhythmic determination.

But I could still hear gunfire. No mistake.

Then I remembered.

It was Thursday, early evening. In Peshawar that was the day they celebrated weddings and there were always fireworks as part of the festivities. Sometimes they'd shoot guns as well.

I lay there on the bed and wondered if it would always be like this or if the dreams would ever go away. Time was supposed to heal all wounds, so they said. I just wished it would get a bloody move on.

I remained prone, eyes closed, to allow time for the throbbing in my head to subside into little more than a dull ache. I hadn't meant to nod off but, somewhat inevitably, the rigours of the past week had brought with them severe fatigue. Sleep had crept into my tired joints like a thief in the night.

To add to my growing discomfort the air in the room, despite the gallant effort of the fan, still carried much of the heat of the day as well as the sour stench of the town that squatted like a privy beyond the half opened shutters. The single cotton sheet under which I reclined was damp with sweat and adhered itself to my body with the loving affinity of a second skin. I lifted it aside, unpeeling it almost. The respite was marginal.

All right, Crow. Make a decision. Do something constructive.

I swung my feet to the floor and, mindful of foraging roaches, for which I have an abiding hatred, I padded barefoot to the window. Pushed back the shutters. Stood out on the tiny balcony.

The panorama wouldn't have rated a page in any of the tour brochures, that was for sure. Most of it was ugly.

Stinking dank alleyways full of dark shadows, some of them moving. But away to the left and lower down the hill I could just about make out the well tended and well protected lawns of Dean's Hotel, a rambling bungalow of an establishment that, despite its rather unprepossessing location, still managed to retain some of the timeless essence of British colonialism, a fading vestige of the Raj.

There was a brief succession of muted explosions and a cascade of sparks followed by the bright orange streaks of tracer in the darkening sky, curving up towards the massive ramparts and dome of the old Balar Hissar fort that dominated the town. Probably one of the resistance groups testing a new consignment of Egyptian-made Kalashnikovs. I watched and listened to the commotion for a short while, glad of the distraction. Entertainment in this neck of the woods was pretty uninspiring even at the best of times.

The bathroom was about the size of a cupboard and just as gloomy. After relieving myself I reached over the stained and cracked enamel tub and turned on the shower. The water was vaguely rust coloured and tepid. I made my customary check for lizards and other wild life before stepping under the nozzle. The spray was weak and intermittent but I could feel the torpor of a few moments before begin to seep away. I raised my head, directing the insipid flow on to my face and chest then took up the small rectangle of goo that passed for the soap and lathered myself until my skin began to burn.

Rinsed, I turned off the water and left the tub. The grey-white towel was coarse and frayed and rasped across my back like sandpaper. It was like being dried off with a bunch of birch twigs. Invigorating if you were into that sort of thing. I'm not. I gave up.

I caught a glimpse of myself in the small square of cracked mirror. Couldn't honestly say that I was

11

impressed with the view. One thing was for sure. Any laughter lines I might have had had long since run out of gags. Still, look on the bright side, Crow. The wrong side of forty and no grey hairs. Think positive, that's my motto. At least it has been since I reached forty.

I scratched chin stubble. There was no one to impress. So sod it.

Got dressed. Short-sleeved cotton shirt, faded Levi's. Hardly a picture of sartorial elegance. Noticed that the stitching along the seams of my scuffed Adidas was coming adrift. Ah, well. Took the worn and much creased brown leather windcheater off the hook on the back of the door, shrugged it on. Let myself out of the room.

Downstairs the squalid box room that passed for a lobby was deserted apart from an emaciated dog that was dozing in a corner, ears twitching. In a back room a transistor radio was blaring away in tinny abandon. Hardly the Hilton but the place was cheap. As far as I knew I was the only European in the dive. A fact which didn't surprise me a whole lot. I dropped my key on the reception desk and hit the street. I think the mongrel opened one lazy eye and watched me depart but I wasn't sure.

Peshawar is the capital of Pakistan's North West Frontier Province. The town lies in a humid depression at the foot of the mountains at the eastern end of the Khyber Pass. It's a fetid sprawl of a place, permanently enveloped in a haze of dust and flies and, like all frontier towns, it's something of a crossroads. Generations of exotic travellers have quartered here. Afghan kings, the hordes of Genghis Khan, soldiers of Alexander the Great, traders from the east. Its bustling streets and crowded bazaars continue to reflect its vibrant history. The majority of the population are Pathans but within the melting pot reside Uzbeks, Chitralis, Punjabis, Tadjiks. Added to which was a growing number of refugees from across the border and a motley collection of western interlopers come to cash in on the war. British, German, French, American.

Dodging the traffic is something of an art form. Gaudy Leyland buses and decrepit Bedford trucks vie for right of way with bicycles, bullock carts, camels, donkeys and nippy motorized trishaws with engines that sound like buzz-saws going berserk.

Needless to say, the noise is ferocious. And the smells are something else. Not many of them are pleasant. Grilled meats, choking diesel fumes, rich spices, over-ripe fruit, and shit. Mostly shit.

Dean's Hotel is a haven of sorts. A tranquil oasis. I left the street and the bedlam behind and walked through the lobby into the lounge. I wondered if this was going to be my last visit.

For the past few weeks I'd been doing fetch and carry charters for the International Committee of the Red Cross, shuttling ICRC officials between Islamabad and Peshawar's many refugee encampments, along with food and medical supplies. Now, I was more or less killing time until the next contract, whatever and whenever that was likely to be. Nothing had turned up as yet, which was why I tended to frequent Dean's. In Peshawar there wasn't a whole lot of night life and at least the seats in the lounge were comfortable, a darned sight better than the hard bed in my cramped hotel room, at any rate.

I headed for the Permit Room, the only place in Pakistan where you could imbibe intoxicating liquor. A sobering thought, literally. The rest of the country is dry. A few familiar faces were dotted around. Not surprisingly most of them belonged to journalists. I suppose that was a testimony to the old adage that the press corps found itself unable to function without the lubricating constituent of alcohol.

13

The click clack of backgammon counters indicated that the Swiss TV crew was still ensconced. The camera crew had approached me two days before. They wanted me to fly them to and fro along the Durand Line in the hope of latching on to one of the Mujehadeen supply caravans but, so far, all they'd done was complain about the food and play endless games of backgammon in the lounge. There had been rumours – later oft proven fact – of Soviet air strikes against a number of the more remote refugee camps and I'd wondered if perhaps the Swiss were resorting to their reputation for neutrality which, in plain terms, meant they were too damned nervous to venture near the war zone. Unlike the French and British teams who had been only too keen to penetrate across the border into the high valleys to try and secure footage of Hind gunships attacking Afghan guerilla strongholds. All for the sake of a five-minute slot on prime-time news, they'd gone in togged up like the Wolf of Kabul; extras in a low budget B movie.

I could sense that the backgammon players were trying to merge with the wallpaper, which meant that they were still in two minds over the feasibility of their assignment. I feigned indifference. If they wanted to play silly buggers that was up to them. It was quite likely that I'd have died of old age before the TV unit got its act together.

The predators were out in some force. They always were. They were inevitable. They loped into war zones like jackals, drawn by the scent of blood. Sundry carpet-baggers preying on other people's misfortunes like carrion. They took on various forms.

One of the oddest had been the woman. Blonde and of indeterminate age, she'd arrived in town with a lame-brained scheme to sell radio-controlled model aircraft to the Afghan resistance. She'd had the gall to explain to the bewildered rebels that the aircraft could be filled with explosives and used to bomb Russian air bases. Needless to say, neither her plan nor any of her aircraft got off the ground. She vanished into obscurity.

Then there had been the American, Tagg. His appearance had caused something of a stir, too. I remembered him as a stocky, compact type, short black hair with perfect teeth. Funny how some things stick in the mind. Rumour had it that Tagg was CIA, a veteran of the American AID programme in Laos and, lately, Nicaragua. And that was usually a euphemism for one activity: the clandestine recruitment and maintenance of anti-communist guerilla armies. In Indochina it had been the Meo hill tribes, in Central America it's the Contras. On the North West Frontier it could only mean one thing. The Mujehadeen.

It's a well-publicized fact that the CIA provides arms and ammunition to the rebel forces in Afghanistan. Some stories have stated that it's the largest military support operation run by Langley since the Vietnam war. It went without saying that the US government avoided overt involvement by ensuring that the weapons reached the resistance by tortuous routes, via a chain of intermediaries in Europe, Egypt and the Gulf States. In fact many of the weapons supplied were actually Soviet in origin which also helped to cloak the Agency's handiwork. That being the case it would not have been unreasonable to assume that representatives of the Company were on hand to ensure that the weapons reached their destination without mishap.

Then Tagg had disappeared as mysteriously as he had arrived. Giving rise to renewed speculation. A few of the old pros among the foreign correspondents put it down to the machinations of the Pakistan Intelligence Service who'd made it clear to Jack Tagg that his presence in Peshawar was far from welcome. It was assumed that Tagg had moved on to greener pastures. Someone,

15

however, had hinted that he was actually in Afghanistan, training the guerillas in the use of their new artillery. None knew for sure.

Then there were the mercenaries.

The group at the table furthest from the door were tanned, hard men with hungry eyes. They'd glanced up at me when I put in an appearance but, recognizing me as a regular, they'd dismissed my potential immediately.

British mostly; men who'd plied their trade in places like Biafra and Angola. Their usual haunt was the Khyber Intercontinental. Looked like they were slumming again. I eyed them warily as I made my way through the tables. I'd heard that some of the mercs were employed by western intelligence agencies to roam across the border into Afghanistan and bring back items of Soviet hardware such as sections of armour plate from Hind helicopters. Extraction operations these were called. The mercenaries were bad news. I stayed clear of their company. They, like people of Jack Tagg's ilk, tended to attract the attention of the Pakistani security service and that was something I didn't need, thank you very much.

Rasul was at his usual table. Fat, ponderous Rasul who, for a nominal sum, promised to provide guides to take you over the mountains to meet Massoud and the other guerilla leaders in their hidden redoubts. The general consensus, however, was that Rasul was in fact an agent of the Khad, the Kabul regime's security and intelligence apparatus, and he was based in Peshawar to gather information on the various resistance groups who all had their headquarters in the town. It was also rumoured that he was a member of the Khad's assassination bureau, the Sacrificial Directorate, and was there to dispose of any Soviet or Afghan troops who had a mind to defect to the Pakistan side of the Durand Line. Most of the local press corps referred to him as Comrade Greenstreet, after the villainous-looking actor in *The Maltese Falcon*.

There had been times during moments of quiet reflection when I had taken to examining my own motives for being there but my conscience was partly salved by the fact that at least I did have legitimate business in Peshawar. The ICRC contract happened to have cropped up at the time. I'd worked for the Red Cross before; in Bangladesh and Bihar, on flood relief operations. This was just another job, another instalment on the chopper.

'Hey, Crow!'

An arm beckoned from a dark corner.

Mike Farrell was the reporter-in-place for the *Far Eastern Economic Review*. He was a thick-set, pugnacious-looking man in his mid fifties, with one of those craggy, seamed faces that looked not so much lived in as slept in. His gritty features were topped by a balding crown about which curly black hair sprouted untidily. His dark eyes were full of humour but that twinkling cherubic gaze could so easily switch to penetrating examination in a split second. The eyes, it has been said, are the windows to the soul. If that is true then Mike Farrell's soul must have been in constant torment over the images he had witnessed in more than thirty years as a roving correspondent, most of them in war zones. He'd covered every major conflict since Kenya and the Mau Mau campaign. Suez, the Congo, Borneo, Vietnam, Iran, Ulster, the Lebanon and Nicaragua. He'd seen it all, been there with the best of them. With Gall, Pettifer, Cameron and Nicholson. Michael Farrell was a man supreme at his craft. His stories carried the abrasiveness of Pilger and the compassion of Shawcross and Buerk.

I'd first met him a year or so before when we had both been in Bangladesh. There, Farrell had been filing reports on the famine with a conviction that was both chilling and

17

moving for he had, like all first rate journalists, the knack of burrowing beneath the surface of the story to find and expose human frailties in a way that was unique to members of his profession.

Farrell had been in Peshawar for a little over six months on and off, reporting on the action of the resistance movements for the *Review*. He must have had his work cut out for there were at least forty resistance groups and political parties in town and, as if that wasn't enough, Farrell himself had admitted that his by-lines had probably been a series of wasted efforts. This had been a war in which the western media had fast lost interest. Until Afghanistan's Communist leader, Najibullah, announced his offer of a cease-fire to the leaders of the resistance, that was. Whereupon the media circus had trooped obediently back into town like a regimental band. Further temporary interest had been stimulated by Najibullah's attempt to curry favour with western reporters by inviting a group of them to Kabul to attend a press conference at which he generously outlined details of the peace proposal. Mike had been one of those who'd taken up the invitation. I hadn't seen him for quite a while.

We shook hands and I sat down.

'Good to see you, Crow. Here's to your continuing good health.' Farrell raised his glass and waved it in my general direction. Mike's ancestors hailed from County Tyrone. There was still the trace of the Ulsterman in his stretched vowels.

'How's it going, Michael?'

Farrell's face had lapsed into a leery smile. No doubt as a result of the slug of Murree Whisky he'd just taken. It's a local brew and pretty lethal. The smile lasted as long as the next swallow. Farrell's expression had suddenly become one of solemn intensity. He reached over and gripped my arm. 'My boy, I bid thee farewell.'

18

I sighed. 'Don't tell me. You're going over the mountains again. What is it this time? Another exclusive interview with Doctor Death?'

Mike Farrell chuckled. 'Not on your life, old son. I am going home. I am departing this pustule-ridden backwater for the trappings of civilization. Where a man can shower and shave in the privacy of his own home without the stench of camel piss in his nostrils. Not to mention the sheer undiluted pleasure of being able to wrap my clammy hand around a bottle of beer without the risk of getting nabbed by a member of the Muslim Temperance League.'

I'd be sorry to see him go. Farrell had become a part of the scenery almost.

Mike's home was the Crown Colony: Hong Kong. He'd established a foothold there during his coverage of that minor skirmish in South East Asia. Now it was his base. He'd shown me a photograph once; a Chinese woman of delicate beauty, smiling shyly towards his camera.

'That's Annie,' Farrell had explained, his tone gentle, his pleasure obvious. 'She keeps me sane.'

I was glad for him. To tell the truth, I envied him his good fortune at having somewhere to rest his head and clear his mind; his roots. I suppose, most of all, I envied him for having somebody who cared.

'When do you leave?' I felt myself growing maudlin.

'On the morrow,' he replied. 'Faster than a speeding laxative.'

'Good luck,' I said, meaning it.

A slight, white-jacketed figure materialized at the table. A waiter bearing a tray. At attention, as if on dress parade.

I'm not a whisky man. 'Guna karas,' I told him.

The boy zoomed away.

Farrell said, 'I can't say that I'm sorry to be going.' He looked suddenly sad. 'This is still a forgotten war, y'know.

19

Most of the people on this planet couldn't give a tinker's cuss what happens here. Christ! Half·of humanity doesn't even know where Afghanistan is! I'll tell you this; it won't be until the Soviets are dipping their feet in the Strait of Hormuz that anyone'll sit up and take notice. And by that time it'll be too bloody late. Ivan'll have his warm water ports and a stranglehold on the Gulf and the West's oil supplies. That's when everyone'll be yelling, "Why didn't they do something? Why didn't they try to stop them?" And by that time, my old son, you and I will be freezing our balls off in some Godforsaken gulag, where the main topic of conversation every morning will be about who's turn it'll be with the bog paper!'

'What about the cease-fire?' I asked.

'Not worth the bloody paper it's printed on! I . . .' Michael Farrell's tirade was curtailed by the arrival of my drink. Sugar-cane juice, lime, salt, sugar and ice. Very thirst quenching but it was a toss-up which would rot first, stomach or teeth.

'Am I boring you?' I heard Mike say suddenly from what seemed like a great distance.

'No,' I said, staring across the crowded room.

Farrell, having lost his train of thought, followed my diverted gaze.

The suit was very shiny and pin striped and looked suspiciously like World War Two demob issue. Wide lapels, trousers like inverted milk bottles. The occupant of the suit looked as dishevelled as the material he was encased in, but then he had the sort of figure that would have made a Dover Street cutter weep. Small and portly, no neck to speak of, and he walked as if he was wearing carpet slippers. His round face was bisected by a thick grey moustache. His fleshy, middle-aged features were almost Levantine and could have indicated any nationality between Bombay and Budapest.

There was, however, no mistaking the homeland of his companion who looked as if he had strayed from the pages of a Kipling novel. Tall, swarthy, hawk-nosed, with thick greying beard, dressed in the garb of a hill tribesman; turbanned headgear, patched jacket over cotton shirt and baggy pantaloons cut off at the ankles, sandals on his bare feet. A Pathan.

'Well, well,' Farrell muttered. 'Now I wonder what they want?'

'Who are they?'

'Haven't a clue about the guy in the turban,' Farrell grunted. 'Could be Harry Flashman in mufti for all I know, but the tubby little bloke in the Oxfam gear is Doctor Mahmud Habbani. He's Yunis Khalis's right-hand man.'

Well, I knew who Khalis was of course. He headed the Hezb-i-Islami faction, one of the Islamic Alliance resistance groups. His guerillas had been pretty active around Kabul of late. They had inflicted a fair amount of damage on the Soviets. Habbani, on the other hand, was a man that rang no bells.

'Doctor?' I queried. Thinking he didn't look like anyone I'd trust to give me an enema.

'Academic, not medical,' Farrell explained. 'He's a professor of law. Used to teach at Kabul University. He and his wife were among a whole group of intelligentsia rounded up by the Khad back in '84; lawyers, writers, religious leaders, anyone who was considered a threat. Most of them were thrown in Pole-e-Charkhi. That's the big prison complex on the outskirts of Kabul. A hell of a place. It'd make the Black Hole of Calcutta look like a bloody holiday camp. The way I heard it was that the lucky ones were those that got taken out and shot. At least they went quick.

'Anyway. Habbani and the rest were accused of trying

21

to form an underground network. They were interrogated, brutally as you can imagine. Habbani was in there for eleven months before he was released. I attended a press conference he gave not so long ago when he described what went on inside. Graphically. Electric shock treatment, beatings, daily executions. You notice he walks kind of funny? They tied him to a bench and whipped the soles of his feet with wooden staves. Nice huh? He said the torture sessions were supervised by Soviet personnel. The number of suicides was high. Some of the prisoners used nails to cut open their own throats. That's how his wife died. The only thing that kept him going after that was the fact that from his cell he could sometimes hear the sound of fighting between the regime's forces and the Mujehadeen. He may not look like a graduate from the Akim Tamiroff School of Deportment but that man is as tough as old boots. He lost everything; job, home, family, status. All he had left when he came over the mountains like the others were the clothes he stood up in.'

Which more than likely accounted for the tatty state of his suit, I couldn't help thinking.

'I see Fatso's spotted them,' Mike said.

Rasul was sitting in his corner like a toad on a lily pad. Hands clasped over his belly, he eyed the newcomers as they made their way into the room. Whatever his thoughts might have been, his round waxy face was impassive.

The duo were attracting no more than a few curious stares from the punters. If it had been a saloon in the old west the piano player would probably have paused a second in his recital. In the lounge in Dean's there was a short silence, after which throats were cleared, then conversation resumed. Very blasé.

Habbani led the way. His companion appeared hesitant, as if unused to the moderately refined surroundings. He looked as though he would have been more at home

22

perched behind a wild rocky outcrop, squinting down the barrel of an ancient jezail. They made a strange pair right enough.

What was even stranger was the startling fact that they had stopped at our table. Judging by Farrell's slack jaw even he hadn't expected that.

'Mr Crow?' the one identified as Habbani enquired, looking down at me expectantly.

'Not necessarily,' I said.

Undeterred, he added, 'My name is Mahmud Habbani. May we talk?'

His English was very fluent. Another surprise. Maybe he'd invested in a Berlitz Correspondence Course. Life was full of mysteries.

I threw a look at Mike and he rewarded me with a don't-look-at-me-I-didn't-invite-them expression, whereupon Habbani sat down.

I hate it when someone does that, invades my space without so much as a by your leave. 'By all means, take a seat won't you,' I said huffily.

Habbani obviously detected the note of irritation in my voice for he spread his hands in a placatory gesture. 'Forgive the intrusion, Mr Crow, but this is a matter of some urgency. Allow me, by the way, to introduce my friend, Raz Sharif. He is honoured to make your acquaintance.'

I thought then that if Raz Sharif looked honoured, I'd sure hate to meet him when he was pissed off.

'Charmed,' I managed to say. 'This is Michael Farrell.'

'Ah, but of course.' Habbani smiled easily. 'We have met before. During his stay in Peshawar Mr Farrell has been a frequent visitor to our party offices. Such a distinguished journalist has given our cause much publicity.'

Farrell inclined his head in appreciation of the character

reference. Meantime I marked Mahmud Habbani down as a bit of a crawler.

'What can we do for you, Doctor?' I asked, aware that the Pathan had taken up position behind Habbani's left shoulder. It was unobtrusively done but it was a clear indication just what the Pathan's role was. Bodyguard.

Habbani looked apologetic. 'Alas, sir, I am merely a lowly messenger. I am here on behalf of Maulavi Yunis Khalis. He sends greetings and asks if you would be so kind as to accompany me to his headquarters. He has a matter to discuss with you. I regret I cannot divulge anything further.'

His tone implied that walls had ears. I resisted the temptation to cast an eye towards Rasul who was enthroned at his table like a sweating Buddha.

Why not? seemed the obvious question to ask but I was busy thinking that maybe it was another job at last and I didn't want to get off on the wrong foot by antagonizing a prospective employer. As I'd come to discover, contracts weren't exactly thick on the ground.

I looked at Mike Farrell for some kind of assurance that this wasn't a con. Of what sort I couldn't imagine. Still . . .

'What do you reckon, Mike?' I said. 'Do we go?'

Whereupon Habbani butted in, his face full of sorrow. 'I regret that Mr Farrell is not included in the invitation. I mean you no disrespect, my friend,' he added quickly, looking at Mike.

'None taken, old sport,' Mike replied, giving me a sideways glance.

Curiouser and curiouser.

Frankly, I was more than a mite dubious about all this. Notwithstanding the possibility that this could be the prelude to a job offer, I didn't entirely relish the prospect of heading off into the murk in the company of two

24

complete strangers, one of whom looked as if he stole camels for a living. Raz Sharif returned my scrutiny with haughty disdain. It was the look of a proud man, a fighter. Raz Sharif was no spring chicken either. He certainly looked older than Habbani; with his mahogany skin wind seared and cracked like old parchment, he could, in all truth, have been any age between sixty and eighty.

That old man, I thought, can see right into my soul.

What to do? In the end, I think it was the fact that at least Mike knew who Habbani was that settled the question. He'd know where to come and look for me if I ran into trouble. And, let's face it, I was pretty strapped for cash. Another of my mottos is never look a gift horse in the wallet. I shrugged. 'Hell, why not?' I turned to Mike. 'You want to hang on here, until I find out what this is all about?'

'Carry on, old son. Don't mind me.' Mike's tone implied that he didn't seem to have much of a choice.

'Okay, Doc,' I invited. 'Take me to your leader.' And with that merry quip hanging in the air, I stood up.

It was Farrell's muttered aside that made me have second thoughts, but by then it was too late.

''Bye, Crow,' he said. 'Mind how you go.'

25

Chapter Two

It was beginning to resemble a scene from *The King of The Khyber Rifles*. Farrell could at least have had the good grace to warn me what to expect.

Maulavi Yunis Khalis looked impressive, I'll say that for him, albeit a touch theatrical. He must have been closer to Raz Sharif's age than Habbani's, but whereas Raz Sharif was tall and full of dignity, Yunis Khalis was quite stout. He was almost a caricature, a Punch cartoonist's idea of a wily chieftain. Grizzled face, luxuriant beard, turban tilted at a rakish angle, automatic pistol stuck in the wide leather belt that circumnavigated his slight paunch. Sprawled in a battered armchair, he looked like an exotic ruffian in a Victorian melodrama.

He was regarding me with keen interest, stroking his beard as he did so. If I'd been in the stalls I'd have hissed and jeered the man, along with the rest of the kids in the Saturday Cinema Club.

We were in a back room at the party offices of Hezb-i-Islami. Just the four of us in cosy company; Yunis Khalis, his two henchmen, and me. The place wasn't grand. The building appeared to have been an old school house. It had that look and feel to it, along with the musty smell of crushed chalk and old books. Around the peeling walls, ordnance survey maps, dotted with coloured pins and tags, had taken the place of the children's artwork. Chairs lined the room, with Yunis Khalis's armchair being the focal point. Presumably this was where the party held councils of war.

I'd been escorted there along a circuitous route, down

narrow alleyways and winding passages. What's more we'd come on foot. Okay, so I hadn't expected a gleaming limousine but a jaunt through the night clad back streets of Peshawar had never been high on my agenda of experiences not to be missed. The place was a veritable rabbit warren and I was disoriented within a matter of a few hundred yards. I think we actually backtracked a couple of times too, which didn't help. I found this more than a little unnerving because it was pitch dark and the stink was unbelievable and God knows what my feet were putting themselves into. I kept asking myself why I'd agreed to go on this trek in the first place. There were times when I severely doubted my own sanity. This was definitely one of them.

Plus one of my companions had armed himself by then; a fact that did nothing whatsoever to alleviate my growing suspicion that this wasn't the wisest decision I had ever made. In fact, I got to thinking that it was, in all probability, quite the dumbest.

Raz Sharif carried a rifle, which, to my amazement, had been passed to him by the porter back at Dean's. It was evident that the old man had been made to deposit the weapon there while he accompanied Habbani into the hotel, like a gunfighter leaving his Peacemaker at the edge of town. Comparisons with the American West were becoming increasingly apparent. And the old man was, after all, a Pathan, a warrior who believed it was his divine right to bear arms. The light that had appeared momentarily in Raz Sharif's eyes when he regained possession of his Lee Enfield had been proof enough of that belief. A Pathan without a weapon was like a man without a limb.

There was a fair amount of activity in the building when we arrived. I was greeted with cautious stares from the armed guards outside the main doors who never lifted their fingers from the triggers of their Kalashnikov rifles.

For the first time that evening I was actually glad of the company of Raz Sharif and Mahmud Habbani.

A lot of people seemed to be milling about. All men, most of them with weapons. Apart from the guards on the door, everyone appeared to be in high spirits. There was a distinct air of excitement and purpose. Somewhere out of sight a typewriter was being pounded and I thought I detected the rattle of a telex machine. I suspected, also, that the scene was not unusual. Exiled Afghans would frequent the place on a daily basis, anxious for news of the war. Here, Mujehadeen guerillas would be briefed and debriefed before and after their sorties across the border.

I supposed the atmosphere was one that was reflected in the other resistance groups' offices that were dotted around the town. Although I had been working for the ICRC for some time, my contact with the resistance had been limited. I'd seen Mujehadeen fighters in the refugee camps, visiting relatives, and I'd been inside the main hospital and seen the amputees and the paraplegics, crippled and maimed by Kalashnikov bullets and butterfly mines. My knowledge of the hierarchy within the various groups, however, was sketchy; based on hearsay mostly.

I did know that there were two main alliances; the Islamic Alliance and the Islamic Unity, and within those two structures there resided a number of separate organizations. All equally determined to oversee the downfall of the Kabul regime, but in no way were they all united in their military strategy or political aims.

The differences between them were determined by such things as tribal boundaries, ideologies and, perhaps most significant of all, by the personalities of their leaders, for it was the latter who provided credibility for their cause in the eyes of the rest of the world. Credibility resulted in much needed support, not just in weapons and equipment but in propaganda through newspapers, radio and TV.

Yunis Khalis, by all accounts, was undoubtedly one of the most charismatic resistance leaders. I'd been told he lacked the guile of other leaders such as Saiaf and Gailani, who tended, apparently, to extol the virtues of a traditionalist order of government while enjoying some of the more capitalistic traits of western democracy such as apartments in Paris, Gucci loafers and Peugeot cars. Khalis's faction was essentially fundamentalist in its aim; to establish an Islamic order in Afghanistan, but without the fanaticism of people like Hekmatyar and his colleague Qazi Mohammed.

Khalis's group was probably the best organized. His commanders in the field were, with one notable exception, the most professional and efficient in the whole resistance movement. Khalis had growing support, both in Afghanistan and abroad, not least because he was known to accompany his commanders into battle against the Afghan army and its Soviet allies. Quite recently he'd travelled to the UK to drum up aid for the resistance and counter the peace and propaganda tactics emanating from Moscow and Kabul.

Minus his armchair, presumably.

The facilities in the building, it has to be said, had a temporary look about them. I took this to be an indication that the offices were likely to be subjected to lightning raids by the Pakistani Special Branch, which would necessitate hurried departure for new quarters at a moment's notice.

So far, President Zia had remained remarkably tolerant of the activities of the various Afghan resistance groups but he had been under constant pressure from Moscow to clamp down on the guerilla organizations. Already, the Russians had threatened to close the Soviet-built Gudda power station and the massive steel mill in Karachi if Zia didn't support their way of thinking. They could blackmail him into purging his borders of all Afghan rebel bases. With close to three million refugees occupying the camps along the Durand Line, Hezb-i-Islami and the other groups were loath to upset Zia or compromise him in any way. Hence they were prepared to put up with whatever accommodation happened to be available. Even if it did mean there was a possibility of sudden eviction. But they had to watch their step.

The door opened suddenly and an Afghan in dark and flowing robes entered holding a tray bearing some cups.

'Would you care for some tea, Mr Crow?' Mahmud Habbani asked graciously. 'You understand we have no alcohol.'

'Thanks,' I said. It would have been impolite to refuse. God, but I could have murdered a beer though.

During my time in Pakistan I had come to learn that all business is conducted over copious servings of tea, green or black, without milk and very sweet.

The char boy departed. I sipped my tea, shifted in the hard uncomfortable chair, and waited for them to go through the traditional hospitality routine. It gave all of us time to assess one another prior to getting to the point of the exercise.

Mahmud Habbani said, 'We understand you saw service in Vietnam, Mr Crow.' Over the rim of his tea cup he was regarding me with frank, unblinking eyes.

Jesus, this was off the wall! I wondered wildly what the hell else they knew. 'That's right,' I said guardedly.

Vietnam had been more years ago than I cared to remember. Back in the Dark Ages. I couldn't recall offhand who'd said that war was hell but Vietnam confirmed it. Vietnam was Dante's Inferno. To those who served there it was a kind of Armageddon, brutal and bestial.

'You served in the Royal Australian Air Force,' Habbani

added. 'Flying gunships. A most dangerous occupation, sir.'

Christ! Dangerous, I thought, didn't come anywhere near it!

My squadron had flown support for Aussie and Kiwi SAS patrols. I'd flown Hueys, the name given to the Bell UH-I helicopters. The Australians had operated mostly in Phuoc Tuy province, south east of Saigon, out of Fire Support Bases like Nui Dat. The SAS teams often worked in close liaison with American Special Forces and Korean Rangers, taking the war to the enemy in search and destroy missions. In my time I'd airlifted men and equipment into and out of some of the most God-awful country I'd ever encountered; dense rain forest, sun-scorched plateaus, mangrove-matted swampland and mist-shrouded valleys. And, as if that hadn't been enough to give me sleepless nights, I'd also had to contend with midgets in black pyjamas who, for reasons best known only to themselves, had taken an instant exception to my own particular code of survival. Hostile terrain was one thing, hostile natives was quite another. It was bloody anti-social for a start.

'Your tour of duty lasted . . .' Habbani started to say.

I beat him to it. 'A friggin' lifetime,' I said. I wasn't sure but as I raised my voice I thought I saw a spark flare in Raz Sharif's eyes. I didn't need this cross-examination of my CV.

'You sound bitter, Mr Crow.'

'That too,' I said. 'Mostly I was disillusioned. Like the rest of the poor bastards who lived through it, I got to thinking that it wasn't my war.'

A look passed suddenly between Habbani and Yunis Khalis. As if they were worried by my response. I wasn't sure about the resistance leader's command of English at this point. I wondered how he'd managed to follow the discourse so far. No one seemed to be acting as interpreter.

Anyway, it appeared that Habbani was going to be the prompt in this production. He frowned. 'Your experiences must have been profound, I think.'

'You could say that,' I said drily. 'Mostly they were based on sheer terror. I've heard enough about the glory of war to see me through to my dotage. There's nothing remotely glorious about getting your backside blown off, believe me.'

And I should bloody know, matey.

My last mission. After which the bad dreams had begun.

At that time we'd been operating out of Bien Hoa, the US tactical airbase, north east of Saigon, shuttling racoon patrols along Route One and the Cambodian border. Some of the missions bordered on the suicidal. It was bad enough having to manoeuvre the choppers into hastily prepared landing zones the size of pocket handkerchiefs without the additional risk of running into enemy ground fire as well. Unsecured landing zones we called those.

My crew had been sent out to retrieve a returning reconnaissance patrol comprised of Special Forces operatives, a New Zealand SAS observer and a Korean tracker. The recon team had broken squelch to say they were coming under heavy ground fire from Charlie, they had one casualty, and where the fuck was the slick that was supposed to be on hand to pick them up? Unquote.

Trolling the treetops at 110 knots, trying to get a fix on their position, that's where. And it had been like looking for the proverbial needle in a haystack. Inevitable really, seeing as one patch of jungle looked much the same as any other. Mile after mile of rain forest stretched away to the horizon; a vivid green blanket broken only by muddy brown tributaries of the Saigon River twisting and turning back on themselves like worms on a freshly watered lawn.

In that sort of terrain half a dozen men in tiger stripes didn't exactly stand out.

Although I was the first pilot I was in the left-hand seat. I had greater visibility there. The left side of the chopper's instrument panel was cut away and I was able to watch the ground beneath my feet. But I still hadn't been able to spot them. And I was getting anxious. Somewhere below me six hard-pressed men were fast running out of time.

As it happened, we finally struck lucky because the VC opened fire on the helicopter as it passed over their heads. Micky Galvin, my gunner, had barely enough time to bellow, 'INCOMING!' into his helmet mike before bullets began to pepper the Huey.

I pushed on the cyclic and applied hard left rudder to swing us away and Micky began to return fire, pumping rounds out of the side door at an incredible rate, pulverizing the ground. As I banked the chopper I saw the recon team. They appeared to be clinging to the edge of a clearing no bigger than a tennis court tacked on the side of a small hillock away to the right. The Huey swept around and clattered in over the trees. Jacko, the lanky crew chief, was also in on the action now and he had joined Micky in retaliation. My ears were filled with the whine of the turbine and the harsh jabber of the M-60 machine guns. It felt as if my head was being pounded by a jack hammer.

Something wicked slammed into the fuselage beneath us. The chopper shuddered violently and the stick jarred in my hands. Peering out over the stubby nose, I felt suddenly vulnerable, despite my chest protector and the ceramic and steel armour that cloaked the body of the helicopter. I prayed that Galvin and Jacko could keep Charlie's head down long enough for us to complete the extraction.

We pitched in over the treeline. I flared the Huey and we sank. The heels of the skids swished through knee-

33

high elephant scrub. Out of the corner of my eye I saw a handful of men emerge from the trees and sprint towards the chopper, the front runner small and wiry: the Korean Ranger. One of the men had a body slung over his shoulders. He was stumbling under the weight. A second member of the team grabbed him as he fell. Together they dragged their wounded comrade towards the hovering helicopter.

The Korean threw himself aboard and turned to help the others. The side window starred and I flinched instinctively. My hands jerked the controls. The Huey lifted. I moved the collective back down to correct and we started to drift. The controls were fighting back. I swore and levelled us out. The chopper sank once again.

Through the noise and vibration I could hear Jacko screaming at the approaching men.

'FOR CHRIS'SAKES! MOVE IT! MOVE IT!'

The Huey dipped as the remnants of the team scrambled over the sill. Faces blacked with cork and camouflage cream, they looked as if they'd all just crawled out from some deadly conflagration. The injured man – it transpired it was the Kiwi observer – was bundled aboard with scant ceremony. There were muzzle flashes in among the trees. I began to thank God that the VC were only using small arms when I saw the ground explode no more than five yards in front of the chopper's nose. The canopy was showered with debris.

Jesus, they were using bloody mortars!

Over my headphones I heard the wild yell of my co-pilot.

'LET'S GO, SKIPPER! PLEASE!'

Jacko and the Korean were pulling the last man in by the scruff of his neck.

I didn't require any second bidding. I brought in the power, felt the air pressure build up under the rotors as they fought to lift us off the ground. Nose down, the Huey dived forward and I hauled us up and away.

We floated out across the forest. Micky Galvin continued to rake the Viet Cong positions. From the din in the back I knew that the recon team were also adding to the fire power.

I felt the massive blow down in the small of my back, like the kick of a mule. Breath was sucked out of my lungs. Involuntarily my body went into spasm as the shockwave rippled through me. Despite enormous effort on my part I watched my hands slip away from the controls. I could feel myself beginning to drift into the void. In my helmet I heard my co-pilot, Griff, yelling that he had the stick and through a mist of excruciating pain I could dimly make out Jacko shrieking my name over and over as if the stupid bastard thought I might be hard of hearing or something.

I woke up in a field hospital with the worst hangover of my entire life. The nurse told me it was nothing to worry about; probably the effects of the anaesthetic and why didn't I try to get some rest? Which had seemed like the best suggestion I'd had all year. When next I surfaced the headache had worn off, which meant I was then able to concentrate fully on the ache that was beginning to spread through my back like a forest fire. I felt about a hundred and fifty years old. Sleep was a welcome relief.

When I was fully awake and relatively coherent they told me how close it had been. The bullet they had extracted from my back had spent most of its energy burrowing through the rear of my seat before paying me a visit. As it was, the surgeon had to root around for a while until he'd found the offending article and swabbed the resulting damage free of infection. Another inch or so and I would have been trundling myself along the corridors in a wheelchair, on a permanent basis. That little

35

snippet of information had caused a fair amount of perspiration to break out across my already fevered brow.

It was about that time that I learned that the wounded Kiwi hadn't pulled through, which prompted no small measure of self analysis, concerned for the most part with an in-depth examination of my own mortality. A subject which I found time to dwell upon during slack moments of my convalescence which had been spent in the company of a number of agreeable companions in the glitzy bars along Tu Do and under the awning of the bar in the Majestic Hotel, sipping an Amstel and watching the hustle and bustle of the Saigon waterfront. Recuperation brought into focus a realization that I didn't want to end the war as just another name on a marble monument or the tag on the end of an olive green body bag.

So ended my tour. As the 707's wheels finally lifted off the tarmac at Tan Son Nhut, I had no regrets. 'Taking the Big Bird to Paradise' the Americans called it; the Freedom Flight. Going back to the world.

But I was still having nightmares about it.

Mahmud Habbani cut into my thoughts. 'So, you turned freelance after the war, Mr Crow. Not an easy transition, I would have thought?'

The tubby doctor was turning out to be a master of the understatement.

The personal columns of the newspapers and trade magazines had been chock full of abbreviated resumés submitted by hopeful and, in most cases, broke and desperate ex-servicemen anxious to turn their talents towards gainful employment; washed-up ex-RAF pilots were ten-a-penny. It was the old chestnut. Too many applicants for too few jobs.

I'd drifted aimlessly for quite a while, keeping my head above water more by luck than judgement, although still taking every opportunity to keep my hours up; mostly through ferrying work, delivering machines to customers who were either too busy or too damned lazy to do the job themselves.

I'd moved north gradually, up through New South Wales and into Queensland where I'd flown left-hand seat for a while for a small independent operator who specialized in scenic flights around the Gold Coast resorts and along the Tweed valley. The job had also involved providing coastal patrols and fire-watch detail as well as radio reports for the local news stations, 4GG and 2MW, as part of a community service project.

I'd improved my rating somewhat as well as my hours logged and moved into fixed-wing operations, flying Cessnas and Chieftains as well as choppers. I'd been taken on for several months by a high-profile commuter outfit operating out of Coolangatta which ran shuttle services for overpaid executives up and down the coast as far north as Brisbane and as far south as Sydney. I was flying Learjets by then, but it was all a bit sedentary after Nam.

Then I met Wallace.

Clem Wallace was another graduate of Bien Hoa and, five years out of the service, was about as bored as he could be with peacetime flying. As bored as I was, anyway. Which struck us both as pretty bloody amusing considering what we'd been through and what we'd tried to forget. Wallace had put it down to every man having a streak of masochism in him somewhere; it just tended to surface in some people more than it did in others. I'd long figured that the reasoning behind that philosophical gem lay in the fact that Clem had been in his cups at the time, sprawled under a bottle-strewn table in a seedy bar in downtown Madang on the north coast of Papua New Guinea, the two of us having recently completed an extensive geo survey flight along the wilds of the Ramu River.

I couldn't remember the exact date that we'd first teamed up. It was somewhere back in the mists of antiquity and I oft wondered if I'd been either too drunk or too damned foolish to appreciate just what I might have been letting myself in for. Whatever the catalyst, though, we'd had more than our fair share of excitement since, not to mention indiscretions. We'd flown relief medical supplies into the Moluccas and booze into Borneo, vulcanologists across the Makassar Strait and M-16s into the Burmese highlands. We were nursing a dilapidated Beechcraft during those jaunts and most of our profit went into keeping the old bird in the air. We weren't just flying by the seat of our pants, we were surviving by the skin of our teeth. Still, as Clem was often prone to point out, it was a living.

So, I reflected on my past and wondered how Habbani had come by the information. It implied that Yunis Khalis had a very efficient intelligence organization and one which could call upon outside agencies to provide assistance in compiling such a comprehensive dossier on yours truly. Habbani hadn't gotten all this from the Red Cross. Even they hadn't gone into my background that thoroughly.

Presumably Habbani and Yunis Khalis also knew the rest.

I was on my own now. Clem and I had parted company several years ago, without acrimony it must be said. We'd made a few bucks between us, and lost a few too. It had been during one of our more lean times that we'd decided to go our separate ways. It had been rather an emotional farewell really. We'd both been blitzed out of our skulls. As far as I could recollect it had been a heck of a divorce.

38

My share of the settlement had been a colossal hangover and half the proceeds of a stunt contract we'd undertaken for a film company that had hired us to fly an elderly DC-3 on straffing runs over make-believe Japanese troop convoys on the Malay Peninsula. While I had been retained by the studio to transport camera crews on location seeking expeditions around Tasek Dampar and the Pahang River, Clem Wallace had packed his kit bag and flown west in search of his fortune.

We'd kept in touch infrequently. The last I'd heard was that Clem was the personal pilot for some East African president. Then there had been a rumour that Clem had been involved in some sort of assassination plot against his former employer and had been forced to hightail it for cover with a team of European mercenaries. That had been well over a year ago. I hadn't heard from him since. In fact, nobody had.

Now I was flying solo and I was back in helicopters, in the shape of a three-year-old Bell JetRanger which I almost owned. Admittedly, my payments were somewhat erratic but then so was my income. So far, the finance company had been remarkably understanding.

Yunis Khalis murmured to Habbani in Pushtu.

Habbani nodded and said, 'We understand you own a helicopter, Mr Crow.'

Here it comes. 'Most of it,' I said cautiously.

Habbani translated and a smile touched the resistance leader's cheery bearded face.

'We are pleased to hear that, Mr Crow,' Habbani said. 'And is this fine helicopter for hire?'

Yunis Khalis was staring at me intently.

'That depends.'

'On what?' The old armchair creaked in protest as Yunis Khalis shifted his bulk.

'On what you need it for. On how much you're prepared to pay. And is it legal?'

That prompted another brief and whispered discussion in Pushtu between Yunis Khalis and the doctor. Raz Sharif, who so far had remained mute since I'd met him, stood over Yunis Khalis's right shoulder, exuding quiet menace. I studied cobwebs.

Yunis Khalis broke off the conversation with a shake of his hand and regarded me thoughtfully. There was a lot going on behind those eyes, I could sense it.

Habbani said, 'The job is one of transportation, sir. As regards your fee, you would not find us lacking in generosity. Thirdly, we do not consider the job to be in any way illegal.'

To which I said, 'Your idea of what is or isn't legal might not match mine. Suppose we get to the nitty gritty.'

Habbani looked blank. 'Nitty gritty?'

'The point,' I said, not a little impatiently.

'Ah, yes, of course. A light dawned in the doctor's eyes. He chuckled. 'My English . . . you understand.' He waved a hand vaguely.

I waited.

Habbani said, 'Mr Crow, one of our associates, a very important man in the resistance, is seriously ill. We wish you to fly him from Dar Galak to a medical centre where he can receive treatment.'

I relaxed. So that was it. A fetch and carry job. No sweat, guys.

'Well, I see no problem there,' I said. 'I take it that's one of the refugee camps, right? I can't say that I'm familiar with the name but some of those places are a wee bit off the beaten track. I guess I can manage that okay.'

But the room had suddenly gone very quiet and they had this weird look on their faces, as if I hadn't quite

40

grasped what they were getting at. I began to get this strange, uncomfortable feeling.

Habbani cleared his throat. 'Dar Galak,' he said, 'is not a refugee camp exactly.'

A tingling at the back of my neck. I was going to regret asking this, I just knew it.

'What is it, exactly?'

'A village, Mr Crow. It lies close to the confluence of the Kantiwar and the Parun rivers.'

I think my jaw dropped open at that point. I know I was halfway out of my chair before I found my voice. 'You've got to be fucking joking! That's over the border, f'r Chris'sakes! That's in Afghanistan!'

Habbani said softly, 'We know where it is, Mr Crow.'

I was all the way out of my seat by this time, aware that at the sound of my near hysterical shriek, Raz Sharif had shifted his grip on his Lee Enfield. The barrel was now pointing towards my midriff. Any sudden move towards either Yunis Khalis or the doctor on my part and I knew, without a shadow of a doubt, that the old man would kill me.

I moderated my tone, only by a fraction. The initial shock was wearing off. Now, I was just plain angry. 'You're out of your fucking minds! You want me to fly into Afghanistan and airlift somebody back across the border? I can't believe I'm really hearing this! It's a dream, right? Any minute now, I'm going to wake up. C'mon, fellas, reassure me.'

'No dream, Mr Crow,' Habbani said. 'We are very, very serious. We would not have approached you other-wise. We know of your background, your expertise. You flew helicopters in Vietnam.'

'Jesus, so did a lot of other guys. And most of us were scared shitless!'

And I'm still getting the bloody shakes because of it. This was insanity.

Yunis Khalis lost his smile. Gone was the jovial buffoon in fancy dress. Instead, steel was clearly showing through the grainy façade. Grim concern was etched on to the lined face. He muttered to his spokesman.

Habbani cleared his throat. 'We were given your name by a contact in the Red Cross. You are our only hope. There is no one else in Peshawar with your qualifications or experience. We had hoped you would help us. It is a matter of life and death and we are running out of time.'

I shook my head. 'You're all nuts.' I sighed. 'Look, I'm sorry. I guess I should be flattered that you asked me, but it's not on. Now, if you'll excuse me, I think I can find my own way home.'

I started for the door. Only then did Raz Sharif lower his gun. I thought, Farrell isn't going to believe this. Not in a million years.

There were indistinct mutterings behind me. After which Habbani said, 'One hundred thousand dollars, Mr Crow.'

Hand on door. 'Beg pardon?' I said. As if I hadn't heard every frigging syllable, for Christ's sake.

'We will pay you one hundred thousand American dollars or the equivalent in any currency you wish if you accept this job.'

The groaning sound was Yunis Khalis clambering out of his armchair.

'We can even pay you in heroin or gem stones if you would prefer,' Habbani added hurriedly.

I turned then. 'My God! You people must be serious!'

'We wondered what it would take to convince you,' Habbani said. 'At least hear what we have to say.' He smiled hesitantly. 'What can it hurt?'

The idea, of course, was preposterous, sheer unadulterated lunacy. Even if I accepted their offer, which I wouldn't, I'd never live to spend the money.

I stared at them all.

But it wouldn't do any harm to listen, would it?

Well, would it?

Chapter Three

Yunis Khalis and Habbani had a plan. Sort of.

The man they wanted me to airlift out was Muhammed Nur Rafiq, guerilla fighter, commander of the central provinces and a close ally of Ahmadshah Massoud, the most effective Mujehadeen leader inside Afghanistan. Although he was aligned to a different faction – Massoud was a Jamiat commander – Muhammed Nur Rafiq was still regarded as being Little John to Massoud's Robin Hood. Which meant he was someone with a considerable price on his head.

'What's wrong with him?' I asked.

'We suspect hepatitis,' Habbani replied, his tone grave. 'We received word of his condition from a group of refugees who crossed the border only this morning. As you are no doubt aware, there are French medical teams working within the guerilla strongholds. Muhammed Nur Rafiq was seen by one of these teams three days ago. However, the French medics did not have the necessary antibiotics or facilities to treat him effectively. All they could do was transcribe his symptoms and give the information to the refugees for it to be relayed to us when they reached Pakistan.'

'The refugees couldn't have brought him out with them?' But I already knew the answer to that one.

'Impossible. He would not have survived the journey over the mountains. No, our one hope was an airlift. Although I admit that by now we may be too late to save him.'

'I would have thought that was a distinct probability,' I said.

A shadow flitted over the face of the doctor. 'My friend, we have very few men of Muhammed's calibre. I implore you to assist us. Not just for the sake of Muhammed Nur Rafiq, but for the resistance. He is four days away on foot, but in your helicopter that time would be reduced to literally minutes.'

A matter of minutes. One hundred thousand dollars. I thought about that.

'All right,' I replied. 'But what about the Russians then? You think they'll just sit there twiddling their thumbs while we go in and get him? I can't see it somehow. Can you?'

I was really interested to know how they seriously intended to combat the unwelcome attention of the Soviets. Not the latter's ground forces so much as their aerial hardware. In particular the aircraft referred to by the Mujehadeen as the Devil's Chariot; the Mil Mi–24 assault support helicopter. This was a machine with formidable fire power, capable of inflicting massive damage with machine gun, rockets and missiles. Code named 'Hind' by NATO forces, these gunships were the most potent and feared weapon in the Soviet arsenal. Najibullah's peace proposals had in no way curtailed their activities.

'Tomorrow morning, at dawn, Mr Crow, a force of Mujehadeen under the command of Ahmadshah Massoud will launch an attack on the Soviet airbase at Bagram. The raid has been planned for some time. With luck it could divert attention away from the pick-up point.' Habbani waddled over to one of the maps on the wall. 'Come, see,' he urged.

I walked over. Mike Farrell had been right, I reflected. So much for the cease-fire.

Habbani stabbed a podgy finger at a triangular tag on

45

the map. The tag was speared by a pin and coloured red. There were other coloured tags, I saw. Green, blue and yellow. I presumed that they represented the various types of Russian and Afghan military deployment. Air bases, infantry garrisons, fuel dumps, that sort of thing.

'Bagram,' Habbani said.

The red tag showed that the base lay north east of Kabul but south of the Panjsher Valley, Massoud's main area of operation.

'And here,' Habbani said, pointing, 'is Dar Galak.'

I peered beyond the end of the doctor's rather grubby fingernail. Dar Galak was literally a pin prick. The scale told me that the village was some forty-odd miles inside the border, in the high mountains of Nuristan. A hell of a trek, whichever way you looked at it.

But I saw what he was getting at. Dar Galak lay to the east, south of the Katwar Pass. It was possible that the attack on the base would draw the Soviets north, away from the village.

I digested that.

Habbani went on, 'The Russians also maintain troop garrisons and air support bases at Jalalabad and Asadabad.'

Two more positions were pinpointed deep within the maze of contour lines. Now, they did present problems. Jalalabad was south of Bagram. Asadabad lay to the east, on the Kunar River, not far from the Pakistan border and therefore very close to the approach corridor that the chopper would have to take. Correction: that a chopper would have to take if anyone was mad enough to attempt the job.

Yunis Khalis was standing next to me. He studied me with rheumy eyes. He was wheezing slightly and sounded out of breath.

I stared at the map. But what if Massoud and his Afghan fighters could draw the Soviets away from the area?

Making it possible for me to swing in behind the gunships as they headed off away from those bases at Jalalabad and Asadabad, towards Bagram to give assistance to the beleaguered base personnel. Scooting in so fast that the Russians wouldn't even know their air space had been invaded. And I'd be going in low, hugging the slopes. The mountains would mask their radar.

Could it be done?

'How long do you estimate it would take a helicopter to reach Dar Galak?' Habbani asked.

A helicopter? They meant my helicopter, didn't they? I studied the map, thought about it. The one hundred thousand dollar question. 'Taking the terrain into consideration, flat out, maybe twenty-five minutes.'

Say one hour there and back. But by God, that was shifting some and providing they moved their asses at the pick-up point. It wouldn't be healthy to hang around any longer than was necessary.

If I took the job, of course. Which I wouldn't.

One hour, give or take. One hundred grand. It would pay off the outstanding balance on the chopper and leave me with a hefty profit. And I'd be a damned fool to even contemplate it.

'I don't suppose you've consulted with the Pakistani authorities about this little caper?' I said. 'I mean, I can just picture their unconfined joy as we toddle off over the frontier into the wide blue yonder. Politically sensitive would be a fair description of this enterprise. Ye gods! If Zia had the slightest inkling of your plan he'd clap you in irons and throw away the key. You must realize he's got the border monitored, especially after the latest cross-border raids.'

The next bit slayed me. It really did.

'Ah, yes,' Habbani said. 'But you will be going out, my friend, not coming in.'

47

Faced with such irrefutable logic, I could see that any argument I was foolish enough to raise would be snuffed out like a candle flame in the breeze. Somehow, I didn't reckon I'd gain any credits by pointing out that we'd be coming in on the way back. After all, wasn't that the whole point of the bloody exercise?

'We would conceal the helicopter's true destination under cover of a visit to one of the refugee camps on this side of the border,' Habbani explained excitedly. 'By the time the Pakistanis realize you have made a detour it will be too late for them to do anything.' He appeared totally smitten with the ruse. For a second or two the flame of jehad burned in his eyes.

Jehad.

Holy War is how the western media like to term it. A rather convenient translation, lacking perception. Jehad is more than that, much more. It is not simply a matter of picking up a gun and shooting Russian soldiers or rolling grenades under the tracks of their tanks. Jehad is, in many ways, the core of Islam. It's the means by which a Moslem measures belief in his creed. It's the strength of purpose, self denial, sacrifice. It encompasses every aspect of the true faith. It means to strive in the name of Allah to the exclusion of all else. In such a struggle war is an option to be considered only as a means of last resort but for the briefest of moments Mahmud Habbani had been as roused as a general about to lead his warriors into battle.

Detour? I thought. Christ! That was one way of putting it!

I saw they were regarding me closely. The short hairs on the back of my neck prickled. It was a feeling I hadn't had since the squadron briefings back in Nui Dat and Bien Hoa.

Yunis Khalis, who by now had regained the sagging support of his armchair, fixed me with a penetrating stare.

Habbani said, 'Ours is a just cause, my friend. You must see that. We are talking of freedom, the right to choose our own destiny. Will you help us?'

I said nothing. I felt like telling them that it was their destiny not mine. I'd told them earlier that I hadn't considered Vietnam to have been my war. Well, this wasn't my war either. So, don't think about it. Do the sensible thing; turn around and walk out of the room. Go back to the hotel, have a few laughs with Farrell, tell the Swiss TV crew to get stuffed, and bugger off back to Islamabad at first light. To hell with the lot of them.

Instead, I asked them what time they wanted me to go in and get him.

The chopper was out on the tarmac, fuelled, ready to go. It was still dark. But away to the east the horizon was tinged with an orange glow; a prelude to sunrise. To the west lay the mountains. I couldn't distinguish them yet but they were there, huge and rugged, a natural barrier, stretching across the frontier and beyond to the jagged, barren ramparts of the Hindu Kush.

At this early hour the temperature was distinctly cool. Before long though, the airstrip would be simmering in the morning heat. A haze would descend over the field and the distant peaks, by then visible, would sift and shimmer like a reflection on the surface of a pond. The air would become hot and muggy, heavy with the acrid stench of kerosene and shit, which seemed to be a permanent feature of every fly-blown town and village in the region.

Somewhere in the stygian gloom a dog barked. The harsh sound was answered by a chaotic chorus of yapping and yelping, the noise as intrusive as a knife thrust.

I burrowed into my jacket and stamped my feet in an effort to dislodge the chill from my bones.

I'd completed my pre-flight checks under the dim light of a kerosene lamp I'd filched from one of the maintenance sheds. I was awaiting the arrival of Mahmud Habbani. I'd been at the field for a couple of hours, satisfying myself that the chopper had no outstanding maintenance problems. It hadn't of course, I was only looking for a way to pass the time without having to listen to the twanging of my nerve ends.

Before that I'd spent a number of restless hours in my tatty hotel room, catnapping, thinking about the ways I was going to spend the money, wondering whether I should have moved myself along to the Khyber Intercontinental with the other mercenaries. Because that's what I'd just become. Or perhaps it was a case of finding my true level. Maybe, after all this charity work I was just reverting to form.

Farrell, not unnaturally, had been mighty curious, as befitted a good newshound, and had adopted a rather sceptical expression when I told him all they'd wanted me for was to transport a consignment of medical supplies from Peshawar to the refugee camp at Chital Rajat first thing in the morning.

'Bloody funny time to come calling,' had been Farrell's trenchant comment.

To which I had responded by explaining to him that the resistance group had received word that a large number of refugees was due to cross the border sometime in the next couple of days and preparations for their arrival had to be made. And if he believed that he'd believe just about anything. So, he'd rewarded me with an 'oh, yeah' kind of look and added that he hoped I wasn't considering doing something stupid.

'No way,' I'd assured him. But I'd had my fingers crossed behind me so the words hadn't counted. Ho hum.

Then I'd asked him for a favour.

As a guest in Dean's, Farrell had access to a safety deposit box. I handed him a small package the size of a fat pack of cigarettes.

'I'd like you to stash this for me, Mike. I want it safe. I also want to pick it up again in a day or so. I know you're not going to be around but if you could arrange with the desk for me to collect it on your behalf I'd appreciate it.'

Farrell had eyed the package with suspicion. 'It's not dope is it?'

'Of course it's not dope!' I said. 'Do me a bloody favour!'

Actually it was emeralds. A dozen stones, uncut, about twenty-five thousand dollars' worth. The gems are mined in Afghanistan, at Dash-i-Rawat, and their export goes some way towards paying for arms and supplies for the Mujehadeen. They were the down payment. One quarter of my bounty. The remainder on delivery. Habbani had offered me cash or heroin as alternatives. I'd declined the cash because of the bulk and the horse because I didn't use the stuff and I was very much aware of the penalties doled out for trafficking. A long sojourn in a Pakistani gaol was not an experience I welcomed, thank you very much.

I hadn't told Mike what was in the package, nor the value. The newsman would have to remain ignorant. Not least because he'd know that no one in their right mind paid that sort of amount to have a batch of medical supplies flown less than fifty miles. Even the threat of pestilence wouldn't merit that kind of fee.

Still, Farrell had agreed to safeguard the goods, albeit with a certain lack of grace, and that made me feel sufficiently guilty at not taking the man into my confidence. Though, if I pulled the extraction off, Farrell would get first refusal on one humdinger of a scoop. In the end, however, we'd parted on good terms; mostly because Mike would have left by the time I returned and there was

51

every chance we might not meet up again. I went and checked back into my doss house. But after the old-style comfort of Dean's my dingy room had seemed even more squalid and so, unable to sleep, I'd packed my holdall and headed for the field. I'd hitched a ride for most of the way on the back of a Suzuki three-wheeler which had been about as comfortable as sitting astride a chain saw. It had taken several minutes after I'd dismounted for the shrill buzzing in my ears to fade away.

At the airfield I'd actually considered erasing the helicopter's registration markings and altering her livery to give her a new colour scheme; something dun or tan to break up her outline so that she'd merge with the landscape. But I'd dismissed the idea, of course, as totally impractical given the short time I had, not to mention fanciful, because if the Pakistanis caught me heading for the Durand Line sans registration and decked out in a highly suspect paint job they'd put the mockers on the extraction before it had even got off the ground. Literally. And if I was caught on the far side of the frontier with a camouflaged aircraft I might just as well put the barrel of a gun against my head and pull the trigger myself. If I found myself in a position where the Soviets did force me down I planned to tell them that I was off course due to a navaid malfunction and plead the bit about trying to find a refugee camp and could they please take pity on me and point me and my errant helicopter in the right direction, if that wasn't too much trouble. In other words, appeal to their better nature and sense of humanity. Although, if it ever did come to that, I'd be far better employed trying to appeal to their sense of humour. Still, it was about the best I could come up with. In short, Crow: forget the paint, forget the registration details, just keep your bloody fingers crossed.

I wondered if Gary Powers had crossed his fingers

52

before he'd taken off from the CIA's base at Peshawar, prior to his U-2 spy plane getting shot down over the Soviet Union all those years ago. I hoped that quirky reminiscence wasn't some kind of omen.

A truck rumbled out of the night; a big canvas-covered Bedford. This would be Habbani, as expected.

The truck shuddered to a stop, engine popping. The cab doors opened. Habbani stepped down. He was followed by another passenger, a slim, effeminate-looking youth. A third person materialized from the gloom at the rear of the vehicle. I was surprised to see that it was Raz Sharif, moving very quietly for such a big man.

'Good morning, my friend!' Habbani greeted me effusively, proffering his hand. He was wearing a high-collared sheepskin jacket and woollen cap as protection against the morning cold.

Raz Sharif's concession to the cool temperature was a woollen cloak, a chogha, that he wore over his shoulders. His rifle hung across his back. Their slight companion was dressed in what appeared to be an ex-army camouflage smock, two sizes too large, and a cap similar to that worn by the doctor.

The young man regarded me with open curiosity. There was something vaguely unsettling in that frank gaze. I wasn't sure what it was precisely but for a while I found myself wondering what he was doing here. Maybe he was a friend come to see Habbani off. Which set me wondering vaguely about the plump doctor's sexual preferences. Horses for courses, I supposed.

'Not exactly keeping a low profile, are we?' I nodded towards the truck. 'I'm amazed you didn't consider selling tickets. Anyway, I thought you'd be alone.'

Habbani indicated his companion. 'Raz Sharif will accompany you across the border, Mr Crow.'

I blinked. 'Oh, yes? What the hell for?'

53

Habbani seemed surprised I'd bothered to ask. 'Why, for your protection, of course. And I presume you have neither Pushtu nor Farsi? Nor Dari?'

Of course I bloody hadn't. But then Raz Sharif didn't appear to have any English, as I pointed out.

'I speak Inglestan pretty bloody fine!' Raz Sharif muttered darkly, unslinging his rifle. 'I fight with the British Army!'

I stared at him. Expedience made me refrain from asking if the preposition meant that the Pathan had fought alongside the British Army or against it. In any case, Habbani jumped in first.

'Also, Raz Sharif's nephew is the malik, headman of Dar Galak.'

Which pretty well made it game, set and match to the fat doctor. All I could do then was consider how much the additional weight would affect the JetRanger's performance. Extra ballast made all the difference when it came to speed and manoeuvrability; two factors I just might have to rely on if corners got tight.

Well, at least I'd have someone with me who could ask the way if we got lost.

But Habbani hadn't quite finished. He said, 'Forgive my rudeness, Mr Crow. This is Doctor Bonnard. She will also be travelling with you.'

The dull clunk I heard was the sound of my jaw dropping.

Doctor Bonnard? She? As in female? God Almighty!

The slim figure in the camouflage gear moved out of Habbani's shadow. Features became clearer, more defined. A fringe of dark hair peeked out from under the woollen cap. Close up, the face had lost much of the boyishness that had seemed apparent from a distance.

In the gloom it was hard to tell the colour of her eyes, but they were almond shaped, set above a straight nose and lips that were full and slightly parted. A firm jawline, uptilted, indicated a determined trait of character that manifested itself in the critical look she was throwing my way. An open challenge that dared me to make something of it. So it seemed a shame to disappoint her.

'The hell she is! Who says so?' Prudently, I gave her a sideways shrug. 'No offence, love.'

Whereupon I was rewarded with a look that could have stripped paint followed by one word spat contemptuously.

'Merde!'

Then she stuck her hands deep in the pockets of her jacket, about turned, and stalked back to the truck.

French? The name and the expletive told me as much. I watched her go. It wasn't that much of a chore either. There's something about the way a woman walks when she's angry. As if every fibre in her body is drawn as tight as cat gut. Almost with reluctance I turned back to Habbani and waited for an explanation.

Habbani said, 'If Muhammed Nur Rafiq is still alive Doctor Bonnard will assess his condition and administer whatever immediate treatment is necessary in order that he may be brought safely back across the border.'

The girl had reentered the cab of the truck. She seemed to be retrieving something. Seconds later she climbed back down. What looked like a small soft sided travel bag, the sort that stowed neatly under aircraft seats, hung over her shoulder. She began to retrace her steps.

She didn't look like a doctor, that was for sure. In dark slacks, boots, ex-army combat gear and that ridiculous hat she could have been a backpacker looking for a lift to a Nepalese hippy commune.

I viewed her arrival with some speculation. French medical teams had been working with the guerillas for some time; in Peshawar's hospitals, inside the refugee camps, and over the border, within the strongholds of the

Mujehadeen. Most of the nurses and doctors had come out under the patronage of Aide Medicale Internationale and Médecin Sans Frontiers. In Peshawar and the camps they operated under the protective umbrella of the IRC but over the border they were on their own.

Entering Afghanistan was relatively easy. They went in with the supply caravans. Once inside the medics moved with the guerilla bands. They were scattered and few but their presence and the assistance they provided was invaluable. They ran field hospitals and were the only means by which the rebels received medical aid. Their work was often carried out in the most appalling conditions with temporary operating theatres set up in caves or in the shells of bombed-out buildings, where the facilities weren't that much more sophisticated than those employed on the battlefields of Corunna and Balaclava. No MASH units here, no compounds emblazoned with the scarlet cross, no generators to provide light, no adequate means of sterilization. Just the hit and miss reliability of hand-pumped machinery and the vapid glow of hissing kerosene lamps to work by if they were lucky. And antibiotics in constant short supply.

Had the girl been across to the dark side of the Durand Line? Anything was possible.

Despite the fact that female emancipation was a concept not yet wholly accepted in the Islamic world, the war had, to some extent, demolished the barriers of constraint that had existed for centuries. Certainly there had been and still were women doctors working within the guerilla strongholds.

In fact they were able to perform tasks that a male doctor could not.

The Red Cross people had told me that the Mujehadeen were still reluctant to allow a male doctor to tend the wounds of an Afghan woman, particularly if the treatment involved examination of any part of the body normally concealed by clothing. Which meant that any critical damage to chest, abdomen or leg would go untended, with inevitable results. The patient died. So women doctors were, in many instances, vital in saving civilian lives.

But convention, it appeared, was not a one-way street. Conversely the Mujehadeen themselves were quite prepared to submit to treatment by female medics. The reason for this was one of supreme practicality. Treatment, no matter by whom, meant recovery. And recovery restored the ability to kill Russians. Quod erat demonstrandum. Quite definitely.

Nevertheless, how come the resistance had chosen Doctor Bonnard? There were male doctors at hand in Peshawar. It just seemed mighty strange, that was all. Still, look on the bright side, Crow. Doctor Bonnard could well have turned out to have been a dead ringer for Fernandel.

Whatever the reason though, the presence of a doctor did make a certain kind of sense. So, curbing my curiosity and irritation at this unexpected and mounting increase in the JetRanger's payload, I shrugged in weary acceptance of the situation and even managed to force a tight smile in the girl's direction.

Because I hadn't forgotten the mega-bucks they were going to pay me. Ask no questions, right?

'Okay love, I just hope you've got a strong stomach. It could get a bit bumpy and I don't want you throwing up over the upholstery. Now, if we're all quite ready, we'll be on our way.'

Doctor Bonnard looked to be on the verge of firing off another barb. With commendable restraint she clamped her lips firmly and walked past me, head high, towards the helicopter.

Terrific, I thought. All I need is a look-alike for

Catherine Deneuve with the bedside manner of Lucretia Borgia. I caught Raz Sharif's eye and winked. Raz Sharif, for his part, feigned instant and acute myopia.

And stuff you too, mate, I thought savagely. Then I followed them all to the chopper.

Habbani sat in the front with me. Raz Sharif and the girl took their seats in the rear. Raz Sharif's rifle was propped against his knee. Doctor Bonnard's flight bag rested on her lap. I checked everyone was secure and switched on.

The rotors began to turn slowly. Raz Sharif cast a nervous eye at the roof of the cabin as if he expected it to cave in on him at any second. Watching surreptitiously, I saw the old man mouth words and place a gnarled hand on the little leather satchel that hung around his neck. The satchel was a type carried by all Mujehadeen. It held a copy of the Qoran wrapped in silk. It was a Mujehad's most prized possession after his gun. Maybe Raz Sharif hadn't been in an aircraft before. Or then again maybe he had and was merely taking out extra divine insurance against my flying abilities. The girl didn't spare anybody any glances. She kept her eyes glued to the perspex.

After a brief dialogue with the sleepy controller in the tower I received clearance for take off. I hauled back on the collective, twisted in some throttle and the chopper lifted. I depressed the pedal, tilted the cyclic and swung her out across the airfield.

Behind us, dawn was approaching over the distant horizon, chasing our tails as we headed for the foothills and our first stop; the camp at Chital Rajat.

Chapter Four

Approaching in the misty half light, it was difficult to detect the full extent of the camp boundaries. The sprawl of ragged shelters stretched across the floor of the valley and merged with the lower slopes of the dark surrounding hills like some creeping fungus.

Chital Rajat was typical of many of the refugee encampments that had become established along the Pakistan side of the Durand Line. According to Habbani there were some twenty thousand people quartered within the immediate vicinity, all of them having made the arduous trek across the border to escape the danger and the horrors of war. From as far apart as Badakstan in the north and Herat in the far west, they had survived the gruelling journey, alone or in groups; men, women, children, livestock. Taking days, sometimes weeks, to traverse the deserts and the high mountain passes in their bids for freedom.

Upon reaching the sanctuary of the North West Frontier Province the refugees were supplied with food and shelter by the Pakistan government and the relief agencies. And, as each new band of homeless strays arrived, so the settlements grew, quickly becoming permanent fixtures on the landscape.

Like the other camps, most of the dwellings in Chital Rajat were tents provided by the United Nations High Commission for Refugees, but these were gradually giving way to structures of a more substantial nature. Additional building materials had been purloined from the adjacent countryside. Canvas had been replaced by timber and clay. In no time at all the camp had metamorphosed into quite a medium-sized town, a warren of narrow alleyways and cluttered hovels, probably a lot larger than anything the inhabitants had been accustomed to back in their homeland.

To avoid instilling panic in the camp – the refugees tended to associate the noise of a helicopter with the arrival of Russian gunships – Habbani instructed me to land the JetRanger a hundred yards or so outside the main gates, close to a tiny stream, melt water from the encircling mountains.

I complied readily. Although, as the rotors stopped spinning and we climbed out of the chopper, I could tell that our arrival had caused something of a stir. The camp was coming awake fast. I could hear shrill cries of alarm and the tremulous bleating of sheep and goats. Dogs barked lustily.

A few moments elapsed before the gates of the settlement creaked open. A small knot of people emerged; men carrying rifles, some holding lanterns aloft. They peered at us with apprehension and suspicion.

Looking at them I could well appreciate their fear and caution. Even though I'd been up for some time, in the muted light of the pre-dawn it still felt like the middle of the bloody night. Hardly a sociable hour to drop in on anybody.

Slowly the ranks of the reception committee parted and an old man limped forward. His skin was dark and furrowed, his beard full and grey but there was an aura of authority about him.

Habbani lifted his hand in recognition. The gesture was acknowledged. Guns were lowered.

Habbani led the way over.

The old man bowed slightly. 'Salaam aleikum,' he said.

'Aleikum salaam.' Habbani returned the greeting before

making introductions. 'This is Ahmed Badur. He is the headman of Chital Rajat.'

Ahmed Badur nodded gravely at the mention of his name and, after a thorough perusal of us all, rattled off a flow of Farsi.

Habbani translated. 'Ahmed Badur bids you welcome and asks that you permit him the honour of visiting his home to take tea.'

I felt that this was taking our cover story just a little bit too far. Our initial plan had been for Habbani to remain at Chital Rajat. I would then depart with the others, ostensibly for a camp site further north. In reality we would turn back on ourselves and, at zero feet, make a run for the border. With Muhammed Nur Rafiq on board – always assuming that he was still alive by the time we got to him – I would fly the chopper back to the refugee camp and the grateful thanks of Hezb-i-Islami. That being the case I was anxious to get the extraction over and done with. Partaking of light refreshment as if we were at some sort of garden party, hadn't been an item on my agenda.

Habbani must have sensed my hesitation. He added, 'It would be impolite to refuse, my friend. Besides, we have time. It is not yet fully light. Massoud will not have begun his assault on Bagram.'

I jerked my thumb at the JetRanger. 'Thanks, but I'll stay with the chopper.'

Habbani smiled reassuringly. 'Do not worry. Raz Sharif will remain with the helicopter. It will be quite safe. No one will touch it.'

As if to confirm the fact Raz Sharif snapped to smart attention, the Lee Enfield resting against his shoulder as if he was on parade.

So, there didn't seem to be anything else for it. Leaving the Pathan with the aircraft, Doctor Bonnard and I followed Habbani and Ahmed Badur through the rickety gates into the compound. The headman was walking crookedly, favouring his left leg. He had no stick. His gait was ungainly, spastic almost.

We passed the silent gaze of men and women who eyed us from the low doorways of their drab and depressing shacks. Sometimes there was a child half hidden behind its mother's skirts, staring with bold inquisitiveness as we trailed the old man and his bodyguards towards a low-roofed hut screened from its neighbours by a shoulder-high adobe wall. Despite the rough and ready nature of the hut's exterior, inside it was remarkably spacious. Light was admitted through the open door and by a glowing oil lamp suspended from one of the brushwood rafters. Ahmed Badur's bodyguards took up position outside, on either side of the entrance.

Ahmed Badur sat down on one of the rugs that covered the earthen floor, his back supported by one of the large multi-patterned cushions that lay heaped around. At his invitation we followed suit, sitting cross-legged as the tea was brought in, along with a tray bearing a platter of small round nan loaves and a bowl of honey. The wrinkled old woman who served us, presumably Ahmed Badur's wife, withdrew as discreetly as she had appeared, with quiet dignity.

Despite my reservations at the time that was possibly being wasted, I discovered that I was rather hungry. I reminded myself that I hadn't eaten since the day before. I tucked into the warm bread topped off with a scoop of honey, sank two cups of the sweet green tea, and tried not to dwell on the prospect that the repast could well turn out to be the hearty breakfast traditionally enjoyed by the condemned man.

Doctor Bonnard, however, appeared to have lost her appetite. She'd accepted a tiny cup of sabs – only, I suspected, out of deference to our host – but declined the food. Most likely her nerves were reacting as she began to have second thoughts about the wisdom of having volunteered her services to help the cause. Which was understandable. The extraction wasn't exactly going to be a picnic.

And, so far, she hadn't said a word either. At least not since her brief outburst of exasperation back on the tarmac at Peshawar. No doubt she was still hot and bothered by my less than cordial display of welcome after I'd been informed that I'd be burdened with an extra passenger and a woman to boot. Although not so as you'd notice. The outfit she was wearing wasn't doing her any favours. In fact it did nothing for her at all. It was hardly the height of fashion. Frankly, she looked about as chic as a Chitrali goat herder.

But her eyes, I could now tell, were quite captivating.

Unexpectedly, Ahmed Badur reached over and prodded my knee. The old man grinned. His teeth, what was left of them, were very yellow. I feigned polite interest as he launched into what seemed like an interminable monologue accompanied by much head shaking and some enthusiastic gesticulations. Baffled, I waited for Habbani to come to my rescue.

'Ahmed Badur apologizes for the coldness of our welcome. His people recognized the sound of a helicopter and thought it might be the Russians. They were afraid. The gunships have destroyed many of their villages, killed their families, slaughtered their animals. The Shuravi use their helicopters to great effect. They have inflicted terrible damage and are very much feared. He hopes you will understand that no disrespect was intended.' Habbani added, 'As you are aware it is not unknown for the Russians to attack refugee camps on this side of the border.'

I supposed that some sort of reply was expected so I raised my cup to the old boy. 'Any coldness there may have been has been made up for by the warmth of his hospitality.'

My talents were wasted here, I thought. I should have been in the Diplomatic Corps. I could sense that the girl was staring at me, no doubt over-awed by my purple prose. Frankly, I was pretty amazed myself.

Judging by the look of rapture on his face Ahmed Abdur seemed pretty impressed though. He nodded and smiled as Habbani relayed the compliment and lifted his own cup in return. There followed another exchange with Habbani.

Again the latter translated.

'Ahmed Badur wishes you to know that he is especially blessed to receive Doctor Bonnard into his house. Everyone in Chital Rajat is aware of the great service she and the other doctors have performed for the warriors of the jehad. Her name is revered in the villages of the Panjsher. During her stay within the camps of the Mujehadeen she was responsible for saving many lives. From his heart Ahmed Badur thanks you and says he will pray to Allah that you may both return safely from the Country of Light.'

Doctor Bonnard regarded Ahmed Badur solemnly. 'Tell him it is we who are blessed and I hope that before long he will soon be able to return to the Panjsher and lead his people in the fight against the Shuravi. Ahmadshah Massoud will be counting the days until his loyal friend Ahmed Badur is fighting at his side once more. Together they will drive the invaders back over the mountains.'

Ahmed Badur beamed with pleasure.

As well he might. That speech certainly had the edge over my feeble effort. But at least one of my own questions had been answered. She had been over the border, working in the field hospitals. There was obviously a great deal more to Doctor Bonnard than met the eye. Certainly she was not just a pretty face. Which now made her something of an enigma and that made the whole damned business of her involvement very intriguing.

Ahmed Badur looked quite overcome. He looked mesmerized by the girl, as though he couldn't quite believe that she was there with him. He came out of his trance suddenly and in a way that took us all by surprise. Grunting with the effort, he leaned back on his cushions and with a great deliberation began to roll up the left leg of his grey pantaloons. Beside me I heard the girl's sharp intake of breath as she saw what was revealed. Though she must have seen plenty of horrors among the ranks of the injured Mujehadeen she was obviously staggered by this revelation. I felt quite sickened myself when I saw what she was looking at.

Ahmed Badur's calf was one mass of ragged scar tissue. The flesh between the ankle and the knee was puckered and fissured with craters like a lunar landscape. A portion of the muscle appeared to have been chopped away by the blade of a very blunt axe so that only a thin layer of grey skin covered the bone. The nerve damage must have been colossal. No wonder the old fellow's progress was so awkward. It was a marvel he could even stand let alone walk.

'Jesus!' I breathed, transfixed by the gruesome sight.

It was evident from the animation in his ancient face and the tremor in his voice that Ahmed Badur was relating in some detail how he had come by the injury.

'The Russians attacked his village,' Habbani explained. 'As a reprisal for guerilla ambushes on convoys travelling along the Salang Highway. They used rockets and mortars and dropped mines, the ones shaped like butterflies.' Habbani used his hands to draw the shape in the air. 'Many people died. Whole families killed in their homes and in the fields, including one of Ahmed Badur's sons. He himself was hit by shrapnel from a mortar round. Every house was destroyed. Those few who survived collected their belongings and, after burying their dead, came east over the mountains. It was winter and the journey was very dangerous. Ahmed Badur's other two sons came too. They carried Ahmed Badur and his wife on their backs.'

I could only look on in astonishment. I couldn't begin to imagine what it must have been like struggling through those snow bound passes in temperatures that could freeze the blood in a man's veins. It didn't bear thinking about.

The headman spoke again. His voice had a new strength in it.

'His sons have returned to the Panjsher to join Massoud. He hopes they will kill many Russians and avenge the death of their brother,' Habbani said.

I thought that I wouldn't much care to be a Russian who got in their way.

A movement in the doorway then as one of Ahmed Badur's swarthy bodyguards entered the hut. Over the man's shoulders I could tell that it was growing lighter. It was also getting warmer.

The bodyguard bent low and whispered in the headman's ear. Ahmed Badur listened attentively then dismissed the messenger with a curt wave. As the bodyguard left the hut a long drawn out wail broke out over the camp. Unmistakably the cry of a muezzin calling the faithful to morning prayers. The haunting sound rose and fell as it reverberated over the shanty roofs of the settlement. It was a summons that could not be ignored. And it was a clear sign that heralded the arrival of the dawn.

Everyone in the hut rose to their feet, Doctor Bonnard assisting Ahmed Badur, who thanked her gravely before leading the way outside. A pale pink light was beginning to sweep across the plain. Throughout the camp shadowy figures were emerging from their houses, moving about their business. The men were washing, cleaning themselves before performing their prayers. The women were tending the cooking fires. Formless in their dark burqquas, they drifted ghostlike through the coils of smoke like wraiths in a mist. It was eerie yet very peaceful.

Habbani took me to one side. He said softly, 'You will leave after namaz, the saying of prayers. Massoud will also pray before he begins his attack. Please wait by the helicopter until I return. I shall not be long.'

Ahmed Badur approached, bowed, shook my hand. His skin was cracked and very dry. It was like clasping a piece of badly tanned leather. He bowed to the girl also. 'Inshallah,' he said softly and turned away.

Doctor Bonnard and I watched the line of men wind its way through the settlement towards the crude mosque that had been built in one corner of the camp. The men walked quietly, conversing in hushed tones. It was almost as if they were in some kind of hypnotic trance. Ahmed Badur melted into the phalanx of worshippers. Strange to think that the old man, bent and crippled, could exert so much influence over so many people.

'Do you think he'll ever see his village again?' I asked.

'He believes he will,' the girl replied. 'That is enough.' Her voice held a trace of sadness.

'Inshallah?' I said.

She nodded, her eyes following the twisting line. 'Something like that.' She appeared subdued, lost in her own thoughts.

'Come on,' I said. 'Let's get back to the chopper.'

We fell into step and retraced our path to the main gates. The sun was beginning to burn away the mist. It was getting very warm now. The dust was starting to rise.

She had unbuttoned her jacket. Underneath the olive-green smock she was wearing a pale khaki shirt which contrasted greatly with the creamy copper tone of her

67

skin. As we left the confines of the camp she removed her hat and ran her slim fingers through her curls. Her hair wasn't black or dark brown as I had first suspected. It was auburn and the deep russet tint set off her tan to perfection. It was cut long at the back but short at the sides and the semi crop emphasized her firm bone structure, like a picture that was complimented by a well-matched frame. I was able to hazard a more precise guess at her age too. Early thirties, I calculated. And damned attractive, no doubt about that. I realized that I was staring and experienced a brief flush of guilt. I didn't know why that should be and wondered if she was aware of my eyes on her. Probably. Having those looks it was something she must have grown used to.

Sunlight was glancing off the perspex canopy of the helicopter. The aircraft resembled a fat yellow dragonfly. I felt a sudden rush of affection for the chopper. Don't let us down, sweetheart, I thought.

We found Raz Sharif on his knees at the rear of the helicopter. He had spread his cloak on the stony ground. The compass he had used to determine the direction of Mecca, along with his rifle, lay on the cloak beside him. Forehead touching the ground in the act of worship, the Pathan was oblivious to our arrival. Prayer was a ritual performed by the faithful five times a day, irrespective of surrounding distractions. It was a phenomenon that I had still not gotten entirely accustomed to. When faced with such ceaseless devotion I couldn't help but feel like a voyeur, fascinated yet at the same time conscious that I was intruding, albeit unintentionally, on a moment both private and sacrosanct.

The girl evidently felt the same way. We both backed off and moved to the other end of the helicopter, leaving Raz Sharif to his communion.

A silence fell between us. The girl looked westwards, towards the mountains and the border.

'What the hell are you doing here, Doctor?' I asked finally.

She turned and looked at me. There were flecks of green in those eyes, I saw. I had seen them spark in anger. What would they be like in passion? I wondered. Heart stopping, I could imagine.

'I thought we'd been through all that.' Her voice carried a vague huskiness that was as arresting as her steady gaze. She was probably debating the validity of my peace offering. I knew she had no intention of making it easy for me, of course. But I suppose I deserved that.

'You know what I mean,' I said. 'There are plenty of other doctors in Peshawar. Why you?'

Her eyes flashed then. 'You mean why not a man?'

'I didn't say that.'

She sneered. 'Please don't insult my intelligence!'

Bugger that. I held up a restraining hand. 'Back off, love. Cool down. I'm not insulting anyone's intelligence, least of all yours. Or your qualifications, for that matter. I heard what Habbani said in there. You've been on the other side. You've worked in the muck and bullets. You don't have to prove a thing to me, okay?'

'How strange,' she responded archly. 'I thought perhaps I did.' But she was off the boil; cooling to a low simmer.

'Look,' I said. 'Maybe I was out of line earlier. But I wasn't pissed off at you. It was that little twerp, Habbani. I didn't like the way he'd added you to the manifest without telling me. It's my bloody helicopter, f'r Chris'sakes!'

'Please don't shout,' she said curtly, nodding towards Raz Sharif's posterior which was bobbing up and down like a cork in a bathtub. Low droning accompanied the genuflections. 'You will disturb his prayers.'

'Doctor Bonnard,' I said with as much patience as I could muster. 'What I am trying to say, in my own clumsy way, is that out of all the medics I've met who've operated with the rebels, not one has ever felt the need to pay them a return visit. Now, it could be that they were at the head of the queue when the good sense was doled out and you were at the back of the line, but that'd be too easy. Or it could be you've been invited back by popular demand. Which is it? I'd really like to know. I mean, this isn't going to be a sight-seeing trip. Chances are we'll all end up draped around the side of a bloody mountain, or worse.'

Any more remarks like that, I reflected, and I'd have talked myself out of the contract.

'Perhaps I should ask the same question of you, Mr Crow,' she countered shrewdly.

'Ah, well,' I said. 'They're paying me. That's my excuse. What's yours?'

Following that, I fully expected, in the light of our previous exchanges, to be at the receiving end of some remark of contempt. But I was mistaken.

Her expression mirrored the one I had observed during our visit to the house of Ahmed Badur. It was as if her attention was suddenly centred elsewhere and far away. And there was something else there also. In her eyes; an uncertainty tinged with sadness. A vulnerability that she had, up until that moment, made a determined effort to conceal. But now, a telling facet of her true self was revealed. The mask of composure that she had worn so successfully had finally slipped. Under that cool and distant façade there was one very frightened girl. I could sense it.

'It's my brother,' she said. There was a catch in her voice. She tilted her chin in a stubborn effort to prevent me seeing the tears beginning to form.

Beyond the limits of her forlorn gaze, the peaks of the Hindu Kush rose like purple turrets, high and massive.

'What about him?'

'He's over there, somewhere. Missing. I'm going to find him.'

This wasn't what I'd expected. 'He's in Afghanistan? He's a doctor?'

She shook her head. 'A journalist. He was on an assignment for *Le Monde*. He was one of the correspondents invited to attend the press conference given by Doctor Najib. He never came back. I haven't heard from him since.' Her slim shoulders sagged.

I stared at her. My God, no wonder she was subdued, I thought. With something like that hanging over her. The well-publicized exercise in public relations engineered by Najibullah had taken place weeks ago. It had been the same one that Mike Farrell had attended.

I was at a loss for words. Anything I said would inevitably sound trite. 'Wouldn't you have heard if something had happened to him?' I ventured. 'What about the other press people? Didn't you check with any of them to see if they'd seen or heard anything?'

Like Mike Farrell for one.

She replied sadly. 'I tried everybody. It is as if he has vanished off the face of the earth. It is as though he never existed.'

'How about the Red Cross?' I persisted. 'They keep their ears close to the ground over there. Word would have reached them surely?'

'They too have heard nothing,' she replied. 'So, when I found out through a contact in the Hezb that they were trying to find a doctor to cross the border, I offered to go. Habbani knew me. He knew I'd already worked in the Panjsher. I've met Nur Rafiq too. I treated him for a bullet wound in his shoulder about three weeks before I left

71

Massoud's camp. It seemed logical that I should be the one to go with you. Besides . . .' A tight little smile touched her face. '. . . there were not too many volunteers. As you pointed out, no one wants to return to the war. I thought that while we were there I could ask the people in Dar Galak if they had news of Alain. If he was in some sort of trouble it is likely he would have tried to make it to Massoud's headquarters. Someone might have heard something.'

What I had to tell her next wasn't going to be easy.

I said, 'We won't have a lot of time, Doctor. You know we can't afford to hang around any longer than it takes for us to get the guy on board the chopper and get the hell out of there. I hate to say this, but you'll only have a few minutes to ask the question. We'll barely have chance to say hello and goodbye. We won't be socializing. As sure as God made little green apples we won't be stopping for tea.' I added softly, 'Have you thought about what you're going to do if they can't help you?'

Her shoulders slumped. It was as if the thought hadn't occurred to her. 'I don't know,' she admitted in utter dejection, her face crumpling. She looked suddenly out of her depth, child-like.

I took her arm. I could feel her trembling. 'I wish I could help you, Doctor. I really do.'

She wiped her eyes and nodded obliquely.

'Why do you do it?' I asked her. 'Why risk your life to help these people? It's not your war?'

Now, where I had heard that before?

'It isn't yours either,' she said, to prove the irony of my remark.

'But they're paying me, love. I told you that. I'm in it purely for the money. You certainly aren't. So why?'

'Because no one else will bother,' she said.

I recalled then what Mike Farrell had told me. This was

72

a forgotten war. Maybe she was right. Nobody cared, really.

She told me the story then. How she'd gone in like the other teams, with one of the Mujehadeen supply caravans. There had been two of them, both women. It had taken them twelve days from leaving Terrimangal to reach the Panjsher and Massoud's stronghold. Her face had clouded as she'd recalled the memory. The Mujehadeen had threatened to leave them behind at one point because they were holding up the column. They wouldn't have done so, of course, as Nicole Bonnard had found out later from Massoud. The rebel commander had given his men strict instructions that the two women were to be taken in on the guerillas' backs if that was the only way they could make it. Medics were in very short supply over in the Panjsher and in many respects were considered even more important than weapons.

They had set up a field hospital in Astana, at the southern end of the Panjsher valley. There had been a hospital there before they'd arrived but it had been bombed by the Russians. The work was non stop. They were there four months before she and her companion had been forced to leave.

For the most ludicrous of reasons. Despite the common hatred of the communists there was much conflict between the various guerilla groups. One of Massoud's rivals accused him of sleeping with western women. The only women who fitted that description were the doctors. At the same time as this slander was being instigated it was learnt that the Russians were about to launch an offensive on the valley. Diplomatically, Massoud decided that the medics should leave the Panjsher. He arranged an escort to accompany the women out of the country back to Pakistan. The doctors had left reluctantly.

That had been a little over five months ago. Since then

73

Nicole Bonnard had been working among the refugee camps and in the wards of the local hospital.

Footsteps behind us. Raz Sharif, having renewed his pact with God, ready to fight the good fight.

'We go soon, Inglestani?' he asked cheerfully. The Pathan hawked a gob of spit around his gums and spat noisily into the dust.

'Saspo,' I said, wondering where Habbani had got to. Raz Sharif was up and about so namaz must be over. Unless they were taking a collection up at the mosque, or something.

Doctor Bonnard was giving me a confused look. 'You are English? But Doctor Habbani told me you fought in Vietnam. I did not think the British were there.'

'They weren't,' I said. 'Not officially, at any rate.'

In fact, British SAS officers and mercenaries had fought alongside Aussie and Kiwi squadrons attached to the US Special Forces.

'In any case,' I added, 'I've an Australian passport, but I doubt old buggerlugs here would know the difference. As far as he's concerned, we're all the bloody same anyway.'

She considered that for a moment. Abruptly she held out her hand. 'I think we should start again,' she said seriously. 'My name is Nicole Bonnard.' She smiled suddenly. 'Usually it is just Nicole.'

I took her hand. 'Crow,' I said.

An eyebrow was raised. 'Just Crow?'

'Usually,' I said.

She digested the information, accepted it, and smiled again, hesitantly. Her grip, despite her slender hands, was firm. I had suspected it might be. After all, she was a doctor and had performed surgery. She'd need to be capable. More than that in fact. In the dreadful conditions she'd probably had to work under, she'd have to be outstanding.

Habbani appeared at that moment, waddling out of the camp gates like a duck heading for a pond. With him were half a dozen armed men, one of whom was leading a donkey harnessed to the shafts of a small wooden cart. I had the distinct and uneasy feeling that this wasn't the commissary truck.

Habbani, business-like as usual, announced, 'You must leave immediately. Massoud will have begun his attack and the garrisons at Jalalabad and Asadabad will have been alerted. There is no time to lose.' He had removed the sheepskin coat. Small beads of perspiration shone across his forehead.

'Suits me,' I said. 'Let's mount up, folks.'

I was about to board the chopper when I heard Habbani rap out an order. To my total amazement, the man holding the donkey's halter began to back the animal and cart towards the chopper. The cart creaked to a standstill. A rough square of sacking was pulled aside to reveal three oblong crates. The Mujehadeen regarded me expectantly. I stared back. Now what?

'First,' Habbani said. 'My men will load the supplies.'

I thought, hang on a bloody minute.

Habbani was already starting to backpedal nimbly so I reached out and grabbed a corner of his jacket.

'Whoa!' I said. 'Hold it right there. Time out! What bloody supplies?'

The tubby doctor blinked nervously, like a schoolboy caught under the blankets with a torch and a dirty magazine.

'Okay, what gives?' I grated. 'First it's the mad mullah over there, then Florence Nightingale, and now it's cargo. This isn't the Berlin Airlift, sunshine. What's going on?' I called to the girl, 'Half a mo. Could be a change of plan coming up.'

She paused, boot on the sill, 'What is happening?'

'Over to you, mate.' Habbani flinched as I let go of his jacket and gave him a medium-strength prod in the stomach. 'I'm sure we'd all like to know. Especially the friggin' pilot!'

The crates contained essential medical supplies; sterile dressings, bandages, antibiotics, that sort of thing, or so Habbani would have us believe.

Sweat was dribbling over the back of the doctor's grimy collar. And was it my imagination, or did the rest of them look a trifle nervous too? Hell, even the donkey was trying to avoid my eye.

No, I decided. It wasn't my imagination at all. They did look nervous. In fact they were so nervous that in their haste to load the stuff into the helicopter they succeeded in dropping one of the crates off the rear end of the cart. It landed on the ground with a thud and there was a sharp crack as one corner split open. The catastrophe was immediately followed, not unnaturally, by a heated altercation between all six Mujehadeen as everyone tried to tie the blame for the mishap on everyone else, loudly.

Not that I was taking any notice of the row. Because Habbani and I were too busy paying attention to the result of the accident.

A torn piece of grease-proof paper was protruding from the damaged crate and underneath that could be seen the gleam of dull metal.

I sighed. 'Oh, wonderful,' I said. 'That's all I bloody need.' Now knowing for a fact what I'd guessed anyway.

Chapter Five

I viewed the crates with a fast mounting sense of rage. I took hold of Habbani again. This time by the lapels of his mouldy suit. His feet left the ground for a fraction of a second. 'You must think I was born yesterday! Medical supplies, be damned! You reckon I don't know weapons crates when I see them? You want me to fly guns in? Jesus!'

I released Habbani's jacket then because I was suddenly aware of a lull in the rest of the proceedings. The Mujehadeen were looking at me as if I'd grown horns and Raz Sharif was fingering his Lee Enfield as if he meant to use it.

'And you can tell Gunga Din over there that if he doesn't point that fucking cannon somewhere else he'll end up wearing it!' Knowing full well that I was unlikely to make more than a couple of paces before I became just another notch carved into the weathered stock of Raz Sharif's .303.

Habbani, still trying manfully to regain composure and dignity, evaluated that possibility and ordered Raz Sharif to retrain his rifle. I could have sworn that the expression on the Pathan's face was one of sincere regret. The bloodthirsty old bugger had most likely been itching to pull the trigger. As if to illustrate the intention Raz Sharif grinned wolfishly. Not a pleasant sight, by any means.

Habbani took the opportunity to step forward quickly and place a restraining hand on my arm. 'My friend,' he declared fulsomely, 'let me explain. I understand your reaction but believe me when I say that we had no wish to deceive you. It is simply that we looked upon your acceptance of the contract as a fortunate means of killing two birds with one shot.' He gave an ingratiating smile. 'That is the correct saying, yes?'

How I resisted the impulse to lash out and wipe the leer from his face, I'll never know.

I was fuming. And yet perhaps I shouldn't have been so surprised that this should have happened. Because I knew the resistance groups were plagued with problems along their supply routes.

The main supplier of arms and ammunition to the Afghan rebels was the United States. That's right. Who else but good ol' Uncle Sam. This applied to all the groups, not just the Hezb faction but also Jamiat-i-Islami, Harakat Inquilab-i-Islami, the ANLF and the rest. However, despite this commitment, it had been estimated by those in the know that as much as one third of those supplies had so far failed to reach their destination, the camps of the Mujehadeen. The weapons were being siphoned off before the guerillas could take receipt. General suspicion placed the blame on the Pakistan government or even Afghan exiles, which was rather ironic since the latter were trained by the CIA. A fact which, at the time, had served to fuel the fires of speculation surrounding the American, Jack Tagg, and the rumours that had trailed in his muddy wake. Perhaps the stories about him hadn't been so far off the mark after all.

The exiles were known to control the lines along which arms supplies moved. They operated through shipping companies, travel agencies and within a number of Islamic organizations throughout the Middle East. Usually they arranged for weapons to be concealed in containers innocently labelled agricultural equipment, engine parts, or machine tools. These were then dispatched through the resistance offices to the refugee camps and thence across the border by caravan. The authorities in Pakistan had promised that anything designated as relief supplies would be given priority handling through the various ports and airports. But that was in theory. In practice many consignments went astray.

There was just as much scope for corruption within the ranks of the Pakistani customs. I was familiar with their devious machinations. Even the Red Cross materials that I'd been paid to ferry hither and yon hadn't entirely escaped the claws of unscrupulous officials.

It was supposed that the Pakistanis and the exiles were either stockpiling the weapons or else diverting them and selling them for personal gain. The exiles, for example, could easily use their positions within the Islamic organizations to ship the goods out of Pakistan to Malaysia or Indonesia disguised as religious materials. There were regular and quite legitimate shipments of this kind to many Asian countries, especially from the Gulf. The profits from such an enterprise would be great indeed.

So, I could appreciate that having got some of the weapons this far, the resistance was mighty anxious to pass the hardware on to the fighters at the front line as quickly as possible.

A spark flared in Habbani's eyes. 'Mr Crow, the Mujehadeen need those weapons desperately if they are to have any chance of driving the Russians from our country. You will be performing a great service for our cause if you deliver the arms to Dar Galak.'

'I'm already doing your cause a great service, mate. I'm about to fly into bandit country and extract one of your oppos from death's dark door. Or had that little item slipped from your memory? Christ! I don't suppose you'd like me to bomb Kabul on the way home by any chance?'

'That will not be necessary,' Habbani replied, as if he'd taken me seriously. 'Just deliver the weapons please. There is enough room in your helicopter, is there not?' He looked worried.

He wasn't the only one. 'Lack of cargo space wasn't quite the point I was trying to make,' I said icily. 'I was thinking more along the lines of what would happen if the Russians were to force me down. It'd be tough enough trying to con them into believing we were off course due to faulty avionics without having your so-called supplies on board. The fact that I'll have passengers will be bad enough. Trying to justify three crates of ordnance hidden under the rear seats will be out of the fucking question!'

'What makes you so sure that the Soviets will appreciate the difference, Mr Crow?' Habbani responded craftily.

He had me there. 'You mean if they force me down I'm buggered whatever happens, so I may as well take the guns along anyway, right?'

Habbani smiled enigmatically.

Which brought everything neatly into perspective.

I rounded on the girl then, who was looking at us as if she thought we were all certifiable. 'Did you know about this?'

She flushed. 'I . . .'

'Oh, that's just great,' I said bitterly. 'Well, I guess that answers the question. And you call yourself a doctor? My God! Maybe they should call it the Hippocritic Oath after all! I sure walked into this one, didn't I?'

So much for our truce. It looked like it had been a temporary affair only. A pity.

Although there was still time enough for me to walk away. I knew that. Just as I knew that Massoud's guerillas would, even as I was thinking about it, be laying siege to the airbase at Bagram in a bid to draw the wolves away from the fold. And they weren't being paid either. They were paying for the privilege. In blood.

What the hell, anyway?

'You'd better get the stuff on board,' I told them. 'We're wasting time.'

So they loaded the guns.

This time the girl sat in the front, bag clutched to her chest. Raz Sharif, still sneering, I might add, sat with his knees around his ears, sandals resting on the controversial cargo. I slipped my sun specs on, checked safety belts were fastened.

Habbani looked up at me through the open doorway. 'Go with God, Mr Crow.'

'I sincerely hope so,' I said, and closed the door.

By this time our departure had attracted an audience from within the camp. As well as Habbani and his crew there were a dozen or so children who'd come to wave and a couple of scabby mongrels. The extraction was rapidly taking on the trappings of a spectator sport.

The engine noise pitched up to a harsh whine and the blades began to thrash the air. Backs were turned, eyes covered, against the swirling stinging clouds of dust and sand thrown up by the downdraught. The children clapped and laughed gleefully. The dogs barked frantically and turned tail, scooting for the safety of the compound. The helicopter lifted. Habbani, hand protecting his face, shrank beneath us, trog-like in his shiny black suit.

I took the chopper up fast and turned us away. We flew low, skirting the settlement, and headed out across the plain, skimming above the wilderness like a bird. The camp retreated into the haze behind us.

Ahead lay pine-clad foothills and beyond them the mountains, still touched by shadow and, in some places, by cloud which hung over the lower summits like strands of cotton wool.

I took a look at my passengers. The girl was staring dead ahead, wrapped in her own thoughts again, which were probably centred on her brother and the chances of his survival in Russian-occupied territory. Wondering too if the people in Dar Galak would have the news she was seeking and trying not to dwell on the options available to her if they hadn't.

Raz Sharif, in his baggy Pathan pantaloons and turban, looked like a man transported forward in time, out of his natural element. His face was a blend of apprehension and excitement as he contemplated the ground rushing beneath the skids. He looked up suddenly and caught my eye. Showed his teeth again in a rictus grin. I could imagine him inflicting torture; twisting knife into sinew with relish, paring skin away from bone with brutal rapture. This was a man whose forefathers had routed the might of the British Empire a century and a half ago, in the cantonments of Kabul and the desolation of the Jagdalak Pass. Afghanistan was a wild and savage country, inhabited by wild and savage men, as Moscow was finding out only too well.

Soviet designs on Afghanistan weren't anything new, not by a long chalk. Annexation hadn't been something that the Politburo had hatched up overnight. The invasion back on Christmas Eve 1979, when the 105th Guards Airborne Division of the Soviet Army seized Kabul airport, was merely a prelude to the culmination of a battle plan conceived way back by Peter the Great. Then, Russia's goal had been British India. Now it was the ports on the Arabian Sea and access to the Indian Ocean and a chance to compromise the West's oil supplies. The Great Game wasn't over by any means. The rules had simply been updated.

All in all, I reflected, as I brought the JetRanger down to a low hover eight miles out of Chital Rajat, from what I had seen of the country through the windshield of the helicopter, the Ivans were very much welcome to it.

The tops of the mountains did look beautiful though, the highest points probing the clouds like spears. The crests at the extreme limit of my vision were etched in purple. The closer ridges were cast in gold.

Five miles from the frontier, the JetRanger hung suspended above the ground. I held the chopper at this height because I needed to get my bearings from the outline of the hills ahead of us. I had the map open on my knee. I had already traced out our prospective route and I wanted to make certain I picked the right corridor that would take us through the mountains to Dar Galak. We would only get one chance. Once we were in the labyrinth we were committed. Just hope to God that the Minotaur was having the morning off.

And there it was! A gash in the rocky slopes, a narrow defile that would grant us access.

And if ever there was a time for me to have second thoughts and a change of heart then this was it. Behind lay safety. Ahead lay the gauntlet of valleys and the possibility of a confrontation with the Russian gunships. Plus one Muhammed Nur Rafiq, linchpin of the resistance and the ticket to my prosperity.

No contest.

The girl was biting her lip. She flicked me a glance.

You look scared stiff, love, I thought.

There was a glow in the eyes of Raz Sharif, though. The Pathan was clearly enraptured by the view. One hand clutching his rifle, the other touching his leather satchel, the old man smiled dreamily. 'Ah!' he cried suddenly. 'Afghanistan!'

Which at least proved that my navigation was accurate, I thought wryly. I looked around, took a deep breath. 'All right, gang,' I muttered. 'Let's go for it.'

I pushed the cyclic forward slowly, pulled up on the

collective to add power and twisted the throttle. The helicopter began to accelerate.

We crossed the border at fifty feet.

The run was on.

I remembered my first low-level sortie as having been both frightening and exhilarating; rather like sitting in the front car on a roller coaster.

As I swung the helicopter from one valley into the next, the JetRanger reacting to my every hand and foot movement like a thoroughbred race horse, I wondered if Nicole Bonnard felt the same way. It was hard to tell, comparisons being odious, and what have you. She was hunched up in the left-hand seat, teeth and fists clenched in equal measure. The instructors during my training had rated a cadet's first experience in nap of the earth flying as having a high pucker factor. Maybe she was simply scared out of her wits, nothing more simple than that.

Well, she'd have to get used to it.

At times like these, it's almost like you're outside looking in on yourself. You may not be aware of it but it really is a case of flying by instinct. I had mapped out the route in my mind and switched myself into what amounted to automatic mode. I was controlling the chopper by a means that was almost telekinetic. I had become part of the aircraft and the collective, cyclic and pedals had virtually become extensions of my body. My concentration was total.

It had been the same in Nam. Most pilots had it. The ability to immerse themselves into that highly tuned state in which they were able to extract optimum performance from their machines as well as absorb peripheral data, determine if it was offensive or defensive in character and evaluate the necessary response. It's not unlike an adept of the martial arts attaining a state of Ki; mental force transposed as vital and subtle energy. You couldn't rationalize it. At least I couldn't.

There was another comparison with Nam. I was contour flying. Like a cruise missile the JetRanger was hugging every fold and crease along the landscape. It was a nailbiting way to go, but the safest. It cut down the risk of radar entrapment considerably because the chopper's profile was only revealed for the merest fraction of time as I took us closer in to the target. Though in maintaining our low altitude I had probably caused my passengers' hearts to flutter.

Sometimes it must have seemed that the ends of the rotor blades were only a matter of inches away from the rock face. Once or twice, out of the corner of my eye, I had seen the girl shy away from the edge of her seat as we swept under sheer cliffs that blotted out the sunlight like an eclipse. At such moments Raz Sharif was no doubt touching his satchel and mumbling incomprehensible prayers. With the desired result at least. We hadn't hit anything, yet.

In fact it was so easy, it was uncanny. Every time I switched on to a new heading or veered over the next ridge I fully expected the worst. And each time I had been intensely relieved to find our progress unhindered.

I had been pleased to note that as we flew deeper into the mountains so the cloud had descended. That was good because the Russians didn't like to take their Hind helicopters below the valley rims. That made them vulnerable to attack from above. That meant, hopefully, that the gunships would remain above the cloud level. Which would leave us free to sweep along the valley sides undetected.

A couple of times we had flown over the evidence of gunship attack. Bomb craters, shattered tree stumps, ruined houses that were little more than a heap of rubble at the side of an untended orchard, maize fields lying in sad neglect under a spreading carpet of weed and thistle. Of the inhabitants there had been no sign and I had taken that to be an indication that most of the immediate region we had been flying over had been evacuated, probably resulting in a further exodus of refugees. More nomads heading for the sanctuary of the AID settlements. Though, ironically, this wretched state of affairs was surely serving in our favour. For the decline in population meant that the Soviets were less likely to police the area, which would lessen the odds of coming up against an aerial patrol.

To the north the high and formidable crags of the Hindu Kush could occasionally be seen through gaps in the cloud layer, their snow-capped tips shining like ice palaces. While below us the country was quite Alpine in texture, with steep, cedar-covered slopes and rolling meadows. Where the valleys narrowed down into rocky gorges icy rivers tumbled over truck-sized boulders, gouging and eroding the land in relentless passage.

The most hazardous part of the run so far had been the traverse of the Kunar River. Rivers carried with them the risk of adjacent habitation and thus were a probable target for Soviet activity. But we had been lucky. It hadn't taken but a few seconds to power the JetRanger across the churning torrent and turn her up and away and on to the next track without incident. Once across, the land around us rose above fifteen thousand feet, most of it impenetrable to all but mountain sheep and Mujehadeen gun runners en route to Pakistan to pick up more weapons and supplies from the bazaars at Chitral and Garm Chisma. Neither breed would be anxious to advertise their presence to passing aircraft.

And all the time I was wondering how long Massoud and his guerillas could keep the gunships occupied before they were forced to withdraw to their camps in the Panjsher. With luck, for the next thirty minutes or so.

Long enough for us to land, get Nur Rafiq on board and make it back to Pakistan in one piece.

Because, incredibly, we had made it.

We cleared the last sharp ridge and our destination lay below us. Dar Galak, hidden, isolated, like Shangri La.

We went in from the south. The village was an untidy cluster of flat-roofed dwellings perched on the western slope of a sinuous ravine. The buildings overlooked a winding, bubbling tributary of the Parun River. I followed the watercourse upstream, the skids of the JetRanger barely clearing the pebble-strewn banks, and looked for a place to set down.

I could see no immediate sign of life which was hardly surprising. As we had established at Chital Rajat, any helicopter was considered a threat until it proved to be otherwise. And there had been no way that we could have got word to the villagers to let them know that we would be coming in to pick Nur Rafiq up. There hadn't been time. So our unexpected arrival had to be considered hostile. Which was another reason why Raz Sharif was with me. His presence was to convince the inhabitants of Dar Galak that we were friend not foe.

I spotted a flat piece of mossy ground twenty yards from the stream and swung the chopper towards it. The helicopter sank on to the grass. As the engine idled I yelled at my passengers. 'Move yourselves! And keep your heads down!'

They tumbled out, Raz Sharif extricating himself with an alacrity that belied his years. The girl followed him. I remained where I was, my hands at the controls, rotors swishing slowly above me.

Still no sign of life. But we were being watched. I could sense it. Raz Sharif knew it too. So when he called out to the unseen ears he knew there would be a response. In fact it was almost immediate.

There was a shout from on high. Raz Sharif had been recognized. Men were running from the houses. Most wore bandoliers over their shirts. Every man carried a gun. They were a felonious-looking bunch to be sure.

Raz Sharif waved and let out a roar of greeting. With the Lee Enfield in his hands he loped towards the villagers. The girl ran in his wake, bag bumping against her hip. Credentials established, I switched off.

I'd have preferred to keep the aircraft ticking over but the last thing I needed was someone to decapitate themselves on the low-slung blades. So I got out and jogged across the grass. Ahead of me the Pathan was bounding over the pasture like an ibex, calling loudly to his fellow Mujehadeen. I wished I was as nimble at half the old man's age.

By the time I'd caught up with them Raz Sharif had embraced just about everybody in sight and was engaged in animated discussion with the guerillas. There were about fifteen of them and they were all talking at once. There was much brandishing of weapons; Lee Enfields and the inevitable Kalashnikovs. It was a salutation. Raz Sharif was being welcomed back like the prodigal son or, in his case, like a prodigal uncle. There were no women present. I presumed they were either in hiding or else they had been evacuated. The latter would seem to be the most likely option. These were fighting men, with little time or the facilities for camp followers.

Raz Sharif had obviously paved the way for myself and the doctor, informing them why we were there. The men jostled forward to shake hands. The Pathan's face was alive with excitement. 'Welcome to Afghanistan, Inglestani!' he cried.

'Right,' I said. 'Terrific. Now, where's the patient?' Under the circumstances I didn't feel inclined to engage in polite chit chat. I had a job to do. I simply wanted to load up and get out.

Raz Sharif relayed the question and about a dozen index fingers pointed back up the hill. Which told us one thing anyway. The sick man was still alive, presumably. I supposed they could all have been indicating the way to Muhammed Nur Rafiq's burial plot, of course. But that was unlikely. Everyone was in too good a mood.

'Okay, doctor,' I said. 'He's all yours. If the guy's fit to travel I want him down here as fast as they can carry him. Well, don't just stand there, love! Jump to it!'

The girl took off with a couple of the Mujehadeen leading the way and I turned to Raz Sharif. 'Tell them to get the crates out of the helicopter.'

It was one of the men standing at Raz Sharif's side who gave the order. Young, dressed in tombon pants, pirahan shirt and sheepskin waistcoat, with a Kalashnikov slung over his shoulder. I also couldn't help noticing that he was the only man wearing boots; military style with thick soles. As a number of the group ran to do his bidding Raz Sharif beamed proudly and introduced him.

'This is the son of my brother,' he explained. 'Kerim Gul is malik of Dar Galak. Very important person.'

The headman of Dar Galak gave the impression that he was rather embarrassed by the glowing character reference. He was like his uncle; tall and wiry. He looked to be about thirty years of age, perhaps a little younger, and roguishly handsome with a thick black moustache, the ends of which curled up flamboyantly. Warm brown eyes indicated that not too far beneath that hard and sinewy exterior there resided a strong sense of humour. He pumped my hand with genuine enthusiasm and smiled cheerfully. 'Salaam aleikum,' he said. 'You had a good flight, yes?'

Which struck me as funny. It was rather like being met

89

by a Hertz rep on arrival at Kingsford Smith. Kerim's English was pretty fair too. With an infectious grin, he told me why that was.

Kerim, it transpired, had been a student of economics at Kabul University and had, in the course of his studies, and through coming from a wealthy family, been fortunate enough to have visited both the United States and the UK. Then he'd joined the army as an officer cadet. Done well, too, with rapid promotion. He'd been a major by the time the Russians had arrived. Three months after that, he'd had enough, seen the light, and deserted to the Mujehadeen.

'Russians can go and bugger themselves!' Kerim chortled. 'I go to the Panjsher to join Massoud. Now I kill Russians and they all go to bloody hell, yes?'

'Absolutely,' I agreed, wondering where Doctor Bonnard had got to and, more precisely, why the blazes wasn't she getting a frigging move on, for Chris'sakes?

The three crates had been removed from the helicopter and dumped on the grass. Three spindly legged horses were led out and the crates were loaded on their backs. The horses were then driven off the meadow and hobbled under the branches of a willow tree. Soon they would be wending their way through the mountains to Massoud's forward base. By which time we would be back in civilization. Well, Peshawar anyway.

I glanced skywards then and wasn't happy with what I could see. The sun was beginning to break through which meant that the cloud base was dispersing. C'mon, doctor, I fretted, get your finger out, we haven't got all day. I tried not to let my frustration show. We'd already been in the place far longer than I'd intended. Only minutes, admittedly, but it seemed like hours.

There came a sharp cry from above and I followed the sound. The girl was on her way back. She was coming

down the hill, treading carefully. Beside her, two Mujehadeen were lugging the body on a makeshift stretcher
fashioned from what looked like the remains of a wooden
door.

'They come!' Kerim cried, somewhat unnecessarily. He
slapped me on the back. 'You soon be back in Pakistan,
my friend!'

Providing they didn't drop the poor bastard down the
side of the mountain, I thought as I watched the irritatingly
slow descent.

But they finally made it without mishap. Muhammed
Nur Rafiq turned out to be quite a youngster, probably no
older than Kerim Gul. But, from the look of him, he was
certainly in a bad way. His colour was ashen and he
appeared comatose, wrapped baby-like in a threadbare
grey blanket.

'Well?' I asked the girl. 'How is he?'

But she never got the chance to reply.

Because at that precise second all hell broke loose and
Plan A went hurtling right out of the window.

'SHURAVI!'

The scream was followed by a ragged volley of gunfire
and a roll of sound like the rattle of a train in the distance.
The warning came from high on the slope above us and
echoed around the high walls of the ravine.

'RUSSIANS!'

Chapter Six

All eyes turned in horror towards the neck of the valley.

A massive barrage of engine noise was approaching fast. Kerim screamed at his men and the Mujehadeen began to scatter. The stretcher bearers were immediately caught in two minds. Whether to deliver their charge to the helicopter or follow Kerim Gul. I solved their dilemma.

I yelled at the girl. 'Get on board! MOVE IT!' Made a grab for Raz Sharif's sleeve. 'Help us get him in the chopper, dammit!'

Beside me, Nicole Bonnard hesitated then stumbled as I pushed her towards the JetRanger. 'What the hell are you waiting for?' I bellowed. 'GO! GO!'

She began to run.

Raz Sharif and I took a corner of the stretcher and, with the two Mujehadeen in tandem behind, started to follow her.

Then I saw them.

Even from a distance the Soviet gunships appeared huge. Head-on they looked like enormous, grotesque insects, giant mutations, with bubble-like eyes and wings clipped short. Two of them, flying in above and below formation. Coming in at frightening speed.

The nightmare began.

She was twenty yards from the JetRanger when she fell. One moment she was sprinting across the grass, the next she was sprawled on the ground, clutching her ankle, her face a grimace of pain.

Cursing, I abandoned the stretcher party. As Raz Sharif took the additional weight I hauled the girl to her feet and hooked an arm under her shoulder. Strange, but for a brief moment it seemed as if she was reluctant to go, then, like tired contestants in a three-legged race, the inert body of Muhammed Nur Rafiq alongside us, we crabbed towards the chopper.

We were only a matter of yards from the JetRanger but it might just as well have been a hundred miles. In my heart of hearts I knew we weren't going to make it. We hadn't a prayer.

And if the gunner in the leading Hind had any doubt as to what his priorities were he didn't waste any time reaching a decision, he opened fire. And his aim was remarkably accurate.

I heard the rasping snarl, saw the muzzle flash at the mouth of the cannon and the path of the bullets as they stitched their way across the grass towards us. I bawled out a warning and threw myself aside, taking the doctor with me. I hit the earth hard, air exploding from my lungs, felt the ground tremble, dragged my body across the girl's, kept my head down.

Looked up through stems of grass I watched the Jet-Ranger disintegrate under the savage onslaught like a cardboard box in a hailstorm. My senses were bombarded by a tremendous roar as the two gunships battered their way above us and began a sweeping turn to make a second run.

The demolition of the helicopter wasn't the only damage that had been sustained. Only a few feet away the stretcher party lay in gruesome disarray. The grey cocoon that had been Muhammed Nur Rafiq was now a shapeless mass, mangled and blood soaked; the guerilla leader's body had been pulverized beyond recognition, as had the bodies of the two Mujehadeen. They lay in the grass like two tattered rag dolls, limbs twisted and broken like twigs, devastated by shrapnel. Somehow Raz Sharif had survived the attack. The Pathan rose groggily to his feet, scrabbled for his rifle, and screeched in rage. He started to drag at the bullet-ridden corpses as if to urge them back to life. An arm flopped out of the shredded blanket and brushed along the ground. Only it wasn't an arm as such. It was more like a bloody joint of meat that had been carved by a butcher's apprentice. It certainly didn't resemble anything that was remotely human.

And the gunships had completed their turns and were clattering in like airborne tanks.

I raised myself and pulled the girl to her knees. Called across to the old man. 'LEAVE HIM!'

Raz Sharif, blood seeping from a cut on his cheek, heeded the cry and ran over. I looked around for cover. The first priority was to get as far away as we could. Sharpish.

I backed into Kerim. The young headman had run in behind me unseen. One look at the carnage around us and at the remains of the JetRanger told us all we needed to know. The helicopter was beyond salvage. It was as if a grenade had exploded inside a greenhouse. The interior was littered with shards from the windscreen panels. The instruments were a wild tangle of shattered gauges and twisted wires. As for Muhammed Nur Rafiq and the others, there was nothing anyone could do except mourn them. But that would follow later. Together, Kerim and I helped Raz Sharif and the girl away from the stricken aircraft and the four of us stumbled towards the rocks at the base of the hill, searching frantically for shelter.

There was a streak of smoke behind us as the gunships released the first of their S-5 rockets, followed closely by a blistering detonation as what remained of the JetRanger blew apart.

Their main target destroyed, the Soviet helicopters

94

began their assault on the Mujehadeen dwellings. Fierce rocket salvos pummelled the crude buildings to rubble.

The Mujehadeen were being pinned down by the rapid fire power of the Soviet machine guns. A few sporadic bursts from small arms meant that some of the guerillas were retaliating, but with little effect.

I spotted the defile ahead of us and then we were all burrowing into the ground like gophers. I had just enough time to get my bearings before Kerim was gone. The headman was making his way along the slope in a bid to rally his men. The gunships, meanwhile, were sweeping up and along the valley as if they had all the time in the world.

And we had been so damned close to pulling off the rescue, only another two minutes would have seen us out of the valley and on our way home. Back to Peshawar and my one hundred thou.

But some days were diamond and some days were stone. And fate had decreed that the master plan should be thwarted by a brace of rampaging interlopers. To wit: two prime examples of Soviet air power, harnessing between them the destructive force of a battalion of infantry. And whether they were there by accident or design was academic. So what if they had strayed off course? So what if they had decided to indulge themselves in a small peripheral engagement at this tiny isolated hamlet they just happened to know about? Whatever their reason, their arrival had been dramatic, not to say bloody inconvenient.

But it was no use worrying about the maybes and the what ifs. Life was chock full of the if onlys. It was the future I was concerned with, not the past. Not that I expected my future to last beyond the next few minutes or so, mind you.

I knew the Russians would want to get some men on the ground in order to evaluate the presence of an unidentified aircraft in their sector. And to do that they'd have to whittle down the number of guerillas who'd be trying to stop them. Hence the aerial gunnery practice. I thought it unlikely that the Hind pilots had relayed their current involvement to their support base. The mountains could well have stymied any radio transmission.

It was possible that the gunships had troops on board. They each had cabin space for eight fully armed men, which meant that between them they had more than enough manpower and weaponry to fight the Mujehadeen on their own turf, given the size of the guerilla band. And one thing was certain. If they did succeed in landing ground troops their first task would be to get their hands on the pilot of that helicopter they had dealt with so effectively. And that notion was enough to give me severe stomach cramps.

Raz Sharif's attention was directed over my shoulder and by the gleam in his eye and the grimace on that old bearded face I knew the gunships were coming round again. I squirmed down into the burrow and followed the Pathan's gaze.

Bright rays from the sun were now lancing into the ravine and reflecting off the canopies and stubby wings of the Hinds as they swept across the slopes, multiple rocket pods hanging like obscene fruit beneath the camouflage fuselages. As the gruff throb of the engines grew in volume and rolled like thunder along the steep sides of the valley the nose-mounted 12.7mm machine guns began to growl.

Raz Sharif began to mutter to himself in Pushtu and I realized with a start that the old man was praying. The words were from the Qoran. I knew that because I actually recognized them. Unlikely though it was they constituted one of the few phrases of dialect that I'd actually managed to retain. Why they should stick in my mind particularly,

I would be at a loss to define. Just one of those legacies of living and working in a society bound by religious dogma, I suppose. Nevertheless, I understood them.

'Praise to God, the ruler of all people in the world, the most merciful God who, on the Day of Judgement . . .'

I felt the girl suddenly tremble by my side. The Pathan's bass droning was engulfed by a solid wave of sound as, with a ferocious roar and a downdraught that scurried dust into our faces, the two Hind gunships barrelled overhead, spraying mayhem.

Christ, but they were close! Through smarting eyes I could just make out the pilot's pale, helmet-shrouded face as he banked the big helicopter on to another straffing run. In the snout, behind the plexiglass shield, the weapons systems officer was hunched over the trigger of his Gatling gun. How the bastards must have been laughing all the way through to the soles of their fur-lined moon boots, or whatever passed for service issue in the Armeiskaya Aviat-siya these days, at the antics of the Mujehadeen below them, bolting like frightened rabbits across the scree.

By now most of the tribesmen had gained cover among the rocks and were firing back but their weapons were about as effective as pea-shooters against the strength and fire power of the Mi-24s. I winced as I watched two black-robed rebels tumble like dominoes as they were caught in the open by a withering burst from the lead gunship. Face down in the dirt, they looked for all the world to see like cat-mauled crows left to rot.

I couldn't understand why they had abandoned their refuge and exposed themselves to attack. Then it dawned on me.

The horses. They were still out there, under the trees at the edge of the stream, straining at their halters, eyes rolling in fear, unable to move because they were still hobbled. It was a pitiful sight, seeing them bucking wildly,

97

ears pricked as they fought to break their bonds and escape the terrifying deluge of sound that had come upon them like a tornado.

Although the two guerillas had been trying to reach the animals it was probably the weapons they had been trying to save. But, whatever their motive, it was inevitable that their action had only served to draw attention to the hapless beasts.

With cold deliberation, one of the gunships sank into a hover above the stream and the gunner opened fire. The horse nearest the helicopter was tipped back on its haunches as its hindquarters were torn apart in seconds. A second horse slid on to its belly as its legs were cut away.

There was a muttered curse in Pushtu and a commotion as Raz Sharif wormed his way along the ground and watched as the animals were scythed down. He fingered the trigger of his rifle, his body quivering with rage. In the confined space at the entrance to the defile I was unhappily aware of a sour odour emanating from the Pathan's pores. Perhaps fear and anger had triggered some kind of gland secretion but whatever the catalyst it was a bit like sharing the foxhole with a dead goat. Still, given the circumstances I was fully prepared to forgive the old warrior his sanitary indiscretions. The girl was in no condition to complain either. She was too busy keeping her head down.

I peeked around the edge of the nearest boulder. On the valley floor the shell of the JetRanger still smouldered. The gunships were circling like wasps over a picnic hamper. I could see the red star emblem on the sand and duck-egg-green paintwork behind the stumpy wings. The twin air intakes above the cockpits looked like the black eyes of sharp-faced rodents.

As though latching on to a scent they turned in unison and it was as if they were looking directly into my eyes. It was feral the way they began to move slowly up the hillside, as bloodhounds might follow a spoor. Instinctively, I shrank back. The tiny hairs at the back of my neck tingled and cold tendrils of fear slid along my spine. The WOP WOP WOP of the rotors reached an hypnotic cacophony as they approached our redoubt.

And Raz Sharif, the stupid bastard, stood up!

God knows what made him do it. Probably sheer fury at seeing the slaughter of his comrades, taken out like ducks in a fairground shooting gallery. I had felt the man tense as the gunships drew nearer and, before I had fully grasped what was happening, Raz Sharif had scrambled out of the gully.

'Allah o Akbar!' The exultation erupted from the Pathan's throat as he thrust by.

'You fucking idiot!' I screamed, unable to stop him.

The underbellies of the helicopters seemed to fill my field of vision. The noise was tremendous. The sensation was as if the entire hillside was shaking and I was convinced my eardrums were about to burst. The guerillas in the rocks around us were still taking potshots and the sharp crack of rifle fire and the brief staccato bursts from automatic weapons added to the din.

In a moment of startling clarity it was suddenly as if I had been transported back in time to another place, another war zone where, instead of the contest being fought on mountain slopes, the deadly arena was one where the stench of fear and death was accentuated by the sweet smell of the rain forest fermenting after the monsoon. And then, as that terrible feeling of déja-vu began to enclose me, just as abruptly I was back, stranded on that Godforsaken, sun seared stretch of desolation, wishing I'd taken the trouble to wear my brown corduroy fatigues while, at the same time, trying my damnedest to prevent one extremely irate Pushtu tribesman from getting his balls blown off. And I hadn't even got a weapon of my own, for Christ's sake! Nothing to hit back with. Unless I started throwing bloody rocks.

I was halfway to my knees, alarm fast overcoming caution, as Raz Sharif, the tails of his cotton shirt flapping like a raven's wing, clambered over the rocks with the agility of a chamois and levelled his rifle at the nearest gunship. He was ten yards ahead of me and I could see what was going to happen. And there was nothing I could do about it except roll back into the defile, wrap myself around the girl and prepare for the inevitable.

The rate of fire from a Soviet 12.7mm cannon is a thousand rounds a minute but in the open Raz Sharif didn't even last that long. The heavy slugs took him full in the chest, lifting him off his feet, punching him backwards with the force of a mule kick. The Lee Enfield .303 flew from his grasp, the stock splintering like matchwood against the boulders. Raz Sharif's long body crashed back on to the rocks, his upper half little more than a ragged, bloody crater in which white bone gleamed. I turned my eyes away from the crumpled form and to my horror the old man began to squeal, the shrill sound rising to a crescendo as the chopper crews continued to rake the surrounding positions. The combined noise was deafening.

Nicole Bonnard struggled violently in my arms, her gaze transfixed on the Pathan's dreadful wounds. 'We must help him!' she cried, and tried to pull herself away from my desperate grip.

'No!' I tried to stop her.

My attempt failed. She broke free and I watched helplessly as she crawled out of the hole. She was in full view of the Russian gunner. He couldn't miss, not at that range.

I moved fast, bawled at her, 'GET DOWN, DAMMIT!' I was out of the gully, running. Not entirely sure in my own mind what I was planning to do. Try and get her out of the field of fire or something equally heroic. And futile.

My frantic yell was immediately drowned out by a colossal bang that dropped me to my knees and a noise that sounded as if one of the gunships was falling out of the sky. When I looked up I was astounded to discover that was exactly what was occurring.

The SAM-7 had struck the helicopter just behind the exhaust port, ripping away the rotorhead hydraulic control jacks and the pitch control rods. The gunship went down like a house brick dropped from a third-storey window. It hit the ground on its port side, metal buckling and cracking like an eggshell. Then its fuel reserves went up with a boom that reverberated around the ravine like the voice of God.

The effect on the surviving Mi-24 was instantaneous. It accelerated away and went up like a fighter. The comrades hadn't bargained on the Mujehadeen having anything heavier than an AK-47. A SAM-7 surface-to-air missile was a definite infringement of the rules. The big helicopter disappeared around the side of the mountain like a bat out of hell. The rumble of its huge Isotov turboshaft engines dwindled into the distance. An uncanny silence descended over the valley.

The girl was crouching over the wounded Pathan, anguish engraved on her face. But it was too late. There was nothing she could do. There was nothing anyone could do. I got shakily to my feet and surveyed the carnage. The floor of the valley looked like an aviation junkyard. The JetRanger was demolished almost beyond recognition. Oily black smoke spiralled up into the still morning air. Fire had also engulfed the Soviet helicopter. I could hear the snap and crackle of the flames. The airframe had virtually melted away. It now resembled a molten block of plastic.

The Mujehadeen were taking toll of the casualties and retrieving weapons. I heard a shout. Kerim was wending his way down the slope with the missile tube on his shoulder. He looked as happy as a schoolboy who'd saved the innings in a first eleven cricket match; the hero of the hour. He grinned at me, jerked his head at the remnants of the Russian gunship, and spat into the dirt.

Whoever had taught Kerim to fire the weapon had done a fine job. The Mujehadeen hadn't exactly been renowned for their technical expertise when it came to anything more advanced than a Kalashnikov or, on occasion, Chinese 60mm mortars. The fact that Kerim had successfully primed and fired a missile and knocked out a Russian helicopter to boot was proof that the guerillas were receiving some form of advanced weapons training. Maybe the British mercs were involved in something more than appropriating random artifacts of Soviet hardware. Or perhaps Jack Tagg had been conducting evening classes. But that definitely smacked of direct covert involvement by Western intelligence agencies. And the less said about that the better.

The smile did not linger on Kerim's face for long, however. Not when the full extent of the casualties was realized. For, not counting Raz Sharif, the guerillas had lost eight men. Which amounted to half of their group. It was a severe blow.

As the other members of the band carried those killed into the shade of some birch trees by the side of the pasture, Kerim cradled the body of his uncle in his arms. Tears streaked the guerilla's face as he carried the body of the old man down to the meadow and laid it gently on the grass with the rest of the dead. Doctor Bonnard and I followed at a distance. On the way I bent down and helped myself to a gun. One of the Kalashnikovs. Its owner was no longer in need of it. I slipped the webbing strap over my shoulder. Now I didn't feel quite so naked.

Of the surviving rebels, two had received wounds. One of them, who looked about fifteen, had taken a bullet through the arm and was looking quite chuffed about it. I suppose he regarded it as some sort of initiation rite, the silly young sod. It seemed to me a painful way of achieving maturity. The other victim, however, was not so fortunate. His leg wound was a far more serious affair. It was obvious from the amount of blood coating his upper thighs that the bullet had caused extensive damage. Only quick thinking by one of his companions had ensured that he hadn't bled to death. A crude tourniquet had been fashioned out of a length of turban and the magazine from an AK-47. It wasn't BMA standard by any stretch of the imagination but it had proved effective. Not surprisingly, Nicole Bonnard expressed grave concern over the fellow's condition. A brief examination had told her that the artery had indeed been nicked. But all she had time for right then was to reset the tourniquet, plug the wound with a gauze pad that she took from her medical kit and secure it with a length of bandage. She also administered morphine to deaden the pain. There was little doubt, though, that the wound required extensive treatment, and soon.

While the feasibility of that requirement was discussed between Kerim and the doctor, I went to survey the aftermath of the raid.

The body of one of the horses lay in the stream, blood flowing freely from deep gashes in its haunches, staining the water a frothy pink. A weapons crate rested, half submerged, against the animal's flank. Two of the Mujehadeen were struggling to tug it free. Another of the pack animals lay on the bank, forelegs a mess of shattered stumps, its belly a mire of creamy entrails. The third horse had, by some miracle, survived the attack but it stood, nostrils flared, snorting with panic whenever anyone came within a couple of feet. Its precious load remained intact, however, and the Mujehadeen were content to give the poor beast time to calm down while they rescued the remaining crates.

I left them to it and picked my way forlornly through the pile of metal bones that had been the JetRanger. The wreckage was ringed by a blackened circle of scorched grass. Of the helicopter, not a single strut remained undamaged. The same could be said for the Russian gunship, still burning fiercely.

The Mi-24 had been a massive aircraft, dwarfing the JetRanger. The Hind had initially been designed as a multi-role battlefield helicopter with emphasis on it being able to transport front line troops into forward key positions. But with a growing awareness of the effectiveness of armed helicopters in battle zones, as illustrated by the American's use of Air Cav squadrons in Vietnam, its function had been altered drastically into that of an assault support platform. With great effect, as the Afghan guerilla fighters had come to discover only too well and as I had recently witnessed to my own cost.

At least Nicole Bonnard had her bag, dropped in the dash for cover. I was left only with the clothes I stood up in. Nevertheless, despite this and the catastrophic loss of the JetRanger, in the final analysis I knew that we had both been incredibly lucky to have emerged from the fray physically unscathed, barring what amounted to only a few minor cuts and bruises. Which was more than could be said for Kerim and his Mujehadeen.

But there was the worry and the likelihood that the Russians would return. Once the crew of the surviving Mi-24 returned to base and reported the loss of their companions the Soviets would mobilize their forces. They'd pour men and machinery into the area faster than you could say 'do svidanya'. They'd want to salvage what was left, if anything, of their downed helicopter and crew and, most of all, exact vengeance. They'd be looking for blood. And I didn't want to be anywhere in the vicinity when that happened, thank you very much. Neither, I presumed, did any of the others.

I looked over the wreckage of the JetRanger with increasing despair. Felt a light touch on my arm. The girl.

'I am sorry,' she said softly.

'Sorry doesn't really cover it,' I said.

'What are you thinking?' she asked.

'I'm thinking that it's going to be a bloody long walk back to the border.'

'The border!'

I looked at her. 'We're a million light years from home, love. Pretty soon this place is going to be knee deep in Russian ground troops. Take my word for it, neither of us wants to be around when they get here.'

As I said, we were well and truly stranded. Logic therefore dictated that we should try and make for the Durand Line and Pakistan. But it was a long slog to the border and neither of us was equipped for such an arduous journey. But maybe Kerim could provide a couple of his men to act as guides.

Meanwhile, under the trees, rocks from the bed of the stream were being placed on top of the bodies. The task was completed in some haste because, like me, everyone feared the return of the Russians. Tentatively I asked Kerim about guides. Not surprisingly, it wasn't that Kerim wouldn't provide men it was more a case of he couldn't.

'My friend.' The guerilla shook his head sadly. 'Alas, I cannot spare any of my Mujehadeen to take you and the lady beyond the mountains. I am deeply sorry. Besides, that is what the Russians will expect you to do. They will surely try and cut you off. I think you should remain with me and my men. There is – how do you say it? – safety in numbers, yes? You help us take the guns to Massoud. Then we will send you north through the high passes to Pakistan. No Russians there.' Kerim stroked his moustache and smiled. 'Much better, I think.'

I thought about that. I wasn't too thrilled with the idea of a prolonged hike through Afghanistan, particularly in the opposite direction we needed to be in, but I could see Kerim's point. The alternative, of course, was that we should try and make it on our own. But I wasn't that foolish. 'We don't really have much of a choice, do we?' I said grimly. 'Mind you,' I added to Doctor Bonnard. 'I'm open to suggestions.'

None were forthcoming. In fact, if anything, she looked more than a little relieved. I wondered why that should be but then I remembered why she'd taken the job in the first place. This way, I supposed, by sticking with Kerim and his group until they reached Massoud's camp, there was a better chance of her finding out what had become of her brother. There didn't appear to be anything else for it then. It was cut and dried.

'In that case, Kerim my old mate,' I announced, 'it looks very much as if we're in your hands.'

The guerilla beamed. 'Don't worry, mista! We will take good care of you.'

I sincerely hoped so. I really did.

By now the Mujehadeen had managed to load two of the crates on to the back of the remaining horse. They had broken open the third box – the one already damaged in the fall at the refugee camp – and distributed the weapons among themselves. Several of the men, one of whom had already been carrying the SAM rocket launcher, had a couple of the Kalashnikovs slung around their necks. The whole crew was now positively draped with hardware. The girl had her bag and, although I was now equipped

106

with my own gun, I felt very much the odd one out. My offer to carry a couple of extra rifles, however, was politely declined.

The last rock had been placed upon the bodies of the dead guerillas. The end result was a row of small stone pyramids under the trees. Warriors' graves.

Which meant we were ready to leave. But not before the Mujehadeen had left a warning to the Russians.

There hadn't been any troops in the downed Soviet helicopter, just the two crew men. The body of one of them had survived the fire. The helmeted corpse had been discovered down in the stream, several yards away from the wreckage of the Hind gunship. Presumably the poor devil had been tossed out of the aircraft when it exploded. The other crew man had clearly perished in the flames. What was left of this one resembled a rack of pork, slightly undercooked. Skin, blistered and pink, poked through jagged rents in the charred flying suit.

The Mujehadeen stripped the corpse and left it staked out in the meadow. They also cut off the head and placed it upon the mutilated torso. The sightless eyes had turned up on themselves. The veined white muscle had the sheen of glazed marble.

I resisted the urge to vomit. Doctor Bonnard averted her eyes conveniently. God knows what she must have been feeling. But she knew these people. She had known better than to interfere.

And thus, leaving the grim reminder to the Soviets of what they could expect to suffer if they were killed or, worse, captured by their Afghan foe, Kerim led us out of the valley.

Chapter Seven

Even Indiana Jones never had it this bad, I was thinking.

Time had dipped into the afternoon and the temperature must have been somewhere up in the high eighties. It was like walking through a sauna and I was feeling more than a mite bothered.

But then, togged up like a snake charmer's assistant, who the hell wouldn't be?

It had been Kerim's idea, the rogue, and I suppose it made sense. Although, frankly, the thought of changing my appearance hadn't occurred to me at all.

We'd only been on the move for about thirty minutes. The plan being to get as many miles behind us as possible before the Soviets returned to Dar Galak and picked up our tracks. Already I'd worked up quite a sweat. Although I'd taken my jacket off and hung it through the strap of the Kalashnikov I was beginning to wish I'd left the gun behind for someone else to carry. Rivers of perspiration were flowing down my back and my shirt was sodden. Up until then I'd fancied I was in pretty good shape. Maybe I was, compared to a whole lot of people, but in the present company I felt like I was the fat kid who lagged behind in the cross-country run. A bit of a tryer, but bloody useless when it came down to it.

That was when I caught Kerim looking at me with a bemused expression on his face. He was ahead of me and was staring back and shaking his head as if he couldn't quite believe what he was seeing.

He waited for me to catch up. When I got there, he looked me up and down thoughtfully.

'My friend,' he said, stroking his beard, 'this is not good.'

I presumed he was referring to my lack of fitness. I was panting quite a bit at the time.

'To hide from the Russians you must look like an Afghan not a Feringhi,' he said solemnly. 'You wait.'

Kerim called out the Pushtu equivalent of 'time out, you guys!' and I took a breather under a tree while he bounded away towards the panniers on the pack horse. When he returned he was carrying a bundle of clothing which he dumped at my feet.

'You change quick,' he instructed.

I picked up what looked like a long white night shirt and a pair of pantaloons from the pile. They were clean enough but I peered suspiciously at a couple of patches sewn into the material. I wondered what had become of their previous owner but didn't think it was prudent to ask right then.

I saw they were all waiting for me to make a move so I shrugged and started to unbutton my shirt. I heard a couple of sharp intakes of breath. I'd forgotten that the Afghans are more than a bit prudish when it comes to exposing the body. Even in all male company, one doesn't strip off. With Nicole Bonnard standing there looking on, they nearly all went into cardiac arrest.

So I picked up the shirt and pants and went in search of a rock to change behind.

I emerged to a smattering of applause and a selection of ribald comments, none of which I understood but I got their gist well enough. Doctor Bonnard looked to be trying hard to bite her lip.

Kerim clapped his hands. 'Ah, my friend! Now you look like a true Mujehad!'

Which was all very well for him to say. Personally, I thought I looked like a twenty-four-carat berk. But I had to admit that already I felt a lot cooler, particularly in the below-the-waist department. The tombon pantaloons were generously baggy and I had plenty of movement. They were tied around the waist with a draw string. The only part of my own clothing that I had on, apart from my skinnies, were my trainers. I wasn't prepared to give those up. A man has to be allowed to preserve some dignity, after all. I rolled up my windcheater, shirt and Levi's and Kerim stowed them away in one of the pack horse's saddle bags. When everybody had fully recovered from the cabaret I looped the Kalashnikov over my shoulder and we set off again. With me feeling like a spare guest at a fancy-dress party.

Four hours later we still hadn't made it off the bloody mountain. The gradient seemed endless. I wondered how Nicole Bonnard was coping. So far, she'd spent most of the journey keeping an eye on the guy with the leg wound. Ironically, he was being carried on the same rude stretcher that had supported Muhammed Nur Rafiq, with the bearers being switched every hour or so. Their collective stamina must have been incredible. They had borne him over the harshest of terrain without complaint while I, having only myself to worry about, was dog tired.

I trekked across to a large boulder at the side of the trail to rest my bones. I looked up the track and watched the rear end of the pack horse sway around a bend in the hill, hooves clattering on the stones. The drop down the mountain was terrifying but the animal seemed uncon-cerned. It had negotiated the steep paths with the sure-footedness of a mountain goat.

The view was spectacular. The mountains, displayed in serried ranks, stretched into the distance, summits glinting in the sunshine, like the polished shields of some vast army. Above us the sky was clear and so blue it was almost painful to look at it for any length of time. And the stillness was absolute. The sound of our passage seemed the grossest intrusion. It was as if time was suspended. We might have been the only people on the planet.

The two stretcher bearers loped past me, unbowed, intent on their task. Nicole Bonnard followed behind, picking her way carefully. In these conditions it would have been so easy to turn an ankle. And disastrous. One invalid in the party was more than enough to have to try and cope with.

She stopped when she came level, brushed a stray hair from her forehead, gazed breathlessly out over the chasm. 'Beautiful, isn't it?'

I agreed that it was. Took another couple of deep breaths. At this altitude the air was very thin. I was feeling quite light headed.

She rummaged through her bag. Held something out to me. 'Here,' she said. 'This might help.'

'What is it?'

'Glucose.'

I took the proffered tablet and rolled it around my gums to get my saliva glands going. I could feel life beginning to return to my legs.

Nicole Bonnard hadn't needed to go through the same sartorial transformation as I had. To look the part all she'd needed to do was hitch her shirt out of her pants, place her hair up, and put her cap back on. The camouflage smock and the boots had completed the deception. From a distance, apart from the fact that she wasn't carrying a gun, she was indistinguishable from the rest of Kerim's motley crew. It had been the leather windcheater and jeans that had done for me.

Despite the disguise I could see she had a good figure. Curves in all the right places, slim hips, long straight legs. I guess I couldn't have been that far gone to notice such things.

111

There was a yell from ahead.

'Birram! Birram!'

'Let's go! Let's go!' It was Kerim, urging us on. A hard task master but a practical one. Although we had been on the move for half a day, the distance we had covered was still well within the patrol sector of the Russian gunships. We weren't out of the woods yet.

Talking of which, I would gladly have given my eye teeth for a patch of shade. The heat was bouncing off the rocks around us with the intensity of a laser beam and I was starting to get serious cravings for a cold beer. Yet, despite this, I knew that up here, at night, the temperature could drop by as much as ninety degrees. With luck, though, we'd be off the mountain by then. But here was I, wondering where we were going to spend the night, and I didn't even have so much as a bloody toothbrush. So, come on, Crow. Wise up. Forget about cleaning your teeth. Just grit them instead. I sighed and heaved myself off the rock. And off we went. Ever onward.

We came down off the mountain and into the valley in the late afternoon. To a general feeling of relief, most of which emanated from yours truly.

We walked through a grove of mulberry trees. The men helped themselves to fistfuls of the plump fruit and passed them around. They tasted wonderful and I for one suffered no pangs of remorse at depriving the farmer of part of his season's meagre crop.

Kerim called a halt on the bank of a tiny bubbling stream. A village lay close by: Jamalagar. He dispatched a couple of men to scout ahead. The pack horse, having been allowed to drink, was tethered to a bush. The rest of us settled down to wait. I took off my trainers and dipped my feet in the water. It was ice cold but I didn't care. It felt marvellous.

Doctor Bonnard was dispensing care and attention to

various members of the group with the help of salves and Band Aids and such like that she took from her holdall. Blistered feet appeared to be the most common ailment. The Mujehadeen with the leg wound had survived the journey but his condition was still serious, which was hardly surprising considering what he'd been subjected to during the long hot day. There was apparently even some doubt the man would last the night.

Around me the rest of the band tended to their various needs; bathing their tired bodies, treating sores, followed by the obligatory prayers. Namaz over, they dozed under the trees. They hadn't even bothered to put out sentries, I noticed, but no one seemed the least bit concerned. I thought I detected the sound of aircraft engines somewhere in the distance, but from the complete lack of interest shown by the rest of them, perhaps I had imagined it. Ah, well. When in Rome . . .

I closed my eyes and lay back on the grass.

'How are you, my friend?' Kerim plopped down at my side. He had taken his boots off and was dangling his feet in the water.

'Knackered,' I replied, without thinking, and watched his brow furrow immediately. 'Tired,' I followed on hurriedly.

'Ah!' He nodded sagely. 'We will rest soon. My men will find us somewhere to stay and then we will eat. In the village of Jamalagar there is a chai khana.'

Chai khana, I knew, meant tea house. It would have to do. Forget the beer. In Afghanistan, pubs were decidedly thin on the ground. Thin, that is, as in non-existent.

The sun had slipped over the ring of mountains and the light was beginning to fade. Shadows lengthened, dappling the trees under which we lay. There was a calmness in the air. After the calamity at the pick-up point and our subsequent hike over the mountain we were all starting to wind down.

Voices. Someone approaching. The scouts returning. Kerim stood up to greet them. There followed a muttered consultation. Kerim turned back to us and smiled. 'No Russians,' he announced happily. 'We go.'

The good news spread and the call went out.

'Arakat! Arakat!'

'Move on! Move on!'

The prospect of food and shelter spurred all of us into action. Ablutions performed, belongings, along with the pack horse, were hastily collected. Two new stretcher bearers took up the strain. Kerim informed me it was only a short walk to the village. I resisted the urge to let out a cheer.

Some village. Jamalagar consisted of about a dozen stone houses grouped around a tiny square. It was gone dusk by the time we got there – so much for Kerim's short walk – and in twilight the place didn't look exactly welcoming. But then a door opened in one of the buildings and I saw the pale yellow glow of a hurricane lamp. The place began to look cosier by the minute.

The chai khana wasn't much more than a shack built over a metal stove, the flue of which disappeared through a hole in the roof. The floor was beaten earth but a raised platform ran around the room and this was lined with rugs and cushions. We made ourselves comfortable. The stoop-shouldered, wall-eyed proprietor looked about as unprepossessing as the rest of the fixtures and fittings but he jumped to Kerim's bidding at will.

Funnily enough, despite my Ali Baba get-up, I didn't rate so much as half a glance. I could only surmise that he'd gotten so used to the comings and goings of itinerant Europeans that my arrival in his humble establishment was pretty low down his list of the ten most moving

114

experiences of his lifetime. In other words, one more feringhi in off-white pantaloons didn't make a whole heap of difference to his scratch-a-living existence. He did give Nicole Bonnard the once-over though. Mind you, who wouldn't?

The wounded Mujehad was laid out on the platform, his back propped against the wall. I couldn't even tell if he was conscious but I had the feeling that even if he'd shrugged off his mortal coil they'd have brought him inside. It was smoky and cramped. The only one of our party not present was the pack horse. It had been relieved of its burden and taken into a nearby outhouse.

An enormous kettle was brought out and tea was dispensed. The brew was very hot. I sipped cautiously and listened to the guerillas chat amongst themselves. Nicole Bonnard came and sat beside me. She held her cup of tea with both hands and blew gently to cool it. As far as I could tell in the dim light, she looked pale and exhausted.

'How's our friend?' I asked, indicating the injured Mujehad.

'Not good,' she said. 'It is possible he may lose the leg unless we can get him to a field hospital. All I can do for the moment is deaden the pain.' She appeared close to despair.

I could only nod in sympathy; a pathetic acknowledgement of the poor devil's circumstances.

Mine host came in then, bearing food. Bowls of rice, a stew which I guessed was mutton, nan loaves, yoghurt, more tea. It was a feast. Conversation died and was replaced with the sounds of group mastication. I remembered to use only my right hand to pass the food to my lips, the left being reserved for more unhygienic use. After the meal I lay back against the cushions, a blanket over my legs, and listened to the chorus of contented burps and farts that began to permeate the room.

115

Through half-closed eyes I picked out Nicole Bonnard conversing with Kerim in urgent tones. The two of them were crouched over the wounded guerilla, Kerim looking deeply anxious. Finally he nodded briskly. They looked up, saw me watching them.

'What's happening?' I asked.

'I'm worried about Sayyef here,' she replied, indicating the wounded Mujehad. 'The wound needs attention. Kerim has told me that there is a French hospital in the next valley, but that is nearly a full day's walk away. And we couldn't possibly set out before morning. By which time it could be too late.' She bit her lip. 'If something isn't done soon he could lose the leg.'

'You mean if you don't do something soon, don't you?' I said.

She pursed her lips.

'It strikes me, Doctor,' I said, 'that you don't have a whole heap of choice.'

She gazed at me then at Kerim. Made up her mind. The decision was inevitable. She had known that.

The proprietor was summoned. Kerim issued orders. The wall-eyed man nodded and disappeared. He must have had the kettle permanently on the go for he returned less than a couple of minutes later with the vessel in his hands, his palms protected by a rag wrapped around the handle. He placed the kettle at the doctor's side and backed off.

'You need any help?' I pushed my blanket aside.

Nicole Bonnard said, 'Bring the lamp over here.'

I lifted it down from the rafters and took it across. This activity served to alert the rest of the gathering that something momentous was about to happen. Everyone not directly involved in events looked on expectantly. A hush fell on the room.

There was a hook on the wall just above the patient's

116

head. I hung up the lantern and Doctor Bonnard peeled back the blanket that covered the man's thighs. Kerim ripped away the remains of the guerilla's tombon and cut away the crude bandage to expose the wound and we all sat back to examine the damage. Which was considerable.

The edges of the bullet hole were difficult to define because the skin around it was puffy and severely inflamed. Also the lower limb was beginning to turn a sort of grey-blue colour. This despite the fact that Doctor Bonnard had made a point of releasing the tourniquet at regular intervals during our march. And what made it worse was that the bullet was still in there, somewhere.

Nicole Bonnard took her medical kit from her bag. It was very basic. Some kaolin dressings and gauze pads, Band Aids, antiseptic ointments, a small supply of foil-wrapped antibiotics and sedatives, tiny phials which presumably contained more pain-killing solutions, a compact sachet holding scissors, a pair of tweezers, two small scalpels, needles and gut and half a dozen disposable plastic syringes. To my eyes the contents looked pathetically inadequate for the task in hand. But that was hardly her fault. After all, she hadn't really been expecting to perform major surgery, had she?

Meanwhile, Kerim, talking softly, was attempting to reassure the patient. Without much success, mainly because the poor bastard was damned near comatose anyway. Which made me suspect that it was more a case of Kerim trying hard to steel his own nerves for what was about to happen rather than administer comfort to his unfortunate companion.

So, Doctor Bonnard picked on me to assist. Along with two volunteers from the audience.

First she took my hand and placed it high up on the inside of the patient's thigh. I could feel the big blood vessel throbbing away under my fingers.

'You press in here,' she instructed. 'Like this. Very firmly. Until I tell you to let go. That will reduce the blood flow while I drain the wound. If you ease the pressure before I'm ready he could bleed to death before your eyes. Literally.' She held my gaze for several seconds. 'Do you understand?'

My throat was suddenly very dry and constricted. I could only nod.

She told Kerim to hold the patient's shoulders. 'I cannot risk further sedation,' she said. 'He is too close to the edge already. You must hold him down to prevent him moving.' She indicated to the other men that they should secure his ankles.

She laid out her pitiful array of instruments on a corner of the blanket and poured water from the kettle into a shallow clay bowl. Then she dropped the scalpels into the boiling water. Tiny bubbles clung to the slivers of steel, detached themselves and broke the surface of the water. After a minute or two she removed the scalpels with the tweezers and laid them on to a square of clean dressing.

She looked at Kerim then at me. Nodded briefly. Kerim gripped the patient's arms, the others held their end. I bore down on to the pressure point as instructed. Doctor Bonnard took a deep breath and began to loosen the rough tourniquet that she had applied previously.

That part wasn't too difficult. A slight seepage of blood from the wound was all that occurred. So far so good.

Nicole Bonnard picked up a scalpel, selected a bloated section of skin, and sliced down.

Several things happened at once.

Kerim's face turned yellowy-green, which roughly matched the colour of the stuff that bubbled its revolting way out of the hole, the patient spasmed, the man holding the left ankle let go. I lost my grip and a fountain of blood erupted out of the patient's leg like water from a fire hose.

I heard Nicole Bonnard curse violently as I fumbled along the inside of the gore-splattered leg. Everyone else seemed to be shouting too. Then I found the pressure point again, more by luck than judgement, pushed my thumb up hard into his groin. Almost immediately the torrent eased to a trickle. Panic over, for the moment. The noise died down.

The crisis could only have lasted a second or two yet there was blood everywhere. We were covered in it. There was even some on the wall. Another rough day in the Out Patients Dept.

And our patient had lost total consciousness. I can't say I was all that surprised.

I remember reading as a boy in school that during the Napoleonic Wars a good ship's saw-bones could amputate a leg in thirty seconds and cauterize the stump as well.

Nicole Bonnard would have given Nelson's surgeon a run for his money, no doubt about it.

She sliced around the leg as if paring a length of electric wiring. Dark blood and pus creamed out of the wound. The smell was evil. There seemed to be a lot of poison in there, no doubt starting to eat away like maggots on a rotten piece of meat. I tried not to gag. As each section of skin was punctured and cleaned gasps of awe filled the room. The Mujehadeen were impressed with Doctor Bonnard's skill. As I was.

When she had removed all the outward signs of infection from the wound, she used fresh water to bathe the surrounding area, wiped it clean.

Then she went exploring with the tweezers.

She seemed to spend hours digging around in there, like someone rooting for buried treasure. I was starting to get cramp in my wrists.

Suddenly she let out a grunt of satisfaction, turned her hand a couple of degrees and pulled. This led to a succession of slurps and pops followed by a squelchy sucking noise as she hauled the slug out of the rent in the leg.

She worked very quickly then. Swabbed the hole clean, injected the contents of one of the glass phials into the thigh, performed some intricate needlework, smeared antiseptic ointment over another gauze pad, secured it with a fresh bandage, wrapped it around the leg. Eventually she leaned back, breathed a deep sigh, and said we could all ease off. Gently.

We did so with universal relief. Nicole Bonnard drew the blanket up to Sayyef's waist. She dumped the blood-and-pus-sodden bandages into the clay bowl, which was then removed by the proprietor. She poured some of the still hot water into another bowl and, with one of the remaining gauze pads, she cleaned her hands and arms. She offered the rest of us the same facility.

As Kerim cleaned himself I told Nicole Bonnard that she was one hell of a doctor.

She looked down at the wounded guerilla. 'It had to be done,' she said matter of factly. 'But he could still be dead by morning.' She laid her palm across Sayyef's forehead. 'Such a waste,' she added softly. Sadness clouded her eyes.

'You did your best, doctor,' I said. 'Give him a chance. He just might surprise us all.'

There was an expression of peace on the wounded guerilla's face. After all the excitement the rest of the room was beginning to settle down once more. There were grunts and groans as bodies rearranged themselves into some semblance of comfort for the remainder of the night. By their actions they evidently had little doubt that Sayyef would make it. Or perhaps they were simply prepared to place their trust in Allah. As old Ahmed Badur might have said: Inshallah.

'Perhaps,' she conceded. She wiped a stray hair from

her temple. 'He will still require serious attention, more than I could provide here. If he makes it through the night we will take him to the field hospital . . .' Her voice trailed off. She looked shattered.

I retrieved the bowl and pad from Kerim and rubbed the blood from my hands. 'You'd better get some sleep,' I said.

She sat back against the wall and nodded dully.

There seemed to be a sudden shortage of bed space.

'Here.' I dragged a blanket and cushion across. 'Take these.'

She didn't protest when I dropped the cushion behind her head and drew the blanket across her body. By the time I'd got myself under my own rug she was already asleep.

That was the night I discovered that most Afghans snore.

Loudly.

Chapter Eight

I awoke with a crick in my neck and Nicole Bonnard's arm across my chest. I'd known ruder awakenings.

It was early, the very edge of dawn, but I was glad the bulk of the night was over. I had slept fitfully during the first few hours in what had been little more than a series of dozes, interrupted by periods when I just lay there, besieged on all sides by the incessant snuffling, mumbling and coughing of my companions. Exhaustion, thank God, had finally tipped me over the threshold somewhere around midnight, at which time I went out like a light.

Nicole Bonnard took her elbow out of my ribs and the corner of the blanket fell away. She frowned at me, uncomprehending at first. Then she looked around warily, remembered where she was and blinked the sleep out of her eyes.

'What time is it?'

'Don't even ask,' I said. It was a bit chilly. The fire in the stove had long since died. I leaned back against the wall and shivered.

There was a general stirring among the Mujehadeen. Limbs stretching, mouths yawning, fingers scratching. Someone broke wind with gusto. Morning had definitely broken.

She sat up quickly, almost as if she was suddenly embarrassed at having been seen with her defences down. Despite her brief moment of disorientation, however, it was my considered opinion that Doctor Bonnard looked pretty damned fair in the morning. Hair tousled, eyes that looked at you half dreamily as if recalling warm thoughts. It was enough to drive a person under a cold shower.

I watched as one of the Mujehadeen stumbled blearily over his companions towards the door. As he opened it I saw it was in fact almost light. His departure was a signal for the rest of the group to vacate their pits. This was followed by a mass exodus as all of them headed outside, no doubt to find a bush behind which they could perform their necessary morning ablutions.

Kerim must have been up very early indeed because as everybody trooped out he came in, beaming. 'Good morning, my friends! How are you today?'

He looked like the cat who'd swallowed the proverbial cream. I wondered why that was. In my book no one has a right to be that chipper at that time of the day. Then I realized he was holding something behind his back. He saw me looking and announced happily, 'I have brought you presents!'

To my amazement he held out two towels and a small round bar of carbolic soap. Luxuries indeed!

'You see? Now you get room service! Just like the Hilton Hotel!' He thought that was very witty and gurgled with laughter.

While he was still chortling away to himself, Doctor Bonnard took a look at her patient. Sayyef was conscious by now and looking marginally better than he had the night before. He grimaced as Doctor Bonnard probed the area around his wound. Despite his pain, I suspected that, out of all of us, he had probably enjoyed the best night's sleep. And at least his condition hadn't deteriorated, which was something, although Doctor Bonnard, her diagnosis complete, reiterated her recommendation that the wounded man should be delivered to the French medical team as soon as possible.

Kerim agreed readily. Then, waving away Nicole

Bonnard's thanks for the washing articles, he wandered off, hollering for the chai khana's general cook and bottle washer.

Clutching our towels like bathers in a lido, Doctor Bonnard and I headed for the communal bath. The idea of washing had now become a pleasure rather than a chore.

In the rapidly brightening yet cold light of dawn, the village didn't look any better than it had in the gloom of the evening. Nestling among walnut trees, at first glance it seemed a well-concealed place. But that obviously wasn't so. The stone houses were very dilapidated, as if they had been built out of the rubble of a previous town, a clear indication of just how extensive the Russian bombing raids in the region had been.

The stream by which we had rested the afternoon before, ran through the village. It was shallow and not very wide but the current appeared quite swift. A number of the guerillas had beaten us to it and were engaged in washing themselves. There was a distinct ritual to their actions, I noticed. Starting with the face and ending with the crotch, all parts were washed three times. Ablutions by numbers, as it were. At no time did anyone fully remove his clothes either. Now, that took real skill.

Doctor Bonnard expressed her intention of moving upstream to find a spot that offered a bit more privacy. If I'd been Robert Redford, I dare say I'd have followed her about two seconds later but I knew it hadn't been an invitation so I stayed where I was. Besides, knowing how cold the water was likely to be, the idea of total immersion struck me as being above and beyond the call of duty. So, I waded in, ankle deep, lathered and rinsed my hands and face, gasped with shock at the icy touch, and towelled myself dry. I ran a palm over the stubble on my face. It was a reminder that I hadn't shaved for a couple of days.

Most of the Mujehadeen sported beards or moustaches. I was probably beginning to look the part.

After they had washed, the men prayed.

The intonation rose into the still morning air.

'La ilaha illa'llah Mohammedan rasulu'llah . . .'

'There is but one God and Mohammed is the apostle of God . . .'

Et cetera, et cetera.

Nicole Bonnard returned. I'd half expected her to be blue with cold but instead she looked fresh and tingly and lovely. Obviously from hardy stock was our Doctor Bonnard, although as an experienced campaigner in these mountains she'd have gotten used to some of the spartan conditions. She even smiled at me, would you believe? In a moment of quiet companionship we sat together in a patch of warming sunlight. The war might have been a million miles away.

I wondered if the Russians had picked up our trail. Due to Kerim's RSM impersonation, we had made good progress though, and from the Soviets' point of view there must have been a hundred different routes we could have taken. It was also worth bearing in mind that the Afghan guerilla armies controlled over eighty per cent of the country. Movement of the Soviet forces, therefore, was limited to certain areas, at least as far as their ground troops were concerned. The Air Army, however, was a different matter altogether. It had a lot greater ability for one thing. It had the facilities to cover the ground faster and more efficiently using its spotter planes and gunships. Although, as I knew only too well, trying to spot men on the ground, particularly if the latter didn't care to be found, was well nigh impossible in the sort of terrain we were travelling over. That fact gave us a distinct advantage. So we were probably safe for the time being.

Nevertheless, I still wasn't completely enamoured with

the fact that we were heading away from the border. Okay, so I know it made sense and there was safety in numbers and all that, but what really struck a sour chord was the fact that I was moving further away from the twenty-five thousand dollars' worth of emeralds that were burning a hole on the inside of Mike Farrell's safety deposit box back in Dean's Hotel. If I had any future left at all in the big wide world, those emeralds were my deposit on it. Somehow, I didn't think the insurance on the chopper covered the likelihood of having the crap pounded out of it by Soviet gunships.

Which meant that I still owed the finance company the outstanding balance on the bits I hadn't owned. The twenty-five thousand just about covered it. I'd have to settle that little matter before I could even begin to make some sort of living. Well, that was the honest way out, of course. The dishonest way was to play dead, purloin the twenty-five grand, and melt into the ether. Which was all very well until such time as I might want to raise the asking price on another aircraft. Hell, I'm a pilot. I'm not much good for anything else. And how could anyone even think of retiring on a measly twenty-five Ks, for Pete's sake?

This was depressing, Crow. Change the subject.

So, I asked if Kerim and his group had heard anything about her brother. In the excitement of the previous day and the subsequent flight from the valley, I had forgotten all about her reasons for being there.

She didn't answer immediately. It was almost as if I'd trapped her off guard, like a child who'd been caught out by a lie and was trying to recoup some sort of credibility for the slip-up. Or it could have been my imagination working overtime again. Probably it was that my inquiry had suddenly rekindled the doubts and fears that she might never see Alain again. A possibility that, up until that moment, her subconscious mind had only just managed to come to terms with.

I sensed that a barrier had been raised yet again.

'They have heard nothing,' she said.

'I'm sorry.' I was beginning to regret my show of concern. 'I guess you'll have a better chance of learning something the closer we get to Massoud and his camp.'

She gave a quick, almost nervous nod. 'Yes,' she said. 'Perhaps.'

She got up abruptly. I watched her go, damp towel slung over her shoulder. A strange girl. Proud yet vulnerable. It was as if she was afraid of something yet determined to keep any offer of help, comfort, or affection at arm's length. Had anyone ever got through to her? Touched her inside? I wondered about that. I was willing to lay odds that a lot of people had tried. Few, I suspected, had succeeded. And for those that had? Now, there was a thought.

Namaz over, we ate. Breakfast consisted of nan loaves, yoghurt, tea and a yellow gooey substance which Kerim assured me was scrambled eggs. I took his word for it and watched everybody else tuck in. Nan and tea was as much as I could manage at that time of the day. Doctor Bonnard, I saw, felt likewise.

We set off a short while later. The pack horse was back in harness and had been placed in the charge of Talib, the youngster with the arm wound. Sayyef was again litter borne. Our wall-eyed host saw us on our way with a small bow and a handshake. It wasn't until we were a mile or so out of the village that it struck me that he appeared to have been the village's sole inhabitant. I certainly hadn't been aware of anyone else being around. Had there been they would surely have made themselves known before we'd departed.

I mentioned the fact to Kerim.

Kerim nodded sadly. 'The village was bombed by the Russians. His wife and children killed. All the other villagers escaped to Pakistan but Qasi Timur stayed. Now he works for the resistance, providing food and shelter to the Mujehadeen supply caravans as they travel between the border and the Panjsher.'

'Doesn't he fear the Russians will return?' I asked. 'They'll probably kill him, for God's sake!'

Kerim shook his head. 'If the Russians return and kill him he will join his wife and children in Paradise.' He shrugged philosophically. 'So, what is there for him to fear in death?'

I was trying to think of a suitable reply when he added succinctly, 'You do not have to fire a gun to become a Mujehad, my friend.'

Again I was at a loss for words.

We started to gain height. Our path took us over scrubby terraces. It was a while before I realized we were walking through the remains of a vineyard. The grapes had been sadly neglected. A few sorry-looking bunches clung to the scraggy stalks like bloated blood blisters. I picked a couple in passing and spat them out moments later. They were sour. I noticed a couple of the Mujehadeen do the same.

Beyond the vineyard we came to a small clearing where we stopped and looked back down the valley. I could see the stream winding like a snake into the grove of walnut trees. It took me a while to spot the exact site of the village though. It was very well hidden indeed. I thought that its destruction must have come about through indiscriminate bombing rather than a specific attack for it would have taken a sharp-eyed gunner to even see the houses, never mind align his load on them. Which, frankly, made its destruction even more of an outrage.

The cloying smell of pine was heavy in our nostrils as

we climbed fir-clad slopes. Bright sunlight filtered down through the high, cone-laden branches. Even though it was still early in the day and the sun was far from reaching its zenith, their shade was very welcome.

At noon we rested.

Out in the open it was very hot but we found shade in a large cave. We sat under the overhang at its entrance and munched on apples, sweet plums and apricots. I presumed they had been supplied by the old man in the chai khana.

About that time we had our first scare.

It was Talib, our young horse handler, who heard it first, attracting our attention with an urgent cry. We all stared off in the direction to which he was pointing. Then we caught the sound; a dull throb of rotors to the east, followed by the scream of jets. Then came the boom of the explosions and ominous plumes of black smoke rose like mystic vapours above the distant ridge.

Angry mutterings broke out among the Mujehadeen. Kerim narrowed his eyes against the sun's bright glare. It looked as if he was trying to see right through the intervening hills into the valley beyond. I saw the brief flash of sun on metal as one of the attacking aircraft banked high over the dun-coloured hillside and another column of smoke rose into the air like an elongated grey balloon.

Nicole Bonnard bit her lip and stared with fixed intensity towards the jet's target area. I knew what she was thinking; I knew what they were all thinking.

The Russians were on a bombing spree. I wondered if Jamalagar was one of their targets. I thought suddenly of the old man, Qasi Sur Timur, alone and defenceless, sheltering in the ruins of his chai khana as the bombs rained down about him. Or could it be that he had already entered the gates of Paradise?

Then I thought of something else.

I looked over at Kerim. 'Maybe they've picked up our trail. What do you think?'

His expression was grim. 'I think we should move on,' he said.

So we did.

It took us another five hours to reach our destination.

The French field hospital was well hidden. No pun intended.

The valley of Mir Seraj was narrow, heavily wooded, bounded on all sides by high limestone cliffs, and a great place for an ambush.

We were under surveillance from the moment we entered the ravine. Kerim told me so and I didn't doubt it. I had already begun to experience a strange tingling sensation between my shoulder blades so it was kind of reassuring to discover it wasn't just my paranoia. Probably Custer had felt the same way before the Little Big Horn. Small comfort, George Armstrong.

Then I caught the smell of woodsmoke and there was a shout from a lookout on the high ground as Kerim was recognized. Within seconds we were surrounded by what seemed like a battalion of armed men.

We were escorted through the camp, accompanied by raucous greetings, a lot of smiles and much handshaking. I felt like a politician on a canvassing spree. There were a number of women moving among the trees, some carrying cooking utensils, others with stalks of kindling. I even spotted some children playing down by the river.

Then I saw it. Built on a small rise. At first glance it looked as if it had been carved out of the cliff face.

Kerim told me that the watchtower had been built centuries ago, to protect travellers from attack by roving bandits. Indeed it looked very old, what was left of it, and, during its heyday, it must have commanded spectacular views of the valley, which, no doubt, had become a welcome and much valued haven for caravans making their way along the great trade route known as the Silk Road. This would have been a natural place to pitch camp. There was a good water supply from the nearby river, forage for livestock, wood for cooking fires.

But that had been before the earthquake, before the landslide that had dislodged a section of the mountain and sent it crashing and tumbling into the valley, blocking the road as effectively as a cork in a bottle. Since when the travellers had been forced to find a new path through the mountains. Their route had taken them further north. And with them had moved the bandits, following the merchants like wild dogs after a cattle herd. And the watchtower had long since crumbled into ruin and decay. But the ancient storage walls had remained intact.

Protected by the boundary of the rear wall they had been sunk into the rock shelf. Half a dozen deep silos in which would have been stored many months' supply of grain and water. Cool, dark chambers, gouged out of the ground like missile tubes.

Now they had a different use. As recovery wards.

Entrance to the vaults lay in a flight of stone steps which we descended in single file. The two stretcher bearers led the way, Sayyef prostrate between them. It was noticably cooler below ground.

The silos were quite large. They ran in a straight line and were connected by a series of low archways. I judged the height from floor to ceiling to be about fifteen feet. Each gourd-shaped gallery was big enough to hold half a dozen mattresses. Light was admitted into each silo through a circular hole in the roof. Although, with the sun beginning to go down, natural illumination had been replaced by kerosene lamps. As far as I could tell, in the first three compartments we walked through, about half the beds seemed to be occupied. The smell of antiseptic hung in the air. Sayyef was lowered on to an empty mattress.

There were various injuries on show. Some of the men had head wounds, some were bare chested and had heavy blood-smeared bandages wrapped around their stomachs. One man looked to be unharmed until I saw that the blanket under which he lay was curiously flattened below the place where his right knee should have been. Most of the victims called a cheery greeting to Kerim. The rest gazed at us with vacant, unseeing eyes. Evidence of deep shock. I was reminded of the time I'd visited the hospital in Peshawar. The facilities were pretty rudimentary there but nothing compared to this. And yet I knew that these field hospitals were the only places this side of the border where the Mujehadeen could have their wounds tended. These men were the lucky ones. The rest hadn't even made it this far.

I poked my head into the next gallery, and recoiled. It was the woman's ward, if you could call it such. My brief appearance caused a couple of heads to turn listlessly. I was reminded about the confines a male doctor had to work within when faced with female patients. A tragedy. Shrapnel doesn't recognize the same distinction. I was about to withdraw when I noticed, with horror, that two of the mattresses were occupied by children. Small boys. They couldn't have been much older than nine or ten, thin dark faces pinched with pain. The right arm of one of them had been severed below the elbow, the stump bound with gauze. I was suddenly gripped by a wave of anger. I backed away. Their huge round eyes followed me.

A man rose from his seat on one of the beds. He was tall and gangly and dressed much like I was. I thought at first that he was one of the walking wounded but as the light from one of the lamps caught him I realized that under his tan and light beard he was a European. He peered at us uncertainly through a battered pair of wire-framed spectacles.

'Salaam aleikum,' he said politely, and then did a double take and blinked. 'Nicole? Mon Dieu!' He called over his shoulder. 'Paul! Venez ici! Vite!'

'Gilles!'

The girl stepped past me and held out her arms. There followed a swift and somewhat awkward embrace and the rest of us were momentarily forgotten. Kerim twirled his moustache and grinned at me slyly.

They released each other and turned sheepishly to their audience. As they did so a second man appeared through the archway behind them. He too was in Afghan dress. Short and stubby, also bearded. More tears and laughter, hugs all around.

When they'd all quite finished Nicole Bonnard made the introductions.

I had the vague feeling that they had taken me for one of the Mujehadeen at first, as I had them. Though I suppose my rather grubby attire, not to mention my three-day stubble, can't have aided my identification any. I was still carrying the Kalashnikov over my shoulder too, so I must have looked quite disreputable. Once they'd got over the shock, however, they proved to be perfectly amenable.

The tall one was called Gilles Masson and his partner was Paul Le Beq. They had been in Afghanistan for over five months and in Mir Seraj for a little over three. It transpired they had been the team whose original diagnosis of Muhammed nur Rafiq had prompted our extraction attempt. Nicole Bonnard knew them because they'd all travelled from Europe together. They'd all entered Afghanistan at the same time too, but with different caravans. This was their first meeting since then.

Both men spoke fluent English. While Doctor Bonnard and Gilles Masson took a look at Sayyef's leg, Le Beq expressed regret at Nur Rafiq's death. Le Beq had been taken to Dar Galak to tend him. He explained how they had then persuaded the group of refugees heading for the frontier to carry word of Nur Rafiq's condition to the resistance leaders in Peshawar. Although they knew that the guerilla's condition was serious they hadn't really expected anyone to fly in and try to take him out.

Le Beq shook his head with wonder. Smiled at me. 'I think you are either very brave or very foolish. I have not yet decided which.'

'Oh, pretty dumb,' I agreed. 'Definitely pretty bloody dumb.'

He laughed. 'But now it is too late, my friend. Yes?' He slapped me on the shoulder. 'Welcome to the war!'

I wondered how rare that was. A Gaul with a sense of humour.

Maybe it was a sign that things were beginning to look up. If it was it was about bloody time.

And, what's more, Gilles Masson told us that thanks to Nicole Bonnard's prompt treatment the night before, Sayyef wouldn't lose the leg. The news cheered us all, especially Sayyef.

We left him in the care of the doctors' assistant, a cheerful young man called Abu, and Le Beq and Masson took us on a tour of the camp. Kerim had disappeared elsewhere. I guessed he was checking on his men.

Masson and Le Beq had spent their first few months in the country operating a field hospital in the foothills of Kohistan, but, following Russian bombing raids in the area, they had been forced to move south and had joined forces with a band of Mujehadeen gunrunners heading for the border. In the course of their exodus the guerillas had brought them to the valley of Mir Seraj, apparently a watering place much frequented by supply caravans and refugee columns, and here they had set up a field hospital beneath the broken-down walls of the old fort.

'The Russians must know about this place,' I said. 'Aren't you worried they'll launch a raid?'

'They have already done so,' Le Beq said. 'Twice.' He grinned. 'Their aim was abominable!'

I couldn't help but grin myself. Only a Frenchman would have had the nerve to use the word abominable.

Masson cut in. 'We are very secluded here. They dare not risk sending in ground troops as the place is too easily defended. And, as you can see, the walls of the valley are high and quite narrow. The Russians do not like to fly their gunships below the ridges. They are afraid of rocket attack.' He shrugged. 'But sometimes they forget and try to catch us by surprise. So far they have not been successful. Besides, they are more concerned with the revolt further north. The Panjsher is still their big problem. Despite the truce offer the fighting goes on. Only by defeating Massoud and his guerillas will they seriously weaken the resistance movement. By comparison we are a very minor threat.'

'How many people do you have here at the moment?' Nicole Bonnard asked. She spoke in English. For my benefit, I presumed.

'About fifty,' Le Beq said. 'Mostly refugees as you can see.' He waved an arm to encompass the half dozen or so groups dotted around the area beneath the trees. Makeshift shelters and windbreaks had been erected out of blankets and saplings. Some families had found niches within the rubble of the fort. Thin plumes of smoke rose in the air. I detected the aroma of roasting meat and wondered what was going into the pot. Then I heard the faint bleat of a goat and realized they'd even brought their livestock with them. A piquet line had been stretched between a couple of trees to which had been tethered a dozen or so horses.

Camels too, contemplating their surroundings with scornful superiority. The place was beginning to look like an advertisement for Barnum and Bailey's.

I asked him about our welcoming committee; the men brandishing the guns.

'A Mujehadeen supply caravan,' Masson said. 'Heading south to Jalraiz.'

'And the wounded men in the bunkers?'

'Ah, yes,' Le Beq shook his head sadly. 'The victims. Some of them have been here as long as we have. Some are refugees, injured when their villages were bombed. The others are Mujehadeen fighters, left here by their comrades. Some of them will recover sufficiently to return to the war, some will continue their flight to Pakistan. The rest . . .' His voice trailed off.

'What about the women and children?'

Nicole Bonnard shot me a sharp glance. She'd seen the women but not the two boys. She'd been conversing with Masson.

It seemed that the Russians had a nasty habit of scattering booby traps and mines along the routes used by refugees and the guerilla groups. The boy I'd seen in the bunker had gotten his hand blown off by a brightly coloured packet of colouring pens. He was too young to wonder what such an object might be doing in the mountains and his parents hadn't known enough to curb his curiosity.

A tremendous sadness touched Le Beq's eyes. 'The other one was hit by a Russian bullet during an attack on his home village. His spine is damaged. At the moment he is not well enough to continue to the Red Cross centre in Peshawar. In any event, it is unlikely he will ever walk again.'

Masson removed his spectacles, breathed on them, and wiped them fastidiously with the hem of his shirt. You could just sense the tension in him, and the rage. Both doctors were young, not much into their thirties, yet the suffering they had obviously witnessed in the past few months would have served them a lifetime back home.

I didn't ask them why they were there. I'd no doubt have got the same answer as I had from Nicole.

Then I saw something familiar; a line of stone cairns marking the graves of the Shaheed, the martyrs. A green cloth banner had been strung out above them. Daubed on it were inscriptions from the Qoran; passwords to Paradise.

The light was beginning to go and we were on our way back to the underground post-op station when we heard a warning shout from the lookout. Strangers approaching.

Kerim appeared at my shoulder like a djinn. I found that I'd unslung the Kalashnikov and slipped off the safety catch. Around us the Mujehadeen were on red alert. The women and children had melted into the shadows. Suddenly the valley was very quiet as we all listened.

I could hear metal jangling and the laboured clatter of iron-shod hooves on the rocks down by the river. Vague equine shapes coming towards us through the trees, men walking beside them. A small caravan.

There were half a dozen horses, narrow-bellied, lean-limbed creatures, heads bowed and backs ladened. The men leading them were a ragtag bunch, tough looking and heavily armed with automatic weapons. A number of them wore combat jerkins.

The column emerged from the shadows and the features of the men leading the horses became clearer. I picked up vague hostile murmurings from the guerillas around me. Whoever these people were, they weren't particularly welcome.

The fact that they looked like extras in a Sam Peckinpah

western didn't adhere me to them either. A more unsavoury bunch of characters you couldn't wish to meet.

The man working point was obviously their leader. It wasn't his size that gave me that impression because he wasn't much bigger than me, but he had that air of command about him. He also carried with him what I would term a sense of menace that the rest didn't. Especially when you looked into his eyes, which were cold and dark, almost reptilian. He wore a heavy moustache and about a week's worth of stubble. Unlike the rest of his crew, he had no headgear, and I could see that his hair was long and, to my amazement, secured at the back by a band so that it hung in a short pony tail to a point midway between his shoulder blades. He didn't look like any Afghan I'd ever seen. In fact he looked as if he'd have been more at home on a squat Mongol pony, riding the steppes. It was difficult to judge his age but the slight trace of grey in his hair made me think he was in his forties. He looked as hard as nails. A real sweet-heart, you could tell.

He was clad in an olive-green combat jacket and quilted pants tucked into calf-length leather boots. A bandolier was strapped over his chest. He had a Kalashnikov slung over his shoulder. His companions were similarly armed and they were all dressed more or less the same, a mixture of ethnic garb and ex-army surplus; dead scruffy.

Beside me, Kerim muttered something under his breath that I didn't quite catch. I glanced at him for an explanation.

He spat into the dust. 'Heroin smugglers.'

Chapter Nine

It is a well-documented fact that the Golden Crescent, the area comprising Pakistan's North West Frontier Province and the north eastern regions of Afghanistan, has over-taken South East Asia as the chief source of supply of the world's heroin. In Landi Kotal and Dir and Chitral and the other frontier towns where the drug is refined, a kilo of heroin fetches about two hundred US dollars. On the streets of New York the same amount brings in over a million. The syndicates who ship the stuff through Paki-stan to Europe and the East Coast are cleaning up. Smack is big business.

Not that the trade is anything new. They had been growing and transporting opium in these parts for centu-ries, albeit on a fairly modest scale. It wasn't until the cultivation of poppies had been eradicated in Turkey and Iran that the market in Asian horse went through the roof. At one point, in an attempt to undermine the trade, both the US and Britain had tried to fund crop-substitution programmes, but the schemes had proved ineffective. There wasn't nearly so much profit to be made in cotton and tobacco as there was in dope.

Then they tried to put pressure on General Zia; and achieved a modicum of success, too. For, with great enthusiasm, Zia prohibited the use of drugs and all trans-actions in them. All very laudable. Except he had one slight problem. Namely the hostility that existed between Pakistan's central government and the old princedoms of the British Raj; Swat, Chitral, Dir and the Malakand Agency, known collectively as the Merged Areas, who owed allegiance more to tribal law than to the legislative powers and processes of the government in Istanbul. Zia received what could only be described as an almighty brush-off from the tribal territories. And there was absolutely nothing he could do about it. To the tribesmen in these hills smuggling had become a way of life. During the Raj the contraband had been guns. Today it's opium. Why abandon the habits of a lifetime?

The only concession that the tribes had made, as regards Zia's attempts to bring them into line, had been to move the heroin refineries out of Pakistan and over the borders into Afghanistan. Very accommodating of them, really.

In South East Asia it's the Chinese chemists from Hong Kong who run the refineries. On the borders of Afghanistan and Pakistan it's the Shinwaris. Running the finished product across the Durand Line into the NWFP or west into Iran is done by anyone with enough nerve. It's normally the Afridis who pass the stuff into Pakistan but I wasn't sure about the western route. Probably somebody with suicidal tendencies, knowing Khomeini's reputation.

I'd even been approached myself, on occasion. Not unnaturally, having an aircraft at my disposal had made me a target for traffickers. More than once I'd been offered a cash deal to carry smack from Peshawar down to Karachi and Lahore. The offer had usually been made out of the corner of somebody's mouth and in a darkened room and all with the same result. I'd told them to get stuffed. I'd seen enough of drugs in Nam, and the effects they'd had, to stay well clear. The US bases were going through some very bad trips while I was there. More than once I'd had to go in and help airlift out a squad of grunts who'd tried to take a hill doped up to the eyeballs on Chinese White. It wasn't funny, believe me.

As Kerim made his feelings known, I caught the smell. The sweet pungent aroma of unrefined opium oozing from the sacks lashed to the backs of the pack horses was unmistakable.

The man with the pony tail held up a hand and the rest of his scrofulous entourage came to a halt. I could see them eyeing up the Mujehadeen. Warily.

He stepped forward. I noticed he had the barrel of his rifle pointing down so he evidently wasn't taking any risks, especially as he could probably sense the hostility radiating from Kerim and the rest of the guerillas.

His gaze swept over us all, eyes narrowing perceptibly as he tracked over me. When he reached Doctor Bonnard I could almost hear his brain click into overdrive. For her part she returned his stare with cool detachment. He finally settled his sights on Gilles Masson.

'Salaam aleikum.' He spoke slowly, with great deliberation.

'Aleikum salaam,' Gilles Masson replied. Rather cautiously too, I thought.

There followed a brief exchange, with the drug runner pointing back down the line of pack horses and Masson pursing his lips and looking thoughtful. They were conversing in dialect so I couldn't understand a word of it. Although I had the distinct feeling that the newcomer wasn't any more fluent in it than Gilles himself. Funny that, I thought. But the significance didn't hit me at the time. Maybe I was just being inordinately dim. I nudged Kerim. 'What the hell's going on?'

'He seeks permission to pitch camp,' Kerim said. 'It is the custom.'

Agreement reached, Masson nodded. Immediately the smuggler beckoned to the crew behind him and the horses were led past us towards a spot close by the bank of the stream. As he turned to follow them the man rapped out something to one of his companions and the shock of realization went through me like a jolt of electricity.

141

Le Beq had caught my dazed expression. 'You knew!' I said accusingly. 'You bloody knew!'

Le Beq nodded. 'Everyone knows,' he said. 'His name is Rasseikin. Taras Rasseikin.'

No wonder Kerim and his men were so uptight. No wonder I'd detected the man's unfamiliarity with the dialect. No bloody wonder! Not only were these men heroin smugglers, they were also Russians!

I'd heard the stories of course. Who hadn't? About the number of troops who'd deserted from the government's ranks. Afghans mostly; as individuals or as entire platoons or even battalions. Their numbers could be measured in thousands. Sometimes, though, the defectors would come from the ranks of the Red Army itself.

According to Le Beq, the reasons for the defections varied.

Some were conscripts who found themselves unable to accept the discipline meted out by their officers, others were taken as prisoners by the Mujehadeen, choosing to take the faith and join the ranks of the rebels rather than face cruel death at the hands of their captors. Others, more politically aware, had been known to risk captivity in the hope that the Red Cross would secure their releases and intern them in Switzerland, from where they could request asylum. And then there were the ones like Rasseikin.

Rumour had it that Rasseikin was a native of Kazakhstan, and a soldier; a former Staff Sergeant in the elite 105th Guards Airborne Regiment, which made him a veteran of the '79 invasion. Le Beq told me that for some time there had been a growing drug problem among the Soviet occupying forces and that the canny Mujehadeen had actually been trading hashish for weapons in some of the more isolated Russian garrisons. I thought he was having me on but he was dead serious.

Apparently, Rasseikin had been one of the ring leaders

in the distribution of the hash within the main Soviet garrisons in Kabul. When his superiors became suspicious and launched an investigation he deserted and joined the smugglers at their own game. Other men, Afghans and Russians, rallied to his side and over the last eighteen months or so he had gathered around him a small band of followers. Bandits, smugglers and deserters. The latter being, for the most part, of Asian or Muslim cultural origin from areas of the Soviet Union that bordered Afghanistan, such as Uzbekistan and Tadzhikistan. Not surprisingly the Soviet Command in Kabul had put a price on Rasseikin's head.

I thought it a bit strange that Rasseikin and his men should end up in Mir Seraj, given that the valley was frequently used by the Mujehadeen who, as indicated by the reaction of Kerim and his men, couldn't have been enamoured with the presence of Russian soldiers in their midst, be they ex-Red Army or whomever.

Le Beq put me wise.

Mir Seraj was a refuge, a sanctuary; a haven in which to lick one's wounds. At least it was deemed so by the Mujehadeen. The Soviet occupying forces and the Afghan Army didn't honour the definition, of course, but for the various guerilla armies of the resistance Mir Seraj was a neutral zone. The valley offered protection to all who entered it, be they resistance fighters, refugees, brigands, drug runners. The field hospital established by Le Beq and Gilles Masson also served to establish the valley's neutrality and all wounded or injured, no matter from what tribe or army, even Afghan or Soviet defectors if need be, were provided with medical care. The place was the equivalent of Vietnam's 17th Parallel; a DMZ.

Outside the limits of the valley, however, it was still every man for himself. So there was even a code of conduct to follow. A time span of half a day between the departures of opposing factions. It was all very civilized.

A communal eating area had been set up in a corner of the ruined fort. It wasn't exactly Maxim's but, under the circumstances, we weren't that fussy. It had turned cold. There was a big kiln affair in the middle of the room and a fire had been lit so we spread out our blankets around the inside of the walls and tried to keep warm. Needless to say, it was stew again but there was one high-spot of the meal. We'd finished eating and were waiting while the inevitable tea was being served. Gilles Masson got up suddenly and disappeared. He returned bearing a tray with four cups on it, passed me one and winked slyly. When I took my first sip I found out why. Cognac, by God! Pure velvet. A warmth began to spread through me. I drew closer to the fire and asked him in hushed tones how the hell he'd managed to get hold of the stuff,

He chuckled. 'It was brought in for us in our last batch of medical supplies. Purely for medicinal purposes, you understand.'

I took another swallow just to convince myself that I wasn't dreaming. Something close to rapture must have shown on my face because I was suddenly aware that Kerim was giving me one of his sly bemused looks again. I guessed that he must have cottoned on to Masson's little ruse with the tea cups. Knowing the Muslim code, as far as alcohol was concerned, I felt like a nervous customer in a speakeasy, dreading the first knock on the door that would herald a police raid. I actually experienced a momentary and irrational rush of guilt too, as though I was somehow betraying Kerim's trust. Which was pretty damned ludicrous as Kerim was hand-rolling a cigarette at the time and I happened to know that not long ago the Hezb had actually issued a decree which forbade its members from indulging in the dreaded weed. So much for party edicts.

I thought, to hell with it. Took another swig. Felt better.

I watched Nicole Bonnard's face as the spirit touched the back of my throat. She caught my eye and smiled conspiratorially. For a couple of seconds her gaze held mine and in the dancing, flickering light cast by the flames her eyes glowed like bright embers. I felt another sort of glow inside, and it wasn't just from the cognac. Then my nerve broke and the shared moment was gone.

With a convenient sense of timing, Le Beq started to tell me about the problems they'd had with setting up the field hospitals. Most of which had to do with the rough conditions they'd had to work under. That and the fact that both Gilles Masson and himself had had little or no surgical experience. Yet, here they were, having to perform major operations with limited resources and always with the constant threat of Soviet bombardment.

The worst thing they'd had to deal with were internal injuries. Stitching, cauterizing, even amputation was relatively straightforward but it was the damage inside the body, caused by bullet and shell, that had proved to be the most difficult to treat. They had no X-ray equipment so much of the diagnosis was dependent on sight and feel. The Russians used fragmentation bullets which caused tremendous damage when they penetrated human flesh. They turned bone and tissue into spiders' webs but you couldn't tell that just by examining the entry wound. By the time the full extent of the trauma was discovered it was often too late.

Their flow of medical supplies was fairly erratic too, which didn't surprise me, given the gauntlet that the Mujehadeen supply caravans had to run. This resulted in frequent shortages of medicines and equipment. I wondered how, in the midst of all these trials and trubulations, they'd managed to survive this long.

Le Beq's attention drifted past me and out of the corner of my eye I saw Kerim stiffen perceptibly. I knew, without looking, that Rasseikin and his men must have arrived. When my curiosity got the better of me I saw that they'd taken up a corner plot on the far side of the eating area and were conversing among themselves in low tones. Kerim relaxed but I could tell that he was coiled like a panther ready to spring. Out of all of us he seemed to be the one most affected by the smugglers' presence. I knew, however, that while we were in the valley he would honour the neutrality of Mir Seraj. He was bound to do so. It was the code of the Pathans: Pushtunwali.

The code transcends all aspects of the Pathans' way of life and is made up of three main elements. Melmastia: hospitality. When you took someone into your house, you provided not only food and drink, you offered protection against any threat., even if it entailed giving your life for theirs. Nanawati: asylum. A cessation of hostilities, a time for reappraisal. In essence this was what Mir Seraj stood for. Badal: retribution. The most powerful element of the code. The exacting of revenge, at any cost. An eye for an eye.

Judging by the expression on Kerim's face I had the distinct feeling that the last element of the code was the one uppermost in his mind. I asked Le Beq if there was any particular reason for this.

He shrugged. 'Rasseikin is Russian. Kerim Gul hates all Russians.'

Ask a silly question, I suppose.

'So, how come Rasseikin's still alive?' I inquired.

To my surprise, Le Beq smiled. 'Because Rasseikin is

more useful to the resistance alive than dead,' he said, then added, 'For the time being.'

I took another cautious sip at my cognac. I was determined to make it last. 'How come?'

Le Beq declined to answer right away. He stared into the fire for a few moments. 'We are isolated here, cut off. It takes many days sometimes even weeks to get medical supplies through to us. Our two main shortages are blood plasma and . . .' He paused for effect. '. . . morphine.'

It took me a couple of seconds to twig. Morphine. A pain killer, a drug, a derivative of opium.

'Jesus!' I said. 'You get your drugs from Rasseikin?'

Le Beq nodded. 'There have been times when we have availed ourselves of his services, yes.'

'God Almighty,' I said. 'Don't tell me you refine the bloody stuff here?'

Le Beq shook his head. 'There are a number of laboratories scattered around these mountains. Rasseikin and men like him collect the opium and deliver it to the labs. After it has been converted into heroin they then transport it over the border. Sometimes we provide shelter and food for them. In return, they provide us with morphine for our wounded. We take what we can get.'

I could see Kerim's dilemma. Ironically, while the war continued the Russian was safe. Kerim's first loyalty was to the Hezb and his fellow Mujehadeen. For the time being, Rasseikin's activities were actually helping to keep guerillas alive. Presumably, though, if and when the Soviets were driven back into their own country, it would be a different matter. Rasseikin and his fellow deserters, if they were still around, would be fair game.

Le Beq told me that the smugglers also helped to provide the Mujehadeen with intelligence on Soviet troop movements. No doubt Rasseikin still had contacts within the garrison in Kabul who could provide information in

147

exchange for regular supplies of hash and heroin. There was also a market in weapons. Rasseikin exchanged hash for guns which he then sold to the resistance. It appeared that the smuggler had developed an artful appreciation of the capitalist system.

I saw that he'd also developed an appreciation of Nicole Bonnard, too. I could tell that by the way he kept fidgeting in his seat, stealing sneaky eyefuls every time he moved. What I couldn't tell was whether he knew I'd caught him at it.

'Your hackles are showing, my friend,' Le Beq said suddenly. He'd been watching me watching the Russian. 'I trust you are not about to do anything foolish.'

'Who? Me?' I said. 'Not a chance. He'd chew me up and spit me out in little pieces.'

Le Beq chuckled. His gaze slid from me across to Nicole, who was sharing some joke with Gilles Masson on the other side of the fire. 'She is very beautiful, yes?' He scratched his bearded chin.

'Yes,' I agreed. 'Very.'

'There is something between you both?' Le Beq asked, a butter-wouldn't-melt look on his face.

Yeah, a bloody great chasm, mate, I thought. I shook my head.

Le Beq tipped his head on one side and looked at me strangely.

'But you know she has a very high regard for you, Mr Crow,' he said. 'I can tell.'

He had to be joking, I thought. 'You have to be joking,' I said.

Le Beq shook his head. 'I have seen the way she looks at you.'

'You mean like something that she's found stuck to the bottom of her shoe, right?'

Le Beq sighed with exasperation. 'You are blind. You see nothing.'

'And you can, I suppose?' I muttered.

'But of course, my friend. I am French.' He gave me a merry little grin.

What a right berk, I thought.

My own stupid fault, of course. Who else but you, Crow, could end up hundreds of miles from the nearest pub, stuck in riveting conversation with someone who thought he was a cross between Albert bloody Schweitzer and Jean Paul Belmondo?

'I think I'm a wee bit down the list of her priorities at the moment,' I said. 'She's got more important things on her mind. Her brother, for one thing.'

'Her brother?' Le Beq frowned.

'Alain. She's convinced something's happened to him. That's why she came on this caper in the first place.'

Le Beq's face cleared. 'Ah, yes,' he said. 'I remember now. The journalist, no?'

'That's right. You've met him?'

He gave a very Gallic shrug. 'A couple of times. In Peshawar, just before Gilles and I came over the border. I didn't know he was in the country.'

'Seems he's here somewhere,' I said. 'And gone missing. As you can imagine, she's pretty damned worried.'

'But naturally. Mon dieu! And she's come to look for him?' There was unmistakably a note of admiration in his voice.

'You've heard nothing, I take it?'

He shook his head sadly. 'Alas no, my friend. You think perhaps the Russians . . .?'

'Christ knows. She was hoping that we might find somebody who knows something. Somebody here in the valley perhaps.'

Le Beq looked thoughtful. 'Certainly that is possible.

149

Many people pass through here to escape from the fighting. We will make enquiries, never fear.'

A sudden squall of raucous laughter came from behind. Someone in Rasseikin's company had tickled a funny bone. I immediately shot a glance at Kerim. His lips were set in a grim line. It looked as if he was finding it hard to keep his emotions in check.

It was becoming a little too claustrophobic for my liking and a heavy scent was beginning to permeate the room. You didn't have to be a genius to know that somebody was smoking hash. I figured it was one of the smugglers. I needed to clear my head and excused myself to Le Beq.

Outside, the night was cold. Clouds obscured the moon. I sat on one of the tumbled-down segments of wall and wondered how the hell I'd ever let myself be talked into this nonsense.

The first I knew she was there was when her hand touched my shoulder and I damned near went into orbit because I hadn't heard her arrive.

'Jesus!' I muttered, when I came back down. 'What the hell are you trying to do, girl? Scare me to death?'

She looked a bit startled herself. 'I'm sorry. I saw you leave. I came to see if you were all right.'

'I am now. Bloody hell!' I clasped a hand to my heart. It was still working, thank goodness.

She actually had the nerve to grin. 'You see,' she said. 'You are not so tough, I think.'

'I don't ever recall saying I was,' I replied, heartbeat returning to somewhere near normal. 'Whatever gave you that daft idea?'

She went quiet for a few moments, then said softly, 'Because I think we have much in common, you and I.'

'Oh, yeah?' I said. 'And what would that be?'

My response came out somewhat more churlish than I'd intended, with the result that she turned away quickly and

150

looked out over the broken wall, towards the apple grove, where the bright glow of the Mujehadeen campfires winked in the dark like Chinese lanterns.

With her back towards me she said in a small voice, 'We shut people out. We have this ridiculous and naïve belief that we can survive on our own without anybody's help. Perhaps, Crow, we hold our independence too dear. We raise barriers. It's as if we're afraid to let our true feelings show in case it's taken as a sign of weakness. It's an image we try hard to project. A camouflage. Like this jacket.' She pulled abstractedly at her sleeve. 'Sometimes it is not always effective.' As if to ward off the cold she hugged herself.

I wasn't entirely sure how to respond. I put my hand on her shoulder. 'Hey, c'mon, Doc. Don't let the bastards grind you down.'

We were standing very close. She turned in towards me and it just seemed perfectly natural that I should fold my arms around her. She was trembling like a bird.

With her face against my chest, her voice was muffled. 'I have been so frightened.'

The confession was accompanied by a low snuffling sob as the tension welled out of her.

'Makes two of us, love,' I said gently.

I could feel the slow rise and fall of her breasts against me. Soft, pliable, warm. The chill of the night began to steal away. She moved against me and her face lifted. Eyes searching mine. The next move was obviously down to me. So, I took it. I'd have to have been made of stone not to. It was worth the wait. Maybe Le Beq wasn't such a berk after all.

I tasted the salt in her tears, moved down. Finally came up for air about a decade later, disturbed by a sound behind me.

Rasseikin.

The smuggler and his men were leaving the eating area and heading back to their bivouacs. I was standing with my arm around Nicole's shoulder. She moved closer as the half dozen or so men materialized out of the gloom. Some of them, Rasseikin included, were smoking what looked like those long black Russian cheroots. An indication that maybe Rasseikin still had contacts in the Red Army PX or whatever its equivalent. He would seem to have his finger in most everything else.

With his cheroot clenched arrogantly between his teeth, Rasseikin looked even more roguish. He saw us immediately, stopped short, and favoured us with a hard, penetrating stare. I felt like a rabbit mesmerized by a stoat. It was quite chilling.

Then he did something which I didn't expect. He removed the cheroot from his lips and smiled. It was a strange smile though, not open and friendly so much as wily, the smile of someone holding a secret.

He put his head slightly on one side and, with the cheroot held between his first two fingers, he pointed at me.

Then the bastard winked. He actually bloody winked!

And said one word, softly. 'Americanski.'

A coldness spread along my backbone.

Well, no, not exactly, Taras, my old chum. But too damned close for comfort, that was for sure. And he'd known from the moment he'd clapped his hooded eyes on me that I wasn't part of the natural scenery. My tan and stubble and my Pathan pantaloons hadn't fooled him one little bit. My first live Russian had had me marked down for a non-believer from the word go. So much for Kerim's idea of fiendish disguise. And the fact that Rasseikin had caught me making intimate examination of Nicole Bonnard's person probably hadn't aided my cover much either. Even the most liberally minded Afghan wouldn't have been caught in such a compromising situation. And not only with a woman but a western woman to boot. Talk about asking for trouble.

Rasseikin looked me up and down and gave a bemused shake of his head. A deep throaty chuckle emerged from his lips. No doubt, if I'd been in his shoes, the chances are I'd probably have thought it pretty funny as well. He said something to his cronies and wide grins split across dark, bearded faces. Evidently, they were all of the same opinion. I was beginning to feel about as conspicuous as the red-nosed clown at a kid's matinee. Mind you, let's face it, I was dressed for the part.

His next crack was obviously at Nicole's expense, and probably quite lurid in content. You didn't have to be a mind reader to know that. Just the way they all looked at her said as much. In fact they didn't look, so much as mentally undress. I had the distinct feeling that this was purely to see if I would rise to the bait. From the expression on the Russian's face he was just itching for me to make the first aggressive move. With half a dozen of them I knew I wouldn't stand a chance.

But, to my surprise and relief, it didn't come to that. With another all-knowing grin at me, the Russian jammed his cheroot back in his mouth, turned on his heel, and led his crew away. He didn't look back either. I didn't know if that was a good sign or not but if this had been a tennis match it would surely have been advantage: Rasseikin.

Chapter Ten

Dawn . . . again.

Bright, sunny, but definitely a bit on the brisk side. I poked one cautious eye over the side of the rug and squinted around. Nobody about. Quick glance at Rolex. Only five o'clock. F'r crying out loud, didn't anybody ever have a lie in? No doubt the men were out performing namaz. Allah never took a day off, not even Sunday. Why should anybody else?

I felt a sharp nudge in my ribs. Nicole, waking up. We had shared a couple of blankets, tucked up together like Siamese twins. For warmth, nothing else. I suppose we'd probably offended somebody but too damned bad. I wasn't going to freeze to death for anyone which meant that if I was going to curl up next to another body to keep warm it was going to be female and not some hairy Afghan with terminal BO.

One of the women was replenishing the kiln. She was shoving what looked like a huge spatula into its innards. The aroma of freshly baked bread enveloped the camp and a pinkish haze hung over the valley. The place looked like some vast water colour waiting to be framed. The mountains rose out of the mist like huge glistening church domes.

Rasseikin and his men had departed. Kerim told us so when he returned from prayers. No one had seen them go but they must have left very early, certainly before first light. And so far as Kerim was concerned; good riddance.

And it wouldn't be long before we were on our own way out of the sanctuary either. But in this we were bound by the local bye-laws. We had to give the Russian and his men half a day's start. Which meant we couldn't leave until very nearly midday. And that wasn't something I was looking forward to. It meant that we would be marching during the hottest part of the day and so far that had proved to be something at which I was not especially adept.

True to his word, Paul Le Beq had made inquiries among the refugees about Alain Bonnard. But he'd drawn a blank. Mainly because the bulk of this particular band were not from the Kabul region. They were from the west; Jowzjan Province. Hopefully we would pick up better news in the villages further along the trail.

I could tell that Gilles Masson and Le Beq were genuinely grieved to see us depart. I too was sorry to be leaving the relative safety of Mir Seraj. It had been a welcome diversion. For a few hours, at least, the war had seemed a long way off.

Half an hour before noon we said our goodbyes.

Le Beq gripped my hand tightly. 'Take care of her, my friend.'

I nodded.

'Bon chance,' Gilles Masson murmured, his eyes blinking behind the dusty frames of his spectacles. He looked quite overcome.

Behind us, Kerim cleared his throat and spat. It wasn't a comment on the emotional farewell. He was just anxious to be off. He'd said all his goodbyes, including one to Sayyef. He'd promised the lad that he'd collect him up on his return trip.

When we reached the neck of the valley I looked back. Coils of smoke from the cooking fires rose lazily into the air. I could hear birds chattering in the willows down by the river. It seemed quite foolhardy to be leaving such peace and tranquillity behind.

We hadn't been moving very long before it struck me that the land about us looked vaguely familiar. Then I realized, after passing one particular outcrop of rock, that we were actually retracing our steps of the afternoon before. Kerim explained that since the earthquake, all those years ago, Mir Seraj was no longer on the main caravan route. So, to take advantage of the valley's hospitality, we'd had to make a detour south. Therefore, to resume our journey we had first to back track to our turn-off point in order to rejoin the guerilla highway. It took us about an hour to reach the fork in the track, where a single choice awaited us. East to Pakistan. West to the Panjsher.

We turned west. Where else?

Our immediate destination was Jebel Kut, a guerilla camp deep in the hills. Here, Kerim planned to link up with the regional commander, one Sher Khan by name. Apparently Sher Khan was about to move some of his men into the Panjsher in an effort to consolidate Massoud's grip on the area. It seemed logical that we should accompany them. Safety in numbers and all that. Kerim informed me with some pride that he and Sher Khan were, in fact, related. How, I wasn't too sure. Fourth cousin, twice removed on his mother's side or some such permutation. Not that it mattered beyond confirming that almost everybody in Afghanistan seemed to be related by one roundabout way or another. Just one big, happy family.

For a time we kept to the main trail, a winding and dusty artery joining a string of miserable hamlets, all of which showed varying degrees of Russian harassment. Potholes made by cluster bombs, orchards ravaged by napalm, half-demolished houses in which broken rafters and floor beams poked out from the rubble like bleached and twisted bones.

Occasionally we'd pass other people on the road; refugees, Mujehadeen, or locals travelling between villages. We always stopped to exchange news and gossip. Between journeyers this was mandatory practice. For, in a country where there was such an absence of radio, TV and newspapers, this was the only way in which rumour and intelligence about the war could be circulated. Kerim kept us up to date with whatever snippets of information he received along the line. A lot of the time, though, we were on our own. Wayfarers in an alien landscape.

Well, perhaps not entirely on our own. Because I had the distinct impression that we were being watched. By whom I hadn't the slightest idea, it was just that I had that uncomfortable feeling between my shoulder blades again. Paranoia? Maybe. But I hadn't imagined the brief flash I'd seen on the ridge as we turned off the main trail and began our detour towards Jebel Kut. None of the others had spotted it but to me it had seemed as noticeable as a star burst. I knew what it was. The sun's rays striking across metal or the lenses of high-powered field glasses. No doubt about it. We were under observation. I mentioned it to Kerim but to my surprise he didn't seem particularly bothered. It was probably a Mujehadeen lookout, he told me. I remained unconvinced. But he was the boss.

The track was getting decidedly more narrow, the route ahead infinitely more daunting as the mountains began to close in around us. It was an eerie feeling, being hemmed in. Great slabs of rock rose like dungeon walls on either side of the trail, dwarfing us as we wound our way into the canyon. High ridges were darkly visible through the ranks of pine and spruce. The band of blue sky above us was shrinking by the minute. Shadows began to lengthen.

Kerim was breaking trail. I was walking with Nicole. Behind us, Talib was leading the pack horse. The other Mujehadeen were trudging along in silence, strung out in single file. Our footsteps echoed like the slow rattle of dice in a cup. The path was uneven and I was spending a good deal of my time concentrating on where to put my feet.

So I missed seeing where the shot came from.

There was a sharp hollow crack of sound that rebounded along the walls of the canyon like a drum roll. I ducked instinctively and swung around, barely with enough time to catch the glazed expression on Talib's face as the bullet blew away his jawline and the top of his head exploded in a welter of blood and bone. In his dark robes and with his injured limb still strapped up he crashed to the ground like a one-armed paper hanger falling off a ladder.

As a ploy to attract our attention, the shooting of Talib was an outstanding success. But only for a micro-second. We certainly didn't linger over him to express our condolences. Kerim yelled something; probably a warning to hit the dirt. I was already moving. I grabbed Nicole, pulled her towards the cover of the trees at the side of the track, threw myself down on top of her, clawed the Kalashnikov from my shoulder, looked for somewhere to aim it. Couldn't see a bloody thing.

Total panic.

A thought crossed my mind at considerable speed. My suspicions on being followed had at least proved to be correct. The Soviets had caught up with us at last. It was Dar Galak, all over again. Well, we'd had a pretty good run, I suppose. Not much consolation in that, however. Big friggin' deal, in fact.

Almost immediately there came a violent burst of automatic fire. I ducked once more. When I pulled my head out of my shoulders I saw that two more of the Mujehadeen hadn't been able to make cover and had been hit. They lay spreadeagled on the rocks like misshapen scarecrows.

The pack horse was going berserk, legs slipping and a-sliding as it struggled for balance. Stones, dislodged by the animal's hooves, flicked into the air like bird-shot. The beast was vibrating with fear. It looked as if it was going to bolt at any second.

Sprawled unevenly beneath me, Nicole hissed through a mouthful of dirt, 'My God! What is it? What's happening?'

'I think the technical term is bush-whacked. For Christ's sake, keep your head down.'

There was a sudden brief silence, during which the beat of my heart seemed deafening, then I heard a shout followed by the unmistakable sound of automatic weapons being cocked. I raised my head cautiously. About twenty paces further up the trail Kerim was laying down his rifle. The remaining three Mujehadeen were doing the same. They were giving in without a fight. And I could see why. Heavily armed men were stepping out from the trees. We were plainly outnumbered. It would have been lunacy to attempt retaliation.

Then a voice came from above me. Pushtu, Farsi, whatever; it didn't matter which. But the tone and intent was clear. Be a good boy and drop the gun. Or else, I turned slowly.

From my low and ungainly position, my eyes automatically travelled upwards, over dirt-encrusted brown boots, pantaloons, waistcoat, bandolier and pugri cap. All encased around a scurvy-looking individual from whom you'd instinctively know better than to purchase a second-hand motor. Judging by his expression, when the sense of humour was handed out, this one must have been at the end of the queue. And there certainly wasn't anything remotely funny in the way he was holding the AK-47. He was just itching to use it, I could tell. And one other salient feature. He didn't strike me as looking much like Red Army material. So, who were they? Christ! What the hell was going on?

He jerked the muzzle of his rifle and I laid the Kalashnikov down on the rocks; very gently. Another wave. I helped Nicole to her feet and we were herded up the path towards Kerim and the Mujehadeen, all of whom had been made to sit cross legged, hands on their heads.

How quickly our little group had been whittled down. It looked as if the life expectancy of a Mujehadeen wasn't much longer than that of your average crane fly. Twelve out of the original band of sixteen had either been killed or injured. These were unacceptable losses in anyone's book. At this rate, the only one of us who seemed likely to survive the journey was the damned pack horse.

I heard someone laugh then. It wasn't Kerim or what was left of his men. Not unless they were ventriloquists. Nor was it matey behind us, and it certainly wasn't the horse. Dobbin had his head down; obviously trying to avoid eye contact.

A man stepped out from behind the rocks and thrust his way into the circle. Kerim, even under threat as he was, immediately let loose a flood of invective. Whatever he said went right over my head but I presumed it had to do with camels and armpits and infestations and the sexual proclivities of all those assembled therein.

He snarled savagely in my ear, 'Basmachis!'

Bandits.

Definitely not the Russians then, thank God. Well, perhaps.

The man who pushed himself to the fore was obviously their leader; a thin, hatchet-faced individual with atrocious bridgework and a livid scar on the left side of his face that stretched from the corner of his mouth to his hairline. Whoever had tried to repair his face had made a lousy job of it. The stitching along the frayed seams of my trainers was a lot smarter. The inept surgery had served to lift the corner of his mouth in a perpetual sneer. In the charm stakes this one would have been a non runner, scratched at the starting gate.

They made Nicole and me squat down too, hands behind our necks.

'You know this character?' I asked Kerim. I was right next to him. We must have looked like over-age contestants in a kiddies' playground game. Simon says, 'Put your hands on your head and don't move, otherwise we shoot you.' Great fun, what?

Kerim nodded grimly. 'He is called Sikander.' As an after thought, he added, 'A very dangerous man.'

As my eyes strayed over the prostrate forms of the three slaughtered Mujehadeen, I couldn't help but think that the description might just be a mite conservative.

Nicole, beside me, cross legged and pale under her cap, watched nervously as Sikander's men rifled the bodies of the dead guerillas. Sikander himself was more interested in the contents of the crates on the back of the pack horse.

'Afridi bastards!' Kerim hissed through clenched teeth, his dark eyes blazing as the first of the crates was placed on the ground. 'They are of the Zakha Kel.'

This sounded like some sort of masonic brotherhood. In fact, it was a name given to one of the Afridi clans. The Afridis were part of the Pathan tribe, as were the members of Kerim's own clan, the Wazirs. The Afridis had a similar reputation of being formidable fighters. Kerim, apparently anxious to improve my knowledge, added sotto voce that Afridis were noted for their greed and were about as trustworthy as a junkyard dog. Hardly the most reassuring point he could have made, given the circumstances.

Sikander was still trying to open the grounded crate. His men, about a dozen of them all told, not counting the one that was keeping an eye on us, were collecting weapons. They'd gathered up all the AK-47s that Kerim's men had lugged over the mountains and put them in a pile close by. I looked at Kerim and he looked at me. But we'd have been mad to attempt anything. Besides the damned things weren't even loaded.

The crate was finally levered open. The contents were revealed. Gasps of astonishment all round.

It hadn't been only guns that I'd flown in. Rockets too. Stingers, by the looks of them. Absolute proof that the rebels were being kitted out by the Americans. And God knows what roundabout route they had taken before I'd taken them on board,

It was obvious why we had been waylaid. Any supply caravan, no matter how small, would have been counted as fair game by Sikander and men of his ilk. And in our little consignment Sikander had struck paydirt. For in this part of the world, especially, weapons were regarded as currency as well as plunder: a means by which to barter, to repay debts, to assert authority. And, I was hoping, in our case, a means by which we could perhaps bargain for our lives.

Again I wondered how long Sikander and his men had been tracking us before I'd sensed them. Probably since leaving Mir Seraj. Or perhaps even earlier. Not that it mattered. What's done is done. It was what was about to be done that concerned me.

Sikander was chuckling with glee, obviously chuffed to buggery with his booty. His men were passing the rockets around, like cigars at the announcement of a birth in the family. To all intents and purposes it was as if he had forgotten all about us. Only he hadn't, of course. He instructed his men to reload the weapons and swaggered over.

As he approached, Kerim hissed at me from the corner of his mouth, 'Say nothing, my friend!'

The brigand favoured us all with a long, hard stare. His gaze settled on me for a while and swept on, lingering over Nicole, moving up and down her body in a way that was carnal, almost bestial. I felt my stomach turn. A cruel smile played across his uneven face. Then he reached out and ran a hand over her thigh before removing it and placing it over his crotch. Rubbing his hand up and down. He murmured something. Nicole appeared frozen in fear. My own skin crawled.

I saw Kerim give a start and his eyes caught mine in what was some kind of warning. As I hadn't understood anything the bandit had said, the significance of his words escaped me. I didn't know if Nicole had understood either. Her face was a stone mask.

At this snub Sikander gave a lascivious leer and, evidently on a change of tack, rounded on Kerim and fired off what I took to be a round of sharp questions, Kerim answering with a distinct lack of grace. I hoped he wasn't going to push the man too far. I couldn't follow what they were saying but I heard the words Sher Khan and Jebel Kut mentioned a couple of times. That didn't appear to impress Sikander a whole lot.

In fact, just to prove how unimpressed he really was he lifted his gun and blew Kerim's three Mujehadeen to kingdom come.

It was his speed and the couldn't-give-a-damn way he did it that was the most terrifying aspect of the executions. He simply swung around and fired off a burst with his Kalashnikov. None of us were expecting it, least of all the three Mujehadeen, so there wasn't even time for the awareness to register on their faces before they were literally bowled over by the force of the attack. The range was virtually point blank. Little wonder, therefore, that the effects were devastating. Their bodies jerked in epileptic convulsions as the heavy bullets tore them apart before our eyes. Tufts of hair and creamy flesh erupted from their bloodied corpses like chaff in a high wind.

Kerim let out a roar of anger and pain, like a wounded bull cornered by banderillos. He dropped his arms and received a sharp jab in the stomach with the barrel of a Kalashnikov as a reward. His hands returned to the back of his neck. I could tell that he was positively strumming with hate.

I could taste fear then, like bile, sharp and sour. Now it's our turn, I thought. This is it.

It was Nicole who made the next move, however.

God knows what made her react as she did. I could only assume that given her calling and all it entailed, seeing life snuffed out with such little regard tipped her over the edge of reason for that split second.

Before Kerim and I could grasp the scope of her actions she sprang to her feet and rushed at Sikander, tears of rage on her cheeks. She didn't get very far. Horrified, I fully expected Sikander to shoot her. Instead, he backhanded her across the face and she went sprawling.

Kerim, incensed, bellowed again, started to rise.

I yelled, 'You bastard!' I fully intended to follow Kerim's lead at that point, no matter where it led. Saw the barrel of the Kalashnikov turn towards me. Thought, oh, shit.

And Nicole's cap flew off.

Sikander froze, thunderstruck, his eyes popping like rivets. I suddenly understood why. He hadn't known she was a woman! In that ridiculous cap, combat jacket, and no make up, she looked as she had when I'd first seen her. Like a smooth-faced boy. Just the way Sikander liked them. That's what Kerim had realized when Sikander had been making his catamitic overtures. No wonder he hadn't shot her. He hadn't wanted to damage the goods beyond repair, that's why.

The discovery that one of their three surviving captives was of the female persuasion pierced the brains of the gang at something approaching light speed. Immediately, everyone stopped what they were doing and clustered around us like punters at a dog fight. The guns and rockets were forgotten. Without a doubt, this put us into a whole new ball game.

Mindless of the possible consequences, I knocked aside a gun barrel and helped Nicole to her feet. No one tried to stop me. They were all trying to recover from the shock. Nicole sat down again, wiped the blood from her split lip.

'You blithering idiot!' I hissed. 'That was a damned fool thing to do! What the hell did you think you were playing at?'

'He killed them,' she whispered dully. 'He just shot them.' She stared at the dead Mujehadeen as though mesmerized. I put my arm around her shoulders. Waited.

A furious question and answer session then ensued between Sikander and Kerim. Sikander kept flicking looks at us. Finally he went off into a huddle with his men.

I thought, Now what?

'You want to tell us what's going on?' I muttered to Kerim.

'I told him you were both doctors, travelling to the Panjsher. Better that than to explain why you are really here, my friend.'

Well, that made sense. 'And?'

'And now they will decide either to hand us over to the Shuravi or . . .' His voice trailed off.

'Or?' I prompted, trying to ignore the vague feeling of awful premonition.

'Or shoot us,' Kerim finished lamely.

'Oh, wonderful.

Two of Sikander's men were searching the bodies of the recently dispatched guerillas. The limbs of the dead men flopped languidly as the bodies were turned over and ransacked. I heard Kerim growl deep in his throat.

Sikander returned. The crates and their contents had been restored to the pack horse. Which meant they were ready to move out. The bandit grinned, his misshapen mouth looking like a terrible gash in his face. He spoke with Kerim once more.

Kerim looked at us. The expression on his face was almost apologetic. 'They are going to hand us over to the Russians,' he said quietly. 'There is a command post in the next valley. They will leave us there.' He sighed heavily. 'My friend, I think it would have been better if they had decided to shoot us.' Then Kerim smiled a sad smile. 'But at least I will join my brothers in Paradise.'

Which was all very well for Kerim to say. As far as Nicole and I were concerned, wherever it was that Sikander was planning to take us, Paradise wouldn't come anywhere near it.

In fact it was more like purgatory. It was Sikander's lair, or at least one of them. I presumed he had many of them scattered among the surrounding hills. Bolt holes, where he could lie up after a raid, count out his loot, lick his wounds.

The cave was one of a number cut into the hillside. I guessed that the entire area was probably honeycombed with caverns and connecting tunnels. Not that I had any strong desire to go up and explore them. I had other things on my mind. A question of priorities, you might say.

They'd roped us together like a trio of rock climbers. Kerim in front, Nicole in the middle, me as the back marker. Then Sikander had led us into the mountains.

It was his intention to hand deliver us to the Russians in the morning. He wasn't going to risk a night march. During the daytime the Russians held the advantage with their gunships and spotter planes. After sunset the rebels

166

controlled the countryside. Sikander had no intention of walking into a Mujehadeen raiding party. He'd reap his reward in the cold light of day. Hard cash most likely. Or guns.

In every war men like Sikander surface. Making a profit through other men's misery. In an earlier age he'd have been hard at work flogging ration books and petrol coupons. Now, it was trading in his countrymen for a crate of Kalashnikov rifles. Sometimes, I expect, men of his brand receive their come-uppance. Mostly they don't. I sincerely hoped that Sikander would get his. In spades, if Kerim had anything to do with it.

The journey to Sikander's hideaway didn't take long — less than an hour, as it turned out — but it was a hard climb and the light was fading fast. The sky and the mountains were growing darker by the minute as we were herded up through the trees towards the big black openings in the rock. They looked like the entrances to ancient tombs. I hoped that wasn't an omen.

They fed us at least. Food for the fatted calves, probably. Kerim, apparently having accepted his lot, ate with gusto. As I did, funnily enough. Perversely, in spite of our predicament, the walk through the rarefied mountain air had given me an appetite. Besides, I've always been of the opinion that in situations where you never know where your next meal might come from you eat when and what you can. Store energy, that was the rule.

We ate with our fingers, pushing balls of rice around the tin plates to soak up the fat from the stringy goat meat. The meat wasn't only stringy, it was extremely gamey. I trusted the wretched animal hadn't given up without a fight. They hadn't even untied our hands while we ate either. The bonds were beginning to cut into my wrists like leather that had been soaked in brine and left to dry tightly. An untrusting lot, Sikander's crew.

After the food I leaned back against the wall of the cave and considered our chances of escape. Bloody non-existent, as far as I could estimate. Now that we had trekked and eaten we had time on our hands. Time to contemplate the coming day.

Of the three of us, I suspected that Nicole's fate would be the least disagreeable. The Russians had captured French medics in the past. They'd held them for a couple of months and then repatriated them back to France. Smacked their legs and told them not to be naughty boys and girls, in other words.

Neither Kerim nor I could hope to receive the same sort of treatment. Kerim, they would probably subject to a prolonged and very painful sojourn in Pol-e-Charkhi before handing him over to a Khad execution squad. In my case, I doubted they'd even be that lenient. It wouldn't take their interrogators long to discover that not only wasn't I French, but I wasn't that much of a doctor either. I'd be the ultimate proof they needed that Western intelligence services were using foreign mercenaries to train and equip the Mujehadeen. They'd milk the situation for all it was worth and then I'd be hung out to dry. Literally. They'd most likely skin me first.

All that one-bound-and-he-was-free crap is for the story books. It only occurs in romantic fiction. This wasn't the remotest bit romantic. We were in deep shit and no way out of the midden. I hoped Kerim was working on something because my little grey cells had all taken the night off. I looked towards him, hoping for a spark of inspiration. But he had his eyes closed and looked as if he was asleep. Terrific.

I nudged him with my foot. His eyes sprang open.

'You got any ideas?' I whispered.

The nearest guard was about thirty feet away, by the cave entrance. Sikander wasn't taking any chances. The three of us represented a handsome bounty and all he had to do was get us down the mountain at dawn. So he didn't want us getting loose and creating mischief. Hence the gaoler with his automatic rifle. Sikander and the rest of his crew were making themselves comfortable around the fire in the centre of the cavern. There didn't seem to be as many men in evidence as there had been when we'd been held up. I presumed that meant that Sikander had set piquets out beyond the perimeter of the camp. It was going to be a cold night for those who were outside. I hoped the bastards all got frost bite.

Kerim squinted at the guard and the rest of the bandits and pursed his lips. He seemed to be considering the options. While he did that I turned to Nicole. She had her knees drawn up under her chin and was resting her hands on them. Her head was against my shoulder.

'You okay?' I asked.

She looked up, gave a tight, brave little smile. Nodded tiredly.

'We're going to get out of this, love. Don't worry.'

Her expression indicated that pigs might fly.

So much for the morale booster. I went back to Kerim. He caught my glance. His eyes glittered like coals and for the first time I felt a spark of hope.

'We wait,' he said quietly.

Time passed, as they say.

It seemed to take forever for Sikander and his men to settle down for what remained of the night. The guard at the cave entrance was swapped out as, I guessed after some to-ing and fro-ing, were the outer markers. Sikander, in a brief fit of generosity, threw us a trio of sheepskin rugs to ward off the cold that was beginning to seep into the cave. After that he lost interest and returned to his space by the fire. More wood was thrown on to the flames. The place was starting to resemble a boy scout camp. At any

169

moment I half expected them to burst into a rendition of 'Ging Gang Goolee'. From that, though, we were spared.

I don't know what sort of sheep it was that had shed the skin I was lumbered with but it must have been glad to get rid of it. It smelled foul. Still, it was warm. I drew it around me and tried to ease the cramp in my legs.

I must have nodded off. I don't know how long for – an hour or so maybe. I thought at first that it had been the cold that had woken me. Or perhaps it had been something else. I looked around.

Nicole was snuggled against me, breathing gently, and it had probably been some involuntary movement she had made that had caused the sheepskin to slip from my shoulders. I pulled it back over me, grateful for its warmth and her closeness. I saw that the fire had settled into a bed of embers. All the brigands appeared to be asleep.

To my left Kerim was resting with his back to the rock, the sheepskin draped over him. He looked as if he was dozing again. Then I took another startled look. Above the region of his crotch the sheepskin was moving up and down in rapid undulation. I gaped. The last time I'd been privy to a sight like that had been back at the boot camp. They used to tell us then that the cure was to don a pair of boxing gloves, otherwise you'd go blind.

Suddenly his movements ceased and the sheepskin fell away. The first thing I saw was the knife. It was a wicked-looking item, the blade wide at the hilt and tapering in a curve towards a vicious point. I realized then what he'd been doing and what had disturbed me. He'd been holding the hilt of the knife between his knees and sawing his wrists up and down the blade to cut the bonds that tied him. God knows how he'd managed to keep the thing hidden. Although, looking at his clothing I thought it likely that about his person, concealed within the overlap-

170

ping layers of shirt and pantaloons, there were probably enough recesses to hide a complete squad of infantry.

The grin he gave me was positively malevolent. It took him less than a second to lean over and cut the rope around my own wrists. He was doing all the graft. I was working up a sweat just from keeping an eye out for someone who might sound the alarm. I nudged Nicole and, as she came awake, Kerim passed me the knife. I cut the rope at her wrists and handed him the knife back. I looked towards the cave entrance. The guard was hunched on one of the weapons crates, head sunk on to his chest, eyes closed, rifle resting across his knee. He'd obviously nodded off, his grip on the Kalashnikov having relaxed as his body succumbed to sleep. Over by the fire Sikander and the rest of them were wrapped in their partouks, dark shadowy bundles on the ground.

If there was ever to come a time when we would be in with a chance of making a break, this had to be it.

Kerim decided to take out the guard.

I could see that he was weighing up his chances of covering the ground between himself and the target without alerting the man or the rest of Sikander's mob. I willed him to make his move quickly. The telepathy seemed to work. Kerim eased himself into a crouch, took a deep breath.

The guard turned around.

God knows what had alerted him. Kerim had been as silent as a ghost. But the whys and wherefores were academic. Because by this time Kerim was committed. The Pathan had thirty feet to traverse before he dealt with the sentry and he must have known even as he started to uncoil that he hadn't a cat in hell's chance of success. The guard opened his mouth to yell, the Kalashnikov came up and Kerim started his run about a thousand years too late.

Then I saw it.

It started out as a vague shadow, a patch of darkness, over the guard's left shoulder, as if a part of the night had detached itself and formed an amorphous entity that had suddenly taken on human shape. I watched the guard become aware of the presence, start to turn, eyes widening in shock. Then a sinewy arm reached out to embrace the man's neck, pulling it back in one brisk fluid move to expose the jugular and tendons stretched like taut wires. A flash of a blade like a flame lancing across the throat and a viscous fountain of warm black rain as blood erupted.

And the sound of automatic fire shattered the night.

Kerim threw himself to the ground, jaw slack with amazement. Nicole and I did likewise.

The sleeping men around the fire came awake as if a bomb had been dropped in their midst. They broke out of their blankets and scrambled for their weapons. Cries of alarm filled the air. I pushed Nicole behind me, yelled at her to get down. Prostrate, the three of us watched incredulously as Sikander's men ran into a wall of gunfire laid down by the half dozen men who sprinted through the unguarded entrance.

Bright muzzle flashes lit up the walls of the cave. The short sharp bursts of automatic fire were deafening, magnified a hundred times in the confined space, as the attackers picked out their targets with systematic deliberation. Some of Sikander's men were managing to return fire but, in their highly excitable state, their aim was erratic. Bullets straffed the rock above our heads and whined into the darkness. The inside of the cavern must have resembled a Bosch print, being full of dancing leaping figures, jack-knifing as they were cut down, like grotesque break dancers rapping in the energetic throes of death. A body tumbled backwards through the remains of the fire, spewing embers across the floor. Sparks cascaded like Catherine wheels. Someone screamed loudly.

Down alongside me, Kerim was fingering his knife and spitting curses, seeing the action pass him by, incensed at not being a part of it. Then his chance came. I watched one of the bandits swerve out of the line of fire and run towards us, his face a mask of terror. Kerim seized his opportunity and rose from the ground like some awakened genie. The bandit saw his mistake at the last minute and tried to slam on his brakes. Kerim ducked and went in quickly, the blade sweeping around in a vicious uppercut. The man ran on to the blade and the two of them went down together. Kerim pushed himself away from the twitching corpse and wiped the knife on his victim's shirt. He grinned at me, his teeth bared like fangs, and twisted to search for his next mark. A scream launched itself from his throat as he looked for the enemy.

'SIIIKANDERRRRR!'

I had visions of his ending up like Raz Sharif and made a grab for his arm. He threw me off. He wanted blood. No one was going to stand in his way now.

Then we both realized that it might be too late. Because none of the bandits appeared to be moving anymore. They were just shapeless bundles on the floor of the cave, sprawled over darker patches in the sand where the blood was beginning to spread in widening pools.

My ears were ringing as the echoes of gunfire died away. The cavern was filled with drifting gunsmoke. I helped Nicole to her feet, lifting her by the waist. She clung to me, shaking. I became aware of grey figures coming towards us through the half light, like ghosts drifting through patches of marsh gas. Instinctively I shrank back against the cave wall. Kerim moved to my side like a protector.

The eerie forms materialized into half a dozen armed

173

men, dressed in tribal garb. Tough looking, they scanned the shadows for any sign of counter attack. Behind them another figure was silhouetted against the cave entrance. Kerim's bearded jaw sagged open with astonishment as the man's face came into focus. Nicole clutched my arm. I heard her gasp with shock. The wind was taken from my sails too. I recognized the clothes first of all. Combat jacket, quilted pants tucked into leather boots. Bandolier, Kalashnikov. Saturnine features. Moustache, unshaven jowls. Then the hair; long and worn in a tress at the back.

He walked in like he owned the place.

Taras Rasseikin.

Chapter Eleven

If Rasseikin was in any way amused by our dazed expressions he didn't show it. He eyed the knife in Kerim's hand, then the body of the dead brigand. He nudged the corpse with the toe of his boot, turning the body over, pursed his lips and gave a small knowing grunt when he saw the wound, as if admitting a sneaking regard for the method of the kill.

His attention switched to Nicole and me. He spoke brusquely to Kerim in broken Farsi, his dark eyes never leaving our faces. It was as if he was trying to see into the deepest regions of our minds. I felt as if I was being stripped down, layer by layer.

Kerim translated, albeit grudgingly, by the sound of it. 'He asks if either of you are injured.'

'Just shaken,' I said. 'Nothing stirred.'

Kerim frowned. 'I do not understand.'

'Forget It. Rotten joke. Tell him we're okay.'

Kerim relayed the message. The Russian acknowledged our condition with a curt nod, his cold eyes unblinking. Reaching into a pocket of his jacket, he took out a thin black cheroot and lit up, drawing the smoke into his lungs with great satisfaction. He rapped out an order and his men began the body count.

Rasseikin spoke again. He was using Kerim as a conduit. I got to wondering if this was a ploy and that maybe he could speak and understand English more than he was letting on. Although on reflection, I supposed there was no reason why he should have been able to speak any language other than his own. He was obviously having more than enough trouble conversing in the local patois.

'He says we are very fortunate that our paths should have crossed,' Kerim explained. 'One of his men saw the ambush from their look-out point further up the mountain and recognized you as the two ferenghi from Mir Seraj. He says that everyone knows that Sikander and his Basmachis spy for the Shuravi. Sikander is a bounty hunter, trading in the lives of Mujehadeen. Taras Rasseikin guessed that Sikander would plan to deliver us to the command post over the mountain. So he and his men decided to help us.'

The Russian was nodding at all this and puffing at his cheroot. There was something about him that made me wonder how much of the stories about him might be true. Despite his dubious reputation, I detected something of a hidden character behind that villainous appearance. If the military part of his background was only halfway true then under that nefarious exterior there existed an intelligence and a capability that far exceeded the qualities one would normally associate with the terms deserter and drug dealer.

And there were the men with him too.

Studying them as they quartered the area I was struck by how professional they seemed. Even in the chaos of those first few minutes when they launched their attack I hadn't failed to notice that they had carried out their assigned task with the slickness of a well-drilled squad. And, having seen some of Kerim's Mujehadeen in action, this struck me as quite miraculous. Most of the guerillas I'd met so far hadn't taken to the concepts of military discipline all that well. They had the necessary guts and determination, true enough, but they lacked the cohesion that is the essence of all sound military strategy. They usually went in with all guns blazing, with no comprehen-

176

sion of tactics or deployment. But these men were something different. I put it down to a legacy of Rasseikin's army training. They acted as a unit and had made Sikander's bunch look like rank amateurs.

None of the bandits had survived the fire fight. Well, with one apparent and notable exception. We failed to find Sikander's body. It wasn't for the want of searching either, at least not on Kerim's part. What we did discover, though, was a trail of blood stains running from the fire across the floor of the cave towards a narrow, low-roofed passageway in the corner of the chamber.

It was obvious to us all that Sikander would know these tunnels like the veins on the back of his hand. And, unless he'd collapsed through blood loss, it was likely that he was through to the other side of the mountain by now, and still running. No one volunteered, however, to take off after him.

Kerim muttered his vexation and sheathed his knife. He looked like a man whom life had cheated grandly. 'One day,' he grated, 'I will kill Sikander Habib. I will cause him much pain and he will beg me for mercy. But I will kill him.'

I never doubted Kerim for a second.

After further discussion with Rasseikin, Kerim announced, 'He says he will escort us to Jebel Kut.'

The Mujehadeen still looked like someone who was finding it difficult to accept the fact that he and the Russian might both, after all, be on the same side. Or maybe it was a case of Kerim not liking the new rules under which the Great Game was being played. The very idea that he was bound by the Pushtunwali to honour this debt he now owed Rasseikin must have been anathema to him. But he wouldn't break the code. To do so would bring dishonour upon himself and his clan. That would be the gravest sin.

The packhorse had been loaded up again. This was becoming something of a chore for the animal. You could tell by its resigned expression. Especially as it was now taking on extra weight: the guns that had earlier been carried by the recently deceased Mujehadeen. All it really wanted to do was wander away and graze. Still it wouldn't want for company. Although, I had noticed that somewhere along the line since leaving Mir Seraj Rasseikin had relieved his train of the opium, probably at one of the labs that Le Beq had told me about.

And come to think of it, I was getting more than a little hacked off at all this stopping and starting myself. So far, in this fiasco, I'd lost one aircraft, been straffed by Soviet gunships, assisted in field surgery, been set upon by brigands, and been up and down more bloody mountains than Sherpa Tensing. And all I ever really wanted to do was go home. Eventually.

But first: Jebel Kut.

It was the first time that we'd travelled at night. It wasn't much fun. Until I found there was a definite knack to it. When you can't see where you're going the tendency is to walk like a robot with every muscle tensed in case you put a foot wrong. In fact you have to do the opposite and let yourself relax. The body then acts like the gyro-stabilizer on a ship by countering the direction your feet move towards as they slip and slide over the rocks. It's not a style that'd win applause on a fashion show catwalk but it's effective once you get the hang of it.

Rasseikin had led from the off, setting a pace that would have done justice to an SAS route march. He never once relinquished his position at the head of the column either. He was like one of those celluloid frontier scouts that had been hired to lead a wagon train of homesteaders through Indian country. Strong, taciturn, no small talk and a penchant for spitting soggy gobs of chewing tobacco out

178

of the corner of his mouth. Only in Rasseikin's case the baccy had been replaced by a seemingly never ending supply of Russian cheroots. Throughout the journey he was no more than a dark, brooding and slightly hunched shadow moving unevenly ahead of us in the moonlight, never flagging in his stride as he guided us unerringly towards our destination. It was all Nicole and I could do to keep up with the rest of them. For Kerim, of course, it was probably no more arduous than a stroll in the park. The Kalashnikov I was still hauling around was starting to grow heavier by the minute.

We arrived above the rebel camp at dawn.

I recall Mike Farrell once telling me of a fellow journalist's belief why it was that Afghanistan had never fallen under the yoke of the British Empire. It had been because nowhere in the entire country had anybody ever found a patch of ground large enough or flat enough on which to roll out a cricket pitch. If that was so then they'd never discovered Jebel Kut.

Seeing the Mujehadeen stronghold spread below us I was reminded of those isolated hill-top flying strips that had been used to such good effect back in Nam and Laos. The ones that had been hacked out of the jungle by Meo tribesmen acting under the orders of Air America, the airline funded and controlled by the Central Intelligence Agency. The Company had used the crude air strips as RV zones from which to pick up opium from the local hill tribes in exchange for arms and ammunition which were then used by the CIA's mercenary armies against the Viet Cong and the NVA.

Jebel Kut had that same remoteness. It was as if a giant hand had reached down into the heart of the mountains and scooped away a segment of one of the high peaks. The result resembled the remains of a broken tooth; all jagged edges around the side and a flat, hollow depression in the middle. In this case a grass-topped steppe perhaps a mile or two in length and maybe half a mile wide. It was like looking down on to an uncharted island, with the rest of the snow-capped massif soaring above it like the heaving swell of some vast ocean.

Dotted around the edges of the large meadow I could make out some low stone buildings and squares and triangles of black shadow which I realized were some form of canvas shelter. They looked like Bedouin-style tents.

A light mist hung over the ground like a layer of delicate gauze. Through it small distant figures seemed to move as if in slow motion. The tranquillity was suddenly broken by the long drawn out wail of a muezzin calling the faithful to prayer. The cry carried on the still morning air and echoed around the surrounding mountains like a soul in torment, adding a supernatural dimension to the wavering descant. I felt the short hairs on the back of my neck start to prickle.

The smugglers did not accompany us into the valley. Rasseikin and his men left us to make the final descent on our own. I wasn't entirely surprised. Probably the proximity of so many Mujehadeen in one place set him to thinking that it might not be prudent to accompany us into what could amount to the lion's den. I think even Kerim understood that.

Our parting of the ways was a strange affair. We just looked at each other, as if searching for something appropriate to say. In the end we simply shook hands. The Russian's grip was strong and firm. But he never smiled once. Just nodded abruptly as if to say, that's it, chum. My job's done, you're on your own. Then we were dumped at the side of the track like hitchhikers awaiting our next lift while the smugglers went on their way. None of them looked back. The last we saw of them was the rear end of one of their pack horses as it disappeared over the brow of the hill. It was like watching the end of an episode of *The Lone Ranger*, with the hero riding off into the sunset or, in this case, the sunrise, in time to hear someone ask nervously, 'Who was that masked man?'

Taras Rasseikin, that's who. One very singular individual indeed. Soldier. Smuggler. Samaritan. Who hadn't once asked Kerim or me who I was or what the hell I might be doing here. Which was pretty damned weird, I couldn't help thinking.

And with that thought nagging away at me like a terrier on a trouser leg and with Kerim holding the reins of our faithful pack horse, the three of us made our way down towards the rebel stronghold.

The lookouts must have been aware of our approach for quite a while, but they let us get real close before acknowledging our existence.

At first I thought it was a roll of thunder. I stared up at the mountains. Thunder? It didn't seem possible. The mist had cleared and the morning air was clean and crisp. Above us the sky was a beautiful, almost transluscent, shade of blue. Against this porcelain-textured infinity the mountains appeared carved out of glass. Runnels of freshly fallen snow lay etched across them like scratch marks on a crystal decanter. There wasn't a cloud in sight. But the noise was getting louder. A terrifying thought hit me.

Gunships! Christ! They'd found us again. I looked around frantically for somewhere to run and hide. Too late. They were upon us.

But not helicopters.

Horsemen.

They appeared from nowhere. Seeming to rise from an unseen fold in the earth, as if born out of the teeth of the Hydra. Perhaps thirty riders in all, savage-looking men on sweat-streaked horses, the hooves of which had drummed on the ground like the rumble of an approaching storm. It was as if we had passed through a barrier in time. Genghis Khan and Alexander would have faced men like these. They were enough to put the fear of God into anyone.

They brought their mounts under control and formed a semi-circle across our path. Hooves pawed the ground, steam arose from the horses' flanks like smoke. The animals snorted and jostled against each other. Two or three reared nervously but were brought swiftly back under restraint by the heels and whips of their riders. If there was one thing an Afghan was more versed in than fighting, it was horseflesh. These men were the direct descendants of a warrior caste that had, in another era, counted itself among some of the best light cavalry in the world; able to rate as effective as the Comanches or the Cossacks. Quite how they fared against Mi24s and BM-21 multiple rocket launchers, though, I couldn't even begin to imagine. Probably they were as committed as the Polish cavalry had been when the latter had found themselves up against Hitler's Panzer divisions back in World War Two. And just as outmatched, no doubt.

I don't know what it was that Kerim yelled at them. Most likely something along the lines of, 'How do, lads. Guess who?' Whatever it was, it had the desired effect.

A wild yell rent the air and one of the riders dropped to the ground and ran forward. He was about Kerim's own age and of a similar build. The two men embraced. Kerim turned to us, a huge smile on his face.

'My cousin, Jamil,' he said. 'He is the son of Sher Khan, the commander of Jebel Kut.'

Jamil was very dark with tight curly hair, a wispy black beard and very white teeth which he showed in a wide grin.

At least the natives were friendly, I thought. More friendly than I'd anticipated as it turned out. I got a hug from Jamil that just about squeezed the breath from my lungs. Jamil wore a lot of kohl around his eyes, I noticed. I began to wonder a little about Kerim's cousin. Especially when Nicole only received a handshake.

'Welcome, Mista! Welcome!'

'Jamil has very good English,' Kerim said proudly. 'He was fine mechanic with Bakhtar at Kabul airport for three years before the Russians came. He fix anything with an engine, you see.' Jamil's current circumstances seemed light years away from servicing jet engines for the national airline. But then most of the Mujehadeen I'd met hadn't any previous experience of war. Being Afghans it was a skill they'd been born with. It was something inherent within them, like the homing instinct of migrating birds or the habit of the modern domesticated dog to curl around itself before settling down to sleep; a legacy of the wolfhound flattening the rushes in the warlord's keep.

Whatever traits I'd inherited from my ancestors, they surely hadn't included anything remotely equestrian. I don't know how long it had been since I'd ridden a horse, but the last time I'd done so the animal had been piebald and wooden on rockers. And a lot more comfortable, come to think of it. Afghan saddles aren't designed to be ridden in tandem, not unless you've got a special relationship with the guy in front of you, that is. I found that out when the three of us were hoisted up behind a trio of riders for the remainder of the short journey to Shar Khan's HQ. Still, it was either that, or I got off and walked, and I'd had enough of the latter. I gritted my teeth and hung on to Jamil's waist. I hoped, fervently, that this didn't mean the two of us were engaged.

One thing became immediately clear to me. There were a great many fighting men in the camp – the largest concentration of Mujehadeen that I had yet seen, in fact, with most of them, according to Jamil, on their way back to the fighting after recuperation periods in Peshawar and other towns along the Pakistan side of the border. There was a lot of equipment here too, arms and ammunition destined for the front line. Jebel Kut was obviously a staging post of some importance and not just a temporary bivouac. This place was a major transit halt, a strategic support base from where the Mujehadeen relayed men and equipment up the line to the battle zones. Because of that it was well defended against attack, particularly from the air. I saw that a number of anti-aircraft gun emplacements had been gouged out of the granite rocks, ringing the encampment. Concealed beneath webs of camouflage netting and protected by sand-bagged walls Swiss Oerlikons poked their slender muzzles into the sky.

Our route skirted cooking fires, sleeping areas, and piquet lines. A few people called a greeting as we made our way through the camp but in the main we were paid scant attention. Almost everyone was fully engrossed with making preparations for their imminent departure.

Sher Khan's headquarters had been set up in what had been an old chai khana. The low-roofed building was overshadowed by a stand of plane trees, the stringy bark peeling away from slender trunks like advanced dermatitis.

Sher Khan was away tending to matters in another section of the camp so, while Kerim toddled away to tether the pack horse, Jamil showed us our quarters. It was quite large inside, but gloomy. Like an old desert motel down on its luck. What with that and the decor, which I would have described as a cross between Aladdin's treasure cave and a pox doctor's waiting room, the place reminded me of the bazaar back in Peshawar. It was something of a warren. There was one large room reserved for the jirgas, the assemblies or councils of war held by the field commanders, from which a number of dark passages ran through to various corners of the building and off these

184

were several smaller guest rooms. Jamil showed us into a couple of them, usually reserved, so he said, for honoured guests. Massoud often stayed here during his recruiting campaigns, Jamil informed us in hushed tones. I suppose it was the local equivalent of being told that I was about to occupy the four poster that Queen Victoria had utilized during a weekend at Blenheim, or wherever. Nicole and I looked suitably awed. The furniture in each of the cubicles consisted of a narrow framed chapakat bed and an upturned wooden box on which sat a tin bowl, washing for the use of. A couple of faded and very moth-eaten rugs covered the earthen floor. A real home from home.

Jamil then asked us if we'd like to take a hot bath. We stared at him as if he was pulling our legs, although, as I glanced sceptically at Nicole, I could see that she was almost salivating at the thought. In a daze we both nodded. Jamil grinned smugly and beckoned us to follow him.

The 'bath room' was right at the back of the building. It couldn't have been much more than ten feet square. I'd seen bigger outside dunnies. The facilities consisted of a tin bath set on bricks. Next to it was something resembling a camp stove, on top of which rested two enormous urns containing steaming water. In that confined space it was like standing inside a Turkish bath. Jamil looked on anxiously as we surveyed the arrangements. 'Is all right, yes?'

'Is bloody marvellous,' I said, taking it all in like a drunk who'd just hit the jackpot on one of the machines in the local RSL club.

By God, there were even a couple of towels and a tiny bar of soap! Sheer luxury! This was the true extension of Pushtunwali. Melmestia: what's mine is yours. Such unselfish hospitality in these primitive surroundings was positively humbling. Compared to old Qasi Sur Timur's hostelry back in Jamalagar this place rated four stars in the Michelin guide.

Nicole looked up at me and we grinned idiotically at each other. 'Who's first?' she said, unslinging her shoulder bag.

'After you, ma'am.' I bowed in deference.

We left her to it.

'After your bath, you may rest,' Jamil said. 'Then you will meet with Sher Khan.'

'Sounds fine with me,' I replied. I was dog tired after our midnight ramble. I just wanted to lay my head somewhere, along with the rest of my weary bones.

'Later, there will be food,' Jamil said. 'Followed by the game.'

'The game?' I hadn't seen any goal posts that I could recall.

Jamil nodded enthusiastically. 'It is the custom. There will also be singing and dancing and the telling of stories. But first there will be Buzkashi.'

Buzkashi. Now, that was something I had heard of. I realized the significance of the horsemen.

The Afghan national game has been likened to a cross between polo and British bulldog. A free-for-all on horseback. The object of the game was to carry the carcass of a goat down the length of a pitch to a circle without dropping it or having it taken from you. It demanded exceptional horsemanship, strength, stamina, and bravery. There could be as many as a hundred riders in the game at any one time. And anything went. The event had been chosen to take place that afternoon.

As long as they kept the bloody noise down, was my immediate reaction.

I vaguely remember emerging from my soak, par-boiled and perspiring but mercifully relaxed. Didn't even stop to check on Nicole. Crashed out as soon as my head hit the cushions. Instant oblivion. Instant bliss.

Slept for six hours. Then we were taken to meet the boss.

The commander of Jebel Kut was in the council room, flanked by his lieutenants, about a dozen men, of differing ages; from early thirties through to an elderly gent with a face as wizened as a prune and hands mottled and gnarled like the branches of a seasoned oak tree. Kerim was there, too. He smiled a greeting. I got a heavy once-over from the rest of them. Probably because I'd gone through a change of clothes by this time. Jamil had arranged for our grimy travelling garments to be cleaned. Nicole had spare stuff in her bag. I'd been reunited with my shirt, Levi's and leather windcheater. I'd grown used to the Afghan gear, however, and my own clothes seemed quite tight and uncomfortable by comparison. I felt as if I was standing out like the proverbial sore thumb, although I had elected to keep my beard. It was a lot less painful than trying to shave it off.

The scrutiny was continuous as Nicole and I took our seats next to Kerim. We were served tea from a large copper samovar in the middle of the room.

'We have arrived in time,' Kerim whispered as he handed me a cup of tea. 'The day after tomorrow, Sher Khan and his men begin their march to the Panjsher. It will be a difficult journey. It will be a large caravan and therefore will be very hard to conceal, and the Shuravi are very vigilant.'

I glanced surreptitiously at the guerilla chief over the rim of my cup.

From the little I remembered of my few sorties into the works of Kipling, Sher Khan was the name belonging to a tiger of a particular devious bent, full of guile and cunning. I had the sneaking suspicion that, in all probability, the

Sher Khan I was looking at more than lived up to the reputation of his namesake. You don't get to be a Mujehadeen field commander by being Mr Nice Guy.

He was older than I'd expected, though, much older. Massoud was only in his early thirties and I'd supposed that most of his field commanders were the same age. Like Kerim, for instance. Although it wasn't Sher Khan's age that arrested my attention so much as the startling resemblance he bore to the Ayatollah Khomeini. It was quite unnerving. Heavily bearded and dressed almost completely in black, his features were dark and brooding, his eyes penetrating and deep set. The overall effect was extremely forbidding, in such total contrast to his son, Jamil.

There was someone else he reminded me of, too. At first I couldn't put my finger on it, then it suddenly struck me. Raz Sharif! Sher Khan's seamed face had that same gaunt yet haughty look. And then I remembered. Habanni had told me that the malik of Dar Galak, Kerim, was Raz Sharif's nephew. And Kerim had introduced Jamil as his cousin. Which meant that Sher Khan was Raz Sharif's brother, or at least one of them. No wonder there was a resemblance. Further proof that the lineage of families in this country was damned near biblical in proportion.

I continued to study Sher Khan covertly. There's an old proverb which says that Turks make the best friends and the worst enemies. I was fully prepared to believe that the saying applied to Afghans too. This one in particular. I made a mental revision of my opinion of him. No, not so much a tiger. More like an old fox. As in: as crafty as.

Sher Khan spoke. His voice was pitched low, strong and unwavering, belying his ancient looks.

Kerim did the honours.

'Hajii Sher Khan welcomes you to Jebel Kut,' he relayed. 'He asks if you rested well.'

'Very well, thank him.' I took a cautious sip of the sweet green tea. It was a bit sickly for my taste but I was wary to offend by not partaking. I said, 'We are grateful to be here.' Hell, I was grateful to be anywhere they weren't bombing the crap out of me. Only I didn't tell him that.

The old man continued speaking. Kerim allowed himself a wry smile before he translated. 'He understands that your journey to Jebel Kut has not been without incident.'

He can say that again, I thought.

'Tell him,' I said, 'that we regret the death of Mohammed Nur Rafiq and the warrior Raz Sharif.'

Kerim gave me an appreciative look as if to let me know that I'd said the right thing. When he passed on the condolences a murmur went through the assembled guerillas.

Sher Khan nodded gravely and spoke at length.

Kerim said, 'Mohammed Nur Rafiq and Raz Sharif were great fighters. But we do not mourn for them. For why should we mourn brave Mujehadeen whose souls have entered the kingdom of Paradise?'

Why indeed? I mused inwardly.

'Sher Khan asks if you both wish to accompany his Mujehadeen to the Panjsher.'

'I thought that was the general idea?' I said.

'It will be dangerous. The Shuravi will try to stop us.'

'They tried to stop us getting this far,' I said. 'So far, they've failed.' I thought I'd injected the right amount of bravado into my argument.

At this a glimmer of light appeared briefly in Sher Khan's grey eyes and I wondered if perhaps he had a greater command of English than he was prepared to let on. He launched himself into a monologue of Farsi.

'Hajii Sher Khan is seventy-four years old,' Kerim said. 'The Shuravi have offered a reward of one hundred and fifty thousand rupees for his capture, dead or alive. He says they will not succeed while he has Allah and the holy Qoran on his side. He thinks perhaps that for you both to have got this far you also have Allah on your side. Sher Khan will therefore take you to the Panjsher to meet Massoud.'

Like the fairy godmother telling Cinders she shall go to the ball.

Following which we even had the arrival of one of the ugly stepsisters. Well, sort of.

There was a commotion outside. The door opened to admit two of Sher Khan's Mujehadeen. They were certainly excited about something. You could tell by the way they were speaking rapidly to their commander. Sher Khan's hooded eyes flickered briefly as he digested the news. I hadn't a clue what was going on but next to me Kerim, who was listening intently, sat bolt upright as if he'd been charged with a sudden and violent jolt of electricity.

Sher Khan rose swiftly to his feet like a bat flexing its wings, his lieutenants following suit. Kerim pushed past me at a run. I soon saw what had galvanized him into action.

A small knot of armed men were waiting outside. A Mujehadeen patrol.

As Sher Khan appeared in the open doorway the guerillas fell silent and, like a well choreographed team of formation dancers, moved apart.

The man squatting on the ground was in a sorry state indeed. His clothing was torn and dirt encrusted. His right arm was hanging loose. The area of shirt over his right shoulder and upper sleeve was heavily bloodstained. His narrow chest was heaving as weakly as a sparrow's. He looked to be on the point of exhaustion, like an animal sorely run to ground. Eyes, sunken and listless, embedded in a face as drawn and as tired as that of a road runner at the end of a hard race. It was a mutilated face, too, and one that was familiar to us. Beside me, Nicole Bonnard gasped in recognition.

An old adversary.

Sikander Habib. With a face as sour as a dollop of mortal sin.

And yet, despite his predicament, I found myself trying hard not to laugh. Not at his pinched and woebegone expression so much as the fact that he had more chains wrapped around him than Marley's ghost. One thing was for sure. Sikander Habib wasn't going anywhere.

Kerim's breath whistled through his teeth as he withdrew the knife from his belt. His thumb scraped across the blade and Sikander's nostrils twitched as if he could smell the hate that was radiating from his former captive. Kerim stepped forward with a jackal-like snarl.

Only to be restrained by a sharp command from Sher Khan. At first I thought Kerim was going to let his emotions get the better of him but he did sheath the knife. His hackles, however, remained well and truly raised. I could feel the desire for vengeance coming off him like a heat wave.

The young Mujehad in charge of the patrol was looking particularly chuffed with himself. He launched into what I presumed was an explanation of how Sikander had fallen into their hands.

Jamil was standing at my shoulder. He gave me the lowdown.

Sikander had, quite literally, walked into the guerillas. The Mujehadeen had been heading back to base after a night-time sortie to reconnoitre a recently established communist post a couple of valleys away to the west, when this wounded man had blundered into their midst. At first the guerillas had thought Sikander was one of the local militia come to defect and then somebody recognized

191

him as being that wall-eyed son of a diseased whore who, three months previous, had been suspected of trading in a Mujehadeen arms cache to a representative of the Khad for a fistful of rupees and a new Kalashnikov rifle. Sikander had been too weary to put up much of a defence. Added to which he still had a bullet embedded in his right shoulder and was, quite obviously, suffering a great deal of pain and discomfort. A fact which had, no doubt, pleased the members of the Mujehadeen patrol no end as they made their way back to their camp at Jebel Kut, dragging Sikander Habib behind them like an unwholesome afterthought.

I suddenly noticed that Sikander's feet were bare and covered in blood. And he was having difficulty sitting comfortably.

'What's wrong with his feet?' I asked Jamil.

He said grimly, 'They have cut the soles to prevent him running away. His knee, too, has been broken.'

'Jesus!' I breathed. These guys made Torquemada look like an altar boy.

Nicole sucked in her cheeks.

As if to emphasize his utter contempt and loathing for the offender, the Mujehad stepped back and clipped Sikander around the ear with the back of his hand. This brought forth gales of high-pitched, almost girlish laughter from the assembled guerillas, who all tried to get in on the act. One of them took off a sandal and began to thrash the bandit about the neck and shoulders. Sikander took the punishment in silence. I found this mute acceptance of his fate rather unsettling.

I asked Jamil what was to become of the prisoner.

'There will be a trial,' Jamil said matter-of-factly.

Sher Khan and his council went into a huddle. Eventually Sher Khan emerged with the group decision. Jamil's confident surmise had been proved correct. Sikander was

192

to be placed on trial. Which would begin with the summoning of the judge.

They sure as hell weren't wasting any time.

The courtroom was the open air. Several rugs were laid out on the grass under the trees and on these the tribunal took their seats. Nicole and I, as outsiders, were accommodated off to the side. Sikander, still shackled, sat, head bowed, awaiting his fate.

Then the judge arrived.

I say judge. In fact Judge Mohammed Akbar Ghafoor looked more like someone who sold carpets for a living. He was a small, beetle-browed individual, aged about fifty, with petulant lips and a black beard that hung to his breast bone. He was dressed in a grey shirt, matching pantaloons, and a pair of plastic sandals. Not very impressive, in my opinion. But then I'd hardly expected scarlet robes and a wig.

Again Jamil filled me in.

Mohammed Akbar Ghafoor had been chief judge of the Jebel Kut region for the past seven years, ever since the Russian invasion. In that time he appeared to have had his work cut out dispensing summary justice to the infidels. He'd had the dubious distinction of ordering the execution of some six thousand prisoners and the chopping off of over one thousand hands. Even allowing for an exaggeration on Jamil's part I felt this was going some. At that rate the Mujehadeen would soon run out of able-bodied recruits.

'The sentences must be passed according to Islamic law,' Jamil continued, 'upon instruction of the leaders in Peshawar.'

The methods currently favoured were shooting, stoning, and the ritual slitting of the throat. All pretty effective in their own way, I conceded.

193

Based on the judge's track record I didn't rate Sikander's chances of a reprieve as being very high. At which point I couldn't help noticing another man sitting at the judge's right shoulder. Not young but not old, either. Thoughtful – perhaps morose would have described him better – looking as if he had a great weight on his mind. Overtly, not appearing to be contributing very much to the proceedings but plainly anxious to know the final outcome. While the judge was embarking on his opening address to the court I asked Jamil who the man was.

'That,' Jamil said, 'is Toorak, the head executioner.'

I took a closer look. Now identified, Toorak immediately assumed the look of someone who'd have been at home performing the ritual killing in a kosher slaughter house. I began to feel distinctly queasy.

After that I wouldn't have said the trial was a travesty so much as a foregone conclusion. Although, looking at it from the Mujehadeen's point of view, there was little doubt that Sikander was as guilty as they come. Frankly, it was a wonder that he had survived this long. In the end, of course, it was undoubtedly Kerim's testimony that finally did for him.

I think it was the mention of the bandit's mauling of Nicole that tipped the scales. Jamil had kept up a running commentary for our benefit and so it was clear to me why, when Kerim was called to give evidence based on our capture by Sikander and his basmachis, the members of the tribunal began to mutter darkly among themselves.

This was because most of the council were Pathans and the Pathans have a strict moral code regarding women. Put simply it's a matter of hands off to all except the woman's husband. The molestation of Pathan women is, therefore, virtually unknown. So it's a crime that has its own particular emphasis within the sacrosanct constraints of Pushtunwali. They call it tor. The infringement of female chastity. It's punishable by death and there's no precedent for commutation of sentence.

So the verdict was beyond doubt.

They hauled Sikander to his feet. The pain from his broken knee, not to mention his other wounds, must have been agonizing but he didn't cry out. He stood, crippled, swaying slightly as the chains shifted about him, his eyes half closed as if he was on the edge of a self-induced trance. To all intents and purposes he seemed to have lost interest in the proceedings. His stoicism was unnerving, but somehow predictable. For if ever there was one thing I'd learnt about the Afghans, it was that none of them feared mortality. Every man's fate hung upon the divine will of God.

Inshallah.

They led him away. I asked Jamil where to.

'His death,' Jamil replied succinctly. 'Usually he would be taken to another place, somewhere outside the boundaries of Jebel Kut, so a conflict would not arise with any members of his own tribe who may be in the camp.'

'How will it be done?'

'I do not know. That has to be decided by the jirga.' Jamil shrugged. 'Sikander Habib has committed many crimes against the Mujehadeen and by threatening Doctor Bonnard he has brought dishonour upon his tribe.' Jamil's dark expressive eyes flashed. 'I think this time it will be something special.'

Watching Sikander being marched away, I pondered upon Jamil's words. I remembered the Russian that Kerim and his men had left at Dar Garlak, as a warning. It could be that the method of Sikander's execution would be special. But would it be quick?

Chapter Twelve

It was close to kick off.

Or whatever they called the opening move in Buzkashi. There was an atmosphere of barely suppressed excitement around the field. The Melbourne Cup was never like this.

Out of the three hundred or so guerilla fighters in Jebel Kut, about a third made up the number of contestants in the game. It wasn't through desire for non-participation, but a lack of mounts that prevented the remainder from taking part. They had to make do with the role of spectator.

Nicole and I had grandstand seat, alongside Sher Khan and the members of the jirga. Despite our prime position, however, I confess that I was also keeping a weather eye on the horizon for signs of aerial intrusion. Jamil had told me that a couple of years previously a game in Bamian province had been straffed by Soviet gunships. There had been many human casualties and forty horses had to be destroyed. I didn't relish the idea of being caught out in the open like that.

But no one would attack Jebel Kut, so Jamil had assured me. The anti-aircraft guns would see to that. Not entirely convinced, I continued to scan the nearby peaks.

Nicole leaned across and whispered in my ear. 'Where's Kerim?'

I took a look around. 'I don't know.' Which worried me a little. I hadn't seen him for a while. There was a lot of anger in that young man. I hoped he wasn't engaged in some rash enterprise.

A ragged cheer went up. I followed the sound. A lone horseman had ridden out on to the field.

The horse was a magnificent black stallion. Even though I generally plead ignorance when it comes to horseflesh there was no disguising the quality of the animal. It had the appearance of being sculpted from a piece of the finest jet. The rider was Jamil.

He had the look of a man who'd been born in the saddle. In his dark robes and seated on his war horse he seemed to be an extension of the animal. His appearance was a signal for the rest of the game's contestants to take the pitch. They cantered on to the meadow in ragged formation. Not all the horses matched the bloodline of Jamil's steed. The majority of them lacked the stallion's Arab lines but for the most part they were sturdy-looking beasts, at first sight built more for stamina than speed but their stocky frames were deceptive. They could turn on a sixpence and accelerate like a drag racer from a standing start. And they were being handled by experts.

Sher Khan rose from his seat to acknowledge the salutes of the riders. It was time to bring on the goat's carcass.

From the corner of my eye I saw movement to the far right of the field. Another rider, on a grey horse, galloping.

'It's Kerim!' Nicole cried.

Hanging from the pommel of Kerim's sheepskin-covered saddle was the decapitated body of a goat, the black skin sown up like a badly stitched mail bag from a prison workshop. It was hanging against his horse's flank as he spurred the animal towards the centre of the field. The carcass was bigger than I'd expected, bulky, with legs flopping, almost touching the ground. Kerim was supporting it with one hand, his other was guiding the horse.

Kerim dropped the carcass of the goat on to the pitch. Then he trotted to join the rest of the riders.

Sher Khan gave the contestants time to settle their mounts then he swept his hand down in a broad stroke and the game commenced.

There was a wild yell from the spectators as the horsemen surged towards the centre of the field where the goat skin had been dropped.

And the carcass moved.

Nicole saw it first. She gasped with shock. Her fingers clutched at my wrist, digging in tightly. My stomach turned over. No, I thought. It couldn't have been. Hallucination, nothing more. A trick of the eyes. A breeze skimming the field, ruffling the skin, that was all.

It moved again.

Like kittens in a sack on their way to a drowning.

I knew, then, the method of execution, how Sikander was to meet his death. Enfolded in a goat skin, as helpless as a chicken on a spit.

Then he was gone from view, lost under the pounding hooves as, like the cavalry of two opposing armies, the players clashed with a jangle of bridles and cries of inducement from the crowd. In the midst of the mêlée several horses reared violently, hooves boxing the air above the withers of their opponenets. They were brought under control by the knees and whips of their riders who then jostled and bullied their way into the scrimmage in an attempt to pick the goat skin and its grim contents from the ground.

Suddenly there was a scramble in the centre of the pack and a rider broke free. Jamil. He was hanging on to what looked to be one of the goat's hind legs and trying to propel himself towards open ground where he could get up enough speed to carry him around to the goal.

A roar from the edge of the field indicated that he had supporters who were anxious for him to succeed.

I couldn't quite make out how they'd trussed Sikander

up. Then I recalled that they'd broken his knee to prevent him escaping. Maybe that's how they'd done it. A fracture here and there to make his limbs more flexible; maybe dislocated his shoulders out of their sockets and tucked his ankles up behind his knees, then lashed his elbows together and connected ankles to wrists. That way he'd be squeezed into the goatskin like a mental patient in a straitjacket. It was a dreadful form of torture.

Even as the full horror of the scene struck me Jamil was hemmed in by a dozen other horsemen, all trying to reach over and wrestle the carcass from his grasp. Horses snorted and whinnied as hooves cracked indiscriminately against shin bone and flank. Jamil was almost hauled out of the saddle as someone tried to drag the skin away from him. Then he lost his grip and the struggle was renewed as a new player took possession. The spectacle was beginning to resemble some colossal equinal rugby match.

Part of the goat skin had come loose. In the confusion of the contest Sikander Habib was beginning to emerge from the bizarre wrapping like a deformed moth from a chrysalis. I could see that both his elbows had indeed been forced up towards his shoulder blades. They looked like plucked chicken wings. Impossible to tell if he was conscious. I hoped for his own sake that he was not.

There was a sudden surge of horsemen towards the edge of the pitch and a flurry of driving hooves as a dozen riders crashed into one another in a wild and desperate attempt to usurp the horseman holding the remanants of the skin. The crowd bayed like a pack of hounds loosed after a fox.

Nicole sprang to her feet. Her face was ashen. Trembling, fists clenched, she rounded on me. 'Stop them, Crow! For God's sake, stop them! Do something! This is inhuman!' Her face said it all; anger, pain, fear.

I pulled her down fast. 'No, love,' I said. 'It's justice. It might not be our version. But it is theirs.' I kept a tight rein on her wrist. She squirmed to pull away. I held on. 'Dammit, I don't like it any more than you do. Now, for Christ's sake, shut the hell up. Or better still, take a walk. By the look of things, this won't be going on for much longer.'

Her eyes blazed. She shook her arm free.

'You bastard!' she hissed.

Two horses collided in the excitement. The air was filled with heaving bodies and thrashing legs. Clods of mud flew through the air, splattering the front row of spectators. A horse screamed in pain. There was a crack, like the sound of a dead branch snapping. Somebody shrieked loudly. Or it could have been my imagination. It was difficult to hear anything clearly above the sound of the tumbling mounts and riders. The ground rippled with the aftershock.

Okay, so it was inhuman, as she'd said. But I couldn't help thinking about where we might have been if Sikander had had his way, Nicole, Kerim and I would, in all probability, have been contemplating the inside of a KGB interrogation cell by now. Or worse. And I did have the Crow family motto to live up to. To wit: do unto others before they get a chance to do unto you. In short, therefore, and in my book, Sikander, having failed in his effort to do us unto, had got all that his black heart deserved. And I for one had neither the time nor the inclination to grieve over his punishment, awesome though it had proved to be. And if Nicole Bonnard thought for one moment that I was about to stand up as the lone voice of reason in the middle of three hundred riotous Afghan guerillas she had another think coming. I may be prone to bouts of whimsy and rash judgement but I'm not a complete bloody idiot.

As she turned her face away there came another tumultuous clash. It was like the chariot race in *Ben Hur*, where the two main protagonists were battling it out to the death. Two horsemen, neck and neck; between them, Sikander. They were holding the body by the elbows. Sikander's lower half was dragging along the ground, scuffing up dust and horse shit.

One of the riders was Kerim. He was leaning back in his saddle, guiding the grey with his knees as he held on fast to Sikander's arm. The two riders thundered past. What looked like a bloodied piece of meat hanging between them. They broke apart and I'll swear to God that I heard the terrible rending sound as Sikander was literally torn asunder. The onlookers shrieked joyfully and something dropped to the ground; the remnants of the goat skin. It was churned underfoot by the next ruck of horsemen.

I turned away, sickened, but by then Nicole had gone, unable to endure the spectacle any longer. I sensed Sher Khan looking at me. Our eyes met and in that fleeting moment I felt the chill of his gaze. There was a force radiating from him. It was as if I had, at last, caught a glimpse of the man's true character. The old lion, the head of the pride, the patriarch guarding his family as they gorged themselves on a fresh kill. The look that said, this was his domain, we were the trespassers, we stood by his laws, his words, his will.

Behind me, Kerim had succeeded in carrying his grisly trophy to the goal line. The crowd was ecstatic. A few of the Mujehadeen began to fire their rifles into the air.

I got up and made my way through the hubbub, looking for Nicole. I felt sated, strung out. Not high but guilty at having been unable or, perhaps nearer the truth, unwilling to tear myself away from the grim sport. I'd often wondered what it was that could transform a crowd into a mob in a matter of seconds. Now I was close to knowing. Blood lust. Frightening in itself but not half as disturbing as the realization that it's in us all, buried deep, ticking away like a time bomb in a vault, protected within our subconscious, by reason, conscience, call it what you will, biding its time, like a demon awaiting the incantation that will summon it from its lair.

I found her under the trees, tending some of the riders. A number of whom had come a cropper during the game. There were multiple cuts and bruises, a couple of strains, and one broken arm, sustained during one of the more serious collisions between players. A lot of good-natured banter was being knocked back and forth as the tactics of the game were disected.

My reward for tracking her down was a stony glance. It was a good thing looks couldn't kill. I'd have been six feet under otherwise.

'It is over then, the game?' she said.

I nodded. I didn't think it prudent to tell her they were still picking up pieces of Sikander from around the pitch, however. 'You okay?' I asked.

She finished knotting the ends of the sling that she'd fashioned to support her patient's broken arm. The Muje- had toddled off. After twenty yards or so he stopped to remove the sling, wound it around his neck as a bandana, and went off to practise grenade tossing. I wondered if she'd noticed. At least she'd got some of her colour back. She began to fuss over the next man, testing him for cracked ribs. The guerilla suffered the examination in silence, but winced a couple of times as her gentle fingers roved over sore and tender places.

'It was barbaric!' she cried hotly over her shoulder. 'They behaved like wild animals, like wolves fighting over a stray lamb. How could you sit there and watch it?'

'Probably because I was outnumbered,' I replied. 'What the hell did you expect me to do, for Christ's sake? Throw myself over his body?'

202

'You could have spoken with Sher Khan!'

'Oh, yeah? And said what, exactly? You can't do that, mate. It's against the Geneva Convention. You seriously expected that my saying something would have made a difference? Come on, Doctor. You've lived among these people. You know them a darn sight better than I do. D'you think it would have done any good?'

She stopped what she was doing, stared at me hard, knowing in her heart what she knew to be the truth, fully aware that there was only one answer she could possibly give.

'No,' she said, softly. 'No good at all.'

I spread my hands. 'Well, then . . .'

But we never had a chance to take it further because at that moment Jamil arrived on the scene and told me that his father wanted to see me.

I looked at Nicole, tried to read something in her grey-green eyes. But all I saw was a light in them, burning deeply; no hidden messages.

'I'll catch you later,' I said.

She nodded wordlessly and went back to her patient. I stared at her slim back for a second or two then Jamil and I walked over to Sher Khan's billet.

They were all there. Sher Khan, the members of the jirga, and Kerim. Obviously it was a council of war. They were seated in a circle. Before them on the floor was a large ordnance survey map. There was Cyrillic writing around the edges of the sheet, indicating it was Russian in origin. Jamil told me they'd obtained it from a defecting Afghan Army officer. The edges of the map were held down at the four corners by hurricane lamps. The faces of the men in the room were partly illuminated and partly in shadow. The scene had the texture of a Breughel painting.

Kerim cleared a space next to him and I sat down.

'Sher Khan is making plans for the march to the Panjsher,' Kerim explained in a whisper.

He fell silent as Sher Khan pointed to various positions on the map and addressed his men.

'Sher Khan intends for us to head across to the Darra Valley and then cut up to Shawa,' Kerim said. 'There we will deliver the weapons and men to Massoud.'

How long will it take?' I asked.

'Not long, perhaps a day and a half's march. It is not far in distance but the Russians will be quite active in the area.'

Great, I thought. 'And that's the only way we can go?'

'It is the shortest and quickest route.'

My eyes drifted back to the map. Sher Khan was stabbing a point on the grid. I detected a disquiet among the commanders. Sher Khan appeared suddenly very solemn. It was as if he was inviting suggestions from the floor. I cocked an eyebrow at Kerim.

'There is one problem,' Kerim admitted. He pointed to the map. 'The bridge across the Serang Gorge.'

In actual fact it wasn't the bridge so much as the Russian post that was guarding it.

The gorge was named after the river that flowed through it, a raging torrent that was an off-shoot from one of the northern reaches of the Kabul River. The bridge had been constructed in order to save travel time. It was effectively a short cut, lopping off what would have been at least a further two days' march in the journey to the Panjsher. Under normal circumstances the Mujehadeen would have taken the longer route but in this instance, with time being of the essence, they had no choice. Massoud needed the guns and the rockets urgently if he was to consolidate his position in the Panjsher.

Needless to say the Russians had seen the strategic importance of the bridge. Rather than destroy it, and thus remove a useful tool that their own troops could use, they'd decided to put a guard on it instead.

Kerim told me that the original bridge had been built years ago, he couldn't remember precisely when, but certainly before Sher Khan had been born, which damned near made it an antique. Then, it had consisted of little more than a couple of strands of knotted rope. Over the intervening decades, though, it had been added to and modified and strengthened, but by all accounts and by no stretch of the imagination, I gathered that it wasn't exactly in the Sydney Harbour league.

Anyway, the bridge was there and so too were the Russians. They'd sited their observation cum guard post in the remains of an old watch tower, rather like the one back in Mir Seraj. The watch tower was on the other side of the gorge and commanded a clear line of fire down the entire span of the bridge. Their armament consisted of a couple of heavy machine-gun emplacements along with a brace of 82mm mortars. These goodies were well dug in behind the watch tower's defences and would be virtually impossible to shift by frontal assault. And as the only approach path lay along the bridge itself, I could well understand the Mujehadeen's dilemma. Anyone making an attack over the bridge would be mown down before they'd got halfway across.

'What about shelling the place?' I suggested. 'You've got the hardware to do it in the panniers of some of those pack horses out there. Hell, with that Chinese BM-12 you've got you could pulverize the place out of existence.'

The BM-12 was a rocket launcher, a twelve-barrelled affair, a weapon that was a new addition to the Mujehadeen's fire power. I'd spotted the component parts distributed around Sher Khan's camp. Like our Stingers, it had been transported over the mountains. Something like that would reduce the Russian post to rubble in minutes.

Kerim shook his head. 'Alas, my friend, we would lose too much time. We would have to assemble and dismantle the launcher at the gorge itself. By the time we had set it up and commenced the attack we would have lost the element of surprise. The Shuravi would have time to call in reinforcements before we had the chance to dismantle it and resume our journey. Besides, it would be foolish to waste valuable ammunition on such an insignificant target. There are much more worthwhile objectives further north.'

He had a point, all right, but for an insignificant target the command post seemed to have become one very significant obstruction. There had to be a way of surmounting the problem.

'It's a pity you couldn't bomb the bloody place,' I muttered more to myself than to anyone else.

It was as if I'd said 'Open Sesame'.

Kerim and Jamil exchanged looks like a couple of artful dodgers. As if recent plans they had been cultivating had suddenly borne fruit. In fact they were looking extremely pleased with themselves. This was followed by an animated discussion between Jamil, Kerim, and Sher Khan. The latter began looking at me as though I'd suddenly sprouted wings.

Which, in retrospect, might have been considered appropriate, not to say moderately amusing, by those with a particularly deviant sense of humour.

And I started to get that feeling again.

Particularly when Sher Khan drew the rest of his council into the discussion and everybody began talking at once. While I sat there feeling as lonely as an empty grog bottle at an Irish wake. But only for a moment or two because it soon became clear to me that I was rapidly becoming the focus of attention. Rheumy eyes began to regard me speculatively. I plucked desperately at Kerim's sleeve. 'What the hell's going on?' I hissed.

Before he had a chance to reply Sher Khan hoisted himself to his feet and motioned me to do likewise. I creaked upright along with the rest of them.

Kerim said, 'Come, we show you.'

I didn't care for the way he was beginning to grin at me. He and Jamil both. Like happy spastics. Very offputting. Not to say, suspicious.

We all trooped outside.

It was still light although dusk was beginning to creep across the camp. The mountains had turned grey and cumbersome like sleeping giants. Fires had been lit. Food was being prepared. I could hear music too. Though maybe that's being a shade generous. It sounded more like someone beating a couple of twigs against an empty biscuit tin. Over by one of the fires some men were dancing, spinning like tops to the incessant and hypnotic rhythm of the drum.

Nicole was there too. By this time she'd finished dispensing medication and sympathy to the Buzkashi players. She spotted us emerging en masse and homed in, frowning.

'Where are you going?'

At a complete loss, I shrugged. 'Don't ask me, love. I'm only a bloody tourist. Maybe we're all off on a nature ramble.'

Sher Khan and his cronies were setting off across the grass like Moses leading the children of Israel. There didn't seem to be anything else to do except follow them. Well, it wasn't as if I had a pressing engagement anywhere else, right? A bewildered Nicole Bonnard fell into step alongside me and slipped an arm through mine. Another truce declared. I wondered how long this one would last.

I presumed the building we arrived at was a barn of

sorts, a storehouse where they stock-piled fodder for their animals and where they sheltered their flocks during the cold winter months. It was large, built out of stone, with huge wooden rafters over which a latticed roof supported long-dried sods of turf.

I wasn't given a lot of time to admire the architecture, however, before Kerim and Jamil were hustling me forward once again. They pushed me over to the big wooden doors.

Jamil said, 'You see, Mista. You get big surprise!'

I also get very pissed off, mate, I thought. I could tell they wanted me to open the doors.

They were heavy. In the end Kerim and Jamil had to give me a hand. Sher Khan and his entourage looked on expectantly. With a protesting creak from the hinges the doors swung back and the inside of the barn was revealed.

I must have stood there for several minutes trying to get over the shock. Around me everyone had fallen silent. They weren't looking at the contents of the storehouse, they were all concentrating on the stupefied expression on my face.

I found my voice eventually. It emerged from my gullet in a strangled croak.

'Sweet suffering Jesus!'

Of all the things I might have expected to be confronted with, this surely wasn't one of them.

Nicole, mystified by my reaction, crowded in to look over my shoulder. 'What is it?'

'Er . . .' I stared at the apparition before me. It was patently obvious what it was. And I still didn't believe it.

I said, 'What the hell does it look like? It's an aeroplane.'

Chapter Thirteen

Not just any old aeroplane either. An old two-seater bi-plane. A Westland Wapiti to be exact. Well, most of it was. I didn't spot that right off, of course. I was too busy trying to shift my brain out of neutral and into first gear.

Meanwhile, outside, Jamil and Kerim were bouncing around like a couple of lunatic schoolboys.

'Did I not tell you, Mista!' Jamil chortled gleefully. 'Some bloody surprise, yes?'

I felt a bit light headed. Maybe it was the altitude having its effect. 'Right,' I managed to say. 'Oh, abso-friggin'-lutely.'

I couldn't tear my gaze away from the damned thing. I was convinced that if I closed my eyes and opened them again the mirage would have vanished, like a pub in the desert. What in God's name was it doing here? Stuck halfway up a bloody mountain in the middle of nowhere. In a daze I stumbled up to it and reached out a hand. Solid. No dream. It was real.

The aeroplane sat there like some grinning genie recently sprung from a two thousand year old bottle.

Come on, Crow, engage brain. Think about it. I continued to stare stupidly at the aircraft, willing it to give me a clue.

Then I saw the RAF roundel. On the fuselage, below the rear cockpit. Red, white and blue. Faint but unmistakable. Deep down among my little grey cells, something stirred.

What I was seeing was impossible. That's all there was to it.

Or it should have been.

My knowledge was based almost exclusively on the sort of thumb-nail sketch you got on the back of cigarette cards, along the lines of your fifty favourite soccer stars and the flora and fauna of the South American rain forest. In short, a long way from encyclopaedic. What I could remember wouldn't have taxed the recall processes of a five year old.

From the little I could recollect I knew that they'd planned it originally as a replacement for the RAF's war-time bomber, the old DH9A. War-time, that is, as in The Great War, the one that should have been all over by Christmas. Using a number of de Havilland components in the design, the boffins at the Westland factory had come up with a variation on a theme. To wit: a fabric-covered bi-plane powered by a Bristol Jupiter air-cooled radial engine.

Westland had designated the Wapiti as a general-purpose aircraft and in that capacity it had, during its brief life span, served its purpose very well indeed; in various parts of the world, most of them pretty uninviting in both climate and terrain. South Africa, Canada, Australia, Saudi Arabia, Iraq and India. Some had even been sold to the Kwangsi government in China.

But Afghanistan?

Racked my brain on that one.

Remembered vaguely.

It was the sort of *Boys' Own* adventure stuff that we used to read about as kids. *The Eagle* and *Wizard* used to be full of it. Sagas of true British pluck in the face of impossible odds. There used to be a lot more crimson-shaded countries on maps of the world back then, of course.

It has been called the first airlift ever; the fore-runner of Berlin, Dacca and Saigon.

When had it been? 1930? Something like that. And Afghanistan was at war even in those days, in the form of an insurrection sparked by the Mullahs against the then monarch, King Amanullah or some such. Amanullah, recently returned from a grand tour of Europe, had been greatly impressed, apparently, with certain aspects of western culture, in particular the emancipation of women. So impressed, in fact, that he was determined to implement similar sweeping reforms in his own country. Which wasn't the wisest decision he'd ever made. He'd neglected to take into account just how much influence was wielded by his country's religious leaders. In their view the king was moving way beyond the constraints of their formidable and fundamental religion. Too fast, in fact, for his own good.

The unrest soon spread and it wasn't long before the whole country was engulfed in rebellion.

And caught slap bang in the middle was the British Legation in Kabul. There was only one logical way to evacuate the personnel. By air.

Some six hundred civilians of more than a dozen nationalities were eventually airlifted from the British cantonment. By the time it was over the RAF had flown over eighty missions between Kabul and Peshawar using a ragbag collection of aeroplanes: a Hinaidi and Vickers Victorias for the passengers, DH9As and a couple of Wapitis for escort duty.

Which brought us back to this little beauty. Surely to God this wasn't one of the survivors of the airlift? Having, by some supernatural force of happenstance, ended up here on this remote plateau like that squadron of old warbirds left behind by the aliens in Spielberg's *Close Encounters*. That possibility went way beyond the bounds of credibility. Simply not possible. But the damned thing was here, wasn't it?

I reached out again and ran my hands over the mottled fabric of the fuselage, half expecting it to crumble like dust under my fingers. But it didn't. On closer inspection I could see that there had been some modifications made. This aircraft wasn't a pedigree, not one of those original escorts. It was a hybrid.

The success of the Wapitis had encouraged further design developments and a Mark IIA version had been built. Wheras the Mark I had been an all-wooden version the Mark IIs were of an all-metal structure, a much stronger air frame entirely. Which is when the model went into general production to RAF contract. Which is how come I'd recognized the thing in the first place. Because a number of them had been allocated to the Royal Australian Air Force. They'd had one on display back at my old ground school. It hadn't actually flown. It'd just sat there, looking clean and bright and about as innocuous as a plastic model in a toy-shop window.

Later, they'd converted a lot of the Mark IIAs into Wallaces, given the higher powered Pegasus engine and enclosed cockpit. I couldn't see right away what sort of engine this one had on her. It was covered over. The cockpit on this one was still the open model, though, indicating it hadn't been part of a converted batch. Mighty chilly at these altitudes, I shouldn't wonder. In fact mighty chilly at any altitude, come to that. Variations of this little darling had made the first aeroplane flight over the summit of Everest. That must have been like sitting in an ice box for an hour or two. It was like tracing the lineage back to Icarus himself.

I shook my head in wonderment and turned back to Jamil. 'All right, you scheming buggers. Very clever, very amusing. And I give up. You want to tell me what the hell it's doing here?'

Jamil didn't know the full story. Neither did Kerim. It

212

had always been here, as much an integral part of the scenery as the mountains towering above it.

I'd heard tell that the RAF were still using Wapitis in their squadrons based in India right up to the outbreak of World War Two and Wallaces as late as '43. Maybe this was one of theirs. The roundels said as much, but the squadron logo, if there ever had been one, had long since faded.

The armament had been removed too. There should have been a fixed Vickers gun forward and a Lewis gun set up in the rear cockpit. Their absence wasn't exactly surprising, not among this lot of reprobates. The hardware had probably been taken off long long ago.

And talking of taken off . . .

I wondered when she'd last done that. Flown, I mean. Dear Lord, don't tell me she was airworthy as well! The bloody thing was older than I was, for crying out loud!

Although it certainly didn't look it. Even in the fading light of the late afternoon there was something about the machine that made me think I'd just entered some sort of time warp. Okay, she wasn't pristine, by any stretch of the imagination. But there was definitely something about her appearance . . .

We wheeled her out.

It wasn't easy. The simplest way to handle birds like this was rear first. They don't have a wheel at the back, just a skid, so the way to do it was rest the skid on a wooden bogey and pull her backwards. As she was facing outwards we had to lift her at the tail and push her out of the barn. I roped Sher Khan and his council in on this. She was pretty light, but a few of them were struggling by the time we had her in the open. Sher Khan himself hadn't put himself out. He'd stood on the sidelines, spouting encouragement. The rest of his crew perspired with quiet dignity.

She really was in remarkable condition, considering.

Here and there sections of the fabric had come adrift, revealing the metal framework underneath. There were some interesting patches on the fuselage and wings. I made a closer inspection. The patch material looked decidedly familiar. It was canvas.

Jamil chuckled. 'Red Cross tents very good material!'

Holy Christ!

There were toe holes below the front cockpit. I held my breath and climbed up. The cockpit was so cramped, it was like sitting in the side-car of a motor cycle. Basic gauge instrumentation, of course. Fuel, oil pressure, altimeter, clock, air speed indicator and the rest. All gauges in one piece. All needles static. Seat of the pants stuff, though, without doubt. The rear cockpit was even more stark. No seat as such; the gunner spent most of his time standing in the gun ring. There was a sort of tip-up flap arrangement down there, though. I supposed this was to enable him to rest his legs when he got tired. The two crewmen would have conversed through a rubber voice pipe affair, but I couldn't see any sign of it. Long since perished, I presumed.

It was like sitting in a time capsule.

Dead eerie.

I climbed back down. To a reception committee. The way they all crowded around, you'd have thought I'd just flown the Atlantic single handed.

I looked at them and then back at the aeroplane and then back at them again. 'You have got to be fucking joking!' I said.

And then I was immediately struck by a terrible sense of déja-vu, because that's exactly what I'd said to Yunis Khalis and his mate Habbani minutes before I'd taken them up on their job offer. And look where that had landed me.

No wonder Jamil and Kerim were looking so damned

pleased with themselves. No bloody wonder Kerim had insisted that I'd had to travel with his Mujehadeen. This wasn't just a happy coincidence or fate. The sly bastards had planned it all along. They had an aeroplane. All they needed was somebody to fly it.

To fly it?

Oh, my God! They didn't seriously expect for one moment that the damned thing could actually get off the ground? It was a collector's piece, f'r crying out loud! It belonged in a museum. You couldn't just roll it out of its hangar and soar away into the wide blue yonder. Christ! Even if it was the last one off the production line and had been regularly serviced and wrapped in a vacuum, it wouldn't fly. Not after all these years. It was ridiculous. Didn't they realize how ancient the bloody thing was?

'Do you people know how old this crate is?' I yelped. 'Christ! It's so far passed its sell-by date the bloody labels have fallen off! You're all bloody mad!'

'It is very old,' Kerim admitted freely. 'But it is indeed a very fine aeroplane.' He tapped the wing lovingly.

'Right,' I said, wondering how on earth he defined the word 'fine'. 'Now, concentrate on the "old" and watch my lips. There's more chance of you flying to the moon than there is of me, or anyone else for that matter, getting this heap airborne. Okay?'

I became aware of a vague droning over to my left. I realized it was Sher Khan. Kerim listened as the old man spoke then he turned back to me. 'Sher Khan says that you will use this aeroplane to bomb the Shuravi guard post at the bridge. Then we carry the guns to Massoud.'

They just weren't listening, were they? To me this was a clear indication that the guerilla chief was suffering from senile dementia brought on by the altitude and a passion for cups of sweet green tea.

I said, as patiently as I could manage, 'Tell Sher Khan

that, regretfully, this is not possible. This aeroplane is too old.'

Jamil cut in. 'But I am mechanic! I fix!'

Give me strength, I thought. I patted his shoulder. 'Not a chance, old son. Not in a month of Sundays.' I took a last wistful look at the aeroplane, now outlined like a dark swooping bird against the grey sky, and turned to walk away. I could feel a dozen pairs of eyes boring into the back of my neck.

'But, Mista!' Jamil tugged sharply at my sleeve. 'I fix, I tell you! I fix! I work for Bakhtar, you remember? Repair many aeroplanes! Also trucks, Leyland buses, Toyotas! I bloody good mechanic, my friend! See! See! I fix!'

Something in the urgency of his tone stopped me in my tracks. My blood suddenly ran cold as it dawned on me. When he said 'I fix' he hadn't meant he would fix, he'd meant he had fixed. I stared at him. I think my jaw dropped open at that point. As it had done at regular intervals during this expedition.

He had to be having me on. He just had to be. I walked slowly back to the aeroplane.

'Lights,' I said. 'Somebody bring us some lights.'

Jamil told me that the graves were concealed beyond the trees. Two of them. They had been there a long time, covered by tall blue clover in the summer and in the winter months by a blanket of heavy snow. Perhaps some sort of mechanical trouble had forced them down or perhaps they'd landed to avoid inclement weather coming down through the high passes. Whatever the reason they must have been miles off course at the time. No telling why that was. If they'd been part of the Indian Squadron they were way outside their patrol sector. Unless they were on some sort of clandestine mission. Could be they'd simply been delivering the aircraft, part of a consignment flown

216

in from the UK, and been separated from the rest of their unit during adverse visibility. (Were these aeroplanes even delivered to their Middle Eastern squadrons in that way? I'd had the impression that they had been transported by sea.) I hadn't a clue. And it seemed pointless to speculate.

Whatever the reason it must have been a frightening scenario for the pilot and his crewmen. Lost in the mountains in one of the most inhospitable places on earth. To all intents and purposes they might just as well have been dropped off the edge of the world.

Kerim thought it likely that the tribesmen in the vicinity would have tried to hold the plane and its crew for ransom. It wasn't inconceivable, therefore, that the crew had been killed trying to make a break for it, leaving their aircraft in the hands of their captors. The fact that the men had been provided with graves indicated that they had earned the respect of whoever had buried them. And maybe that's how it came to be that the aeroplane was still here, as a bizarre monument to the men who had flown her.

We'd removed the tarp by this time. The engine was revealed as a Jupiter, a nine-cylinder radial job, well tried and tested, a veritable aristocrat among aero engines.

Jamil couldn't remember the exact date when he'd decided to work on the plane. It had been a year or two since, not long after he'd joined the guerilla army. He told me that it had taken him months to break it down to its component parts. A painstaking task, considering he'd done it without referring to a manual of any kind. Naturally, the fuel had long since evaporated away, but the bright lad had acquired more by draining the tanks of a couple of Mi–8 transport helicopters downed by the Mujehadeen a few months previous. The gas was stored in a brace of large metal drums in one corner of the barn.

It wasn't the stripping down of course that had been the problem. It had been the putting back together again. One big three-dimensional jigsaw puzzle. Resulting in the smallest and, so far, totally grounded, non-operational air force in the world. In my own mind I couldn't help but think that the Mujehadeen would have been better off putting their trust in one of that nutty American dame's radio-controlled models.

'Where on earth did you get spare parts for the thing?' I asked when he'd given me the story. I'd suddenly been struck by a brief and quite priceless vision of the Mujehadeen caravans transporting the integral parts of the aeroplane across the mountain by packhorse, like the Chinese rocket launcher, with the entire machine being reassembled by Jamil like some advanced Meccano set.

He shrugged. 'Kabul, Peshawar, Kohat.' Then added with a grin, 'Also Lahore and Islamabad. Mista, anything is possible if you know the right people!'

That didn't come as any great surprise. Most eastern bazaars were pure treasure troves. They made Harrods' claim that you could purchase anything inside their hallowed premises look positively miserly. Spare parts for a fifty year old aeroplane were probably no more scarce than a box of Swan Vestas in a tobacconist's.

The stuff he couldn't buy or steal he'd traded for. With lapis lazuli as currency. The ultramarine-coloured stone was mined north of the Panjsher and transported through the mountains to Pakistan for sale on the international market, to be then cut and fashioned as jewellery. The trade was so healthy that Massoud taxed shipments of lapis lazuli that passed through his territory. This endeavour netted him much needed cash with which to buy guns and equipment for his guerilla army.

We'd rolled the aircraft back into its makeshift hangar. The interior of the barn was now illuminated by hissing hurricane lamps strung from the wooden beams. Jamil, Kerim and I were the only ones there. Sher Khan was off relaying last-minute orders to his cronies. Nicole had been called away to examine an old warrior blighted by stomach cramps. Since her arrival she'd been much in demand among the various hypochondriacs in the camp. An occupational hazard she'd accepted without complaint.

As Jamil tinkered with the engine, I sat in the cockpit and experimented with the controls. I jiggled the stick back and forth and watched, fascinated, as the ailerons and elevators moved hesitantly in their sockets. The rudder, too, was responsive but in need of some lubrication. I was still trying to come to terms with the fact that some parts of the aeroplane actually functioned. But did they really expect the thing to fly?

I said to Kerim, 'Y'know the only thing keeping this dodo together is faith, don't you?'

Kerim smiled. 'Ah, my friend! But can faith not move mountains?'

'Mountains maybe,' I said. 'But it's going to have its work cut out getting this fossil into the air. It won't be faith alone, mate. It'll need a bloody miracle!'

It would also be some sort of bloody miracle if I ever got myself out of this Disney-like escapade, I reflected with grim humour, as I huddled under the sheepskin rug on the charpoy in the tiny guest room at the back of the chai khana.

The three of us had abandoned our labours a couple of hours before. The aeroplane had languished in its hangar for so long already that another day or so wouldn't make a rupee's worth of difference. In any case, I for one was exhausted and anxious to partake of some sack time. It had been a long and gruelling day and, despite having crashed out earlier that same morning, I was still feeling the effects of altitude and the rigours of our forced march through the highlands. Of Nicole there had been no sign. Sensibly, she'd retired long before I'd fallen into my pit.

It was hardly surprising that my attempts to sleep soundly had met with scant success. My mind was still buzzing like a saw following the discovery of the aeroplane so I hadn't been able to relax at all. Being cold hadn't helped. Under my blanket I was fully dressed but it had turned bitter in the night and I didn't dare look at my watch for fear that I would still have an age to wait before the warmth of morning eased its way into my chilled bones. I was half considering carting myself and my bedding along the passage to the council room, where I knew the embers of the evening fire still smouldered. At least I was, until there came a tap on my door.

Followed by a groan from the hinges. By the time my eyes had accustomed themselves to the murk, I could see that my nocturnal visitor was Nicole.

'I'm so cold, Crow,' she said.

She looked it too. She had a blanket wrapped around her and I could see that she too was wearing trousers and jacket, but she was still hugging herself and shivering. She came in and closed the door. 'I couldn't sleep.'

I actually hesitated at that point, which shows how cold it must have been. Although only for a second, or thereabouts.

I lifted the corner of my rug. 'C'mon, then,' I said. 'Get in.'

She tiptoed over and with a sigh slid gratefully under the cover. Snuggling down next to me, she spread her rug on top of mine. Given the size of the bed there wasn't a whole lot of room to move about. Not that I was complaining, for, despite her plea, she felt warm and soft. She nestled into the crook of my arm. I could feel my temperature beginning to rise. And not just my temperature.

She knew.

It took several moments before she moved against me, cautiously at first and then with assurance, stretching her body along mine, like a cat. Her arms circled my chest. I could feel the pounding of her heart. Or it might have been mine. It was racing fast enough for two. She lifted her face and looked into my eyes for several long seconds.

Her voice was husky and urgent. 'Warm me, Crow,' she said.

So I did.

I think it was something we'd both expected would happen, given time. And, because of that, neither of us felt any of the inhibitions that could, oft times, accompany those initial tentative and tender moments of mutual exploration. What was taking place was a chemistry. It was a blending of emotion, a harmony. It was natural and right. And, above all, inevitable.

Warmed by anticipation we shed our clothes. Naked, her body was fine and sleek, her legs endless, her breasts firm and deceptively full for one so slender. Her nipples were hard beneath the tips of my fingers as I stroked her. She raised herself over me, reached down, took my firmness and guided me to her moist opening. She moaned softly as we came together, her lips covering mine, grey-green eyes closed; small animal cries of pleasure sounded deep at the back of her throat. She came very quickly.

Afterwards, we lay together, the perspiration turning cold on our skin as the heat from our bodies dissipated in the darkness. Her right leg lay across my thighs, enfolding me. Her head lay on my shoulder. It was as if we were moulded as one.

We existed in silence for a time as if floating in some strange and soothing dimension. Then she stirred.

'Will the aeroplane fly?' she asked.

'God knows,' I said. I wasn't entirely sure that I wanted it to, if the truth were known.

I could sense that she was looking up at me, as if seeking a more reassuring response.

'Okay,' I conceded. 'An outside chance. Maybe.'

She adjusted herself into a more comfortable position. 'And you will fly it for them?'

I said nothing.

'You're mad, Crow.' She raised herself on one elbow. The sheepskin slipped from one creamy shoulder. 'You'll kill yourself.'

That, I conceded also, was entirely possible. No, I thought immediately, amend that. Entirely probable, more like.

She turned away from me then. Pulled the corner of the rug over herself. At first I thought her movements were due to the fact that she was cold. But she wasn't shivering, she was crying. Which shook me a bit. So I reached for her. 'Hey, come on, Doc, it'll be a breeze.'

Zero effect. I'd have made a lousy insurance salesman. But perhaps it wasn't the likelihood of my imminent demise that had triggered this reaction, but something else.

'You want to talk about it?'

Maybe it concerned her brother, Alain. She hadn't referred to him all the time we'd been in the camp. I wondered if she'd gleaned any more information about his whereabouts from Sher Khan's guerillas.

She didn't answer. I cupped her shoulder and brought her around to face me. 'Nicole? What is it?'

I touched her face, felt a dampness from the tears that streaked her cheeks. Before I could speak, she put a finger to my lips.

Her gaze transfixed me.

'Please, Crow. Do not ask. I cannot tell you.'

I stared at her.

'Remember,' she said. 'No matter what happens . . .' Her voice trailed off.

The confusion must have shown clearly on my face for she clutched me, fiercely. 'Please, Crow. No recriminations, do not give me cause to regret tonight. We have something special, you and I. No one can take that away from us, no matter what the future may bring.' She buried her head on my chest once more. Her body trembled. 'Please, Crow,' she whispered in a still, small voice. 'Just hold me.'

I did as she asked. Gradually her trembling subsided as she drifted into an uneasy sleep. 'No matter what the future may bring,' she'd said. As I lay there with my arm around her shoulder I wondered if any of us even had a future to begin with.

Jamil had transferred the fuel into the Wapiti's tanks and once more the old bird had been rolled out of her hangar. In the bright morning sunshine, she seemed to have lost some of the dowdy plumage that had cloaked her the evening before. I was amazed at the lack of rust on her. Strange that.

I recalled a conversation I'd had with a doctor back in Peshawar about his time among the Mujehadeen camps tending the wounded. He'd said that following operations the patients had hardly suffered any post-operative infection. The doctor had put the reason down to the strong ultraviolet light in the mountains. I wondered if that had anything to do with it. The air was very thin and unpolluted this high up. Provided the aircraft had remained under shelter it couldn't have been exposed to too many rust-inducing conditions. For the Wapiti time had stood still. Maybe there was such a place as Shangri La after all. Tibet obviously didn't hold the monopoly to Hilton's mythical hideaway.

223

In fact the only things marring her outline were the dark and irregular patches of tent canvas that speckled her fuselage. Despite these blemishes, however, there was something strong and reassuring about her. She looked eager to stretch her wings.

I asked Jamil if he'd checked the ignition and plugs and was rewarded with a do-me-a-favour expression which I took to indicate the affirmative. That being the case, there was no putting off the moment any further. I climbed aboard.

There wasn't the remotest chance I was going to take off. I'd made that perfectly clear to everyone concerned. I mean it wasn't as if the engine would even fire for God's sake. But I felt obliged to humour them, of course. And if, by some miracle, the engine actually started? Well, erm . . . I was sure I'd think of something. Either way, I didn't see the point of trying to kill myself any sooner than was absolutely necessary.

I was wearing my leather windcheater. All I needed to complete my wardrobe was a flying helmet and white silk scarf. I adjusted myself in the seat and took a look around. I had an audience. Sher Khan was there. So, too, were Kerim and Nicole. In fact most of the camp looked as if it had turned out to watch the fun. I hoped they wouldn't be too disappointed when the whole thing ended in dismal failure. Well, they couldn't say that I hadn't warned them.

There were a couple of ways to start the engine, both of them strenuous. The Wapiti had starting handles. Which meant that some poor bugger had to perch on the lower wing and crank the blessed thing in the hope that the engine fired and he didn't tip backwards into the spinning prop. The prop was huge, more than fifteen feet long, so one man couldn't turn it on his own. This necessitated the formation of a small tug of war team. The team held on to a rope which was attached to a net-like contraption that was cupped around the tip of the lower blade. At the pilot's signal everyone pulled like mad and, hey presto, the prop turned and the engine fired. I couldn't see either of these options occurring, frankly. In fact, I knew for a fact one of them wouldn't. We hadn't been able to find the starting handles.

I hadn't a clue about the mixture. Like everything else it would have to be a case of trial and error. I guessed the fuel from the Russian helicopters would be richer than the original specifications. At least I'd managed to locate the priming pump, which was something in my favour. I looked out to starboard. Four Mujehadeen were standing there holding a length of rope with a loop dangling on the end of it. They looked about as convinced as I did that it was going to work. I nodded to Jamil and they looped the rope around the end of the propeller.

The throttle lever was housed under the cockpit coaming. I held it and raised an arm. The tug of war team braced themselves. A hush of expectation ran around the crowd.

I dropped my arm. 'Contact!'

No response whatsoever.

'For Christ's sake!' I yelled. 'Pull the sodding rope!'

The four guerillas heaved themselves backwards. Two of them fell over.

Nothing. Not a spark. Bugger all, in fact.

Much as I'd expected. Jamil yelled at his men to replace the starting rope. Everybody took up the strain once more. I primed the pump. Another hush.

Dropped my arm again. Same result. In the ensuing vacuum I heard Jamil swear violently. The prop was looped for the third attempt. This, I thought, was going to be a complete waste of time. I got ready with the throttle lever. Kerim yelled. The team jerked backwards.

Someone coughed.

225

Or something. I watched, mesmerized, as a faint tendril of blue smoke trailed over the upper wing and vanished against the azure sky.

Holy Christ!

'Again!' I bellowed at Jamil. 'Hurry, dammit!'

The team sprang in like demented jack-in-the-boxes. I closed my eyes. Come on, sweetheart. Come on!

The rope went taut, knuckles white.

'NOW!' I screamed.

The team flung itself against the rope.

And she fired. Swear to God, she did. Frantically, I slammed open the throttle. The engine gave a great hacking cough and then we were drowned in the throaty roar. The aeroplane shuddered and started to move forward. Which was when I discovered one of the Wapiti's weak points. It didn't have any brakes.

By some miracle, in the din, as I eased the throttle back, I managed to indicate to Jamil that some of his men should hang on to the wings to stop the momentum. That gave them time to drop a couple of logs in front of the wheels to act as chocks.

I sat there for what seemed like a lifetime, trying to take in the event. The rest of them were bouncing around like a troop of delinquent pogo-stick dancers. Even Nicole. Some of the Mujehadeen were firing their guns into the air, the sharp reports echoing around the plateau.

Dear God, I thought. Now what do I do? I took in the sea of bedlam about me.

Nothing else for it.

I steadied one hand on the stick, felt her straining like a dog on the leash. Poked around into my jacket, extracted my sun specs. Slipped them on. Took a long, deep breath. Saw Jamil staring at me with the intensity of a mongrel poised to go after a stick. Bellowed the immortal words.

'Chocks away!'

Went for it.

The main thought that shot through my mind was that I'd have to make sure that I kept her tail down. If I didn't the end of the enormous prop was liable to touch the ground and I'd be performing somersaults like an Olympic gymnast.

The throttle was open only a fraction yet we were jogging across the grass at a nice clip. There was hardly a breath of wind over the field. Given that, I wondered how much runway I'd need.

A fraction over three hundred yards, as it happened. She wallowed like a porpoise as I lifted her off and I suspected that, flown solo and free of the weight of a rear gunner, she very likely had a tendency to be nose heavy. Before taking her up I should have thought of adding some sort of ballast to simulate the weight of a second crewman. Too late now, though. So I spent a few interesting moments sorting that out and trying to calculate her stalling speed in the event I over compensated. Discovered it was around 60 mph. When I'd done that I began to get the true feel of her.

I didn't go mad.

Started out with a low circuit of the camp. Two hundred feet, speed around 80 mph. I swept over the crowd of upturned faces and waving hands. Hoping, as I did so, that no one would get carried away and loose off the magazine of his AK-47. The ignominy of being shot out of the sky by my own side wouldn't be something I'd live down in a hurry. My barnstorming passed off without a hitch. Confidence rising, I eased her up another two thousand feet.

Then I took her through her paces. Turns, glides, stalls. With the exception of the latter the engine droned on effortlessly with the monotony of a steady heartbeat.

She flew! She bloody flew!

Nothing short of miraculous. Jamil, I was now firmly convinced beyond any shadow of a doubt, was some sort of mechanical genius. I'd tell him when I got down.

At that height the sky was brilliant and clear with the mountains outlined as sharp as razor blades. The largest ones seemed startlingly close. The scenery was breathtaking, visibility astounding.

Or it was until the oil started coming at me. A snag with radial engines, I recalled. The stuff was spurting back along the fuselage from the rocker box on the top cylinder. It had started to obscure the windscreen in front of me. I felt some of it splash my cheek. A good thing I'd worn the glasses.

Time to take her down.

I slipped in over the ring of anti-aircraft guns and traversed the meadow at around 70 mph, with the tail trimmer wound back to give me forward pressure on the stick. She went in as steady as a rock. At 60 mph I eased the stick back gently. She landed a wee bit heavy, kept going, with the tail skid bouncing along like a skateboard on pebbles. Two hundred yards further on she stopped.

Turned off. The silence was deafening.

I was surrounded. Jamil virtually dragged me out of the cockpit. He pounded me on the back. 'You see, Mista! Now we have our own air force! We kill even more Shuravi! We pay them back some of their own medicine! We bomb them to fakking pieces and bits!'

It was the 'we' that got me. Seeing as I was the only daft bugger who could fly the bloody thing. Terrific, I thought wearily. Lumbered yourself again, Crow. Right?

Sher Khan led his men out at dusk. Thus the arms caravan would travel most of the way under cover of darkness, arriving at the Serang Gorge at dawn. Which was when they wanted me to fly in and drop my bombs.

228

Before they left, though, we had another council of war.

With Kerim and Jamil acting as interpreters, Sher Khan outlined his master plan.

We had the maps out again. As they were the product of Soviet military cartographers the previous owners had very kindly indicated the locations of their listening posts and garrisons. The post at the Serang Gorge had been circled in red. To assist me the Mujehadeen had also constructed a three-dimensional model of the gorge and its approaches out of mud and sand in a hollow below the veranda of the chai khana. Kerim was stepping over the main features like Gulliver in Lilliput. He had a long stick in his hand and was using it to point out notable features.

'Here is Jebel Kut,' he said, jabbing a flattened circle of mud with the point of his stick. 'And this is the route our caravans will take.' He indicated a runnel in the dust and transposed the information on the ordnance sheet. 'You see?'

I nodded.

He continued. 'We will travel up this valley.' The end of his pointer scuffed along the ground in a tight zigzag, which I took to indicate a steep incline across the valley slope. 'The Serang Gorge is here.' Kerim jabbed with the stick. The bridge across the gorge was represented by a small double line of pebbles, the fort by a large rock. 'We will arrive on the far side of the bridge one hour before dawn. The darkness will conceal us. At sun up, my friend, you will attack the Russian command post. When the Shuravi's guns are destroyed we will cross the bridge in safety and go on to join Massoud at his stronghold.'

It sounded dead easy, the way he said it. A piece of cake. Fly in, catch the buggers with their pants down, strafe them out of existence, fly back out again. Nothing to it, right?

I looked at the model then back at the map. Took note of the scale, calculated distance and flying time. Ten, maybe twelve minutes. A journey that, because of their numbers and the terrain, would take the Mujehadeen supply caravan most of the night. Nevertheless ten minutes would seem a lifetime in the Wapiti. They'd hear me coming from miles away. They'd have time to call up air support. I tried not to think about my chances if I ran into the patrol sector of a Russian gunship. Slim and no mistake. I'd stand about as much chance of outrunning the thing as would a three-legged mule of winning the Melbourne Cup. And I sure as hell couldn't outgun a Mi-24. I had only one advantage.

Surprise.

Nicole didn't look back. We'd said our goodbyes. She had clung to me for a long while. It had seemed to me that, for the second time, she was trying desperately to conceal her tears. Finally we broke apart. She kissed me, held her palm against my cheek. 'Take care, Crow.' She gave a wan smile. 'Remember, no matter what happens . . .' Abruptly she turned away. I watched her until the tail end of the caravan had disappeared out of sight. It felt as if a part of me had departed with her. Maybe it had.

Jamil was waiting for me up at the hangar. He was going to be my crewman, my rear gunner. And he looked chuffed to buggery about it, too. I couldn't imagine why.

I had wondered where they were going to get the bombs from. Silly of me. I needn't have worried. To the Mujehadeen bombs were no problem.

The Wapiti could carry a bomb load of up to 500 lbs. The Mujehadeen hadn't any bombs of their own so the logical solution was to improvise. I was going to drop mortar rounds, 60mm jobs. The aircraft had the facility to drop four missiles so Jamil had designed his own cluster bombs. Each little package contained two mortar rounds, taped together and fused for instantaneous detonation on impact. Linked as they were to the bomb release mechanism by an ingenious system of racks, wires and pulleys they looked a bit Heath Robinson-like hanging under the fuselage, like plums on bits of string, but they'd do the business, hopefully.

Normally the gunner would have doubled as bomb aimer. The bomb sight was situated below a sliding panel in the floor of the rear cockpit. The bomb aimer lay flat on the floor of his compartment, sited through the slit and gave instructions to the pilot. The pilot released the bombs by means of a lever down by his left knee. A real hit and miss affair, no pun intended.

Which was why I was going to do the aiming myself. Jamil was going along solely to watch my back. You only really required a bomb aimer for high and medium level bombing, from, say, 6,000 to 12,000 feet. Forget that. I was going in low and fast, probably less than one hundred feet above the target.

Which could prove interesting. At that height there had to be two viable scenarios. It either was going to be the greatest success for right against might since Gibson's lot punctured the Moehne dam or else the most spectacular airborne balls up since Arnhem.

It had also occurred to me that Jamil might just have been selected as my crewman for a reason other than defence. I had the sneaking suspicion that he might have been chosen to keep an eye on me.

Probably due to a crack I'd made earlier. After I'd asked them what would happen to the Wapiti if the raid was a success.

Blank looks from all concerned.

'All right,' I'd told them. 'I'll make a pact with you. I

take out the fort and you let me take the plane. I'll use her to make a run for the frontier.'

Huddled consultation this time. But they'd agreed. They didn't really have a choice. It was that or no deal. And then I'd pitched in with the joke. Along the lines of what was to stop me taking off and flying the Wapiti to Pakistan anyway.

To which Kerim had laughed and replied, 'Because, my friend, you are an honourable man.'

Yeah, well, I thought. Ahem. Quite.

Chapter Fourteen

Morning intruded like an inconsiderate guest. Much too soon.

It was still dark when Jamil came for me. Not that I needed rousing. I'd been awake for hours, attempting to stall the inevitable. Kerim might well have deemed me honourable but that hadn't meant that I'd experienced the sleep of the just.

Jamil had thoughtfully provided me with a sheepskin jacket. I slipped it on and followed him outside. We stumbled up to the barn. The mountains were etched against the grainy sky like a tinted lithograph. It was certainly cold and I could feel the dew soaking through the sides of my trainers as we coaxed the Wapiti out of her snug hangar. She emerged hesitantly into the morning like a bather about to take a dip in an ice-bound pond.

Time for the last-minute run-through. Jamil stripped off the engine cover and checked the plugs and ignition harness. I ran through the controls. Then we checked the armament.

We didn't have the Lewis gun, of course. To redress the balance Jamil had equipped himself with a brace of AK-47s. If we ran into trouble I could see he was going to have his work cut out.

But she was looking good, even down to her new logo. I didn't know how effective it would be, of course. There was no way of telling until we were off and running. I'd had the idea the previous night, when we'd been rigging the bomb. I'd been reminded of the preparations I'd made when getting the JetRanger ready and the discarded plan to disguise her registration. On the Wapiti it might not be such a bad notion. I'd asked Jamil if he had any paint. Like red, for instance. He hadn't. I suppose that would have been too much to expect, even amongst his odds and ends. So we had to improvise.

We sacrificed a goat. Jamil slit the animal's throat and hung the carcass over an empty cooking pot to drain the blood. Then we tried it out.

Close up it wouldn't have fooled anybody, but then we wouldn't be getting that close would we? Maybe it would give us an edge. That's all I asked. That's why I used the blood to daub the stars on either side of her fuselage and underneath her lower wings, bracketed by meaningless registration numbers. Faded red stars, five pointed, just like the ones on the sides of the Armeiskaya Aviatsiya's helicopter gunships. Well, okay, so it wasn't perfect, but every little helped, yes, no?

The darkness was slipping away. The sky was beginning to turn pink. We had CAVOK. Aviator-speak for ceiling and visibility okay. Sod's Law dictated we would have. I wasn't getting out of it that easily. Perish the thought.

It was time.

Jamil climbed aboard and I passed him the guns. He rested them down by his feet and gave me the thumbs-up sign.

I followed suit. Our tug of war team was standing by. Jamil had briefed them thoroughly. It took them only two tries to start us up.

She ran unevenly at first, missing a couple of beats, as did my heart, but settled down to a steady throb and I could feel her vibrating, anxious to be off. There was a breeze running across the field. I taxied her out and turned her into the wind.

This time the aeroplane was fully ladened. Our take-off was long. She lifted finally, sluggishly, held down by the drag caused by the load in our bomb racks and the weight of my crewman. I took us on a slow circuit of the field to check the engine temperature and pressure. All A-OK. Then I eased her up slowly, levelling out at three thousand feet.

I felt a tap on my shoulder. Twisted around. Jamil was having the time of his life. Standing in the rear cockpit, a huge grin splitting his face from ear to ear. Happy as Larry. Silly sod.

A ribbon of oil streaked across the windshield. I'd anticipated that happening and felt for the rag that I'd shoved down by the side of my seat. Finding it, I reached forward and wiped the glass clean.

The wind was light. The sun had not yet warmed the air sufficiently to cause turbulence. The old war horse was running as sweet as a nut.

We'd been in the air for six minutes when the gorge came into sight through the spinning arc of the prop. A deep dark slash in the terrain below us. I turned us fifteen degrees to port, banked and side slipped down. The hills and mountains towered above us. Below our wings deep fissures ran across the ground like claw marks. The largest of them was our objective. Kerim's directions, through use of the model and the Russian maps, had led me straight to it.

At that level the surrounding peaks blocked the sun. As we dived into the canyon it was like entering the bowels of hell, a fearful place, full of shadows and jagged outcrops. I went lower. We sank below the rim of the gorge. Behind me I sensed Jamil had gone quiet.

Eight minutes.

Nine minutes.

The rock formation around us was starting to cause some interesting updraughts. The struts and wires in the wings began to strum and pop like an orchestra tuning up. Far below us the river gleamed like molten silver.

Then I saw it. Dead ahead. Timber built. Spanning the abyss like a spider's web. At that distance it looked remarkably fragile. Its length didn't seem to be much longer than the wing span of the Wapiti.

Our speed was nudging 100mph. I gained altitude, saw the dark shadow along the wings and fuselage retreat as we lifted into the path of the sun now risen above the summits behind us. At the same time our target came into view.

I could see the Mujehadeen's problem immediately. The Russian post was situated on a flat-topped promontory overlooking the gorge. The ground between its walls and the bridge was totally devoid of cover. There wasn't a hope in hell that the guerillas could cross the bridge from their side and bypass the post without being seen. A classic Mexican stand off, it seemed.

The complex itself was exactly as described by Kerim in his briefing. A blockhouse, constructed in the shape of a square, wood-built watchtowers at each corner housing machine-gun positions. Above one of the towers an array of radio aerials. Behind me, I heard Jamil cocking the guns.

I couldn't see Sher Khan's caravan and I didn't strain myself looking. They'd be hidden on their side of the gorge, up among the rocks, eyes no doubt glued in my direction. They'd know when it was time to make their move.

I wondered what time the Russians sounded reveille. If we could hit them before they'd got their boots on, so much the better. And the sooner the better, too.

Now that I'd pinpointed our objective I lost height, taking us below the lip of the gorge once more. I wanted us on top of the post before they realized they were being attacked. Our one advantage lay in the fact that although the occupants of the post couldn't help but hear and see us coming the last thing they'd expect would to be on the receiving end of a bomb strike. To their knowledge the Mujehadeen didn't have air power. They'd see us and, despite not recognizing us, for a few short moments they'd see the red star emblem and assume it was one of their own aircraft, very likely a spotter plane. By the time they'd cottoned on it'd be too late. Well, maybe.

We'd find out soon enough.

The bridge loomed through the arc of the prop. The sides of the gorge shrank inwards until it seemed that the tips of the Wapiti's wings would scrape the rock face. I hadn't left much room; barely ten feet to spare on either side. I could almost feel my grey hairs multiplying at a rate of knots. As we passed under the slender wooden span I hauled back on the stick and we rose out of the gorge and into the sunshine like a phoenix arising from the ashes. The post was directly below us. By waiting until the last possible minute to show our colours fully, I hadn't allowed the post's occupants enough reaction time. I banked and took us around the perimeter of the walls to give them an opportunity to spot the markings on the fuselage. Then I waved and jiggled the wings. Nothing other than a friendly greeting to show we were all comrades together. A minor deviation in what would appear to be a routine reconnaisance sortie.

Someone was up and waving back. One of the gun crew in the tower. I waggled the wings again, took us out across the mountain slope. Gained height, and brought her round in a tight turn. I closed the throttle, banked over and we dived out of the sun.

As our speed built up I dropped my left hand down to the bomb release. The wind began to sing through the wires in the wings. The target grew like Topsy as we went in.

I was going for the radio antennae first. That way they wouldn't be able to call in assistance.

A screeching in my ear. Jamil, carried away. Howling like a loon.

Target coming up very fast. In the absence of a forward bomb sight I had bracketed the radio mast between the rocker boxes of the two top cylinders of the engine. I began to wish that I'd made some dummy runs over the camp at Jebel Kut. I'd have known what sort of accuracy I could have expected. Too late now, though, dammit.

The walls were coming up at me like an express train. Our speed was touching 120mph. We couldn't have been much more than seventy feet above the top of the gun tower, with the radio mast bisecting the rocker boxes, when I pulled the bomb release. I slammed my hand back to the throttle, opened the engine up and we barrelled out over the opposite wall of the post in a climbing turn.

I heard the explosion come from somewhere over my left shoulder and then Jamil began to yell wildly. I twisted around. Jamil was craning over the side of the fuselage, his fist raised in triumph. 'Allah O Akbar!' he roared.

There seemed to be a great deal of smoke and flame down there, along with a heap of confusion. We'd made what looked like a direct hit, more by luck than judgement, but the antennae had gone, that much was clear, along with part of the inner building, presumably the part that had housed the radio room. I could see men running around like termites disturbed in a nest. They hadn't known what had hit them. Strike one to the Mujehadeen, by Allah!

I knew we had to go in again quickly, while they were still reeling, before they had time to muster their forces into some sort of order. Kerim had told me that the bulk of personnel in the post was made up from a squad of Afghan militia, with a couple of regular army officers and one Soviet commander. I hoped that much was true. There was a wealth of difference between the type of reception we could expect from the ragbag troops that usually made up the militia and a detachment of Soviet infantry.

We went down out of the sun again. I was going for the gun tower this time. Smoke from the post was drifting up into the air. It beckoned us as if we were a moth being drawn towards a naked flame. Something struck the port wing. I saw a rent appear in the fabric. They were firing up at us now. Small arms fire only. They hadn't been able to elevate the guns in the tower. The last thing they'd expected was attack from the air. The Singapore Syndrome had found another victim.

We were slightly higher this time but I applied the same technique. Waited until we were almost on top of the target before tugging the release.

Bombs gone. As we swept around Jamil began to rake the post with his AK-47. Another detonation and part of an outer wall caved in as if toppled by an earthquake. From our lofty view it was like watching a slow motion film. The tower began to slant crookedly. A body cartwheeled down and the structure gave way like a tree falling on a hillside.

We came around for the third run and by this time they were ready for us. It was like flying down Duck Alley. There was still a lot of panic down in the post but someone had got his act together and was coordinating retaliation. Bullets were coming at us like rockets at Chinese New Year. Common sense, not to mention cold fear, was telling me to pull out of it but the Mujehadeen had yet to cross the gorge and they couldn't do it with the post's guns still operating. I had to risk one more try at silencing them.

And all I needed was for some hawk-eyed Afghan machine gunner to line up on the mortars left in our bomb racks and Jamil and I would be shrugging off our mortal coils faster than you could blink an eye. I was slamming the Wapiti from side to side in a vain attempt to avoid the incoming flak. Our attack was also hampered by the target slipping in and out of view through the pall of smoke that was hanging over it.

It was sheer panic more than anything that finally urged me to release the last two bomb loads. My world was filled with the roar of the big Jupiter engine, the crash of explosions and the harsh rattle of Jamil firing his AK-47 as I tilted the nose and let the mortars fall. In that final moment as the bombs left their racks I felt something slam into the underside of the fuselage. The Wapiti was actually lifted in mid air and a shockwave rippled the fabric beneath my feet. For a brief second I lost her. Then, almost as abruptly, she picked up and I hauled back on the stick, pulling her up and away. It was like grabbing the collar of a reluctant bull mastiff and dragging it out of a pit battle. It didn't want to go.

Someone else didn't want us to go either. We were hit again, starboard side this time. To my horror I watched the lower wing explode upwards, struts snapping like twigs in a gale. Gorbachev was supposed to have pulled out most of his anti-aircraft troops, for Christ's sake. Some bright spark had obviously neglected to pass the directive to the commander of the Serang military post. His boys were doing a pretty good job, considering.

Too damned good, in fact.

The last shot, lucky or not, removed a goodly section of engine casing. The next second my windscreen was full of oil and my ears full of the sound of screaming. Jamil had been hit.

The aeroplane began to die around me.

There are, basically, two options open to you when your aircraft starts to disintegrate. You either look for a soft place to put down in as near to one piece as you can manage, or else you bale out. Slight problem here, however. No parachutes. Even if there had been, I couldn't desert Jamil. I had no idea how badly he had been hit, either. Though by twisting in my cramped seat I could see he was in a bad way. He was slumped forward over the gun ring. The Kalashnikov he had been using had fallen out over the side. I tried yelling at him but got no response.

Down below us, there had been some response to our last bombing run. I could see small figures running across the bridge. Sher Khan's guerillas were attacking the post on foot. I saw the concentrated flash of grenade explosions. I had given them the edge. They were finishing the job, clearing the route for their arms caravan. Well, at least some good had come out of our efforts.

The engine began to cough and splutter in earnest, jolting me out of my observations. The starboard aileron seemed to be operating on faith alone. We were fast running out of time.

I dismissed the idea of heading back to Jebel Kut. We'd never have made it. I'd have to find somewhere closer, a lot closer. Took a look over the side. Nothing but rocks and more rocks, of every size and shape, all of them uninviting and lethal to injured aeroplanes. Then I saw the road.

Road?

Well, it wasn't exactly the Trans Australian Highway, in fact it was more of a footpath, but at that moment it was as welcome as a cold beer in a heat wave. And beggars couldn't be choosers. I began a gentle sinking right-hand turn. Then, as if on a given signal, the engine died.

Contrary to popular belief, when an engine stops the aeroplane to which it is attached does not immediately plunge out of the sky. It does it gradually, in a glide, providing it's in capable hands. And providing the rest of the aeroplane is in reasonably good condition. The rest of the Wapiti wasn't, however. It looked precisely what it should have looked like having come through a small war. A mess.

By this time, though, I'd taken us considerably lower. We were floating some three hundred feet or so above the topsoil, about as graceful as a ruptured duck. And she was dropping fast. Unlike my pulse rate which was galloping away like a runaway train. Also I seemed to have lost my ability to generate saliva.

I was having my work cut out to keep her nose up. The Wapiti, on the other hand, was trying its damnedest to go in head first. And to make matters considerably worse I'd lost the bloody road.

We went in over the tops of the trees in eerie silence. Only not quite silence for I could actually hear wires grinding and twanging as I manipulated the control surfaces to try and keep us level. Most disconcerting.

I was looking frantically for flat ground. Roads, river beds, table tops, anything. Then there was an abrupt break in the treeline and I saw it. A clearing, not much more than the width of a fire break, about one hundred yards long which was miles shorter than the minimum length recommended for emergency landings. Would she stop in that distance? She'd bloody well have to.

I was fighting to keep her nose up. Our speed was only about 65 but it seemed a hell of a lot faster. I had the stick so far back into my stomach it felt as though my ribs were cracking.

As landings go, it wasn't perfect by any means. Call it one out of ten for artistic interpretation. She went in like a flying bathtub. And kept right on going. And with no brakes there wasn't a damned thing I could do about it. The fact that we didn't have any undercarriage, though, was probably an asset because the bottom of the fuselage slamming along the ground helped slow us down. It also meant we stood less of a chance of being upended nose first when the prop dug in. Height off the ground in relation to the force exerted on the end of the propeller, or some such theory. It must have been that jolt I'd felt after our last run over the post that had removed the landing gear. At the time I'd had no way of checking what damage had been done. Under normal circumstances, in a situation like that, the rear gunner would have got down and taken a look-see through the slide in the bottom of the fuselage. Jamil, having been wounded by person or persons unknown, was in no condition to assist. He was well out of it. Good thing too. He hadn't been able to see the complete cock-up I'd made of our touchdown.

Anyway, the little that remained of our undercarriage was sheered away by the force of the Wapiti hitting the deck. Then we were bouncing along like a pebble skimming the top of a pond, careering over the rocks with all the grace of a fat man performing a belly flop. The noise was a cross between ten Cadillacs going through a car press and Godzilla having one of his frequent domestic tiffs with King Kong. Just one long, gut-wrenching, ear-splitting scream of metal being pulverized. Or the screaming could have been me.

She started to slide away then, like a tobaggan on the Cresta Run, heading for the trees. I was hanging on to the stick like grim death. You're gonna die, Crow, I thought. There was a colossal wrench as the port wing was scythed away and for one split second we were airborne again.

There was barely time for the sensation to register before we hit terra firma once more with a resounding crash that drove the breath from my body and the side of the cockpit into my ribs. Then we met the trees coming the other way. Somewhere in the belt of undergrowth we came to a halt. Violently. What was left of the wings crumpled up like a concertina, the windscreen, blackened with oil, starred and cracked like an eggshell, and I was thrown forward like a stone from a ballista. My forehead came up against something hard and unyielding and I felt the warm stickiness of blood break out across my scalp.

Funny, the thoughts that strike you in time of crisis. Nothing like a joke to relieve the stress of pain. Like what was the last thing to go through the gnat's mind when it was hit by the car windscreen? Answer: Its arsehole. I knew how the gnat felt. I couldn't understand why that should strike me as being especially hysterical, but it did. Hanging there in the middle of all that tortured metal my only coherent thought was that if I was going to die I might just as well die laughing. I was still trying to rationalize as to why I should have been blessed with such a morbid sense of humour when the mist began to close in around me.

I began to struggle. Suddenly I didn't want to die. Not just yet. I had things to do, places to go, people to see. It was so unfair, dammit. And I hadn't even spent any of the bloody money yet, f'r Christ's sake . . .

In a way, the darkness was a relief.

Chapter Fifteen

I was drowning. Sort of. It was as if I was under water, not sinking but suspended in some kind of weird limbo. I tried to move but couldn't. My arms and legs wouldn't obey my brain commands. Above me, through the turquoise luminescence, I could see strange dark amorphous blobs drifting in and out of view. Boats, I thought. Then I realized they were faces, out of focus, floating like ethereal spirits on the edge of some dark and murky underworld. My head was splitting. Did drowning people suffer headaches? I wondered.

Then I started to levitate. Moving up out of the darkness into the light. There was somebody up there trying to help me. I could sense hands reaching out to guide me to safety. Someone was calling my name, softly. They were a long way off but drawing closer all the time. It was like following a source of light down a long tunnel. I began to home in.

'Crow?' A woman's voice, gentle, like a caress. 'Crow?'

A face swam into view. Grey-green eyes, framed by auburn hair.

Nicole.

'Thank God,' she whispered. She laid her palm against my cheek. It felt cool, like a healing balm.

'Jesus,' I said through a mouthful of bird grit. 'My head hurts.'

I began to focus. I was lying on a straw mattress. The room was simple. Four stone walls, a few cushions, and a couple of faded rugs covered the floor.

'Where the hell am I?' Hardly the most original question

in the world, I'll admit. I tried to raise myself. It was something of an effort.

'Do Ab,' Nicole said. 'A village. At the head of the Darra Valley. We have reached the Panjsher, Crow. We've made it.'

I closed my eyes, the sunshine lancing in through the tiny window was too damned bright. My head felt as if it was going to drop off and roll across the floor. To prevent that happening I sank back on to the mattress.

'Crow?' There was some urgency to her voice.

'Don't panic, Doc. I'm still here,' I muttered. 'Just.' My entire body was one long sensation of aches and pains.

Then I remembered. I opened my eyes again, quickly. 'Jamil? Did he . . .?'

She shook her head. 'No,' she said gently. 'He didn't make it. I'm sorry.'

'The crash?'

She reached for my hand. 'I think he was already dead. There was evidence of massive bullet wounds to his lower abdomen. There was nothing you could have done to save him.'

Except left him behind, I thought.

I extricated my tongue from the roof of my mouth. Rubbed the back of my hand across my dry lips. Discovered that someone had been busy with a razor, too. My beard was gone. 'How did I get here?'

'Sher Khan's men carried you. They found the aeroplane – what was left of it – and pulled you out. We made a litter and brought you with us.'

'And Jamil?'

'Him too. He was buried yesterday.'

Yesterday? I sat up then. Too quickly. My head reeled. 'Christ! How long have I been out?'

'We crossed the bridge two days ago. Lie down.'

'Two days!' I lay down.

246

'You have at least three cracked ribs, a dozen stitches in your scalp, and severe concussion. You have been remarkably lucky.'

'Feels like it,' I said, wincing. I wondered vaguely what time of the day it was.

She leaned forward and kissed me. Her lips were soft and warm. 'Try and get some sleep.' She let go of my hand and stood up. When she reached the door she turned. 'I've missed you, Crow,' she said.

But I only half heard her. Like a patient under anaesthetic I slipped away again.

On her second visit she wasn't alone. I'd been conscious for a while and had spent the time trying to get my bearings. It was still light outside and quite warm. By that I guessed it was sometime in the afternoon. I'd also made a foolish attempt to stand and take a look outside and I'd even got as far as sitting up and putting my feet on the ground before it dawned on me that perhaps it wasn't such a good idea after all. I felt instantly nauseous and sagged back down again. By the time the room had slowed to a moderate spin Nicole and the rest of my visitors had arrived.

Kerim pumped my hand. A wide grin split his dark and handsome face. 'Welcome to the Panjsher, my friend! I am indeed happy to see you alive and well!'

'You and me both,' I assured him.

I didn't quite know how to respond to Sher Khan. And my dilemma must have shown for with great perception he bent over the mattress, held my eyes with an unblinking gaze and grasped my hands between his own. He spoke softly and with great solemnity.

'Sher Khan bids you swift recovery from your wounds,' Kerim said.

'Please tell him how much I regret the death of his son,' I replied. 'Jamil was a brave warrior, a true Mujehad.'

Sher Khan received the eulogy with a grave nod. He spoke again. Despite the sorrow he must have been feeling I saw there was a bright light in his eyes.

'Sher Khan says that it was the will of Allah,' Kerim translated. 'Jamil has now joined the ranks of the shaheed. He has entered Paradise.'

Sher Khan released my hand and backed away and I became aware of the third man standing behind him.

He was young and slim, slightly stoop shouldered, with a thin and rather pale face. His moustache and beard, although dark, were quite wispy. His nose was long and prominent. His eyes, however, were what held the attention. Quick and bright, giving an intelligent cast to his features. He was dressed in khaki; combat jacket and trousers tucked into a pair of black Russian army boots, similar to the ones worn by Kerim. A flat Chitrali cap was perched at an angle on his head and a black and white checked scarf hung around his neck. Under the jacket, and barely concealed, I saw the strap of a shoulder holster and the butt of an automatic pistol nestling beneath his left armpit.

Nicole said, 'Crow, this is Commander Massoud.'

I was face to face with a legend.

Ahmadshah Massoud was only thirty-three yet it has been said that of all the guerilla commanders fighting in Afghanistan he alone had the capacity to become a national leader. As he came across and shook my hand it wasn't difficult to see why. There was a distinct aura about him, no doubt about it. You could tell by the atmosphere in the room, in the deference shown by Kerim and Sher Khan. He smiled and as our palms met I could have sworn that I felt a current of energy flow through me. It was as though I had been charged by the man's charisma. I was in the presence of someone remarkable. I knew it instinctively.

The most celebrated rebel leader in the resistance. This

248

was the man who had held the Russian forces at bay for seven long years from his redoubt in the Panjsher. Survivor of at least ten major offensives launched by the Soviet High Command in Kabul. His successes against the Russians were flames in the beacon of hope held by all Afghans that one day the communist invaders would be defeated.

To my surprise he spoke in French, obviously addressing Nicole.

'Massoud hopes you are comfortable. If there is anything you require, you have only to ask,' she said.

'Tell him thanks. I'm sorry to have to put him to so much trouble.'

Nicole relayed the message. Massoud smiled, almost shyly, I thought. He spoke again.

'He says that it is no trouble and he is glad to meet you at last. He thanks you for bringing in the guns and rockets and helping Sher Khan and his men transport the weapons over the mountains.'

'Aw, shucks,' I said. 'Nothing to it.'

Massoud chuckled when told what I'd said. He shook my hand again and gave a small salute before leaving the room. Kerim and Sher Khan followed him out.

'How's the head?' Nicole asked.

'Throbbing nicely,' I said. 'How come he speaks French?'

She gave me a brief biography.

Massoud's family were Tadjiks. As a younger man he'd attended the French-run Istiqlal Lycée in Kabul. Hence his ability with the language. He'd then gone to the city polytechnic to study engineering for three years. In '73, when Daoud, the former prime minster, seized power Massoud had been instrumental in organizing anti-communist resistance in the Panjsher region. Following the failure of the coup Massoud had fled to Pakistan where he studied guerilla warfare. He returned to Kabul in 1979.

Then, following the Russian invasion, he moved back to the Panjsher to organize resistance for the second time. His training in Pakistan had proved invaluable.

In the seven years since the December invasion Massoud's reputation and power had spread outwards. He had succeeded in uniting a number of the northern provinces and his influence even extended into the highest echelons of the Afghan army. As his successes against the Shuravi multiplied so did the number of men who flocked to his banner. It was due mainly to his high profile that the resistance had been able to secure help, both financial and military, from western countries, in particular the USA. Without him as a figurehead it was unlikely that the guerillas would have received such generous funding and hardware.

Small wonder the Russians had such a high price on his head.

Food arrived then. Oiled nan and a pot of milk tea, a beverage not commonly served. It was considered something of a delicacy and had been sent with Massoud's compliments. I ate a little then slept a great deal.

It took a further two days for my headaches to subside. By that time I was able to stand and move around without feeling the need to stop and lie down every five minutes to recover from my exertions. My post-op care was attended to by Nicole who had also taken the opportunity to establish a field surgery in one of the small outhouses. Once I was up and about she was able to devote more of her time to dealing with the local populace who were far more deserving of her skills than I was. Left to my own devices, I used the time to take stock of my surroundings.

Of Massoud there was no sign. I learnt that he and his men, Kerim and Sher Khan included, had left the village and travelled north. Their objective was the destruction of a number of Soviet security posts at a place called Farkhar, not far from the Russian border. Massoud had taken a large force with him, some two hundred fighters in all, many of them guerillas who'd accompanied Sher Khan from the rebel transit base at Jebel Kut.

While the guerilla leader was away life in the valley appeared to return to some semblance of normality. At least it seemed so to my eyes. It was a fertile place. Small terraced fields surrounded by a jumble of low stone walls, fed by an ingenious system of narrow irrigation channels, dotted the landscape. The main crops appeared to be wheat and maize but there were also orchards of apricots and mulberries in abundance. Despite the valley's restless history it had the appearance of a place untouched by war. An illusion, however. Despite appearances to the contrary, food was scarce. Further north there were rumours of famine and this southern part of the valley was preparing for a new influx of refugees which would inevitably increase the burden on the local farmers. It was a fact that a number of families, made homeless by Russian attacks, had already found shelter among the caves in the nearby hills.

The Mujehadeen were gone for three days. When they returned Kerim told us how it had taken them over thirty hours to complete their mission. There had been five security posts in all. It had taken them less than three hours to subdue the first four into submission. The last post had proved to be the most heavily defended. It had been manned by a contingent of the secret police, the Khad. It wasn't surprising, therefore, that they had chosen to fight rather than surrender.

Massoud had controlled the battle from the summit of a hill overlooking the enemy positions. He had been in constant touch with his field commanders by means of radios and had been able to direct every attack as it was carried out.

In the end the Khad garrison had fought to the last man. The Mujehadeen had lost eight of their number dead, and thirty wounded. According to Kerim, the other side had suffered tremendous losses. Over one hundred men dead. The guerillas had taken over fifty prisoners, many of them no more than teenagers, all reluctant conscripts in the Afghan army. The Mujehadeen had given them the opportunity to change sides. None of them refused the offer. A wise decision, I would have thought.

From conversations with Kerim I learnt how Massoud was constantly on the move, never spending more than a few days at any one location. He generally travelled with a bodyguard, always varying his route. A very careful man. Doubtless this was the reason he had survived for so long.

His energy was quite prodigious for he had the knack of seeming to be everywhere at once. He involved himself with everything. Whether it was the assessment of tax levels on emerald shipments or supervising weapons training for new recruits he applied himself to each task with a dedication that was staggering.

Massoud held court on the veranda of a house down by the river. There, in the company of his lieutenants, he sifted through letters and messages delivered to him from all parts of the country, dispatching replies as he deemed necessary. Sometimes he received personal visitations. I was a spectator on one occasion. The deputation consisted of an old guy, an elder from a village to the west of Do Ab.

Kerim was there with me. He chuckled as he described to me the conversation that was taking place.

'There are some hooligans in the old man's village,' Kerim explained. 'Bully boys who taunt the old people and who are lazy and good for nothing. They think they can get away with it because all the warriors are away fighting with Massoud. The old man is asking Commander Massoud to help him deal with the young thugs. He is asking for protection.'

I watched Massoud's long and thoughtful face break out into a gentle smile as the elder explained the problem and put forward his appeal. The incident must have been way down the guerilla leader's list of priorities yet he listened attentively to what the old man had to say and gave the case as much consideration as if it had been the most important problem he had been confronted with. In the end he gave his judgement and wrote out a letter for the elder to take back to his village. I guessed it was something along the lines of a warrant, warning the hooligans that they should cease their activities on pain of incurring the wrath of Commander Massoud and his Mujehadeen. Satisfied, the old man thanked Massoud gravely. The guerilla leader helped the old boy to his feet and watched with concern as the emissary walked down the street to begin the long walk back to his home.

Massoud: the people's champion. Guerilla leader. Father confessor. A man of integrity, a good listener. Western politicians could learn a great deal from him, I reflected.

He spotted me watching him, spoke to one of his men. The man eyed me, nodded, and lumbered over.

Kerim listened to the envoy and said, 'Commander Massoud asks you to join him.'

I got up and walked across, Kerim beside me. Massoud shook hands and indicated a space next to him on the blanket. Kerim and I sat down.

'The commander asks how you are feeling,' Kerim said. 'He hopes you are well and he is sorry he has been unable to visit you before.'

I responded with some aimless pleasantry and our conversation continued apace, although stilted, somewhat inevitably, by my inability with the language. Massoud was using Farsi and sometimes Kerim's translations took a bit of time, prolonged, I suspected, by his enthusiastic tendency to embellish every utterance with a charade that would have done justice to Marcel Marceau. To my embarrassment it was clear that the circumstances surrounding my arrival in the Panjsher were fast becoming the stuff of which legends are made. I could tell this by the kind of looks I was starting to get from the rebel commander and the members of his council. When Kerim mimed the outstretched wings of a bird and impersonated the noise of a machine gun – I presumed this was meant to illustrate the bombing raid in the Wapiti – his audience, until that moment spellbound, began to look at me as if I was unhinged.

I could see their point.

Eventually I did manage to get a word in edgeways, while Kerim made a pause for breath, and found out from Massoud that the Mujehadeen had lost twenty-one men in the attack on Bagram. The Russians, however, had lost nine aircraft and an unknown number of personnel and, despite their losses, the guerillas considered the raid to have been a success. At least in one respect, Massoud told me, Muhammed Nur Rafiq's death had been avenged.

It seemed to me that the death toll had been a high price to pay. But Massoud was philosophical. It was the will of Allah. And, although Nur Rafiq had been an integral part of the resistance movement and therefore a hard man to replace, there were plenty willing to pick up the baton.

Looking around me at the intensity on the faces of his lieutenants, I could well believe it.

I changed tack then and asked Massoud why the Mujehadeen had rejected Najibullah's truce proposal. Wasn't he tired of the war?

'We will never tire. We will not stop fighting until the Soviets withdraw all their troops out of Afghanistan,'

Massoud said vehemently. 'We in the resistance do not recognize the Kabul regime therefore any proposals from their side are meaningless. The revolution must continue.'

'What about international opinion?' I asked him. 'You could lose support from the people who see the offer of a ceasefire as a means to end the war. General Zia for one.'

A half smile played across Massoud's face. 'We are fighting for our independence. We have no time for international opinion. Did the Shuravi care about international opinion when they invaded our homeland and destroyed our villages, our women and children, our crops and our livestock? No, my friend. They did not. Besides, the Americans will continue to support us. And President Zia depends on the Americans to provide him with weapons for his army. He cannot afford to offend the United States. Zia is a puppet. He will not turn against us.'

I said, 'The Russians have promised to withdraw their troops. Doesn't that count for something?'

'That was for propaganda purposes only,' Massoud replied. 'The Shuravi's proposal was for a pull-out spread over two years. They should be thinking of months not years. After all, they do not have far to go. It would not be like the Americans pulling out of Vietnam.'

And how about Najibullah's promise to pardon all the officers and soldiers of the Afghan army who'd deserted and joined the rebels? I pointed out. Wouldn't that scheme undermine the foundation of the resistance?

Massoud said, 'As long as there remains one Mujehad who has the strength to lift his gun the struggle to liberate our country will continue.'

But could he guarantee that his source of weapons and supplies would not dry up?

Massoud chuckled. 'My friend, we obtain almost eighty per cent of our weapons from the Russians. As long as they remain in Afghanistan weapons will not be a problem. And the Chinese and the Americans will always step in with more. With American Stingers and the will of Allah on our side, how can we lose?'

Game, set and match, I reasoned.

The dialogue took another turn then. Massoud had summoned me for a reason. He told me he'd learnt from his agents within the Kabul High Command that the Russians were set to launch yet another offensive against the rebel bases in the Panjsher from both north and south. He had therefore decided that as I was now mobile Nicole and I should begin our journey back to Pakistan.

Good-oh. I seconded the notion. I told Massoud I'd alert Nicole. Massoud said he'd let me know the timing of our departure. An escort would be provided. We parted company and I went looking for Nicole to pass on the plan.

She was in the surgery. Her face was flushed. Her hands were shaking. It wasn't anything to do with my news. It was something entirely different. She'd received word about her brother. Alain was alive.

Chapter Sixteen

He said his name was Jassim. He was a cripple.

There were many such men among the ranks of the guerillas. Victims of Russian bombings and engagements with the occupying ground forces. I'd seen them in hospital wards in Peshawar and the underground wells in Mir Seraj. Men with the most appalling wounds; many of them disfigured by the loss of a limb. A hand, an arm, or, as in the case of Jassim Rana, a leg.

Personally, I thought that Jassim looked a bit shifty. He was young; not much out of his teens, I guessed, with dark, rather nervous eyes that blinked constantly like a blackbird's and didn't quite meet your gaze. Small and wiry, too, he had the build of a bookie's runner. Only he wouldn't be doing that much running. Not any more. Not with his right leg blown off at the knee. He'd received the wound during a Russian attack, several months before, on Caris Mir, a village lying to the north of Kabul. Despite his injury, however, Jassim, accompanied and aided by a handful of companions, had managed to escape into the hills.

How he had survived the journey across the mountains to Pakistan defied credulity. But survive it he had. It had taken him ten days to reach the border village of Parachinar. From Parachinar an ambulance had transported him, along with other wounded guerillas, to the hospital at Peshawar. There, a Swiss surgeon had operated on what had been left of his leg. Then, following a short period of recuperation, Jassim had been taken to the workshop to be fitted with a new limb. A month later he had returned to the Panjsher to fight.

The device was called a Jaipur Foot. A crude but ingenious contraption forged from metal, wood and leather. The foot part, flexible from the ankle down, was made of extremely strong rubber and thus was able to withstand the heavy punishment it would suffer in the mountainous terrain. There had been various versions of these artificial limbs tried out and most of them had been far too sophisticated to last more than a few weeks at a time. It was not uncommon for a patient, once mobile, to turn about and head back across the border to rejoin the war. Wearing one of the state of the art aluminium prosthetics meant that the guy got about three miles down the track before the thing fell apart. Sturdiness and simplicity were the answer. They needed something that could be easily repaired, if the need arose, in the villages back home. The Jaipur Foot, as its name implied, had been discovered by Red Cross officials in India. They had taken the design back to the hospital at Peshawar and adapted an Afghan version.

Jassim's foot, though, had been causing him some recent discomfort. It had sustained damage during a recent skirmish with a patrol of Afghan militia on the road outside Omarz. Consequently the stump had become badly chafed and infection had set in. The local blacksmith had managed to reshape the metal framework which had taken care of the mechanical side of things and Jassim, having heard about Nicole's surgery, had called in asking for ointment to soothe the tender flesh.

He was sitting on one of the charpoys, strapping the limb to his thigh when I arrived. The end of his leg, I saw, was a smooth and hairless dome. He slid the bald pink stump into the cup of the false leg and tightened the restraining straps. It looked extremely cumbersome but he stood up nimbly enough and with the wide leg of his tombon concealing the caliper-like appliance there was no way of telling that he was deformed. Only when he walked was it apparent that something was wrong for he still had that slight hip-rolling gait that was common to most amputees. That apart, he appeared to have borne the trauma of his injury extremely well and his only desire now, he had told Nicole, was to resume his part in the war against the communists.

But, first, he had a tale to tell.

Jassim, it transpired, hailed from a village to the south west, called Hajat, in the mountains beyond Rokha. He had brought word that for a period of weeks a stranger had been sheltering there. Not a Mujehad nor a refugee, but a European. The stranger had arrived in the village sick and weak and with a remarkable story. It appeared he had been arrested by the Russians in Kabul and sentenced to a term in Pol-e-Charkhi for attempting to smuggle film of Russian troop movements out of the country. By a miracle, however, on the day he was to begin his sentence, the Afghan army squad detailed to escort him to the prison had been ambushed by a party of Mujehadeen. In the ensuing firefight the Mujehadeen had snatched the prisoner. The Russians, however, had given chase and, in the confusion, the guerillas and their charge had become separated. Alone, the man had been on the run ever since, relying on anti-government sympathizers to shelter and protect him. Eventually he had fallen in with a small family group of refugees heading north, away from the capital. Together they had made their way towards the Panjsher.

It was bad luck that their arrival in the valley had coincided with one of the Soviets' frequent bombing raids.

In the aftermath of the raid the Russians had taken control of the area and established an advance HQ. The European and his companions had been forced to move further up into the hills to avoid capture.

As the Russians spread themselves along the valley, the fugitives had retreated deeper into the mountains. They had then been isolated at Hajat, cut off by the Soviet ground forces and the last of the winter snow falls.

Then Massoud's Mujehadeen had regained a temporary foothold in the region prior to the new and imminent Russian offensive and, with Jassim acting as guide, the fugitives had at last been able to descend into the lower valley. There, the party had split up. The refugees had ensconced themselves in the caverns with the other nomads. The European, on the other hand, had been anxious to continue his escape to Pakistan.

At the present time he was sheltering in a village the other side of Kenj, not much more than half a day's march away. He was planning to return to the border along the same route that we ourselves would be taking.

So it was true after all; miracles did happen. Maybe.

Because, as stories went, this one was pretty interesting. But what made her so sure it was her brother?

'This,' she said. She was unable to hide the break in her voice. 'The man gave it to Jassim as payment for leading him out of the mountains.'

It was a gold ring. She held it in the palm of her hand, it was like a signet ring. Etched into the metal was a symbol. It was one I recognized. The twin-barred Cross of Lorraine.

'It was our grandfather's,' Nicole said softly. 'He fought with the Free French Army. He gave this to Alain on my brother's fifteenth birthday. See?'

She turned the ring around. Inside, carved minutely, were two initials: A. B.

I looked at her. 'You're sure?' A family heirloom appeared, on the face of it, to be an over generous price to pay for such a service. But, given the circumstances, I supposed Alain Bonnard must have been pretty desperate and pretty damned grateful. It had probably been the one possession of any value with which he had been able to show his gratitude. Even as I posed the question, I knew that it had to be rhetorical.

Her fist closed around the ring, gripping tight. She nodded. 'Oh, yes. It is Alain.'

She began to tremble then, her eyes closed. Tears brimmed.

I sat her down on one of the beds. I was conscious of Jassim looking on subserviently, like Uriah Heep.

'Hey, c'mon, love.' I placed my arm around her shoulders. 'It's okay now. You've found him. He's alive. It's what you came here for, right?' I could feel the tension in her. She was drawn as tight as a bow string.

She turned to face me and the look in her eyes pierced me like a knife. I had been expecting joy; relief certainly. Instead there was something else. I sensed trepidation, perhaps fear. My God, I thought, she looks scared stiff.

My feelings must have been evident for she glanced away, a little too quickly for the move to appear natural. It was as if she had no wish to meet my gaze and for one brief moment I felt the hand of doubt reach out and run cold fingers along my spine. Like an itch that I couldn't scratch, the sensation lingered tantalizingly beyond my reach and then, as if plucked out of my stream of conscious thought, it was gone. Almost. Something remained, some awareness that all was not as it should be. I don't know what, but it was there all the same, under the surface; something malignant. A premonition.

'We'd better tell Massoud,' I said.

We found the rebel commander sitting down by the bank of the river, in the company of some of his council. He offered us seats and listened intently as Nicole divulged her information. She showed him the ring. He turned it around in his slim hands and handed it back. He looked thoughtful, cast a glance at his lieutenants. They conversed briefly. Massoud seemed to be expressing some doubt. Kerim, in attendance as ever, frowned as he explained Massoud's concern.

Qum, the village where Alain Bonnard had chosen to lie low prior to his run for the border, had, by many accounts, lain deserted for some time; ever since the last big bombing raid in the region, when most of the village's twenty or so houses had been destroyed. What happened then was that most of the inhabitants had slipped away over the mountains. Those that stayed, the young men mostly, had moved into the lower reaches of the valley and joined the Mujehadeen. The village had, to all intents and purposes, been abandoned.

At that point, Jassim who'd accompanied us to Massoud's quarters, interjected.

It was true, he said, that the villagers of Qum had departed but their places had been taken by a number of refugee families from the northern provinces who'd fled south looking for sanctuary. It was they who were at the present time looking after the feringhi.

Again Massoud looked thoughtful. I could see that he was weighing up the pros and cons of the argument. Finally, after further consultation with his men, he nodded and spoke to Nicole.

Nicole shook his hand, smiled hesitantly. She got to her feet.

'What did he say?' I took her arm.

'He will take us,' she said.

It was then that I felt the relief in her voice. Even so there was a dullness in her eyes which I couldn't account for. Again I was struck by that small niggling element of doubt. But there wasn't anything that I could do about it.

The decision to leave having been reached, there was no time to waste. Nicole and I would begin our trek to the border the next day, at first light. With Massoud. If Alain Bonnard was still in the village the rebel commander planned to place all three of us under the protection of a Pakistan-bound caravan, carrying emeralds and lapis lazuli over the mountains to market in Peshawar.

We left after morning prayer, when the sun was still low over the eastern peaks. Sher Khan was there to see us off. He took my hand gravely. 'Salaam aleikim,' he murmured.

He embraced me then, Afghan style. As he held me I felt the strength of his body and in that spontaneous moment of warmth I experienced a tremendous surge of affection for this ancient and proud warrior.

And peace to you, old man, I thought, as we broke apart.

Because we were travelling in such exalted company we were blessed with transport: Massoud's purloined Russian Gaz jeep. The vehicle looked a bit decrepit; like something that had lost an argument with a minefield. The chassis was exceedingly bent, the windscreen was peppered with bullet holes and there were some interesting dark stains on the seats, the origins of which I didn't intend to dwell over. Beggars, as they say, can't be choosers. On behalf of my feet, however, I gave thanks to whichever celestial deity had chosen to watch over me.

I began to renounce my vows about half a mile down the track. Massoud's driver would have given Emmerson Fittipaldi heartburn. I'd swear he was the only driver I'd ever known who actually aimed for the potholes. There were six of us altogether so it was a tight squeeze. There was Massoud; Maftoon, his chauffeur cum bodyguard, a huge bearded ruffian festooned with more weaponry than the entire Afrika Korps; the indispensable Kerim; Nicole; me; and bringing up the rear and hanging on by the straps of his Jaipur Foot, Jassim Rana. Jassim it was who would guide us the last part of the way to our destination.

We set off at a pace that would have done justice to a competitor in the Lombard Rally. At the first bend Maftoon nearly lost three of us. It was only Jassim's frantic yelping that made him slow down to a sedate warp factor three. If anyone was going to deprive the resistance of its most capable commander it was likely to be the great man's own minder. I wondered how that was likely to figure in the annals of the revolution.

What was figuring largely was the amount of debris littering the wayside, most of it Russian.

The stony river bank was lined with military junk. At one point we passed what looked like the remains of an entire convoy; a couple of trackless and turretless T-55 tanks, several burnt-out lorries and half a dozen BTR 60s, Soviet armoured personnel carriers. The vehicles were now nothing more than scrap metal. Many were simply blackened and gutted hulks, others appeared to be in fair condition except for the fact that some of the APCs were upside down. They looked like dead armadillos.

They weren't the only evidence of conflict in the valley. The countryside bore all the signs of intense bombing activity. Huge craters dotted the landscape and the few buildings that remained all showed the scars that were a clear illustration of the accuracy of Russian shelling. Fighting here, Massoud told us as the jeep bounced and jolted along the track, had been particularly intense.

The village of Kenj was a dump. Most of it having been made so by the last Russian offensive. It had taken the Mujehadeen nearly a month to wrest it from enemy hands. So by the time they had chased the Shuravi out of the valley there wasn't a whole lot left of the place. We didn't linger but crossed the river and carried on. Massoud, inevitably, was recognized. A number of people shouted and waved.

We had to stop several times and take cover under the trees. This was due to the frequency of Russian patrols that had suddenly become regular occurrences. Massoud explained that this was quite common during the days leading up to each new offensive. The helicopter gunships and SU-25s, the Soviet equivalent of the American A-10 Tankbusters, were flown low over the villages and used to draw enemy fire. That way the Soviets could pinpoint rebel-held positions. The SU-25s were bad news, Massoud said. It was almost impossible to detect the things until they were directly overhead.

We lay dug in by the side of the jeep and listened to the gunships clatter across the face of the mountains. Somewhere in the distance there could be heard the dull crump of explosions. Further along the valley the Russians were straffing rebel-held villages. It was the softening-up process prior to a ground assault. It was a clear indication that Massoud's intention to expedite our departure from the area had been the correct one.

Beyond Kenj the road, such as it was, followed the river and continued up to Dasht-i-Riwat where it petered out like an abandoned branch line on some suburban railway system. After that it would be one long footslog – or, if we were lucky, a horseback ride – to the border; up through Paryan, across the mountains to Kantiwar and then north through Nuristan to Garm Chisma. It was the same route as that undertaken by a western film crew several months before. They'd travelled to the Panjsher to film Massoud and his Mujehadeen in action for a documentary to be screened on British TV.

Our journey proper, however, would begin later, after we'd picked up Alain. To do that we had to make a detour.

It was getting harder, even for the four-wheel drive. For a while we had been backtracking one of the tributaries of the Panjsher and, naturally, travelling upstream, the trail had been getting steeper. If it went on like this for much longer we'd have to leave the jeep and continue on foot.

But we were getting close. The track was beginning to level out and there were distinct traces of human habitation in the area. The land had been hacked into terraces and orchards had been planted. Peach trees and mulberries. But they carried all the signs of neglect; peeling bark, wizened and dehydrated fruit. There was no one left to reap the harvest. A small stream bubbled out of the rocks and tinkled brightly down through the rocky pasture. A rough trestle bridge forded the water and this led directly on to the main street. The wooden supports rattled and creaked alarmingly as the ladened jeep trundled over them.

We drove into the village and I could see immediately why Massoud had had his doubts about the likelihood of there being anybody there.

Qum, from what I could see of it, looked, well . . . pretty qwummy. Like a ghost town in a John Ford western. The only additional requirement would have

266

been tufts of tumbleweed bouncing along the main street and the creak of the saloon doors. There was no doubt that the village had taken a pasting. Hardly a building had been left unscathed. The houses that hadn't actually fallen down completely had more holes in them than a Swiss cheese. A dusty and desolate place. It had about it the bleak air of a windswept graveyard.

Even Maftoon was looking a bit wary. Which concerned me because he looked like the kind of man who could leap buildings in a single bound and crack walnuts between his eyelids. If he was worried, I was worried.

And it occurred to me that Jassim, too, was looking distinctly uneasy, like a horse about to bolt.

Maybe we should all have taken our cue from him there and then and run like hell. But we didn't.

At least we were all armed, with the exception of Nicole. I'd repossessed the Kalashnikov and I was glad I had. Holding it gave me a small ray of comfort that if anything nasty was to happen I'd have some means of defending myself.

Maftoon parked the jeep in the tiny square and we climbed out.

If there were any fugitives in the place it was debatable whether they would have shown themselves. Especially at the sound of a motor engine. The Mujehadeen didn't possess too many vehicles and the logical fear to anyone in hiding would have been that the visitors were a Russian patrol. So I wasn't surprised that nobody had come bounding out with garlands and a brass band. Even so, if someone was in residence a lookout would surely have been posted and Massoud would have been recognized. So, if that was the case, where was everybody? It looked as if we had come on a wild goose chase after all.

Looking around, it was noticeable that there was one

building which, although pitted and gouged by rocket fire, still had the outward appearance of being in one piece. The mosque. It was set up on the side of the hill, above the rest of the village. There were ominous cracks radiating across its eggshell-like dome and the columns either side of the archway leading to its dark interior bore the indentations of many bullets, as livid as smallpox scars. In tiny villages such as these mosques weren't just places of worship they were gathering places, emergency centres where the villagers assembled in times of crisis.

A logical place to look. Sure enough, Jassim pointed up the hill and spoke rapidly to Massoud. Massoud nodded and gestured for Jassim to lead the way.

'He says that perhaps everyone is hiding in the mosque,' Kerim translated.

'Alain too?' Nicole asked him quickly.

'That is where Jassim saw him last,' Kerim replied.

We set off after Jassim who was clomping up the hill like a small and tatty version of Long John Silver. Nicole stuck close to me. She looked pale and nervous. Probably afraid of what we might find up there, I suspected.

Close up, the hallmarks of decay that distance had temporarily concealed were now sadly apparent. At one time the building had probably been whitewashed and pristine but now, with the passing of the years and the constant effects of Russian shelling, the mosque looked shabby and neglected. The outside walls were grey, chipped and peeling like layers of wet cardboard. The place looked about as welcoming as a crypt.

We entered cautiously.

Inside the mosque it was dark and cool, like a vault. Above us the dome looked like the inside of a giant helmet. There was a single round hole at the top, through which was admitted a shaft of sunlight that pierced the sepulchral gloom like the beam of a torch. In the beam tiny particles of dust tumbled and spun like minute acrobatic insects.

There was a row of wooden charpoys against the far wall. On one of them lay the figure of a man, partially covered by a thin woollen blanket, his back towards us.

Nicole gave a cry. 'Alain!'

She ran forward. As she did so I heard a click behind me and something hard jammed itself into the small of my back. I was suddenly aware of figures detaching themselves rapidly from the shadows along the walls. Kerim swore violently as the barrel of a Kalashnikov was dug into his ribs. Out of the silence a harsh voice barked a command in Farsi. I saw Massoud stiffen. Then he reached inside his jacket and very slowly drew out his pistol and dropped it on the floor. Beside me I heard the clatter of Kerim's Kalashnikov hitting the tiles. Maftoon and I followed suit. We didn't have any choice. Gun barrels radiated around us like the spokes of a wheel. I took in the ill-fitting uniforms, the fur-trimmed caps, the weapons. Fear twisted like a serpent in my belly.

Soldiers. Afghan militia.

Others, too. Not in uniform but in civilian dress; combat jackets, pantaloons, pugri headgear, bandoliers criss-crossing their chests, a few of them bearded. Dressed like Mujehadeen. Something about them stirred in my memory, something which brought their identity into sharp focus. I looked over to the bed and the man lying on it, half concealed. Nicole was there, reaching out. As she did so, the figure stirred and the blanket was lifted aside. Nicole let out a sharp gasp and reacted as if she had been stung. She backed away, shaking her head, recoiling. The man raised himself, sat up, turned around, and we stared at each other. The shock hit me. The short hairs rose on

269

the back of my neck. On this occasion there was no enigmatic smile. This time it was deadly serious. Previously, he had saved my life. This time he looked ready to take it.

The Russian.

Taras Rasseikin. Again.

Chapter Seventeen

It occurred to me that I couldn't see Jassim. But there was a very good reason for that, as I found out. He was behind me. He was the one who'd stuck his gun in my back. And he was looking pretty damned pleased with himself, too. Not surprising really. He'd sprung the trap very well indeed, the devious little bastard.

'Salaam aleikum.' A voice spoke from the darkness.

Footsteps on the cool tiles.

He swaggered into the circle of light cast by the beam coming from the hole in the dome above him. He was no Afghan. Nor a member of the militia. That was all too apparent. This one was a regular. The real thing. One of Gorbachev's finest. You could tell by his bearing and by the fact that his uniform was cut a whole lot better than everybody else's. That and the insignia on his collar denoting him as an officer.

Medium height, iron-grey hair cut short. He had the palest grey eyes I'd ever seen. Almost colourless, like his features, which were set as stern and as rigid as a Kabuki mask. Not particularly old, though, despite the grey. Early forties at a guess; perhaps even his late thirties. He could have been cast from the same mould as Rasseikin. Another hard man. A professional. No doubt about it.

He had a gun all of his own. An automatic pistol, similar to a Browning. Put on the spot, I'd have said a Czech CZ-75 9mm. Very capable. Like its owner, probably.

'You had us a little worried, Doctor,' the newcomer remarked, the bottom half of his mask cracking slightly.

The attempt at a smile, however, did not extend to his eyes. 'We were not certain you would make it. My congratulations.' He spoke in English. Heavily accented. Somewhere east of the Urals, I guessed. His tone carried all the bonhomie of a host greeting a tardy guest at a cocktail party.

Nicole swung around. Pale and livid, she cried angrily, 'Where is Alain. Where is my brother?'

The reply was curt. 'I regret he has been detained for a while longer, Doctor. My apologies.' You could tell he was just heartbroken.

Nicole's face registered a depth of confusion and pain that was immeasurable. Her face crumpled as the significance of the betrayal hit her like a fist.

Without allowing her the chance to respond, even if she had been able to, our captor turned his attention away from her, towards me, his eyes at once narrow and calculating. 'You,' he said quietly, 'must be the pilot; Crow.'

I felt the cold rush of adrenalin at the casual identification.

'Permit me to introduce myself,' he said, the mask now firmly back in place. 'I am Trevkin. Colonel Arkady Trevkin, of the Chief Intelligence Directorate of the General Staff.'

He sounded as if he was to address a class at the Georgia Military Academy. As soon as he announced himself, though, I knew we had a real problem. Trevkin wasn't just Red Army. He'd identified himself as someone special. Chief Intelligence Directorate could only mean one thing. The Glavnoye Razvedyvatelnoye Upravleniye. GRU; Soviet Military Intelligence. I don't know much about the promotional prospects in the Soviet High Command but he seemed a mite young for a colonel. It meant he'd either got friends in high places or else he'd acquitted himself well in some past endeavour. Maybe both.

His gaze turned and drifted passed me. He raised the pistol, pointed it. 'And this,' he said, 'is the man we have been waiting for. The terrorist leader, Ahmadshah Massoud. These other two . . .' He flicked a speculative glance at Maftoon and Kerim. '. . . I do not know.'

He turned back to me and commented, matter-of-factly, 'You are of course acquainted with Sergeant Rasseikin.'

'We've met,' I said.

At the mention of his name Rasseikin's dark eyes flickered. He'd picked up his machine pistol and was holding it nonchalantly in his arms as a mother might cradle a baby.

Trevkin smiled, breaking the lamina for the second time. He had a gold filling, I saw. Top set, left-hand side. 'You look a little confused, my friend. Would you like me to explain?'

'I wouldn't want to put you to any trouble, Colonel,' I said, thinking that considering the circumstances I was coming across like some laconic Raymond Chandler private eye. However, what I sounded like and what I felt like were two complete opposites. What I felt like doing was making a running leap for the door. But I wasn't about to tell Trevkin that, of course. I had no desire to be pursued by a 9mm parabellum bullet. I didn't want to be pursued by any kind of bullet, frankly.

He responded chummily. 'Oh it is no trouble, believe me. No trouble at all. And it will help pass the time while we wait for the transport.' He cast an eye to his wrist.

I didn't much like the sound of that either. I wondered how the others were doing. Kerim was probably following this dazzling repartee quite well. Massoud and Maftoon, however, were merely spectators.

273

'In fact,' Trevkin said, 'why don't you tell them, Doctor?'

Nicole hadn't moved from the side of the charpoy. The look on her face transfixed me. If someone could be described as being stricken by both grief and guilt it was Nicole Bonnard. 'I'm sorry, Crow,' she whispered. A tear trickled slowly down her cheek. 'They gave me no choice.'

I stared at her, at Trevkin's men, at Kerim, Maftoon and Massoud. 'Oh, my Christ,' I breathed, my throat suddenly dry. 'What the hell have you done?'

Redundant question. She'd led us here. She and Jassim.

'I had to do it!' she replied. She choked back a sob. 'I had to!'

Trevkin cut in, 'It was a GRU operation all along, my friend, right from the very beginning.'

Returning his pistol to its holster on his belt, he reached into a pocket of his jacket. His hand emerged holding a metallic cigarette case. He helped himself to a cigarette and lit up with a small silver lighter. Returning the case and lighter to his pocket, he inhaled, blew out smoke and picked a shred of tobacco from his lower lip. Very theatrical. He was like a parent about to settle down and read his kids a cosy bedtime story. Only this story, I thought, would probably keep me awake nights.

It must have seemed like a wise strategy at the time; announcing a ceasefire only weeks before the Geneva peace talks. That way Moscow had hoped to increase international support for the Kabul regime which, on the face of it, was now actively seeking an early political and peaceful settlement. At the same time public opinion would swing away from the resistance and thus undermine the tenuous unity of the guerilla organizations. The theory, however, had not been supported in practice.

It hadn't taken Moscow long to latch on to the cold hard fact that the truce was to be short lived.

Within days of Najibullah announcing the commencement of the six-month ceasefire squads of guerillas had been dispatched across the border to strike at military positions in Kabul, Khanchahar and Jalalabad. Three key government posts had been subjected to intense rocket and mortar attacks. As far as the resistance was concerned Najibullah's proposal had been nothing but a propaganda exercise. It was their avowed intention to continue the armed struggle against the forces of oppression, liberate Afghanistan, form an interim government, prepare the establishment of an Afghan parliament and draw up a new constitution. Which was a roundabout way of telling Najibullah that he had another think coming. He could stick his ceasefire proposal where the sun never shone.

That was just the beginning. For then the terror campaign had begun in earnest. Car bombs had exploded in Kabul and two government officials appointed to carry out the new policy of reconciliation were killed in Kunduz and Nangarhar provinces. Lately, of course, there had also been Massoud's raid on the base at Bagram and the posts at Farkhar. What these events amounted to was a warning, an indication that cooperation between the various guerilla groups inside Afghanistan was increasing. And that's what had worried Moscow more than anything else. Far from undermining the resistance the ceasefire had, if anything, urged it into taking even more extreme action.

Which meant that something crucial had to be attempted. A tactic that could literally wipe out all resistance in the country in one fell swoop. Something massive that would demoralize the guerilla army into complete submission.

There was only one solution.

Of all the resistance commanders in Afghanistan there was just one of whom Moscow was truly afraid. The man who had united the northern provinces and forged links with guerilla bands throughout the entire country; the man who had his own agents in the Kabul High Command, a sharp thorn in Moscow's flesh. Ahmadshah Massoud.

Capture Massoud and the entire resistance movement would crumble. That was the directive. The GRU would accomplish it.

There was only one problem. Massoud was too well protected. A survivor of countless offensives on his stronghold in the Panjsher, a military raid on his position would undoubtedly fail. And the man was careful, always on the move. Never alone, never spending more than two nights in the same place, always changing his routine. A very difficult target. So, how to achieve the objective? Answer, subterfuge. If the Russians couldn't go in and get him. Massoud had to go to the Russians. Mohammed to the mountain. Literally.

But Moscow needed the right kind of bait.

And in Alain Bonnard they found it.

In the beginning the GRU had never heard of Bonnard. But they knew all about his sister; from their agents in the Khad, the Afghan secret service. The Khad's main brief was to wage a war of assassination against the Mujehadeen across the border in Pakistan and create unrest along the North West Frontier in an effort to destabilize the Pakistani government's hold on Peshawar and the surrounding district. The Khad's actions in this respect had been numerous. It had been responsible for the murders of over half a dozen Mujehadeen commanders, the bombing of the control room of the local television station, instigating student riots, and even the harassment of foreign relief agency workers. Khad agents also monitored the movements of medical teams across the Durand Line and relayed the information to their controllers in Kabul. Which meant that both the KGB and the GRU had a file on Doctor Nicole Bonnard, as they had on all the other western physicians who'd infiltrated Afghanistan to work within the guerilla camps. It was information the Soviet High Command kept in abeyance; for a rainy day.

That rainy day came within days of the ceasefire. When Najibullah invited western journalists to Kabul to attend a press conference and hear Moscow's version of the truce details.

It was inevitable that Moscow Centre would do a security check on those press men requesting entry permits. When Alain Bonnard's name jumped on to the computer screens alarm bells rang. A simple cross check revealed the family link. The information was relayed back to Soviet Military Intelligence in Kabul and the plan was hatched. The insidious GRU apparatus slid into action.

Alain Bonnard's incarceration had been accomplished only hours after his arrival in the Afghan capital. The press corps had been herded from pillar to post, granted interviews, taken on tours of the city. In the general mêlée, what with the confusion over the transport requirements and the rest, it hadn't been difficult to separate Bonnard from the main phalanx of journalists. Once the rest of his colleagues had been split into smaller groups Bonnard's absence from the scene had not been noticed.

Round one to the GRU.

They held on to Alain Bonnard for three weeks before delegating Khad agents to make contact with Nicole. She was working in the main hospital in Peshawar at the time. We have your brother, she'd been told. She could have him back alive if she performed a certain task. If she refused the offer her brother would die; she would never see him again. What choice had she?

The Khad had outlined its requirements. Nicole had worked in the Panjsher. She had met Massoud, treated his men, gained his trust. Her task was to lull the guerilla leader into the arms of the GRU. As a reward she could have Alain back in one piece.

What the GRU needed was a legitimate reason and opportunity for her to return to the Panjsher as soon as possible. As proof that fortune shines not only on the righteous, the opportunity presented itself in the shape of Mohammed Nur Rafiq, Massoud's fellow commander, the man that Yunis Khalis and Habbani had wanted me to airlift out. The resistance needed a doctor. Nicole Bonnard was on her way.

'Timing,' Trevkin said, 'was the most important factor. We had to ensure that Doctor Bonnard was stranded in rebel territory. We . . .'

'How the hell could you guarantee . . .?' I began. And then it hit me. 'Christ!' I said. 'That's why we didn't run into any opposition on the way in! You'd cleared our path! No wonder it was so bloody easy! Jesus! And the gunships were waiting for us!'

Trevkin nodded approvingly. A teacher acknowledging a bright pupil. 'We monitored your progress all the way, Crow. The attack at Dar Galak was all part of the deception. In order for Doctor Bonnard to remain in Afghanistan we had to remove her means of escape. Your helicopter. We had to make it appear that the attack was spontaneous and that the aircraft had been destroyed before she had a chance to get to it.'

'I presume it would have helped considerably if I'd been in the helicopter at the time?' I said.

Trevkin's reply was grudgingly given. 'It would appear you lead a charmed life, my friend.'

Not only me, I reflected. My blood ran cold as I remembered how I'd yelled at Nicole and pushed her towards the JetRanger as the two gunships commenced their attack, seeing her trip as the Russian helicopter opened fire and not realizing that she had fallen by design not accident. She must have been terrified, knowing that she was safer out in the open, in full view of the Russian gunners, because their orders would have been very precise: on no account harm the woman. She was vital to the operation.

'Until now,' I said.

Trevkin nodded. 'Quite so,' he murmured thoughtfully. 'Until now.'

I wondered what dark imaginings were weaving their way through his cold mind. Most of them probably had to do with my future, or the lack of it. Looking back, I could, I suppose, have counted myself lucky that I'd made it this far. Considering.

It hadn't been a bad ruse. The Soviets had obviously known I'd be carrying weapons in the chopper. They'd known that once the Mujehadeen had taken possession of the cargo the guerillas' main aim would be to deliver the stuff to Massoud. That being so it was logical that they'd prefer to take Nicole with them rather than risk splitting their forces to escort her back to the border. If they had offered to take her back over the Durand Line no doubt she'd have insisted she went with them to the Panjsher in order to continue the search for her brother. And Nicole, for her part, had fuelled the deception well. She'd followed her script to the letter. It had worked out exactly as the GRU had planned. Once she'd arrived in the Panjsher all she'd had to do was await the arrival of her contact saying Alain had been 'found'.

Trevkin must have waited until the last possible moment to make his play. In picking Qum as the place of rendezvous he had chosen wisely. The village was well off the beaten track and deserted. He and his men had probably slipped in during the hours of darkness, their movements covered by the general build-up of troops involved in the new offensive.

Then Trevkin had sent his messenger; the messenger that Nicole, in her briefing, would have been told to expect. Someone who would be carrying her brother's ring as proof of identity.

Enter Jassim. Armed with details of the delivery point and her final instructions. His arrival serving to maintain the fiction about her brother's disappearance right to the end. Even down to Alain's supposed flight from capture that would have done justice to a thriller writer's wildest imagination

If the GRU's plan did have a weak point it was the method by which Nicole planned to deliver Massoud to the Russians. But in that she had boxed clever. She had played on Massoud's sense of honour. In asking the guerilla commander to escort her to the village she had relied on the debt he owed her for her part in the attempt to rescue Muhammed Nur Rafiq and for the medical attention she had bestowed on his Mujehadeen. To have refused her his help would have meant he would have lost respect. To an Afghan that would have been unthinkable.

He had been led into the hands of his enemies like a sacrificial lamb to the slaughter.

'Tell me, Colonel,' I said, 'I don't suppose it was part of the grand design to have one of your helicopters blown

280

out of the sky. So far this little scheme of yours has proved pretty bloody expensive to your side, wouldn't you say?'

Trevkin responded silkily. 'A minor setback only. As we have achieved our objective, I would view it as part of our acceptable losses.

'Oh, boy,' I muttered, 'I just bet you were a wow at the Academy, Colonel. Acceptable losses? One Mi–24? Jesus!'

'I must admit, however,' Trevkin remarked somewhat brightly, 'that you gave us a few anxious moments along the way. If it hadn't been for the prompt action of Sergeant Rasseikin and his men you would not be here at all. We were rather concerned.'

He must have been referring to the little contretemps we'd had with Sikander and his brigands. I thought about that and, despite our predicament, I couldn't help but feel a moment of wry humour. If Sikander had carried out his intention of selling us to the Russians, Trevkin's master plan would have gone down the drain scuppered by his own side! Wonderful! I'd loved to have been a fly on the wall should he have had to explain that to his superiors.

Rasseikin, I presumed, had been tracking us all the way from Dar Galak. His brief had been, no doubt, to smooth our passage. That feeling I'd had of being followed after leaving Mir Seraj hadn't been my imagination, nor, on reflection, had it been Sikander Habib. It had been Rasseikin. And his arrival at Mir Seraj had simply been a means by which he'd been able to get a closer look at the person he had been ordered to protect.

'Are you familiar with the Vysotniki, Crow?' Trevkin blew a smoke ring into the air. He watched it float into the gloom and dissolve. 'Or the Spetsnaz perhaps? Sergeant Rasseikin is something of an expert in his craft.'

That accounted for his appearance, I thought. The affectations, the pony tail, the varied weaponry, the

281

slovenly façade. And, above all, the neat way he and his men had taken out Sikander's scabby bunch. It had struck me at the time that they had seemed just a mite too efficient for itinerants.

The Vysotniki or Spetsnaz were the Soviet Special Forces, the Red Army's equivalent of the SAS and the Green Berets. Crack soldiers and officers, specializing in deep penetration, recon and intelligence operations. Like their US and British counterparts they lived off the land and took the war to the enemy. They adapted to their surroundings like chameleons. Or, in Taras Rasseikin's case, like heroin smugglers.

You had to hand it to them, it was a clever way of gathering information from the populace. Oh, the Afghans would have been suspicious at first, no doubt, particularly as the smugglers were led by a Russian. But he was a deserter and a drug smuggler and therefore just as anxious to avoid confrontation with government forces as were the Afghans. Over the months, as he plied his dubious trade through the mountains and valleys he and his band had become accepted as part of the normal traffic in the region. Not especially welcome or entirely trusted perhaps but tolerated nonetheless and able to move at will through hamlet and town. And all the while Rasseikin would have been passing intelligence on guerilla movements back to Kabul. A clever operation, no doubt about it.

Trevkin chuckled unexpectedly. The sound was like small bones cracking. 'You know, you have caused us a great deal of inconvenience, my friend, during your travels.'

'We do what we can, Colonel,' I said.

He shook his head in wonder. 'For some time we had heard rumours that the rebels had some sort of secret weapon but never for a single moment did we expect it to materialize. And that it should be an aeroplane, of all things!' He chuckled again. 'I understand that the High Command in Kabul is still recovering from the shock.'

It occurred to me that I knew exactly how the High Command felt.

'A quite remarkable feat of airmanship, Crow. I believe the machine was something of an oddity?'

'The only oddity, Colonel,' I said, 'was the idiot driving it. Still, it did the trick, though, didn't it?'

Suddenly Trevkin wasn't smiling anymore. His eyes seemed to suddenly change colour, from pale grey to jet black. 'Your pathetic attempt at levity, Crow, does you no justice. You will be made accountable for your actions. Put bluntly you have engaged in an act of war against the Soviet Union and its ally, the democratic state of Afghanistan. I would advise you that the penalty for such an action will be severe indeed.'

'So, what happens now, Colonel?' I said. 'Thumb screws?'

Trevkin said archly, 'Nothing so dramatic. I suspect you have been watching too many American films. Nobody uses thumb screws anymore. They are far too crude. We have much more . . . how shall I put it? . . . refined methods of interrogation.'

I didn't much care for the word 'interrogation'. It had definite connotations, none of them very pleasant.

Trevkin's thoughts must have mirrored my own. 'Why, Crow, you seem to have lost your sense of humour.' He lifted his eyebrows in mock astonishment. 'Why is that? Are you telling me you have only now realized just how serious your position is? Surely you didn't expect us to let you walk free, did you? You are not that naïve?'

'So, give me a clue, Colonel. I hate surprises.'

'Clues? Well, you may rest assured, my friend, we do have some very interesting plans for you. Moscow does not take kindly to the activities of foreign mercenaries, especially when they are acting against our own interests.

'Oh, we know all about you, Crow,' Trevkin continued, obviously warming to the subject, 'and your contacts with the American Central Intelligence Agency. What is that expression? Ah, yes, I remember. Your sins have found you out, no? Well your sins, Crow, have been found out and they will be revealed when you stand trial for your crimes against the legitimate and democratic government of Afghanistan. Your presence will be a prime example of how the West is financing the sabotage and terror campaign employed by the anti-government forces based in Pakistan.'

He sounded as if he'd been rehearsing the speech for days. Next he would be berating me about Western decadence and telling me all about the peace-loving peoples of the Union of Soviet Socialist Republics and how they were all striving towards universal harmony, believing only in the freedom of mankind and the Kamchatka equivalent of mom's apple pie. Spare me that, Colonel, please.

I wondered what might be going through Massoud's mind at this point. While I'd been keeping up this merry banter with Colonel Trevkin the guerilla leader had remained silent, watching the proceedings through calm brown eyes. So far he had appeared remarkably unmoved by events; appearing to have accepted the circumstances in which he found himself with fatalistic detachment. I found that somewhat unnerving. He'd gained himself a reputation as a man of action. I hoped to God he wasn't going to go down without a fight. Although, surrounded as we were by Trevkin and his squad, I didn't see what choice he had. One thing Massoud wasn't was stupid. Maybe he was just waiting for the right moment to make his move. Maybe.

My thoughts were interrupted by a noise from outside; the grinding rumble of a heavy vehicle. The noise was evidently the signal that Trevkin had been expecting. He took one last drag on his cigarette and flicked the butt on to the floor. Grinding the stub into the ground, he glanced through the open door and drew his pistol from his belt.

'Our transport has arrived,' he announced. 'Time to leave, I think.'

'D'you mind me asking where it is taking us?' I asked.

'Not far. You are all to be flown to Kabul. There is a small airfield and military post a few miles from here. An aircraft is waiting there to pick us up. We will complete the first part of the journey by road, under escort.'

Trevkin then rapped out an order to his men, some of whom ran outside, presumably to check that the coast was clear. The rest of the squad remained inside the mosque and kept us covered.

Nicole had moved towards the door, a new expression of hope on her face. As if she was expecting her brother to stroll through like an airline passenger emerging from the green channel. I watched her wilt visibly as she realized that wasn't going to happen.

In a weak voice she said, 'Where is he?'

Trevkin sighed. 'Your brother will not be coming, Doctor.'

'Oh, God,' she breathed. 'What have you done with him?' There was a mounting trace of hysteria in her voice.

Trevkin said, 'Personally I did nothing to him, Doctor. I didn't have to. It had already been done.'

I felt the cold chill of impending doom.

'What do you mean?' She stared at him, her voice barely audible.

Trevkin said, 'Your brother is dead.'

Chapter Eighteen

For a moment I thought she was going to fall. I started towards her and felt the muzzle of Jassim's gun press into my kidneys.

'No . . .' She hugged herself, shook her head as if to banish the terrible visions that had entered her mind. 'They said he would not be harmed. They promised!'

Trevkin regarded her with something akin to pity. He shrugged offhandedly. 'They lied.' He turned for the door.

Nicole Bonnard went berserk.

With a dreadful cry she hurled herself at the Russian and for the briefest second the attention of the soldiers around us was distracted.

With a speed that defied measure Kerim drew his knife from its scabbard beneath his shirt and in less time than it took to blink he had slit open Jassim's throat. Jassim went down like a slaughtered calf, the Kalashnikov slipping from his lifeless fingers. I twisted desperately and made a grab for it. Pain flared along my injured ribs. I ignored it. From the corner of my eye I was aware of Maftoon thrusting the body of Massoud behind him as, with a wild bellow of rage, he threw himself towards Rasseikin.

Rasseikin shot him before he'd moved two paces. The Russian didn't even bother to aim as such. He simply swung his machine pistol up and fired. Maftoon ran into the bullets. He was dead before he hit the ground.

The rapid burst of gunfire crashed around the room like thunder. There was an acrid stench of cordite. In that second of awareness I knew I wasn't going to make it either. I was miles too slow. Kerim was already moving towards another target, one of the militia men, the blade of his knife catching fire as it tracked through the column of sunlight in the corner of the room. Massoud was rolling away and clawing for his own discarded gun. But neither of them was any quicker. Light from the open doorway was blocked as the men outside returned at a run. The noise of machine pistols being cocked echoed around the confined space like a death-rattle. Too late, Crow. Far too bloody late.

Rasseikin's finger was already tightening on the trigger of his gun and I realized, as I continued to claw hopelessly for Jassim's discarded weapon, that I was looking death in the face. Rasseikin's knuckles whitened.

'NIET!'

The order slammed around the walls.

Trevkin had hold of Nicole's hair. She was on her knees and he was twisting his fist around as though he was wringing out a shirt. Nicole had her eyes closed. Her mouth was open in a silent scream of pain.

Kerim and I froze, as did Massoud, locked into immobility like a trio of waxworks.

The Pathan caught my eye; the question hung in the air. Did we go for them anyway? I shook my head, glanced over at Massoud. Saw the tension gripping his body. No. Leave it.

Kerim dropped his knife, a savage reluctance in his expression.

We raised our hands slowly and placed them behind our necks.

'Stupid!' Trevkin snarled. 'Very, very stupid.'

He came towards us, dragging Nicole with him. 'I ought to kill you, Crow, you and these . . . these vermin!

But I have orders. They want you in Kabul. They want you all very badly. I intend to deliver you there.'

He let go of Nicole's hair and she fell forward towards me. I reached out and dragged her upright. She sagged against my shoulder, all cried out, her hurt spent. Trevkin glanced down at Maftoon's body with undisguised distaste. He stirred it with his foot. Beside me, Massoud growled under his breath. Trevkin walked over to Jassim's corpse and awarded it a brief perusal before stepping towards the door.

'Another acceptable loss, Colonel?' I inquired lightly.

He ignored me and spoke to somebody outside. One of the militia men came in with four sets of steel bracelets. Then they manacled our wrists. Trevkin watched the proceedings carefully. Satisfied that we no longer posed a threat he nodded at Rasseikin and we were herded outside into the square.

The vehicle was a BTR-152. A squat, six-wheeled armoured personnel carrier. There were also two Gaz jeeps. The newer-looking one was Trevkin's, the other was the one we'd arrived in. Trevkin boarded the first jeep in line and stood surveying the scene like Erwin Rommel. He wasn't sporting the sand visors but you could tell he was after the same intrepid effect. He called Rasseikin to him and spoke at some length. Rasseikin saluted casually and backed away, summoning his men. Evidently they weren't coming with us.

I wondered why that was and then it occurred to me that Rasseikin had completed only the first half of his mission.

The Soviets had timed their new offensive to coincide with the climax to the GRU operation. As of this moment the resistance had been relieved of its most able commander. And it would be Rasseikin's duty to spread the word among the people that Massoud had been captured. He and his men would begin to sow the seeds of panic and uncertainty among the ranks of the Mujehadeen. The terrible news would spread like wild fire. With Massoud taken, the first rifts in the guerilla hierarchy would begin to appear. The Russians would be able to move in without the fear of concerted resistance. Where there had once been cohesion there would now be rivalry, giving way to distrust and then fear as the unity of the various rebel groups began to disintegrate. Before long, inter-tribal warfare would have engulfed the country once more, taking priority over the fight against the invaders, making it easier for the Kabul regime to divide and conquer the various resistance factions. Allied to this, the agents of the Khad would no doubt intensify their policy of assassination and terror across the border, driving the Afghan leaders in exile towards a multilateral acceptance of Najibullah's offer of a truce and a subsequent laying down of arms. The concept was frightening in its inevitability.

We were prodded towards the APC and the rear door was swung open. The interior of the vehicle was lined with bench seats, facing inwards. I had to help Nicole up. They sat us against the right bulkhead, away from the door. Half a dozen of Trevkin's men climbed in after us and took their seats. The remainder split themselves between the two jeeps.

It was like sitting in a tomb. There was a distinct feeling of claustrophobia made even more acute as the door began to close. My last view of the scene outside was of Taras Rasseikin. He was watching me. As the gap around the edge of the door narrowed I saw him raise his hand to his forehead in a final mocking salute. Then the hatch slammed shut like the lid of a coffin.

The lights came on and we began to move. The big

vehicle shambled forward like a tired rhino. One of the soldiers stood up and opened a square hatch in the roof. Instinctively the four of us raised our faces to the light source as if hoping that the effect of the angled sunlight would, by some miracle, erase the sense of foreboding that gripped our minds.

I felt drained, mentally and physically. The edges of the steel bracelets were cutting into my wrists. I glanced at the others. Massoud and Kerim were sitting opposite me. Kerim's eyes were half closed. Sunshine slanting through the open hatch above us played across his face. He looked completely relaxed. Massoud was looking gloomy but when he looked up and caught my eye a shy smile crept over his face and he gave me a philosophical shrug. It was the look of a man who had played the game, thrown the wrong combination of dice, and lost. No recriminations, just resignation.

Nicole was leaning with her head against the side of the hull. Her eyes were red rimmed, her pose listless. The chain of my manacles clinked as I touched her. 'Why didn't you tell us what was going on?'

The BTR lurched suddenly and my back jarred against the stanchion behind me. Nicole's body swayed in her seat as she regained her balance. 'How could I?' she replied with complete despondency. 'They told me I would never see Alain again.'

I knew it would be cruel and quite futile to point out that she still wouldn't although at the time she'd made her pact with the Khad agents she couldn't possibly have known of the outcome to her complicity. It was clear that guilt seasoned with knowledge of the GRU treachery would now be eating her up inside. And that would be almost as hard a cross to bear as the acceptance of her brother's death.

'Remember,' she'd said. 'No matter what happens.' I recalled her words to me. Only now did they make sense. Dear God; the pain she must have been feeling, carrying, as she had been, the full weight of her deceit since she'd left Pakistan.

Alain Bonnard's fate had been sealed the moment the GRU had put their plan into action. As I thought about that another, almost as uncomfortable, thought struck me. Someone else's fate had been sealed also. That of the man they had sent me in to airlift out of the country in the first place. Muhammed Nur Rafiq. I asked Nicole Bonnard what the prognosis would have been had he not been killed in the air attack. She had known before we'd taken off from Peshawar that there had never been the slightest chance that the man would have been flown out of Afghanistan to safety.

'We would have taken him to Mir Seraj,' she said 'or . . .' She fell silent.

A terrible understanding gripped me. 'Jesus,' I breathed. 'You mean you'd have killed him?'

'That's what they wanted me to do,' she whispered. 'With an overdose of morphine. I told them I wouldn't do it.'

In the final analysis, of course, the decision had been taken out of her hands. But I thought of the full extent of the nightmare she must have been going through. My nightmares were day dreams by comparison.

She spoke to Massoud then, hesitantly, in French. I guessed she was trying to make atonement. Her voice was breaking and fresh tears began to well in her eyes. Massoud listened to her, his head on one side. Watching him closely I could see the compassion in his eyes. He had lost family and friends in the years of fighting. He must have known what she had been through; what she was going through. He waited until she had finished then he spoke slowly and softly, also in French. He seemed to be reassuring her. He reached to his neck and removed his scarf. Then he passed it to her and watched with concern as she wiped the tears from her cheeks. She went to return it to him but he shook his head and indicated that she should keep it. She smiled tentatively, gratefully, and slipped it around her own neck.

'I'm scared, Crow,' she said, resting her head against my shoulder. 'I think they are going to kill us too.'

'If they are,' I said, 'they're wasting an awful lot of petrol. They could have done the job back in the village and left us there. Besides they'll get more mileage out of us alive than dead. You heard the colonel. They want us badly, he said.'

She was silent for a while. The engine of the APC clanked and roared as it negotiated the mountain road. I had a sudden desire to stick my head out of the hatch and look to see where we were going. It was like being on one of those mystery tours where only the driver knows the destination. The difference here of course was that we all knew where we were going to end up. That took the fun out of the ride for sure.

There was something I had to know. Something I hadn't yet asked her. I said, 'Who was your contact?'

She stared at me. 'What?'

It had to have been someone close to the resistance. Someone who'd been privy to the plot to airlift Muhammed Nur Rafiq out of Afghanistan; who'd been confident enough to guess that I'd accept the contract and then alert the Soviets that I'd be going in by chopper to bring him out, taking Nicole Bonnard with me. There could be only one answer. When I repeated the question. Nicole confirmed it.

293

'It was the doctor,' she said. 'Doctor Habbani.'

I nodded tiredly. I had suspected as much. It couldn't have been anybody else. So Habbani was an agent of the Khad, I reasoned. A mole deep inside the resistance organization with the ear of all the main leaders. Probably using fat Rasul as a conduit by which to relay messages to his masters in Kabul and Moscow Centre. His background as fictitious as that of Jassim Rana and Alain Bonnard's bid for freedom. The GRU had trained their men well, it appeared. Very well indeed.

Jassim was dead but Habbani would continue his mission, gnawing away at the resistance from within. Festering inside the Hezb like a cancer.

She interrupted my thoughts, asking softly, 'Do you really work for the CIA, Crow?'

I stared at her. I was right out of flip remarks. 'No, love.'

'But you know people who do?' She had obviously taken heed of Colonel Trevkin's diatribe back in the mosque.

'A long time ago,' I said. 'Not any more.'

'Trevkin doesn't think so.'

'Trevkin's a moron,' I said. 'He's after brownie points. He's probably after a cushy number somewhere. Military attaché in Washington, I shouldn't wonder. He'd say anything to get out of his present tour of duty.'

He's also exceedingly dangerous, I thought grimly.

I could see how his mind had been working. I wondered how I'd cope with being a film star. Because they'd have cameras there, of course. Footage of the Western mercenary paid by the Americans and working among the rebels would be relayed around the world. Proof that Western intelligence agencies were financing the insurrection. I wouldn't be in the same league as Gary Powers, of course, but I'd be up there in the GRU's Hall of Fame, my face on the front pages of the world's press. I presumed they'd want me to sign some confession, make a public statement apologizing for my actions, renounce the resistance, et cetera. Then what?

Something I recalled from my days in Nam. It concerned some of the men who carried the title MIA: missing in action. A meeting with a man in Saigon. A man called Codey. Now, he had been CIA. A radio operator who had been responsible for monitoring VC broadcasts. One of his functions had been to track the movements of American prisoners of war captured by the North Vietnamese. In particular, aircrew. He'd been able to do it by homing in on VC radio traffic. Knowing the general vicinity of downed US aircraft he was virtually able to pinpoint the moment of capture by the messages coming in over the radio. Once the airmen were in enemy hands he could, by tuning in to Charlie's broadcasts, track the route taken by prisoner and escort. Generally he could put names to the crewmen who'd been picked up. He told me they had a file on these airmen. A special file.

The VC had a tendency to shoot prisoners or put them in isolated jungle stockades. With aircrew it was different. Aircrew were specialists, technicians, particularly if they were navigating officers. These men were in command of multi-million-dollar pieces of hardware; state of the art aircraft. The VC didn't shoot people like that, they were too valuable. They delivered them to people who would tap into that knowledge and use it to further their own technical know how. The names of the airmen in Codey's special file had a set of initials after them. The letter signified that a specific fate awaited them. The initials were M.B. They stood for Moscow Bound. It was another way of saying they disappeared into thin air.

Not that I was any kind of technical wizard. I wasn't. I was an out of work chopper pilot. And I wasn't Moscow Bound either. But I had this terrible feeling that Kabul Bound meant the same thing. I was going to disappear too.

The explosion, when it came, sounded enormous and very close.

The first thought that plummeted into my brain was that we'd struck a mine. But I realized a second later that it hadn't been our vehicle that had been hit.

We had travelled without further incident up until that point. True, our progress had been a bit erratic due to the state of the terrain but the APC was heavy enough to withstand the deepest potholes. It had been an uncomfortable ride. Despite the open hatch, it had been hot and cramped in the personnel carrier's metal hull, jolted at every turn of the wheels. I wasn't sure how far we had come since leaving Qum. We hadn't been moving for that long and the velocity of the APC wasn't exactly terminal. So, when the jeep in front of us ran into the sharp end of the RPG-7 our own driver had time to react.

He slammed on the brakes and I braced myself against the hull as we slewed across the track. Nicole screamed and grabbed hold of my arm. Kerim and Massoud were thrown out of their seats. They landed on the floor at my feet in a tangle of arms and legs and jangling manacles. Our guards were yelling at each other. I thought, if they're going to start shooting inside this heap we're all going to meet our respective makers.

From outside came the harsh rattle of automatic fire and the sound of men shouting. Bullets clanged off the hull of the APC, whining into the distance like fast-disappearing hornets. Someone screamed and there followed the dull crump of an impacting missile.

Inside the APC it was pandemonium. Massoud and Kerim had extricated themselves from their undignified position on the floor. At the other end of the vehicle the militiamen were loudly involved in deciding who should open the rear hatch first. None of them seemed too keen to play hero. But I knew what they were thinking. They were thinking what it would be like trapped inside the APC if someone outside decided to let off another RPG. Those things could penetrate 12in armour plate. The effect of a hit in such a confined space was, to say the least, messy. It turned living flesh into pink gruel.

Then someone dropped a grenade through the top hatch and that did the trick.

I was aware of a shadow passing over my head, blotting out the sunlight and then something small and cylindrical dropped at my feet and rolled away down the length of the floor.

It could well be that my heart ceased to beat at that point. I know only that in the microsecond that seemed to stretch into an eternity freezing terror paralyzed my vocal cords.

Then I screamed.

'GRENADE!'

And threw myself over Nicole's soft body in a ludicrous attempt to protect her from the blast.

The militiamen, eyes popping with fear, shrieked and hurled themselves out of the rear door while the driver and commander disappeared through their own entry ports like greased piglets. Into a withering hail of bullets. My ears rang with the screams of the dying men and the hammering bursts of automatic fire. At the same time my brain was telling me that I was still alive and the grenade hadn't gone off.

I raised my head cautiously and squinted down the vehicle. The grenade had rolled to a stop against the rear bulkhead. It lay there, dormant, like a discarded tin of tobacco. This isn't happening, I thought.

The door crashed back against the hull of the APC and a dark character in shapeless Afghan dress roared at me.

'Birram! Birram! Let's go. Let's go!'

A hand reached out and picked up the grenade. The cylinder disappeared into the folds of the man's pantaloons. I hauled Nicole to her knees and thrust her towards the hatch. Massoud and Kerim tumbled after her. I crawled behind them, poked my head out into the fresh air. A hand grabbed at my collar and I was dragged unceremoniously into the dirt.

I landed on my side, the steel bracelets glancing off my knee. I cursed violently and struggled to sit up. The four of us made a sorry little huddle in the road. But we didn't look half as sorry as the bodies of our guards. They lay spread eagled and blood stained, their weapons beside them. They hadn't stood a chance.

We were surrounded.

Men in the dress of Mujehadeen. They were stripping the bodies of the militiamen and picking up weapons. A figure loomed over me. I looked up into the face of the man who'd dragged me from the APC. About my own age, stocky, compact, short black hair. He was also dressed completely in black with bandoliers slung across his chest. He glared down at me.

'You gonna squat there all day, fella? Or d'you wanna get your ass into gear?'

I peered up at him, at the Kalashnikov in his hands, the shoulder holster with automatic pistol under his left armpit. Tanned, square-jawed, teeth just perfect examples of the orthodontist's art. Hollywood's idea of a freedom fighter.

I sighed. 'Hello, Tagg,' I said wearily. 'Fancy meeting you here.'

Chapter Nineteen

Trevkin's jeep lay on its side, bonnet open, engine parts spewing across the dirt track like the innards of a disembowelled turtle. The shell of the vehicle was burnt and blackened like a brick of charcoal. Bodies lay scattered about it. Splashes of blood ran dark across the ground or formed small pools that seeped into the grey earth like water into a sponge. I spotted Trevkin's body. The GRU man lay face down, one arm outstretched, the other twisted somewhere beneath him. A scarlet trickle had emerged from under his head and was meandering away between the cracks in the topsoil.

The second jeep had careered into a clump of foliage at the edge of the track. It had collected a few more bullet holes in its chassis and windscreen but apart from that it looked relatively undamaged. The driver, however, lay hunched over the steering wheel, unseeing eyes gazing bleakly into the middle distance. He had been shot in the chest.

Someone had found the keys to the bracelets. I rubbed my wrists vigorously to restore circulation. Nicole was still looking dazed. Kerim and Massoud, ever practical, were retrieving their confiscated weapons.

Tagg was directing his men like a sergeant major. There were about a dozen of them and they were working fast, gathering guns and ammunition that could be used at a later date.

'Birram! Come on, move it!' he urged them. He was addressing them in both English and Farsi, switching from one to the other without hesitation. 'Bala! Grab the gear! Shift yourselves, f'r Chris'sakes!' He caught me watching him. 'You too, birdman. Make yourself useful.'

So, one mystery had been solved at least. This was where Jackson Tagg had ended up. The rumours about him had, it appeared, some foundation. The American was involved with the resistance. And Trevkin, had he lived, would no doubt have been well pleased to have seen his suspicions confirmed. I did have contacts with the CIA after all. For the moment, anyway. Unless Tagg was working freelance.

I caught the AK-47 that Kerim threw to me, checked the magazine was secure.

Tagg was watching me. 'How're you doing?'

'Oh, great,' I muttered. 'Absolutely fucking tremendous.' I purloined a spare magazine from a passing Mujehad and stuck it in my belt. Then I told him it was a neat trick he'd pulled with the dud grenade.

He chuckled. 'Gets 'em every time. Suckers!'

Then I asked him what the hell he was doing there.

'Dumb question, Crow. I've just been saving your ass.'

'Mine in particular?'

He grinned. 'Well, maybe not yours directly.' He jerked his head at Massoud. 'But his certainly. You could say I'm trying to protect Uncle Sam's interests.'

'I take it that means you're here on Company business?' I said.

He squinted at me hard. 'Bright boy, aren't you, Crow?'

'I have my moments.'

He sighed. 'Let's just say that Washington has six hundred million dollars' worth of aid riding on these fellas; Massoud in particular. They wanted somebody to check on their investment.'

'And you're the man?'

He nodded. 'I'm the man.'

Some euphemism, checking Washington's investment. Tagg was quite obviously engaged in a lot more than that. Such as training the Mujehadeen in the use of shoulder-held Stinger, Blowpipe and SAM-7 anti-aircraft missile launchers for example. Like the one Kerim had used to such devastating effect at Dar Galak. Men like Tagg had a tendency to crop up in every country where the USA felt that its interests were being threatened by the ogres of Communism. In Nam he'd have been with the SOG; in Central America he'd have been working with the FDN. His title would have been the same: military advisor, a euphemism in itself. In effect it meant that Tagg was as much a soldier of fortune as the mercenaries that frequented the Permit room at Dean's Hotel. The only difference being that Tagg's paymaster was the American government. He was here to train the guerillas to kill Russians. He'd been working among the rebel camps in the Panjsher for weeks, supervising the distribution and use of the newly arrived consignments of Stingers and the other weapons the Mujehadeen had been able to lay their hands on.

But, by Christ, he'd succeeded in keeping a low profile. In the days we had spent in the valley not once had we been given any indication that the American was in the area. But he knew we were there all right. He'd been keeping tabs on us. Lucky for us he had been.

Tagg and a Mujehadeen patrol had been on a scouting mission to determine Soviet troop deployment in the valley. One of Tagg's point men had witnessed the springing of the GRU trap. He'd contacted Tagg by field radio and the CIA man had reacted quickly to set up his ambush along Trevkin's escape route.

Massoud approached us, Kerim at his shoulder. The

301

guerilla leader smiled and shook Tagg's hand. He addressed the American in Farsi, presumably expressing his thanks for his deliverance from Trevkin's clutches.

'You're welcome,' Tagg replied in English.

Christ, I thought. If he tells him to have a nice day, I'm probably going to throw up.

Instead Tagg said briskly, 'Okay, let's get the hell out of here. Someone's gonna be wondering where you've all gotten to. Ivan will be sending out spotters.'

'Where are we going?' I asked. I looked around for Nicole. She was behind me. 'You okay?'

She nodded and stared at the American.

'This is Tagg,' I said. 'Our hero.'

'Doctor,' Tagg acknowledged her brusquely, obviously well aware of who she was. He continued, 'Massoud rejoins his men. You and the doctor get taken to Paryan. There's a Mujehadeen convoy heading for the border tonight.' He added dryly, 'If that's fine by you?'

'Spot on,' I said.

'Right,' Tagg announced. 'Let's move.'

The report of the pistol shot rang out sharp and clear, like one block of wood striking another. Everybody scattered, except Massoud. He pitched forward into my arms like a man tripping over a kerbstone in the street, his narrow face registering total shock as the bullet entered his back.

The Mujehadeen panicked; there was no other way to describe their response. At the sight of their fallen commander they cried out in alarm, jabbering at each other like madmen as they tried to shield him from further harm and pinpoint the source of this new and unexpected attack. Kerim fell away, taking Nicole with him. But it was Tagg who tuned in and responded quicker than anybody. He turned very fast, his machine pistol in his hands. As I

302

began to lower Massoud's body to the ground I saw where the shot had come from.

Trevkin. He wasn't dead. He'd been playing possum, biding his time, awaiting his chance. Now he'd retaliated, with a vengeance.

The Russian had raised himself on one hand and drawn his gun from the holster on his waist. Blood masked his face. He was bracing himself for another shot when Tagg fired.

Tagg's bullet blew away Trevkin's face in a crimson spray of blood, skull fragments and grey brain matter and the GRU man's corpse slid backwards across the road.

By the time the echoes of the shots had died away people had begun to crowd around. Nicole arrived first, followed by Tagg.

Massoud's face was lined with pain. Nicole helped me turn him gently on to his side. Massoud groaned as the movement aggravated the hurt inside him.

'How bad?' There was a cold hard urgency in Tagg's inquiry as he bent a knee beside us. It wasn't that the American was being unduly blunt, he was being practical. Although it had seemed like hours since he and his men had ambushed our convoy it had, in fact, been something like six or seven minutes. But in this situation that was a long time. It wasn't inconceivable that hostile ears had picked up the sounds of the gun battle and even now were heading to investigate. Rasseikin and his men to name but a few. Tagg didn't want to be around if and when they got here.

Nicole shook her head helplessly. 'I don't know.' She was moving her hand around under Massoud's jacket, assessing damage. She withdrew her hand. It came away with blood on it.

'What the hell do you mean you don't know?' Tagg barked. 'You're a fucking doctor, for Christ's sake!'

'I mean I can't tell you!' Her voice rose sharply. 'The bullet seems to be in very deep. There is no exit wound.'

'Jesus, lady! Can't you do something? Anything?' Tagg shouted.

'What do you suggest?' she shot back at him. 'Do you want me to open him up and operate here? Don't be so foolish! He needs serious attention. Much more than I can provide.'

Tagg crunched his fist into the ground in exasperation. The American stared angrily down at Massoud as though the wounded guerilla leader had invited the calamity purely as a means of providing him with the maximum amount of inconvenience.

'Shit!' The expletive exploded from between Tagg's gritted teeth with undeniable force.

His concern was affecting the Mujehadeen. It was clear from the looks on their faces that they were becoming increasingly jumpy. They were milling around like frightened sheep. We were going to have to come up with something pretty damned fast.

'Can we move him?' Tagg asked Nicole suddenly.

On the face of it I thought that was a pretty bloody silly question. We didn't really have any choice. We'd have to move him. We couldn't stay where we were, that was for certain. But there wasn't a friendly medical facility within miles. And, with the Russians moving their forces into the valley we'd have a hard time carrying a wounded man through their lines. They'd run us to earth within hours. Not that we even had hours when it came down to it. Massoud was obviously badly hurt. Judging by his sweat-encrusted brow, we didn't have much time at all. This

304

man was going to die very soon unless someone used their brain. We all knew that.

Tagg didn't give Nicole a chance to reply. He stood up quickly. 'Okay,' he said. 'Here's what we'll do.'

We all waited.

Tagg said, 'We'll fly him out.'

Nicole and I stared up at him. Eventually I found my voice. 'What?'

'You heard,' Tagg replied.

'I heard it,' I said. 'But I don't believe it. Who the hell are you thinking of using? The Red Cross?' And then I thought, Oh, Jesus, no.

'That's right, Crow. You've got it. You're supposed to be some kind of hotshot pilot. Now's the time to prove it. Hell, with a name like yours, it should be a piece of cake.'

'You've got to be fucking joking, Tagg. Where are we going to find an aircraft?'

'You've got a short attention span,' he grated. 'There's one waiting for us, remember?'

Bloody blimey, I thought. Trevkin's master plan.

'Okay, wise-ass,' Tagg said. 'You got a better idea?'

Not right off the top of my head I hadn't, no.

'Look, people,' Tagg said. 'While we're debating the issue here, Ivan's closing in. The doctor tells us Massoud's in a bad way. Chances are he might not even make it. So it strikes me we got a few options. Now we can stay here while the young lady performs crude field surgery, with not much chance of success; or we can try and make it through the Russian lines to one of those French field stations; or we could even sit here and fend off Soviet ground forces while we wait for him to die. Which would give us an extended life span of about ten seconds. Alternatively we can try and hijack an aeroplane and fly him to Pakistan. Which is it to be?' He turned to me.

305

'How far d'you reckon we are from the border, birdman? And how long would it take us?'

We were, in actuality, probably less than one hundred miles from the Durand Line, when it came down to it. As the crow flew, of course, but I refrained from saying that to Tagg. I didn't want him to get the impression that I was being facetious. Meanwhile the clock was ticking away. I thought about it. 'Depends on the aircraft,' I said. 'And you'd have to allow for contingencies, of course.'

'Like what?'

'Like having to negotiate the entire width of the Hindu Kush at ground level while the Russians try to shoot our balls off.'

'But it's still the quickest way we'll be able to get him to a proper medical facility, right? Short of handing him over to the Russians, that is.'

Put bluntly like that I couldn't argue with him. In pure minutes and seconds Tagg was absolutely correct. But we'd have to be stark staring mad to even contemplate it. Now, where had I heard that before?

'Right,' Tagg said into the ensuing silence. 'That settles it. Here's what we'll do.'

Tagg outlined his plan in the carnage of the Mujehadeen ambush. And promptly ran into one big snag.

The Mujehadeen weren't at all happy at the thought of us flying their commander anywhere, much less out of the country. Tagg hadn't thought of that, had he?

In the end it was Kerim who came to Tagg's rescue. From where I was standing it seemed that the young Pathan was lambasting the devil out of his fellow guerillas. Tagg was sticking his four penn'th into the pot too. As far as I could gather, the main thrust of their argument amounted to one simple question. What would the resistance rather have: one live commander or one dead martyr?

306

Grudgingly, the men started to come around. They did so only because Kerim swore to them he would accompany Massoud to safety. He would take full responsibility for the rebel commander's life.

And yet I couldn't help thinking that, ironically, the GRU plan was pretty close to fruition. With the curtain about to rise on the new Russian offensive the fighters in the Panjsher were going to be without their leader after all. If we did manage to spirit Massoud over the border and the Russians launched their attack, would his men be able to hold out until he returned? If he ever did.

Either way, we had to move quickly.

Massoud was carried gently to the APC and placed carefully along the seats on one side of the hull. Nicole went with him. The wounded guerilla leader had been wrapped inside some of the Mujehadeen cloaks to cushion him against the bumps and jolts he would undoubtedly suffer during the ride down to the Russian military post where, Trevkin had told us, the aircraft scheduled to transport us to Kabul would be waiting.

Next we retook possession of Massoud's jeep, reversing it back on to the track and dumping its contents; the driver's stiffening corpse.

Then we stripped the dead. That was the worst part.

The difficulty was finding enough uniforms that didn't carry bloodstains. In the end, and surprisingly, we retrieved five, mostly removed from bodies that had suffered only head wounds and one or two where the bullet holes could be concealed by strategically held weapons and liberal daubings of dirt and dust from the road surface.

The uniforms were for those of us who were going to travel in the open. Which meant me, Tagg, Kerim, and two of Tagg's unbearded Mujehadeen. He'd picked me because he wanted someone to watch his back. I was flattered but bemused. He evidently didn't have a great deal of faith in the men he had with him. Maybe he had a point. The Afghans had already shown that they had a distinct tendency to get over excited in a fire fight and often lacked coordination. Tagg said he wanted someone with him who would do exactly as he ordered without getting carried away in the heat of the moment. I took that as a backhanded compliment.

Tagg wore Trevkin's uniform. It was the one that mattered more than the others because it carried the colonel's insignia; the authority that, with luck, would get us through the gates. It also carried a fair splattering of the colonel's life blood, a legacy of the head shot that had killed him. But the traces were situated for the main part around the collar and they could be hidden by one of the Mujehadeen scarves. This colonel was, after all, a member of the GRU. No one would be likely to question his dress code. His cap, oddly enough, we had discovered intact on the floor of the jeep. It had fallen there during the attack and was conveniently unmarked save for the sweat stains around the band on the inside of the brim. Tagg didn't seem to be too bothered about that when he put it on.

The jacket fitted him well enough. He was of a similar build to the dead Russian which had been a bonus we couldn't disregard and I had to admit, as I buttoned myself into my own jacket, that he looked the part.

'There is one thing, Tagg,' I said.

He was busy strapping on Trevkin's belt and holster. 'What's that, birdman?'

'Anyone here speak Russian?'

There was a pregnant pause. Everybody who'd understood my question looked at everybody else.

Tagg pulled the belt in a notch. 'Yeah,' he said, not batting an eyelid. 'I do.'

I sighed. It figured he would. Dumb question, really.

'Just a thought,' I murmured, chastened.

Tagg nodded, unperturbed. He looked up. 'Everyone set?'

We were something of an assortment. Like a job lot at an army recruitment centre. Half in uniform, half out of it. I was reminded of Rasseikin's Spetsnaz squad. We looked just as unsavoury. Kerim was scratching around under one armpit and grumbling about the fit of the khaki jacket. Out of his Mujehad garb he looked like a fish out of water. I could tell he was itching to tear the jacket off, literally. The other two Mujehadeen looked equally as fetching.

Tagg split us up. The Mujehadeen not in uniform were to travel inside the APC, hidden from view. One of Tagg's uniformed men would drive it. The rest of us would ride in the jeep; Tagg and a driver in the front, Kerim and me in the rear.

'Okay,' Tagg said when we were ready. 'Let's go kick some ass.' He sounded as gung ho as John Wayne hitting the sands at Iwo Jima.

The Afghan Army, I soon discovered, had a great deal more than the inhospitable countryside and the wily Mujehadeen to contend with. Their uniforms for a start. The material itched like buggery.

The jeep bounced across a shallow gully in the track and my backside took momentary flight. I winced as I came down to land and felt an immediate release of perspiration dampen my armpits. The tight jacket collar was beginning to develop all the comfort of a serge garotte. The trousers fitted even worse. Perversely I had chosen to wear them over my jeans. Uncomfortable wasn't the word. I'd drawn a line at donning the boots though. I was still wearing my trainers. Sitting in the back of the jeep, my feet hidden from casual view, I hoped that no one would bother to look that far down. I reckoned glumly that not only had I scaled more mountains than Sherpa Tensing, I'd also been through more costume changes than Laurence Olivier.

Twenty yards behind the end of our tail pipe the APC was chasing our exhaust fumes like a dogged buffalo. I wondered how Massoud was coping. Nicole too. She'd had more than her fair share of woe in the last few hours. So far, her endurance had proved remarkable.

Tagg halted the convoy in the shade of some trees just below a small ridge. We took Trevkin's field glasses and went to reconnoitre. We crawled to the crest of the hill and looked down on to the valley. Below us lay the airfield.

Tagg passed me the glasses. Details sprang into sharp relief. It looked very much a makeshift affair with one narrow strip of runway stretching along the floor of the valley like a dirt road in a desert, which wasn't so very far from fact. There were no permanent buildings in evidence, only a few Quonset-style huts set behind a wire perimeter fence at one end of the runway. Standing apart from them was a group of military vehicles; a couple of T-62 tanks and three personnel carriers. Alongside these was parked a big Zil-157 radio truck attached to a trailer-mounted PAR and radio antennae. I moved the glasses a fraction and my throat went dry.

Mi-24s. A brace of them. They squatted on the dusty ground like two fat beetles. Tagg had spotted them already. 'There's our way out,' he whispered. Adroitly aware of my silence, he glanced across. 'What's up, birdman? Cat got your tongue?'

'You've got to be out of your fucking tree, Tagg!' I stared at him, disbelief accounting for the shrillness in my voice. 'You want us to steal one of their gunships?'

This wasn't what I'd had in mind at all. I'd been expecting the aircraft to be some sort of transport plane; an Antonov maybe, something like that. A Hind? No frigging way!

Tagg gripped my arm like a vice. His eyes blazed. 'Now, you listen to me, Crow. We've got one sick man back there. This is his only chance! Dammit, this country's only chance! You know what'll happen to these people if Massoud kicks the bucket? It'll go down the fucking tubes! That happens and Gorbachev's next stop'll be Iran, maybe even Pakistan. Then he'll have his warm water ports and both sides of the Gulf and a stranglehold on the oil routes. That's out of the fucking question, Crow! That's unacceptable!'

I shook him free, 'Christ, Tagg! You slay me, you really do! Your government's bloody paranoid, you stupid prick! Why can't you stay the hell out of other people's business. You've screwed up in so many countries you can't see straight. Chile, Nam, Central America. You name it and the Company's sticky fingers are always there. Why don't you just back off for once? Give us all a break! You couldn't give a toss for that poor sod. All you're interested in is opening up the area for a new Macdonald's franchise. Massoud's just another one of your pawns, you pious bastard!'

Tagg's jaw dropped open at this point. Then he found his voice. 'Okay, Crow,' he said abruptly. 'You've had your say, you've got it off your chest. Now that we've finished debating US foreign policy, are you going to fly us out of here or not?'

I glared at him.

311

'Hey, Crow,' he said placatingly. 'Ease up. C'mon, guy, I'm just doing my job, okay?'

I opened my mouth but no words came out. I picked up the glasses and took a second look at the field. Fuck you, Tagg, I thought.

In my ear Tagg said seductively, 'What if I offered you a little incentive?'

I put down the glasses.

'Do you know how much one of those babies would be worth to Uncle Sam?' he asked, inclining his head towards the two helicopters.

I closed my eyes. But that didn't blot out his next utterance.

'Half a million, Crow.' He paused as the words sank in. 'Think about it.'

I opened my eyes slowly. Blinked. 'Dollars?'

'No, yen, asshole! Of course I mean dollars. US dollars. Greenbacks. Hell, we've been after one of those machines for a long time. We had a go for one in Nicaragua about four months ago. Entrusted the job to a couple of ex-Air America mercs working for Setco. Only Ortega's boys got wise and our two fellas had to abort the mission. They were on a contract for the same amount. As far as I know the deal's still open.'

I breathed deeply. Half a million. I took another look at the gunships. I was conscious that while I was doing so there was a man dying less than twenty paces behind me.

'All right, Tagg.' I handed him back the field glasses. 'Let's get it over with before I change my mind. And remember this,' I jerked my thumb at the APC, 'I'm doing it for him, not your damned state department.'

Tagg eyed me sceptically. 'You mean you're not interested in the dough?'

We crabbed away from the top of the ridge and regained

our feet. I brushed soil from my jacket and gave a resigned shrug. I said, 'Let's just say it'll help subsidize my success.'

He slapped my shoulder and grinned wickedly. 'Attaboy!'

We ran back to the vehicles. Inside the APC it was hot and airless. 'How's he doing?' I asked Nicole.

'He's holding on,' she said. 'I don't know how.' She wiped Massoud's forehead with a length of scarf. 'What's happening?'

'We're going in,' I said. 'We're going to steal one of their helicopters.'

Her eyes widened with fear. 'God, Crow, I'm frightened.'

I looked at her. 'I know, love,' I said. 'So am I.'

Chapter Twenty

I asked Tagg why he was grinning.

'You ever read poetry, Crow?'

A strange answer. I told him it wasn't one of my vices and wondered where he was leading me.

'Tennyson,' he said and waited for the penny to drop.

I only knew of two poems penned by him. One of them was 'The Charge of The Light Brigade'. The other one wasn't. But I saw what Tagg was getting at. The significance of our actions had not escaped me.

'Into the valley of Death . . .' I murmured.

Tagg nodded. 'Right first time, Crow. Kind of hits you, don't it?'

Yeah, very whimsical, I told him. I was suddenly conscious that the knuckles on the hand gripping the butt of my Kalashnikov had turned white. If ever a man was dismayed, it was me. And Kerim. The Pathan was muttering something in my ear. He had his hand tucked inside the top of his army tunic. I guessed he was clasping his copy of the Qoran contained in the pouch strung around his neck. He was praying. All things considered, I thought he had good reason. Cannons to the right of us, cannons to the left of us. Russian ones, like in the poem.

We passed tanks dug into the ground like burrowing animals, turrets extending like the snouts of strange subterranean rodents about to emerge from their setts. A small convoy of half a dozen trucks went by us, some of them ladened with soldiers, others with munitions. It was evident that the airfield, although not yet fully established, was destined to become a major staging point for the new Soviet advance. The odds were beginning to stack up like building bricks.

But nobody challenged us. In Russian and Afghan uniforms, in a Russian vehicle, why should they? We were invisible. We breezed through.

Where the runway began there had been a village once, long ago. Now the houses were flattened, laid waste by Russian bombing. The fields either side of the main road had dried to a harsh stubbled plain. The irrigation ditches were redundant. They ran along the edges of the barren acreage; a ribbon of dried-out trenches reminiscent of other, more ancient, battlefields.

Under pretext of stopping to examine one of the jeep's perfectly sound tyres we pulled in to the side of the track and Tagg gave us the once over. He told Kerim to fasten the top button on his jacket, ordered me to straighten my cap, my stitches were showing. I studied the opposition.

Ahead of us the airfield was protected from the outside world by a ten-foot-high perimeter fence. A guard post and a tilting wooden barrier sealed off the main entrance. From where we were situated there appeared to be two men on sentry duty. At the moment there wasn't a whole lot for them to guard. Except for the two helicopters. They were parked about two hundred yards inside the fence. Even at that distance they looked enormous and intimidating. Tagg unfastened the flap on his pistol holster. He took out the gun and placed it under his right thigh. Then we went for broke.

By my reckoning they should have been expecting Trevkin. After all they were holding an aircraft for him. So there was an outside possibility that they would automatically raise the barrier as we approached. But they didn't.

Instead, the sentry stepped out from the side of the road and flagged us down. At this stage I was conscious that the only noise louder than the rumble of the APC's engine behind me was the rhythmic hammering of my heart. I felt a bead of sweat trickle like a teardrop down the side of my face. Inside the crotch of my jeans my skin began to prickle. Daniel must have felt like this on his way into the lions' den.

The tread of the sentry as he walked slowly up to the side of the jeep sounded as loud as a measured drum beat. I looked for his partner. And found him studying us through the window of the sentry box. I couldn't see his features clearly due to the sun's reflection on the glass. But I knew he was looking at me. I could feel it. The palms of my hands had turned damp and clammy.

The nearest guard looked as if he wasn't long out of short trousers but already he had that slightly stiff-legged cocky kind of stroll common to almost everyone in a peaked cap who'd been delegated any kind of authority, even if it meant asking a full colonel to produce his identity papers. With his fur hat on his head he looked as if he was auditioning for the role of Davy Crockett. Only his gun wasn't a Brown Bess, it was an AK-47. He was carrying it slung over his right shoulder. The salute, when it came, was adequate. He gave us a slow once over and spoke to Tagg. There was a certain deference in his voice but I could still tell that he was asking Tagg what our business was.

Tagg's Russian was good. At least it sounded so to me. I didn't have a clue, of course, what it sounded like to the sentry. For all I knew Tagg could have been asking him what time the next bus left for Leninskiy Prospekt. But there was authority in his voice and whatever he'd said it seemed to have worked. The sentry stepped back, saluted again, and walked over to the bulbous end of the wooden barrier.

Sweet Jesus, I thought. We're in!

Which was when the second guard stepped into view which just went to prove that life could be a real bitch.

This one was of a different breed. Older, wiser, more cynical, and probably harbouring a deep grudge against anybody higher up the echelons of rank than he was. And he didn't give a damn who knew it either.

The first thing he did was to tell his apprentice to take his hand away from the pole. Then he sauntered over.

When he extended his palm to Tagg I knew he was asking for some sort of ID. The younger man might have been intimidated by Tagg's badges of rank but not this one. He was going by the book.

Tagg was carrying Trevkin's ID. It was in his top pocket. He'd established that much after he'd commandeered the uniform. The problem was that although the American might have matched the GRU man physically, facially they were poles apart. One look at Trevkin's photograph would reveal that fact.

I started to ease my finger around the trigger of my gun. Tagg shrugged, handed the sentry his ID and slid his right hand down under his thigh.

And one of the tanks inside the perimeter fence blew up.

We'd been expecting it to happen; the guards hadn't. Both of them swung around in horror as the T-62's turret billowed in orange flame. Tagg drew his pistol from beneath his thigh and shot the older guard in the head. The sentry's features disintegrated and he sagged backwards, the look of amazement still transfixed to the segments of his face that remained intact. Trevkin's useless identity papers fell from his fingers and fluttered to the ground. The second, younger man, driven by confusion and panic, was trying to slip his rifle off his shoulder when Kerim raised his own Kalashnikov and fired. The savage burst ripped into the youth's chest, lifting him off the ground in ungainly flight. Kerim roared in defiance.

Tagg was out of the jeep and running for the barrier. As he pushed down on the weighted end of the pole he waved us through, screaming, 'GO GO!' The jeep surged forward, Tagg leaping on board as we went past him. Behind us the Mujehadeen driving the APC floored the gas pedal and both vehicles roared on to the airfield.

There came another explosion and a second tank exploded.

Tagg had trained his men well.

We'd dropped them off when we'd stopped by the field earlier. Six of them from the back of the APC. Under cover of the hull of the personnel carrier they had entered the dried-up irrigation ditch and crawled along its course until they were in range of the tanks parked inside the perimeter wire. Armed with the RPG-7 rocket launcher, they'd waited.

We had known we might need a diversion to get us into the airfield. Some ruse to draw the sentries' attention away from our arrival. The APC had worked like a Trojan Horse, carrying within its steel belly the half dozen warriors that would breach the gates of the city. Or, in our case, the way into the airfield.

Soldiers were emerging from the huts and running towards the main gates and the blazing tanks. Cries of alarm could be heard above the crackle of the flames and the noise of our progress across the airfield. Somewhere a siren was wailing. Incredibly no one seemed interested in us as we headed for the two helicopters. My spine was being jolted like a spring as we bounced across the grass

318

towards the helipads. It wasn't doing my damaged ribs any good either.

Our driver slammed on the brakes and the jeep skidded in a semi-circle with the APC swerving in behind. Tagg scrambled out of the jeep, yelling at the driver to back the personnel carrier up to the nearest helicopter. At least Tagg had chosen the right one. Its partner had most of its port engine cowling unhinged.

Tagg pushed me out of the jeep towards the chopper. 'Start her up, dammit!'

I threw off my cap and ran like hell.

The helicopter was an ugly, bulbous-looking machine, squatting on its tricycle undercarriage like some grotesque insect. I'd heard tell that its crew referred to it as the Gorbach, the Hunchback. The nickname was certainly apt. The five rotor blades drooped over the fuselage like folded skeins of membrane. Close up the four rocket launchers slung under the stubby wings resembled huge seed pods. At the end of each wing sat two Swatter anti-tank missiles. This particular gunship was loaded for bear.

These aircraft had two operating crew: pilot and weapons systems officer. The seats were arranged in tandem, with the pilot occupying the rear elevated position. Each crew member had his own entry port. The pilot had a door, the gunner a canopy that opened above his seat.

The door to the pilot's cockpit was open. I'd almost reached it when its former occupant ran into view around the nose of the chopper. He was carrying his helmet and buttoning up his flying suit. I don't know who was more surprised; him or me. He must have been expecting either Trevkin or his crewman but possibly not in so much of a hurry. His jaw sagged open in amazement as he saw me. He took one look at me, the APC, the people being helped from the back of it, another, longer, look at my Adidas trainers, and then he started to have second thoughts.

I didn't even hesitate. I swung the butt of the Kalashnikov against the side of his head. There was a sickening crunch and he went down like a felled tree. I grabbed for his helmet, threw the rifle through the cockpit door, clawed my way up the side of the fuselage, clambered into the seat, and closed the hatch behind me.

It was like being folded inside a suit of body armour. Compared to this the JetRanger was about as sophisticated as a lawnmower. And the latter didn't have all its gauges noted in Cyrillic either. I should have expected this of course. For all the assistance it rendered that language could just as well have been Martian. Where the hell was Tagg when I needed him? Heart pounding like a jack hammer, I stared at the instrument consoles in front of me, searching for familiar-looking displays and switches. Some of their functions were obvious, some of them not so. Okay, Crow, let's see what you've got. Compass; stabilizer; VDU to display height, speed and attitude; fuel; mixture; oil pressure; temperature; engine and rotor speed. So far so good. The rest I'd have to work out later. Necessity dictated it was going to be a crash course.

Tagg and the other two Mujehadeen were pulling Nicole Bonnard towards the helicopter. The doors to the main passenger cabin were on the port side of the fuselage, an above and below arrangement that looked like a gaping maw. While Tagg and his men were taking care of Nicole, Kerim was carrying Massoud in his arms. He was holding the wounded guerilla like a baby. I felt the helicopter settle as they got on board and a whining sound as the doors started to close then Tagg reemerged and ran to the snout of the chopper. He pulled himself up into the front compartment.

320

'What the hell are you waiting for, Crow?' he roared at me through the perspex. 'Your fucking pension? Get this mother started!' He reached up and hauled down on the canopy above his head. Already I could imagine his hands gliding across the controls on his own instrument panel.

I wasted valuable seconds putting the headgear on, hollering at Tagg to follow suit. There had been a helmet hanging down by his seat. I looked for the radio cord, found what I hoped was the right piece of flex, plugged it in. Hoped that Tagg had done the same. I also hoped to God that the basic design for Soviet helicopters wasn't any different than anybody else's.

I scanned the console above my head for the rest of the switches and gauges that I thought I might recognize. The seconds seemed to be passing like hours. I took a guess at the master switch, pressed what I thought might be the radio trigger and heard the last part of Tagg's sentence demanding to know what the fuck I'd been doing with myself for the past five minutes. It hadn't been five minutes, of course, but about a million times longer.

Okay, go for it.

Fuel valve open. Throttle closed. Check pressure. Adjust mixture. Where the hell was the bloody lever? Ignition switch. Starter.

Grabbed the cyclic with my right hand and the collective with my left, said something like, 'Please, God,' squeezed the button on the collective.

Nothing. Dead silence.

Except for Tagg screeching in my headphone. 'GET US THE FUCK OUT OF HERE, CROW!'

Tried again. Closed my eyes as I did so. Heard the whine of the starter motor. A shadow moved above me. I looked up. Through the top of the canopy the rotors were starting a slow revolution. A sudden and violent hissing noise. The fire had caught in the turbine. Needles in gauges flickered into life. The blades whipped into a blur above us.

I heard Tagg shout, 'They're coming, Crow! They're coming, for Christ's sake!'

They were too. A squad of them, pelting over the field like a charge of cavalry. In two jeeps, racing to intercept our take-off.

Forget bloody procedure run-through. I pulled the collective up and the gunship rose back on its haunches as the nose wheel lifted off the ground. The rudders thudded loudly as they increased their pitch. I raised the collective a notch further and the rear wheels came off. Then I pushed the cyclic forward and the gunship nosed up like a shark heading for the surface of the ocean.

My ears were bombarded by a terrific rumble of sound. Tagg was firing the nose cannon. He'd sighted over the snout of the helicopter and his aim was spot on. The leading jeep ran into the hail of shells and I saw bodies explode out of it like offal tossed from a pail. Tagg was whooping in my ears as he continued to squeeze the trigger. Then I hauled up on the collective, twisted in more power and shoved the cyclic forward. We began a slow acceleration over the field like an express train leaving its platform.

'Radar!' Tagg yelled.

I saw what he meant and swung the helicopter around. It was the first serious manoeuvre I'd committed. The response to the control imput wasn't anything to write home about. She was definitely a mite sluggish. I got her lined up for him, though.

Tagg sighted and squeezed the trigger on his gun control column. The 57mm rocket left the pod beneath our port wing and streaked across the grass towards its target.

Three hundred metres away the PAR trailer blew apart with a roar, followed by the gas tank of the Zil truck.

There was tremendous power in the machine, I could feel it through the columns. The prototypes of these gunships had been responsible for setting speed records of over 200 mph. I was sitting in the most potent combat helicopter in the world. And it was all mine.

Bullets were peppering the body of the chopper. Small arms fire only. The titanium armour shell that encased the front and rear crew compartments was well able to deflect the strike of a slug fired from an AK-47. Nevertheless things were getting a little too hot for comfort. Somebody would be burning a hole in the ether advising his HQ that one of his helicopters had been hijacked. Somewhere squadrons would be scrambling.

Below us, the ground was a hive of activity. Figures were converging on the wrecked vehicles, attempting to douse the flames, their efforts frustrated by the sporadic sniping of Tagg's guerillas concealed in the ditches outside the perimeter wire. I could see dead bodies on the ground. The Mujehadeen were making their shots count. Before long, though, the enemy would summon enough resolve to counter-attack. I was torn between going to the guerillas' assistance and making our getaway. Tagg solved my decision when I voiced my thoughts. Massoud's survival took priority. The Mujehadeen could take care of themselves. In other words, Crow, move your ass.

Say no more.

Gaining height, I pointed our nose north towards the mountains and twisted in more throttle. In the mountains we would be safe for a while, protected by the terrain, invisible to radar. I needed the time to familiarize myself with the aircraft, in partiucular the gunship's defensive systems. At the moment we were immensely vulnerable.

It was a foregone conclusion that they'd send somebody after us. If, or – as was more likely – when, they caught up with us I wanted to be ready.

'Tagg?' I called to him through the mike.

'Yo!' His response came quickly. He sounded as if he was enjoying himself.

'Any problems?'

His reply came after a short dry chuckle. 'Yeah, I could do with a leak.'

'You should have gone before we came out,' I said. 'Twerp.'

'Up yours, buddy,' came the immediate answer.

I wondered how it was in the back. There had to be a way I could communicate with them.

I pressed the radio trigger. 'Nicole? If you can hear me I want you to try and talk to me. There should be a microphone and receiver in the cabin. Probably on the wall. Have a look. Chances are it'll look something like a transistor radio. See if you can find it. Press a few switches. I'll tell you if you're coming through.' I clicked off, wondering if she'd heard me.

There was no reply. Damn. I tried reaching her again. I triggered the radio switch a couple of times in quick succession in case there was some sort of console affair back there with a light on it, something that might flash and attract her notice.

My eyes flickered to the compass on the instrument panel. We were off course and heading more north than east. I corrected our bearing. We'd been off the deck for about six minutes. The enemy would probably be airborne by now, and chasing.

There was a sudden squawk in my ear.

'Crow?' Nicole, calling urgently.

'I'm here.'

'What's happening?'

'You tell me,' I said.

In a muffled voice she told me that they'd unearthed the morphine in the chopper's medical kit. Massoud was now strapped down and under sedation. Kerim and the other Mujehadeen were watching over him. Then she asked me how long it would take us to reach the border.

I said I wasn't sure. Maybe forty minutes. I told her to look after her patient, I'd talk to her later. Then I clicked over to Tagg.

'You there?' I asked him.

'Where else?' he replied.

We were flying along a narrow valley. The sun was three o'clock high, decorating the white peaks with slashes of gold and silver. We were travelling about halfway up the hillside, on the shadowed side. In those conditions we couldn't go flat out. I had to keep our speed down in order to be able to maintain manoeuvrability in the tight confines of the canyon. I had been right in my initial impression of the helicopter's performance. The Hind was slow to respond to the controls. It wasn't nippy like the JetRanger. Nap of the earth flying in this bird was out of the question. It just didn't react fast enough. I didn't want to sacrifice stealth for speed, however, which meant I had to keep below the ridges and meet the change in the scenery as we came upon it. We weren't doing much more than 90 knots, a little over 100mph.

By this time, though, I'd worked out how to use some of the navaids.

Most of the gismos in the aircraft were pretty advanced and beyond my ken. I'd last flown a combat helicopter fifteen years ago and there had been a lot of changes in avionics in that time. Some of this stuff I'd only heard about or read about in trade mags.

I'd tuned in to the projected map display without too much aggravation; likewise the radar and radar warning receiver. I wondered about that. These birds were big. Their radar signatures would be pretty conspicuous. I wanted to be able to spot if anything was homing in on our tail. If it was, the helicopter had various means to combat it.

The Hind had ECM capability in the shape of chaff and flare dispensers. They were housed below the fuselage, forward of the tail skid. The idea was to eject the chaff in order to create a radar signature greater than the helicopter itself. If they sent missiles after us, based on their own radar transmissions the flares, in their turn, would cause the missile guidance system to run amok. In the same way the IRCM system pumped out IR radiation at a pulsed frequency, which also caused the missile seeker head to give up and break its lock on the target. Which meant us.

The gunship also carried FLIR sensors and low light TV but we wouldn't be in the air long enough to warrant their use. Besides, I had only a rough idea of how to use them anyway. In any case if we were still airborne come night time it meant my navigation was way off beam. It also meant we'd be flying on empty fuel tanks.

So much for our defences. Our attack capability was also very impressive.

This particular version carried a lethal combination of weapons. The nose cannon was a four-barrelled 12.7mm Gatling gun, capable of inflicting extreme damage as some of us had witnessed at Dar Galak and also in the way Tagg had taken out the jeep back at the airfield. The pylons at the tip of each wing each supported two At-2 Swatter missiles, the inner pylons carried the UV-16-57 rocket launchers. All I needed now was somebody who knew how to use them. It was time to call Tagg again.

'Still hanging in here, birdman. What's the problem?' Very laconic.

'That little display back at the field; was that skill or a fluke?'

'You trying to insult me, Crow?'

'Don't ponce around, Tagg,' I scolded him. 'Just tell me.'

'If it's got a trigger and can kill people,' he said matter-of-factly, 'I can use it.'

'Okay,' I said. 'The hardware's all yours. I've got enough problems just flying this thing without trying to read the bloody instuctions.'

'Thanks,' Tagg said. '. . . I think.'

'Don't mention it. What's Russian for ejector seat?'

Tagg laughed. He didn't know the question had been half serious.

Below us the terrain was changing. The hillsides were getting steeper, the mountains rising higher, the snowline drawing closer. Tight in against the ridges, the turbulence intensified. We were flying along the updraught side of the valleys. The helicopter was pretty heavily laden with passengers and armament so the free lift effect was giving us valuable assistance. I knew we needed all the help we could get.

Because they had found us.

It had taken them just seventeen minutes.

Chapter Twenty-One

A moving helicopter isn't an easy target to acquire on radar, especially from a fixed-wing aeroplane over-flying it at a thousand feet per second. Radar impulses reflecting off the rotor blades tend to produce conflicting radar returns. The tracking radar can't handle it. It gets confused by the mass of signals. And the kind of terrain we were traversing didn't help either. Ground emits heat, especially sunlight reflecting off snow. Nevertheless the blip on the radar warning receiver was like a stab to the heart.

Whatever the pursuing aircraft was it was moving fast. It had to be either a Flogger or an SU-25 Frogfoot, most likely following some carefully devised search pattern. The fighter would be using doppler radar, enabling it to look down into the valleys as it passed over them. It would be trying to pick up our signature and the IR emission from our exhausts. Hopefully the suppressors over the chopper's jetpipes would cut down the amount of heat being radiated from the engines. We'd find out soon enough.

I looked up through the windscreen and a cold hand grabbed at my intestines and twisted as I watched the vapour trail streak across the blue sky like a fast-moving distress flare. Compared to the fighter we seemed to be moving in reverse. But had they picked us up and relayed the information? I had to assume the answer was yes.

In many respects a helicopter has a distinct advantage over a jet fighter when it comes to open engagement. It's all down to manoeuvrability. In confined areas and low altitude, the fighter just can't compete. It was more than likely, therefore, that the pilot above us wasn't going to get involved but was acting as a spotter. Which meant he had reserves on the sidelines waiting to be sent in.

The mountains masked their approach. By the time the RWR had picked them up they were on my tail, running fast. I watched them through the rearview mirror.

There were two of them. Hinds; sister ships to the bird I was flying. Fully armed. I could see the heavy ordnance slung below their wing pylons. Looking at them through the mirrors there was no sense of speed in their movement. It was as if they were floating, suspended behind us, hanging by some invisible thread, like twin swords of Damocles. Deadly. A chill crept along the length of my spine.

I said hoarsely to Tagg, 'We've got company.'

'I hear you,' he replied. 'Where?'

'On our heels. Two of them. Six o'clock high.'

'Shit!'

I was wondering why they hadn't blasted us out of the sky when, without warning, there was a sharp crackle of static from the UHF. I jumped in my seat. I was more strung out than I'd thought.

The voice that came through sounded quite reasonable. In a heavily marked accent it said in English, 'I wish to speak to the pilot of the stolen helicopter.'

This was followed by an expectant silence.

Tagg clicked in. 'Tell them to fuck off.'

I didn't get the chance to pass his message on. The voice came through again. 'If you do not reply to this message you will be shot down. I repeat, I wish to speak to the pilot.'

I was holding our speed around ninety knots. We had

329

been in the air for twenty-one minutes. My brain was transmitting signals. Stall them, it said. For as long as possible.

I said, 'This is the pilot.' I eased the cyclic forward and our nose dropped a fraction. Imperceptibly we began to accelerate. I applied tentative pressure to the right pedal. The slopes on our port side began to slide gently away. A glance in the mirror told me that the two hounding gunships had followed suit.

The UHF rustled like crinkled tin foil. 'You are known as Crow. That is correct?'

I didn't reply. I was too busy considering the possibilities. Or the conspicuous lack of them.

'This is Major Gregori Kazin speaking,' the disembodied voice continued. 'I believe we have met before, you and I.'

I felt a tingle run along the back of my neck.

Dar Galak.

'A most interesting encounter,' he went on. 'As you no doubt recall. This time I would prefer that we should come to a rather more civilized agreement concerning our mutual survival.' There was a slight pause then he said, 'I am therefore ordering you to decrease your airspeed and turn the helicopter around. You will be escorted to the nearest airfield where you will be placed under arrest. Failure to carry out my order will result in the destruction of your aircraft. Do you understand?'

'This time,' Tagg said, 'I'd definitely tell him to fuck off.'

I ignored the interruption. I waited until I was sure impatience had set in before I replied. 'I hear you, Major.'

Kazin said sternly, 'You must turn around at once.'

I let him stew for several more seconds before I responded. 'I'm thinking about it,' I said. I hoped to God that Tagg was as good with weapons as he'd led me to believe. We'd only get the one chance.

We were passing over scattered and ever widening patches of snow. Around us the mountains of the Hindu Kush rose like giant waterfalls. I felt the gunship wallow in the thin air as we hit a patch of turbulence caused by a downdraught from the upwind side of the ridge over on our starboard wing. It caught our pursuers also. The two Mi-24s staggered slightly as the invisible wash cut down through their rotor blades.

Kazin's voice broke through the band of static like an axe blade. He was getting a trifle agitated. 'I will not warn you again! You will alter course immediately!' Then, for a moment, he sounded quite contrite as he added, 'You cannot escape, believe me. Turn back before it is too late.'

We were now almost directly over the centre line of the valley with Kazin and his wingman some seventy feet behind us. It was now or never. I clicked the radio trigger, snapped out a warning for everyone on board to hold on. Then I did something really bloody dangerous.

In training they call it critical testing. You could see why. I eased my left hand round to the back of the collective, at the same time keeping the lever itself as steady as possible. Made sure we were all stable. Then I gripped the neck of the collective, wrenched the throttle closed, and jammed the lever towards the floor. I'd simulated engine failure. It was like running into a wall. The nose went down and we dived like a brick. Someone yelled in my ear. Tagg, swearing violently.

Through the upper segment of my windscreen I saw that he hadn't been the only one to be taken unawares.

Our rapid deceleration had forced the two chasing gunships to overshoot us. As their twin shadows blotted out the sunlight above us I opened the throttle. Power restored, I corrected the yaw to the right and pulled the nose back. The chopper hung in the air for a millennium before the snout came up and it began to rise like a breaching whale and the Russian helicopters broke across our field of vision, showing their undersides like basking hammerheads.

I screamed at Tagg.

'FIRE, DAMMIT!'

Tagg hadn't lied about his abilities. His reaction speed was extraordinary. I'd hardly got the words out of my mouth before he began shooting. As I brought the helicopter upright I could see that he was bang on target. The burst from the nose cannon raked the nearest gunship from stem to stern, culminating in a massive concentration of fire power across the slender boom of the gunship's rear fuselage. I watched in awe as the Hind's rear rotor hub disintegrated like matchwood, shearing the drive shaft and blowing away a section of the tail pylon.

Without the compensations of the tail rotor the enemy gunship was helpless. The job of the tail rotor is to counteract the driving force of the main rotor blades, known as torque. Without the tail rotor the main body of the helicopter will simply revolve the opposite way to the main blades. Violently. Result: the helicopter spirals down to the bedrock like a bird with a broken wing. Which is what happened here.

The second gunship was already turning away rapidly while trying to gain height and spoil Tagg's aim. Meanwhile I was applying full left rudder to swing us away from a possible counter-attack. From my side window I followed the track of the crippled helicopter as it spun out of control. It was whipping round and round like a lead weight on a piece of string. It hit the rocks below with a thunderous detonation and a bright bloom of orange flame. I heard Tagg cackle with glee in my earphones as I slung the chopper towards a cleft in the side of the valley. Below us the remains of the gunship exploded impotently against the snow-clad side of the mountain.

I pressed the radio trigger, enquired urgently, 'Everyone okay? Nicole?'

Breathlessly she answered. 'We're all right. My God, Crow, what happened?'

Shut in the rear cabin with limited field of vision they hadn't even been aware of the other helicopters. Hearing only my last minute cry of alarm and the awesome shift in the trim of the chopper they must have been wondering what on earth was going on. They must have thought we were going to crash.

'Massoud . . .?' I was searching frantically for the other gunship. Couldn't see it at all. Maybe it was coming up astern. Above our blind spot, intent on revenge.

It seemed a long time before she replied. 'He's still alive. One of the others has bruised himself badly. Kerim has been sick.'

So much for the damage report. Bruises would heal and Kerim would survive the embarrassment. But how Massoud was still with us was beyond me. Maybe the man was immortal after all. But the fight wasn't over yet; not by a long chalk. As Tagg reminded me.

'Crow!' his voice rattled my eardrums. 'The bastard's coming back!'

I knew that already. Because the RWR had gone berserk. It was pulsing like an out of control pace-maker. Which meant the target was very close. The read-out from the screen told me, in fact, that he was less than three thousand yards ahead, coming at us from the two o'clock position, closing very fast. To have been aware of that

Tagg must have been tracking him by sight all the time. Not a bad feat given the distance.

And, somehow, I knew it would be Kazin at the controls. And he would be very very angry. He'd lost two wingmen because of me. He'd be burning.

Which was probably why he fired the missile too soon.

I saw the brief glow of flame as the Grail left its pylon. At two thousand yards the missile flight time to impact would be about seven seconds. It didn't give us very long to effect countermeasures.

I was already slamming us down towards the ground. Assuming that the missile had an IR terminal homing device, it would be streaking for our jetpipes. I wanted to provide it with an overwhelming heat source. And there was only one way to do that. Use ground heat and release our flares. Like pretty damned quickly. Always provided I pressed the right bloody button of course.

Fifty yards out from its pylon the missile's booster motor ignited, thrusting the Grail towards us like a sling shot.

There was a set of switches alongside the console holding the RWR and IR jammer. They were protected by red hinged caps. I flicked the caps up. If I'd got it wrong I wouldn't be permitted the luxury of a second chance. So, no time to rationalize. I punched the buttons, banked the helicopter hard to port, and prayed. The Hind keeled over like a capsizing boat, the wing tip barely clearing the hillside, and a glorious incandescent arc of fire burst around us as the flares ignited. Something streaked past our tail rotor and we all felt the blast of the explosion as the confused warhead scythed through the decoys and struck the rock below us.

Thank you, God.

Tagg began to fire the cannon.

The other chopper was curving away. Tagg missed his target by a mile. I tipped us to starboard. We levelled out and boomed off across the valley floor. We began to pick up speed again. Automatically I adjusted our course towards the north east. I looked at the clock. We seemed to have been airborne for hours. In fact it had been thirty-two minutes. Kazin would be calling in for reinforcements. We were running out of time. The border might just as well have been on the dark side of the moon.

'I've lost him!' I heard Tagg call through my earphones.

I cursed and craned my neck around to stare out of the windscreen. Radar and RWR were ominously mute. Where the hell was he? Concealed behind some fold in the ground or some rocky outcrop? Like an Indian lying in ambush at a bend in the trail? Come on, Kazin. Don't leave me in suspense, dammit. Show yourself!

He must have heard me.

The RWR pulsed with the sudden energy of a life support machine reactivated by the resuscitation of a patient, indicating that we had just been illuminated by Kazin's radar. My sensors told me that he was very close. I'd only just realized how close when the attack came.

God, he was coming in fast! From out of nowhere, it seemed. Barrelling into view around a thick turret of rock that rose out of the floor of the canyon like a twenty-storey building. Sweat erupted. I had time only to pull up and slam us into an abrupt wingover as the bullets from Kazin's nose cannon ripped through the thin air like arrows of molten lava; the significance of which hit me like a sledgehammer. He was using tracer! (Yes, you can see the damned stuff in daylight.) In horror I watched the bright rods of fire ripple past our nose and strike the side of the rock like exploding Very rockets.

And Tagg was returning fire. The four-barrelled gun in

the chin turret below him was spewing out rounds at a ferocious rate towards the massive helicopter that was veering away from us to begin another turn and assault. But it was too late.

Kazin had gauged his attack well and I just hadn't had the time nor the expertise to take sufficient evasive action. The tail end of his cannon burst caught us high up, slamming into the rotor head fairing and along the length of the starboard cowling. It turned most of the starboard compressor units into scrap metal. The helicopter gave a violent shudder, like a boat caught in a force ten gale. This time the engine failure was for real.

Hardly time to react. She began to sink beneath me.

I heard Tagg grunt in my earphones. I yelled at him to shut the fuck up. In fact I was yelling at everybody to shut up. Distractions I didn't need.

Come on, Crow! Do something!

As adrenalin pumped its way into my system I pushed the collective down fast to neutralize the angle of pitch. I had to maintain the spin of the rotors otherwise they'd fold up like a broken fan and we'd go in like a kami-kaze gannet. To maintain an even trim I had to keep the pitch of the blades flat. That way the blades revolved, provided lift, and the helicopter descended in a controlled glide. When it works it's called autorotation. When it doesn't work it's called a total bloody write off.

And, like a winged Nemesis, somewhere above me, Kazin's gunship was circling like a vulture over a carcass, waiting to pick over the remains.

At least, it should have been.

Because, in all the fever and excitement of that sudden and final onslaught, Tagg had, by some miracle, managed to extend to the major a taste of his own medicine. He'd released all our rockets.

336

Maybe he'd been able to sight off as he fired or, most probably, it had been the last desperate gamble of a man who, unable to accept defeat and yet, knowing we were dead, had refused to give in without a fight.

Even as I grappled with the wayward controls of our own machine I had but a second to catch sight of the missiles as they spurted away from our wing pylons in pursuit of Kazin's gunship. They cascaded out like a shower of meteorites.

Kazin must have realized he was being tracked. But he was too late. He'd assumed that because our aircraft was equipped only with air-to-ground capability he was safe from everything except our cannon. He was wrong. And he paid for his arrogance. He tried to counter the threat by releasing his flares but he was too late. There wasn't much he could do in the face of such fire power. Each of our rocket pods held sixteen missiles, less the one Tagg had used against the radar truck. All the flares in the Armeiskaya Aviatsiya's arsenal wouldn't have saved Gregori Kazin.

At least half the missiles went astray. The remainder were on target. They accelerated up into the centre of the flare pattern like an angry swarm of killer bees. They didn't even falter. They bracketed Kazin's gunship and the huge helicopter erupted in one brilliant, eye-scorching ball of fire.

And then I was concentrating totally on the controls because we were still going down, fast.

Good news and bad news. The good news was that the ground wasn't much more than three hundred feet below us. The bad news was that not much of it was flat. We had, I estimated, fifteen seconds, maybe less, to impact.

But we were gliding now. Going in at around forty knots. And I was still looking feverishly for a decent

337

landing site. The view was about as bleak as a Siberian winter. All I could see were steep, snow-speckled hillsides and sharp outcrops of black rock rearing towards us like rows of jagged teeth. There didn't seem to be much vegetation other than the occasional wind-seared and forlorn stand of trees; dwarf-cedar and stunted pine. I began to experience another sense of déja-vu. That same strange feeling I'd had in the cockpit of the Wapiti; a sense of timelessness as we continued our eerie descent.

We sank in over a spine-shaped ridge and I spotted sanctuary. An acre of snow-dusted scree lying on the leeward slope of a razor-backed escarpment. It was likely to be our only chance at a safe and obstacle-free touch-down.

Amazingly, at ninety feet we were still on an even trim. I lowered the undercarriage; the grating sound gnawing through the soles of my feet as the wheels locked. Fifty feet above the surface I pulled the cyclic back, flaring the chopper, trying to decrease our approach velocity. Still too bloody fast, Crow. I eased the cyclic back another fraction.

Still dropping.

Thirty feet. Ground closing. Rapidly.

Twenty.

Ten. And visibility was almost obscured as the whirling blades whipped a pocket of soft surface snow into opaque powdery mist around us.

Five feet.

With the tail rotor almost on the deck I eased in the last of the pitch. The main gear touched. The snout dropped abruptly, the nose wheel slamming into the ground with a crunch that made my teeth rattle. Then we began to slide. But not for long. The weight of the helicopter settled, the wheels gripped and we came to an abrupt and canted rest across the bottom of the slope. The snow cloud began to dissipate.

I sat back, closed my eyes, felt the tension drain out of my pores. I took a couple of long deep breaths, removed my helmet, pushed open the starboard door, retrieved the rifle, and tumbled out of the helicopter.

Leaving Tagg to effect his own exit from the forward compartment, I made my way around to the main cabin door. Where we had ended up, the snow – what there was of it – wasn't especially deep but in parts it was still well over the tops of my trainers, so by the time I'd reached the door my feet were wet through and cold. We'd also landed on the shaded side of the valley. Out of the sun it was more than a trifle nippy.

The segments of the door swung open and I climbed into the cabin. With a sharp cry of relief Nicole fell into my arms. She clutched me tightly. Pain flared along my still sensitive rib cage.

Reluctantly I eased her away. 'Everyone all right?' I looked for Kerim. He was a bit green. So were the other two. But they'd live.

Massoud was wrapped in blankets like an Egyptian mummy. Only his face was showing. His complexion was grey, his breathing was very shallow. He looked terrible. Like Muhammed Nur Rafiq had done when they'd brought him down off the mountain at Dar Galak.

What I had to tell them next wasn't going to make him feel any better. It wasn't going to win me any fans either.

'Bring him out,' I said.

Nicole gasped and grabbed my arm. 'We can't move him!'

'We've got to. We can't leave him. They're still looking for us. We have to get out of here.'

339

She stared out at the mountains and the snow and rocks. It all looked pretty inhospitable. 'Where to?'

'Anywhere.' I looked at Kerim then. 'He's your man. It's your decision.'

Kerim didn't hesitate.

'We walk. I will carry him.'

I hadn't expected him to say anything less. Kerim Gul had told Massoud's men that he would protect him. The Pathan had an obligation that he had sworn to fulfil.

'All right,' I said, 'But hurry.' I got back out and looked for Tagg. But he was having problems getting his hatch open. I slung the rifle over my shoulder and went to give him a hand.

I grabbed the handle on the canopy and yanked it violently. The hatch swung back and Tagg let out a sigh of relief. He looked exhausted. No, not exhausted, I realized. Something else. He stared up at me, a strange half grin on his face.

'Guess what?' he said huskily.

Then I saw the blood.

One of Kazin's shells had found their target. And the armour plating along the underside of the gunship's body hadn't been any use at all in deflecting the stray projectile that had punched its hot cruel way through the starboard hull of the gunner's compartment, ricocheted up and out of the forward control panel, and, almost as an after-thought, pulverized most of Tagg's left hip for good measure. His voice in my headphones earlier had been the signal that he'd been hit.

'The son of a bitch got me!' Tagg said. He sounded surprised more than anything else, as if put out at the effrontery of his counterpart in Kazin's helicopter. His eyes squeezed shut as a spasm of hurt racked him. I yelled for Nicole. She came running.

There wasn't a damned thing she could do, of course. Tagg knew that. He knew we'd never be able to lift him out. The compartment was so cramped that there wasn't even enough room for Nicole to administer any sort of first aid. Tagg was going to bleed to death.

Nicole took off the scarf that Massoud had given her. She passed it to Tagg. Instructed him to try and staunch the bleeding. Tagg folded the scarf into a square wad and pushed it into the wound. His hand came away scarlet with gore.

Nicole looked at me, gave a swift and silent shake of her head as an understanding of Tagg's condition passed between us, and climbed back down to the ground.

'Massoud?' Tagg spoke through clenched teeth. 'He still with us?'

I nodded. I didn't add that it was only by a very narrow margin.

Tagg clicked his tongue in admiration and gave a small smile. 'What a guy!' His head dropped forward on to his chest.

For one awful moment I thought he'd gone. I reached down and touched him gently. His head jerked up. His eyes focussed, swimming with pain. 'You guys had better get out of here,' he muttered. Then he grinned again. 'I guess you've blown the half mill, Crow. COD terms only, birdman.'

'Next time, Jack,' I said.

He nodded tiredly. 'Yeah, sure.'

I said, 'Someone's going to be here pretty soon. They'll know we've come down. They'll want to come in and finish us off.'

'Then they're gonna be fuckin' disappointed, aren't they?' he grunted.

I felt a touch on my leg. Nicole. Behind her were the

341

three Mujehadeen. Like me, they were still in their militia uniforms. Kerim was carrying Massoud pick-a-back style. The guerilla leader was hunched inside the blankets, his hands looped around Kerim's neck. He looked very tiny, very fragile, like a small child.

It had been hardly more than sixty minutes since Trevkin's bullet had penetrated his body. Not long, but time enough for severe trauma to have been induced into nerve and tissue. For that reason it was almost impossible to believe he was still breathing. His eyes, I saw, were open. Only just. They were glazed, the pupils dilated by the morphine administered by Nicole. The man looked comatose, and close to death. But there was no way that Kerim was going to leave him to the Russians.

'Give me one of the rifles,' Tagg said.

I passed him mine.

He checked the magazine, the blood on his hands smearing the grained stock. 'Maybe I can hold them off for a while.'

Unlikely, I thought. He could hardly hold the damned gun.

I started to step down when he called me back. 'Hey, birdman, you might as well take these.' He was lifting something from around his neck. Trevkin's field glasses. He handed them up to me. 'They'll come in useful I guess.'

I took them from him.

'One more thing, Crow,' he murmured.

'What's that?'

'When you get home you can pass on a message to State.'

'A message?'

'Yeah,' he said. 'You can tell 'em that the armour plating

342

on an Mi-24 ain't worth shit.' He started to laugh. Grimaced as the pain caught hold.

'I'll tell them,' I said.

'Right,' he murmured. 'Now, what are you waiting for? Get the fuck outta here. You're making the place look untidy.'

I hesitated but he'd already dismissed me. He was busy trying to hold on to the rifle and ease himself into a comfortable position.

I got down and joined the others. I looped the leather strap of the field glasses over my head. Kerim handed over his rifle. He needed both arms free to support Massoud's body.

'Which way?' I asked him.

The Pathan nodded towards a fold in the high ground, to where a ragged belt of pine trees ranged across a cleft between two cloud-shrouded ridges. 'East,' he said. 'To Pakistan.'

I looked up, caught my last sight of Tagg watching us through the side window, knowing without a shadow of a doubt that we were leaving him to die. Kazin had been out of contact for too long. They'd send someone to look for him. To look for us too. And it wouldn't take them long to get here. When they did arrive Tagg, if he was still alive, would try and hold them off, to give us time to put some distance between ourselves and the hounds. I wondered how much time we had and how far we would get.

It took us a little over ten minutes to reach the ridge. Progress could have been easier. Breathing, at least for Nicole and me, was somewhat laboured due to the altitude. After all we were up around twelve thousand feet. The rough militia trousers I was wearing over my jeans had become even more of a burden. I took them off and hid them at the side of the trail. After that I felt a lot more comfortable.

At the top of the slope, beneath the shelter of the trees, I turned and looked back. The stranded hull of the gunship lay tilted in the shadow of the mountain like a beached whale. I thought of Tagg slumped in the turret watching his warm blood drain away. Had the rifle become too heavy and awkward to hold? Or had the gun already slipped from his lifeless hands? Had his head fallen on to his chest for the last time in dreamless sleep?

My thoughts were interrupted by the low throb of distant rotors. We had time only to duck into the cover of the trees as the Mi-24 helicopter swept into the valley and began to circle like a buzzard over the marooned Hind.

We should have taken off there and then but I found myself mesmerized by the activity below us. I unslung the field glasses and crawled forward for a better view. I was conscious of Kerim urging me to hurry and come away but I couldn't ignore the events that were happening down there.

The gunship had landed. Through the glasses I watched half a dozen tiny figures jump from the chopper's main cabin and converge on the grounded Hind. All in combat gear, fully armed. Russian troops.

Half the troopers bracketed the main doors, the rest approached the pilot's compartment. They were very careful. They could see that both crew hatches were open and they weren't taking any chances. When they finally closed in they did so very quickly. Hurriedly they checked the main cabin. Found nothing. Moved on.

Then they discovered Tagg.

I saw one of the soldiers raise himself slowly over the sill of the forward hatchway and then his gun swung up. He gestured swiftly to his companions. A second later the

344

fuselage was swarming with men. They were like ants devouring a dead moth.

It took two men to lift Tagg out of the forward turret. It was the thought of that shattered hip bone dragging over the edge of the hatch that caused my nerve endings to grate like fingernails being raked down a blackboard. So he hadn't been able to hang on after all. He had lost too much blood. He had been too weak.

They dumped his body on the ground like a piece of old sacking. Beside me, through clenched teeth, Nicole drew in a sharp breath.

One of the soldiers toed Tagg's body with his boot. He did it the way a beachcomber might nudge a piece of driftwood on the sea shore; with a sort of idle curiosity. There followed an animated discussion during which someone else flung out an arm as if to indicate that we could have gone anywhere.

Just keep thinking that, my son, I thought. Please

I was still studying them through the glasses. So when Tagg lifted his hand I saw it plain as day. He was still alive!

In his fevered state Tagg must have thought he was reaching for a weapon, the rifle. But of course that had been removed by one of the soldiers. The American was lying on his back, arms moving feebly like the legs of a beetle skewered by a pin. I suppose they must have known immediately that he wasn't going to be of any use to them.

So they finished him where he lay.

It was nothing short of cold-blooded execution. I watched one of the soldiers – I presumed he was the officer in charge – draw his pistol from the button-down holster at his side and point it at Tagg's body. The sound of the

345

single shot hung flatly in the still air. Tagg's corpse twitched once and lay still.

Nicole gave a low moan as though she was in pain and buried her face in her hands.

The officer holstered his gun and began issuing orders. Then the soldiers formed a skirmish line. They were beginning a search pattern.

It didn't take them long to find what they were looking for either. Through the glasses I saw one of them raise his hand and point to the ground then up towards the crest of the hill where we lay watching them. The rest of the squad gathered around him. One of the troopers ran over to the helicopter and issued instructions to the crew. The gunship's rotor began to turn. It lifted and wheeled about, completing one low circuit of the landing site. Then it accelerated up and away. I realized immediately that it was heading straight for us. I hissed at everyone to keep down and we buried ourselves under the trees as the huge helicopter thundered overhead. My attention returned to the troops in the valley. It was much as I had expected. Having picked up our tracks in the snow they were following our spoor. Ranged in a line abreast they began to climb the slope towards us.

Chapter Twenty-Two

Time to move.

But not before a thought had crossed my mind. Maybe a couple of us should stay behind to try and hold them off. To give the others time to get away. And then I considered the implications. Two against six? Bugger that for a game of soldiers.

I crawled back into the trees, pulling Nicole with me. 'I think we ought to get out of here,' I said. 'Now.'

I don't ever recall seeing four people look more relieved.

We couldn't move fast of course. Not with Kerim carrying Massoud. But at least it was downhill all the way. I had no means of telling how far the belt of forest extended, though. It could have been a hundred square miles for all I knew. But while it lasted it gave us cover and therefore an opportunity to conceal our tracks and put time and distance between ourselves and our pursuers. Maybe.

Kerim and the two Mujehadeen settled into a sort of loping stride. Nicole and I kept up as best we could. My chest, meanwhile, was killing me. I'd obviously aggravated my damaged ribs during the flight in the helicopter. The altitude wasn't helping much either. But we were descending fast. Also the undergrowth was becoming more dense as we left the snowline behind. And somewhere ahead of us I was sure I could hear water.

The woods ended abruptly, as if someone had suddenly raised a curtain. The river stretched before us. It was broad, perhaps fifty metres across, and flowing quite fast.

The banks were wide, too, and covered with pebbles. A number of narrow, gravel-strewn islets rose above the surface in the middle of the river. Vegetation had taken hold on a few of them in the shape of spindly gorse-like bushes. Other weeds sprouted up from between the stones. At any other time the view would probably have been quite picturesque. But not now. We had more pressing matters to attend to than make brief halts to admire the scenery.

But Kerim was grinning like a Cheshire cat as he pointed across to the far side.

'There!' he cried. 'Pakistan!'

His words sank in. Relief soared through me. We'd made it, by Christ! One hundred metres away lay sanctuary. I felt like shouting out loud. Nicole gripped my arm, her eyes bright with elation.

The sound of a bullet striking the human body is very distinctive. It comes as a smart *thwack* as lead and steel meet flesh. It is unmistakable. As is the sound that precedes it.

I heard the crack of the shot followed by the wincing thump of the bullet hitting home. A yard away from me one of the Mujehadeen grunted with pain, jack-knifed violently and crashed to the ground. Even as we turned towards him a second shot rang out. I grabbed for Nicole as the other Mujehadeen fell away, his chest a bloom of scarlet as the slug shattered his sternum. He tumbled down in slow motion, feet sliding away beneath him. He struck the ground in a ripple of pebbles.

Twenty paces away from us a man stepped out from the trees. He was carrying an assault rifle. He stood watching us, his stance casual, almost arrogant, his dark skin and long hair giving him the look of a half-breed Apache scout, straight out of a Hollywood western. I was the only one left who was armed. But I never had the chance to bring my own weapon to bear. At that range he'd have to be the worst shot in the world not to hit what he was aiming at. And I knew he wasn't that.

Not this one. Not Rasseikin.

You had to hand it to him; he was a persistent bastard. And smart. Boy, was he ever. He'd anticipated every move we'd made. All he'd needed to do was to get to the river first and then cut off our line of retreat. So he must have been in the helicopter, the one that had flown into the valley after us. The one containing the squad of troopers who, even now, were closing in astern, like a row of beaters thrashing the undergrowth, driving us into the gunsight of this one-man shooting party.

With a sob of despair, Nicole crumpled to her knees. All hope of our deliverance dashed like a ship on the rocks.

I let the Kalashnikov fall to the ground and gazed out across the river. So near and yet so far. The hopelessness of our situation overwhelmed me. I felt anger, too, at the fact that none of us had given the Soviets credit for thinking this far ahead. We had run right into the snare and Rasseikin had drawn the noose tight around us with all the precision of an expert poacher.

And he was alone. He was that damned sure of himself.

Kerim's face said it all. If he hadn't been carrying Massoud he'd have gone for Rasseikin there and then. With his bare hands given half a chance. And the Russian knew it. So he wasn't going to give the Pathan the opportunity.

Rasseikin drew closer and motioned with the gun. Kerim, with Massoud draped over his shoulders like an old knapsack, stepped from the edge of the water. The Pathan shot me a speculative glance as if to ask, what now? I shrugged resignedly. What could we do? Not a whole hell of a lot, it seemed to me.

I started to wonder where the Soviet helicopter might be lurking. Somewhere close but not so near that we'd have spotted it when we reached open ground. It had dropped Rasseikin off and then slipped away beyond the trees out of sight, no doubt waiting to be summoned in like a gundog called to heel. Rasseikin, however, didn't appear to have a radio with him. But the soldiers sweeping the woods behind us would have. Once they'd put in an appearance the Hind would be contacted and they'd swing in to pick us up.

As if to echo my thoughts Rasseikin stole a quick look towards the densely wooded hill above us. He was wondering what was keeping them. So was I. They couldn't have been that far behind us; certainly near enough to have heard the shots that had killed our escorts. Their tardiness was only prolonging the agony.

I helped Nicole to her feet. She gave a brave but sad smile. 'Oh, Crow,' she murmured softly. 'We were so close.'

Rasseikin spoke.

He addressed Kerin in Farsi. From his actions I could see he wanted the Pathan to relinquish his burden. Then he turned to Nicole and me. Whatever he said was in Russian this time. We didn't understand that any better but we took it to mean he wanted us to assist.

With Rasseikin watching every move we eased Massoud off Kerim's back and laid the guerilla leader gently on the damp pebbles. As we did so the edge of the blanket fell away and Massoud's racked and pale features were fully revealed. When the identity of the injured man became clear Rasseikin's eyebrows very nearly took off. He hadn't expected this at all. The true value of his haul had suddenly reached new dimensions. He'd struck the mother lode.

The Russian gave Kerim another directive and, with a slightly rueful expression on his face, Kerim took the knife out of his shirt and tossed it on to the ground. Rasseikin had a good memory. He'd remembered the speed with which Kerim had dispatched Jassim back in the mosque at Qum. He had no intention of ending up the same way.

Then he shot Kerim a question. I guessed he was inquiring after Massoud's condition. Cradling Massoud in his arm, Kerim's answer was understandably curt. Rasseikin's response was to jerk his head at Nicole. He knew she was a doctor. He wanted an up-to-date diagnosis. I crouched down with her as she examined the wounded guerilla. I could tell that the end was very near. What faint glimmer of light there had been in the young rebel commander's eyes was fading rapidly. Like a dim beacon on a faraway hilltop.

I looked at Nicole for confirmation.

'He's dying, Crow,' she said, leaning towards me slightly.

And with her back to the Russian and thus shielding her hands with her body, she passed me the gun.

I didn't latch on at first. Then, heartbeat accelerating like a starship leaving Earth's orbit, my palm closed on the automatic's dulled blue metal and my fingers slipped around the smooth walnut grip. Massoud's Browning! Sweet Jesus. She must have removed his pistol and shoulder holster during the journey in the helicopter. She'd had the weapon on her all the time! Hidden deep in the pocket of her combat jacket.

I flicked a quick glance at Kerim. For confirmation. Alerting him that I was going to make a move. A nerve twitched in his cheek. He nodded imperceptibly. I felt him tense like a spring.

Rasseikin was about fifteen feet away. At some point during the time that Nicole had been examining Massoud he'd helped himself to one of his cheroots. The thin black cigar drooped languidly from his lips. He narrowed his eyes fractionally as the smoke drifted up past his face. The rifle barrel rested alongside his right thigh.

Do it now, Crow. Don't think about it. Do it.

I came up fast, the gun gripped in both hands, and Rasseikin whirled to meet me. He saw the pistol and the Kalashnikov swept up, his finger tightening white on the trigger. He was too late.

I shot him twice. The first bullet hit him in the lower half of his chest, punching him backwards, the rifle spinning from his hands. As he started to topple, his eyes still widening with shock, I fired again and his jaw exploded as the second bullet took him under the chin, lifting him off his feet, removing the top of his skull like a hammer hitting an egg shell.

Before the boom of the shots had died away I was pushing Nicole towards the river. 'Run!' I cried. 'For Christ's sakes, run!'

Kerim scooped up Massoud into his arms and followed her as she stumbled into the water. I tucked the Browning into my belt and retrieved the Kalashnikov and, as an afterthought, Kerim's knife. I slung the AK-47 over my shoulder then I ran over to Rasseikin's splayed corpse. His eyes were still open. They gazed up at me in sightless bafflement. His rifle lay by one outflung arm. I picked it up and sprinted for the river.

The water was freezing. Hardly surprising as less than an hour ago it had been snow. Even so I gasped at the shock of it.

We were less than halfway across when my eye was caught by a sudden movement at the edge of my field of vision and the first of the Soviet commandos ran from the trees behind us.

I heard the shouts as we were spotted and the section of stream through which I was attempting to wade instantly assumed the consistency of quicksand. Ten yards in front of me Kerim and Nicole were struggling through the calf-deep water like exhausted marathon runners. The first shots came then, sounding like distant fire crackers exploding. No one was hit but they weren't that far off target. And cover was virtually non existent. Except . . .

A long flattened reach of pebbles broke the surface of the stream ahead of us. About fifteen yards long and featureless save for the stranded tree trunk that lay across its narrowest part, both ends half submerged in the water. I yelled at the others to take refuge behind it.

Shots peppered the surface of the water, plucking at my heels as I threw Kerim his dagger and one of the rifles and scrambled in beside him. I'd only just got my head down as the next fusillade struck the log and wood and sand erupted around us like tiny bomb bursts.

This whole thing, I thought, wiping grit out of my eyes, was getting beyond a bloody joke. The river swirled past us on either side. Pakistan was now less than twenty metres away. It might as well have been twenty miles.

I raised the Kalashnikov over the top of the tree trunk, sighted on one of the moving figures, and fired off a couple of rounds. I missed. My efforts were answered by a dozen sharp bursts of automatic fire. The harsh sound echoed across the river. Kerim squirmed himself into a firing position and returned the compliment. We were lying in a shallow depression behind the tree trunk. There was a gap below the bottom of the trunk through which we could see the river bank. Kerim and I scooped away some of the stones to give ourselves a better view.

The soldiers had taken up defensive positions and lay concealed behind convenient rocks. Rasseikin's body lay where it had fallen. In isolation. I eased one eye over the top of the stones. One of the troopers was trying to make a name for himself by sneaking forward on his belly. I gave him a three-round burst and gained a great deal of satisfaction at hearing the shrill cry as my shots found their mark. The trooper's body spasmed once and lay still.

One down. Five left. Rotten odds.

One fact was abundantly clear. We couldn't stay where we were.

So . . .

Nicole was huddled foetus-like between us, her body covering Massoud's. She stared at me.

'You okay?'

She nodded quickly.

'Think you can make it to the other side?'

She twisted around and took a look. Immediately across from us, a wedge of trees grew close to the edge of the water. They would provide cover once we reached the bank. If we reached the bank.

'What are you going to do?' she gasped. Fear was mirrored in her expression.

'I'm going to try and keep their heads down while you and Kerim make a run for it.'

'For God's sake, Crow! No!' She reached out as if to grab my arm. And ducked immediately as someone, impatient at the lack of action, loosed off half a magazine in our direction. Bullets thudded into the ground and the tree at our backs.

Kerim glanced at me and grimaced. He wasn't too keen on the odds either.

'You'll have to take one of the rifles,' I said. 'That way you can cover me when I come after you.' Nicole knew that meant her, Kerim couldn't manage a weapon and Massoud at the same time.

They looked at each other in mute understanding that this was the only choice we were all likely to be given.

Kerim passed her the rifle. Her look implored me to reconsider. 'Crow . . .'

I pushed her away gently. 'Go on, Doc. Bugger off.'

She reached up, touching my face with her palm. There was a trace of mist in her eyes. 'I'll be waiting, Crow,' she said hoarsely.

They got ready.

I took out the AK's magazine and checked the load. Two thirds full. Twenty rounds. Not much. But better than nothing.

I took a deep breath.

'Now,' I said.

I sat up quickly and began shooting. Three-shot bursts. Timed. Kerim swept Massoud into his arms once again and then they were off and running.

I heard a cry from one of the troopers and a couple of them ran out into the open. Maybe they thought we were all making a run for it. They discovered their mistake too late. I raked them as they emerged from shelter. The bullets hit chest high and they fell away like discarded dolls. That left three. And I was out of ammunition. Except for the pistol.

But Kerim and Nicole were safe.

As I ducked down behind the log I saw them enter the trees on the far side of the river. Kerim was staggering. Whether it was due to the weight he was carrying or whether he'd been hit or just twisted his ankle, I couldn't

355

tell. But they were there, that was the main thing. They'd
made it. Its usefulness spent, I hurled the rifle aside.

Whereupon the air was filled with the roar and clatter of
aero engines and the huge Russian gunship rose into view
above the trees and wheeled down towards me like an
awesome bird of prey.

At that moment I knew I was dead.

Or I was if I didn't move fast.

Across the water, Kerim appeared with the rifle at his
shoulder. He jammed himself into the fork of a tree,
waved once, and I realized if I didn't go then, I never
would.

Twenty metres. That was all. Not far at all really.

Not far? Christ.

I thought, frig it. What the hell, anyway . . .

Kerim started shooting as soon as I was up. I began zig-
zagging about the same time. The Hind was some thousand yards off and coming in exceedingly fast with enough
noise to wake the dead, Rasseikin included. I heard the
snarl of the cannon and the tree behind which I had taken
cover became instant kindling. Kerim was screaming at
me to lift my feet up and I was doing my best to oblige
him but it was bloody difficult because I'd been damned
near out of breath before I'd even started my run.

So I didn't quite make it. The fact is, with less than ten
yards to go, I zigged when I should have zagged.

It was like being hit by a battering ram. I felt a stunning
blow behind my right shoulder and I was shoved forward
as though fired from a catapult. My legs were still moving
but I wasn't going anywhere except down and the water
was coming up to meet me very fast. I went in hard and
then I went under. It was bloody cold.

Someone screamed as I went in and then the water
closed over my head and there followed several seconds of

frenzied confusion during which time I lost interest in everything save for the excruciating pain spreading along my arm and down my right side as I made feeble attempts to establish which way was up.

I managed to right myself with my good arm and as my head broke water and I took in air I heard another urgent cry as Nicole launched herself into the stream and began to splash her way frantically towards me.

'Crow!' she screamed again, a look of abject terror on her face.

'No!' I yelled. 'Get back! Get back!' But my words were swept away by the current as I lost my balance for the second time. I took in another mouthful of water, horribly aware that the stream was turning pink around me.

But she wasn't listening. She was still coming.

I never heard the sound of the shot. I don't think she did either. They say you never hear the one with your name on it. And, anyway, nothing could compete with the thunderous clamour of the Russian gunship as it lunged in for the kill.

It was as if she had run into a glass wall. The bullet hit her and she paused in mid-stride and hung there as though frozen in some kind of force field before gravity took over, pitching her backwards into the water, her eyes registering the pain and the surprise as the shock wave travelled through her system.

She was less than a yard from me, hand reaching for mine as the shadow passed over her face like a cloud. I kicked myself towards her and caught her sleeve with my left hand. I pulled her to me and drew her in. I held her and looked up through waves of agony to find the helicopter hanging in the air above us.

And I began to hallucinate. Because it wasn't the same helicopter. I stared at the aircraft hovering overhead. The

357

High Command in Kabul must have wanted us something terrible, I thought wildly, to justify sending two choppers after us. A Hind and an Mi-8, no less. And then I tuned in properly and my brain went into turmoil as I realized I'd been mistaken. It wasn't an Mi-8 at all. In fact it wasn't even Russian. It was an SA 330 Puma, an Anglo–French job. Very similar in design except that the Puma had a thicker tail boom.

Then I saw the roundels.

It was the cavalry. Or as good as.

Pakistani Air Force. A border surveillance patrol. No doubt scrambled from their base at Chitral in order to discover why there was so much frenzied activity along their northern border region and, now, even more anxious to find out just why their country's air space was being encroached upon by the Soviet Air Army.

But they were too bloody late, damn them.

The two aircraft were nose to nose in open confrontation; each challenging the other to make a move. There was probably less than thirty feet between the ends of their rotor blades. The din was colossal. The downdraught buffeted me on all sides, driving spray into my eyes as I clutched Nicole's limp body to mine. We were clasped together like children frightened by a thunderstorm.

'Crow . . .' Her voice was faint, barely discernible through the tumultuous barrage of engine noise coming from overhead.

'It's all right,' I said. 'It's all right. I've got you now.'

She opened her eyes. They were beautiful and filled with light.

She shivered. 'It hurts, Crow,' she said.

I felt the sting of tears on my cheek.

A cold hand reached up slowly and gently wiped them away.

'Remember,' she whispered. 'No matter what happens . . .'

Her voice faltered and her head fell against me.

The Puma was no match for the Hind, not when it came down to a fight. But neither ship commander would have wanted to commit himself to initiating an attack and risking an international incident that would have set the wires humming all the way between Islamabad and Moscow.

Russian nerves were the first to break.

The Hind retreated. The Puma, true to its namesake and secure in its authority, continued to hiss and snarl as it defended its territory. The gunship backed away. It gained its own side of the river and hovered momentarily as if deciding what course of action to take. Finally it began to descend. The survivors of the patrol emerged from cover and ran towards it. I hung on to Nicole's body and watched as the Russian soldiers gathered their dead. Rasseikin's corpse was retrieved last of all. The cabin doors of the Soviet helicopter swung shut. With a heavy whine the Hind's turbines increased their pitch and the gunship rose abruptly and slid around. It accelerated. Skimming the side of the hill it turned west into the mountains and disappeared from view like a dog running from a fight, tail between its legs.

The Puma continued to hover then it dropped slowly towards our side of the river. As soon as it touched down, the rear doors slid back and a helmeted figure in a khaki jumpsuit appeared in the opening. He waved urgently.

I tried to stand up but I found it impossible. And I had no movement in my right arm. I could feel Nicole slipping away from me into the river. I yelled for Kerim and he threw his rifle aside and came running. Or at least limping. I was on my knees in the stream. The crew man from the

359

helicopter was coming too. But I was losing my grip. I couldn't hold on any longer. I couldn't see too well either. My head slid under the water.

Then strong arms caught me. 'Nicole . . .' I called her name and tried to reach her but our hands slid apart. It was Kerim's face I saw before I blacked out, filled with immeasurable sadness.

The pain revived me. And the noise.

Not content with trying to bore a red hot poker into my shoulder, they were also attempting to drive a road drill into my brain. At least that's what it seemed like. I could feel the vibrations all the way from my feet through to my tonsils. It was engine clatter. I was in the Puma.

I was lying on my left side, my back supported by some means, I couldn't make out how. I was in no state to turn around to try and find out either.

Kerim was seated with his back to the bulkhead. The Pathan looked as if he was asleep. His head was nodding on his chest. I noticed that he was still wearing the bottom half of the militia uniform. There was blood all down his right leg.

At the aft end of the bay there was a long bundle, wrapped in what looked like black canvas. I knew what it was. I'd carried them in Nam. It was a body bag.

Nicole.

I closed my eyes quickly in an effort to quell the fresh tears that I couldn't hope to stem and, in doing so, my mind was filled with visions that were too dark, too dreadful to contemplate. I focussed again.

Massoud was lying next to me. He, too, was lying on his side, still half covered by a blanket. Somebody in the crew had fixed up an IV drip. It floated above him like an umbilical cord. The rebel commander's eyes were closed.

Ironic, I thought, watching him. They'd sent me into Afghanistan to bring out one resistance leader. It had taken me damned near twelve days and I'd come out with the wrong bloody one. Some extraction.

Massoud opened his eyes.

I could see he was still pretty much out of it and having difficulty relating to his surroundings. By rights he shouldn't have been relating to anything. He should have been dead.

Then his eyes caught mine. Movement then. I watched as he tried to extend his left arm. Slowly at first, and then with grim determination his hand reached the deck and, with fingers probing, began to inch, with infinite slowness, across the floor of the bay. His eyes never left mine. I could see the muscles in his jaw tighten as he willed his body to obey the commands of his brain.

I lifted my right arm slowly and felt the tendons begin to tear. But I was beyond pain. My hand slid to the deck. I reached out towards him, feeling for him. Our fingertips brushed. Another inch. My hand turned in to meet the clasp.

A shy smile touched Massoud's face. Sweat coated his brow.

Our hands touched, gripped.

And held.

It was over.

Almost.

I watched as the tug trundled across the tarmac towards the gleaming Learjet. Saw them load the casket on board. The coordinator signalled all clear, the pilot raised a hand and the door closed.

I stood by the jeep as the aircraft pushed back from the stand and taxied on to the apron, paintwork catching the sunlight as it turned on to the runway. It lined itself up and waited patiently for the final word from the tower. It came. The pilot opened the throttles, the engine pitch rose to a high whine and the aircraft vibrated momentarily as the brakes held. Finally it began to roll, gathering speed as it fought to leave the ground behind. It lifted finally, banked and began to climb. Another brief flash of silver as the wings caught the sun and it was gone, like a graceful bird in flight.

Nicole was going home.

I turned to the man standing behind me. 'All right, Major,' I said. 'Let's go.'

Major Niaz Tariq nodded silently and slid into the driver's seat. I got in beside him. He was a big man, a Sikh. Bearded, with soulful brown eyes. I sensed his awkwardness as he engaged gear and steered us out towards the military sector of the field to where the chopper was waiting. They'd already started the engines by the time we got there.

The major got out of the jeep with me. At the aircraft steps he said, 'Have a safe flight, Mr Crow.'

'Thanks.' We shook hands. Left handed. My right was still in a sling.

'You will be met on your arrival,' he added. 'Your transfer time in Islamabad will be approximately forty-five minutes. We have arranged for you to board your departing flight before the other passengers.'

I nodded.

'Goodbye,' he said. I could see he was resisting the urge to salute. But he actually looked sorry to see me go.

After all it's not every day you get to chaperone a deportee. Maybe he wanted the tender moment to last.

I wasn't only a deportee, I was also something of an

embarrassment. Well, you had to look at it from their point of view.

Refugees they could handle. They'd seen enough of those to last them a lifetime. They usually palmed them off on to one of the relief agencies. Our little party, consisting as it did of two Europeans and two Afghan nationals, all of whom were suffering from gunshot wounds of varying degrees, however, was quite another matter. Especially as our arrival had entailed a somewhat hurried, not to say traumatic, transit of the Durand Line, involving the rather unwelcome attention of one Russian gunship and a severely depleted squad of Russian infantry. The Pakistanis were not amused.

And then when they'd established our identities the shit really hit the fan. So they decided to keep the news and circumstances of our arrival under wraps from the general public. The alternative, of course, would have been to accede to the covert requests they had undoubtedly received from Kabul to throw us back across the frontier.

But Zia wouldn't have agreed to that, not at any price. Not with the Americans breathing down his neck and the world's media still ensconced in the province's capital. So, they'd locked us away like a dotty old aunt in a high tower, away from prying eyes. Until Massoud and I were mobile and the powers-that-be had decided what to do with us.

There had been some consolation. The window of my room in the base infirmary at Chitral had had a terrific view of the mountains. They'd told me that on a clear day, I'd be able to see Tirich Mir, all twenty-five thousand feet of it. I saw it once. Rising towards heaven, summit blazing like Ezekiel's chariot. Even from fifty miles away it was breathtaking. Better than staring at the ceiling at any rate.

Then the word came down from on high.

They handed Nicole's body over to Aide Medicale Internationale, the French medical organization that had arranged her original passage. The organization had arranged the charter of a plane to take her home. I still don't know for sure what story the Pakistanis had fabricated to account for her death. I believe they told the Aide Medicale director that she had been operating a clinic in one of the refugee camps in the Kurram Agency when it was straffed by Afghan jets on a cross-border air strike. At least that would account for the manner in which she had died, were her family to demand an autopsy after her body had arrived home.

Kerim and Massoud they handed back to the resistance. I'd said my goodbyes to them two days ago, back at Chitral. Kerim was walking with a stick by that time but I guessed he wouldn't be for long. Massoud was on his feet within five days of our arrival. He was astounding. I swear to God that the man had the constitution of an ox. The surgeon who'd treated me had told me, in between removing Nicole's stitches from my scalp, that only the guerilla's incredible stamina and Nicole's care had enabled the rebel commander to survive the rigours of the flight in the gunship and our final hike over the mountain. The morphine and the altitude had slowed down his metabolic rate sufficiently to diminish the speed of his blood flow which, in turn, had accelerated clotting, thus avoiding terminal blood loss. Truly a miracle. As old Ahmed Badur might have said: Inshallah.

Me? Well, they wanted me out. By the first plane. It didn't matter where to. Hence the military escort. Major Tariq. He was the first leg of the relay team that would see me through the formalities all the way to the boarding gate of the Qantas flight that they had me booked on, eastbound ex Karachi.

But at least the Pakistanis had agreed to let me accompany Nicole's coffin on the short flight back down to Peshawar. It had not been the best of farewells. They never are.

True to Major Tariq's word I was met on my arrival at Islamabad – a captain this time – and escorted to the PIA flight. I had a seat in the front. There were another twenty minutes still to go before they started boarding the rest of the passengers so I had the pick of the morning's newspapers that had been provided for our reading pleasure. I helped myself to copies of the *Pakistan Times* and the *Karachi Morning News*. As my escort chatted up one of the flight crew my attention was grabbed by two stories.

Both were in the *Pakistan Times*. The first one in a paragraph tucked away on the second page.

Soviet forces in Afghanistan had launched a new offensive on the Panjsher Valley amidst rumours that the commander of the Panjsher region, Ahmadshah Massoud, had suffered serious wounding during an attack on a Soviet military installation. These reports were strenuously denied by a Mujehad spokesman, who also stressed that initial Russian advances into the valley had been averted by vigorous rebel activity.

I wondered about that. Massoud and Kerim would be over the border by now and heading west with more weapons and ammunition for their fighters. But the Panjsher was at least ten days away on foot, perhaps less if they travelled at night as well. Could the rebels hold out that long without their most able commander? I hoped to God they could.

What they really needed was someone to fly him in, of

365

course. Cutting a ten-day journey down to a matter of minutes . . .

Whoa, hold it, Crow, I thought. This is where you came in. Besides, hadn't you forgotten something?

No. I hadn't forgotten a damned thing. In fact I'd remembered only too well.

One small matter of a package. About the size of a pack of cigarettes. Still in the safe at Dean's. I hadn't even been paid for the first bloody job yet, had I?

I was into the second story when they began to board the passengers.

This one concerned murder.

It appeared that the Khad assassination squads had been active in Peshawar again. Their latest victim had been one of the Hezb-i-Islami faction, Doctor Mahmud Habbani. Habbani had been gunned down by an unknown assailant shortly after leaving the Hezb headquarters in order to attend a secret meeting with Mujehadeen commanders. The information had been confirmed by Pakistani Intelligence.

I put the paper down and gazed out of the window. The aircraft had been closed up. We were pushing away from the blocks. Fire tenders and empty baggage trolleys slid by the wing. I reached up and adjusted the air vent above my seat. My thoughts strayed back to that last news item.

Frankly, I was a little surprised.

I felt sure Kerim would have used his knife . . .

END

At the time of writing the following information is fact.

Dr Ahmadzai Najibullah, former head of the Khad, continues to hold the post of Secretary of the People's Democratic Party of Afghanistan, the PDPA.

Maulavi Yunis Khalis remains the leader of the Hezb-i-Islami faction of the Islamic Alliance resistance group, based in Peshawar, capital of the North West Frontier Province of Pakistan.

Ahamadshah Massoud of the Jamiat-i-Islami resistance group, commander of the guerilla forces in the Panjsher Valley, is still, by far, the most potent and respected rebel leader in Afghanistan. The Russians haven't caught him yet. I hope to God they never do.

March 1987 – JM